I DIDN'T KILL HER
BUT THAT MAY HAVE BEEN SHORTSIGHTED

A DONNA LEIGH MYSTERY BY ROBIN LEEMANN DONOVAN
(2nd in a series of Donna Leigh Mysteries)

When you learn that a former colleague, one from very early on in your career and from a whole different part of the country is dead, it stuns you. But when you learn that she was murdered in the very city where you now reside – stunned doesn't even begin to describe it. And that means Donna Leigh, a menopausal ad exec, will be forced to jump into the fray in order to keep herself off the suspect list once again! Join Donna for some laughs, as she once again employs her effective but unorthodox sleuthing to keep herself one step ahead of the handcuffs.

Published by Gracie Dancer LLC
www.rldonovan.com

Printed in the United States of America

Cover Design by Heather McCain, Bozell
Formatting by Sheryl Ann Hayes, Bozell
Cover Photography Copyright © by Scott Drickey

ISBN 978 1 943976 00 3
First Edition

[CHAPTER 1]

It was Wednesday and I was running a bit late. I ran across the south parking lot with purse and tote bag in one hand and 12-pack of Diet Orange Sunkist in the other. Burdened with an unwieldy load, I moved precariously through both the front door and the outer lobby entrance. Once inside I wound my way around the tall wooden, teepee-like structures that served both as organic art installations and intimate meeting pods and veered past rows of sleek wood and black laminate desk units carefully balancing my parcels. Upon reaching my desk, I dumped the load and logged on to my computer. The meeting reminder popped up with a 'bing' to confirm a 10:00 A.M. conference call, reminding me to reread the project file before jumping on the call.

I noticed my message light blinking and hoped it would be something quick. I'd have to hustle if I was going to review that file. The message was from Ken Farley. It had been years since I'd given Ken a thought. He and I had worked together at an ad agency in southern Connecticut for a number of years, which now seemed like a lifetime ago. The message was oddly cryptic.

"Wow Donna, that must have been some shock for you, huh? All things considered, you must be really torn about how to feel. I'd sure love to know what you're thinking."

I couldn't imagine what on earth he could be talking about.

Oh well, no point in taxing my brain. I might as well just call him. Logic would dictate that I wait until AFTER the conference call to indulge my curiosity, but I'd never been a slave to logic.

Once on the phone, Ken was no less cryptic. I put up with about two minutes of his nonstop gibberish before I started to lose my temper.

"Hey Ken, what the hell are you talking about?!"

My impatience seemed to help him focus.

"You mean you haven't heard?" he asked.

"Guess not." I tried to hide my annoyance. "Why don't you fill me in?"

"Your old buddy Betty Jean bought the farm!"

"Thornton?"

"That's what I'm saying," Ken pressed, "you didn't hear about it?"

"How would I have heard about it all the way out here in Omaha?" He really could be thick sometimes.

"Man, Donna, You're not saying you didn't know she moved to Omaha three months ago?"

The man was talking pure nonsense now. Betty Jean and I had worked together for several years when I was in Connecticut. After my move to Omaha ten years earlier I had seen neither hide nor hair of BJ. In fact, it had probably been another two years prior to that. Not seeing BJ was definitely how I liked it. The thought of her moving to the Heartland? I would never buy that! She fancied herself a big city "player" and a fashionista. There was no way she was moving to Omaha, Nebraska.

I harbor no such fancies. Having lived my whole life as an Easterner, I virtually leapt at the opportunity to join the prestigious advertising firm, Marcel, when the call came from an overzealous recruiter. Once I knew it was Marcel there was no looking back. If that meant a move to Omaha – so be it! At the time, I had no way of knowing that public holding company shell games would result in my opportunity to buy the very advertising brand I had respected from afar for so many years. Now, my partners and I were charged with the sacred task of taking this revered icon of communication into the next phase of marketing.

BJ's self-delusion did not stop at her perceived importance in the world of business. She also considered herself to be fashion-forward in the extreme. She was right about extreme. On the fashion side of the equation, she and I could not have been more different. Tailored black business was my wardrobe staple. Admittedly it wasn't exactly groundbreaking, but at least I'd never arrived at a business dinner attired in a white linen jumpsuit, festooned from neck to toe with twelve-inch tall basketball players as had my former nemesis, Betty Jean. In my humble opinion, she could not have looked more ridiculous if she'd been wearing the 50-gallon garbage drum parked by the side door. Yet she faced a sea of Brooks Brothers clad marketers with a smug, almost arrogant, smile on her self-satisfied face. She perused the room to ensure that everyone had taken notice of her latest fashion statement. A lingering glance must have sated her obsessive desire for attention; there was no denying that every eye in the room rested on her. That was one amazing thing about BJ. She lacked the ability to discern a difference between genuine admiration, as *rarely as that occurred*, from a thinly veiled attempt to keep from laughing in her face. It was that blissful ignorance which enabled her to bask in delusions of imagined grandeur as she stood there in her outrageous garb and preened. I almost envied her that.

Now Ken was saying BJ is dead? It just wasn't sinking in. This had to be some kind of a lame joke. It was hard enough to accept that she was dead much less that she had died in, of all places, Omaha, Nebraska, my home.

3

"Ken, I'm sure you're mistaken. You of all people should know that Betty Jean would no sooner move to Omaha than I would move to Appalachia...."

"That's where you're wrong, Donna," Ken persisted, "She did move to Omaha, and now she's dead."

My head was starting to hurt with a building pressure; in my estimation it had already reached skull-cracking capacity. It's probably important to note that I'm not at all prone to exaggeration. I heard what Ken was saying, it still wasn't sinking in. In the past, Ken had always been a good source of information. A career PR guy, he took pride in knowing not only what was going on, but why. Maybe it was time to shut up and let him fill in the blanks. Shutting up was not my best thing!

"I honestly can't believe you didn't know BJ was in Omaha," Ken continued, "she'd been telling everyone she was moving there so the two of you could go into business together. In fact, an article ran in the *Times Courier* just as she was preparing to move."

Ken took a slight break here. Good thing because I was pretty sure I felt something pop in my head. If there was bleeding in the brain I'd want to clear the line and dial 911. My life must have flashed before my eyes because I started seeing images of the past. I had worked with Betty Jean at my first advertising agency, the one I joined after making the move from teaching English. She was my immediate supervisor. And she hated my guts. Her supervisory skills consisted of emotional abuse and abject criticism. I even learned that at times she'd fabricated work order memos addressed to me but never delivered, so she could complain about my incompetence. She was often heard announcing to anyone within earshot that I'd "lost yet another memo." I would never have had proof of this duplicity had it not been for her sloppy work habits.

4

Inadvertently leaving evidence of betrayal in various unfinished stages around the agency, my fair-minded colleagues found several of these gems and ultimately pieced together a clear picture of her draconian master plan. I shuddered as I recalled that disconcerting time in my early career. It was a hard lesson learned: talent and brains are not always enough; there are people who will expend energy to deliberately hurt others. Although I was to see additional proof of this occasionally over the years, the motivation behind such cowardly behavior continues to baffle me.

Even with conclusive proof in hand, my vindication was subdued at best. When you're as slippery as BJ it isn't tough to weasel out of even the tightest of jams. It didn't hurt that she was handling all the media for our largest aerospace account, and the boss needed her more than she did me. This was the lesson in office politics, which formed that little bit of paranoid edge that would serve me well as I climbed the advertising ladder. We damn sure never learned about the mean streets in my naively innocent days of teaching high school.

Remarkably, I let this torture continue for about three and a half years. To the uninitiated I would appear to have been an idiot not to have gotten the hell out of there ASAP; but in the dog-eat-dog world of the ad business, I was industriously building my resume and skill set by learning as much as humanly possible at one of the two most acclaimed ad agencies in Connecticut. I was loathe to jeopardize this rare opportunity; to do so would have been career suicide. At any rate, over time even BJ had to acknowledge that I was a reliable and talented employee, a fact that only served to make it easy for her to dump all her work on me, so she did.

No, going into business with Betty Jean would never be a consideration for me, although she did approach me, indirectly, about starting a business together while I was still working in the New Haven market. My answer back then had been a resounding "no," and the years had done nothing to change how I felt on that issue. Besides, my partners and I already owned Marcel. Even if BJ and I hadn't had a history of hostility, I would never have convinced them to allow her to waltz in as a fourth owner.

"Ken, you're sure this isn't some lame practical joke?" I asked, grabbing my iPad and heading into the nearest conference room. I gently latched the door behind me, adjusted my earpiece, and waited for Ken's response.

My hasty dash for privacy may have been a bit late, but our thin-walled conference rooms generally failed to provide an ideal sound barrier anyway. Folks seated near them were constantly reminding us nothing uttered within their walls was ever truly private – unless you whispered and blasted the fan simultaneously. We were often reduced to improvised sign language and cryptic notes in order to contain the content of our meeting within the walls of those conference rooms. Nevertheless, I felt compelled to give it my best shot.

Several months earlier, Marcel had moved corporate headquarters from comfortable, new construction suburbia into a classic, historic, downtown loft, replete with high ceilings, crumbling exposed brick and ancient pipes, the latter occasionally causing unwelcome, not to mention malodorously unpleasant, surprises. These same pipes periodically released a toxic drip, wreaking havoc on both technology and paperwork; it was the Chinese water torture `a la Omaha.

We had ditched our old fashioned, isolated executive offices and opted for a more collaborative and integrated environment, which worked great to energize the creative atmosphere. The lack of private spaces and soundproofing, however, posed its share of challenges.

"I'm dead serious, Donna... oh, Jeez, that was tacky," Ken offered.

So typically Ken. Even in a crisis he couldn't stop with the dorky jokes.

"Wow, it's hard to believe BJ is really dead," I hesitated. "Where did she die?"

"From what I heard, it was in the NoDo office she was renting to house your new joint venture – I assume that's the northern end of your downtown district. But Donna," Ken continued, "they're saying she was murdered."

It had seemed so real, but that last bombshell convinced me that Ken's call had to be nothing more than a bizarre dream, meaning I must still be home in bed all safe and sound. I was feeling relief that the whole Ken 'blast from the past' would invariably boil down to a food induced nightmare – no more late night gherkin pickles for me.

But then it started again.

"Donna, are you still there?" he whispered.

"Wouldn't have expected to be dreaming about Betty Jean and Ken," I mused.

"You're not dreaming, Donna. It's all real," Ken assured me.

"Can't be," I countered. "I've gone all these years never knowing anyone who was murdered. And now, within a few month's time, two of the women who have labored to make my working life a living hell have been murdered right here, practically in my back yard. Do you know the statistical probability of something like that? "

"Would it help if you went online and checked one of your local news sites? Go ahead, I'll wait," Ken urged.

I didn't really know what I hoped to accomplish but I

grabbed my iPad and typed the URL of one of our local news sources. Up jumped an article about a recently murdered transplant from Connecticut. Crap, that meant I had to start believing this insanity might actually be real. If what Ken was saying was true, I had once again unwittingly become a major player in a murder investigation. My head was definitely hurting.

If I was having trouble convincing my old pal Ken that I didn't know what BJ had been up to, how was I going to convince Warren? Detective Warren was in charge of murder investigations in Omaha. I knew her from a recent murder investigation in which I'd unintentionally played a fairly major role. The "Vic" (as most cop show buffs know, that's the term we use for "victim" in law enforcement) had also been a former co-worker, Claire Dockens. The rocky history she and I had had involved me in her murder investigation, in spades. In order to clear myself, my colleague Kyle (another Dockens dissenter) and I had gone about trying to help solve the crime. While in retrospect I believe my involvement only added to the chaos, most folks insist I singlehandedly solved the mystery. Now, mere months after life had settled down again, here was another murder for which I would almost certainly be the prime suspect. I wasn't sure I was up to that 10 a.m. client call after all.

I hastily concluded my call with Ken, thanking him for getting me up to speed on an extremely disturbing situation, and promised to keep him apprised as the investigation unfolded.

As I pushed open the French door leading out of the compact conference room, I caught an odd swoosh of movement out of the corner of my eye. It was followed by a gut-wrenching clatter. My eye followed the swoosh to a strange pile of moving, jean-and-sweater clad human extremities struggling for an apparently unattainable goal.

"Did you get all that?" I asked as I casually strolled toward my desk. Clearly Babs and Peg, who had provided a good percentage of the brains and more than enough of the muscle in my journey through the last murder investigation, were already gearing up to jump into the fray once again. One glance told me that "my girls" had been leaning into a free-standing bookshelf in an attempt to get close enough to hear the scoop. My hasty exit must have upset their proverbial applecart. It's not like it was the first time. Guess those walls weren't thin enough for some people.

Had I any remaining doubts of the veracity of this assumption, they were erased by the roomful of hysterical laughter that accompanied me back to my workspace.

"Have a nice trip, ladies?" I heard from across the room. I just shook my head.

That's when I spotted Kyle sauntering over to my desk as he fought to regain his composure. Unlike the majority of the staff who delighted in making Babs and Peg realize the full humiliation of their eavesdropping calamity, Kyle would never want to make them feel worse than they already did; he was a genuinely nice guy!

On top of his extreme niceness, Kyle always looked so put together. The day must have been filled with internal meetings as he was dressed in the 'brunch on Fisherman's Wharf' elegant, business casual style that was his stock in trade. Beautiful clothing sized perfectly to frame his fit and toned physique. His pale yellow silk trousers and button down beach style short-sleeved shirt were the perfect compliments to his stylishly coifed blond tresses. I lost no time in filling him in on the whole Thornton problem.

"Unbelievable," Kyle said. "How could something like this

happen again so soon?" And as an afterthought, "Don't worry, Donna, we'll figure this one out together, just like last time!"

God bless Kyle. Kyle Thoroughgood was my crime-solving partner, as well as my colleague and friend. I could count on him for anything. Last time he and I had both expected to be suspects, since we'd both had rocky relationships with the murdered woman. Surprisingly, we didn't get much heat from the cops. I slipped easily back into the sleuthing zone so the cop lingo just came naturally.

This time Kyle was willing to jump right in with both feet, even though he'd never heard of the "vic" until right at that moment. If I remembered correctly from our last adventure this would be an incredibly time consuming little hobby, and it had been grueling on Kyle to actively participate in the investigation without falling behind on his unrelenting work schedule. Kyle was our GM so he was actively involved with virtually all of our clients.

"You know, now that I think of it, I do remember hearing about that murder on the news. The details sounded very, very odd. Maybe you should call Warren before she has a chance to come after you."

Probably good advice. But not something I looked forward to doing.

[CHAPTER 2]

After thinking it through, I lost no time in calling Detective Warren. Maybe, if I took a proactive role, the Omaha homicide team would be less likely to place me at the top of their suspect list. Warren was a career cop in her early-thirties with brains and street smarts. Physically she gave Castle's Detective Beckett a run for her money, but on the whole she was a lot sharper than Kate. It would be difficult to finesse any details of the murder out of her, but I was confident my finessing skills were up to the challenge.

"Well now, Ms. Leigh," Detective Warren mused, "I have to admit it surprised me to learn that you're featured prominently in this recent murder. Am I wrong in seeing a trend here?"

Okay, I guess I had that coming. I mean let's face it: being knee-deep in two back-to-back murder investigations was probably no big deal if you were a crack dealer, but it had to be somewhat out of the ordinary for your average ad agency owner. I was guessing the fact that I'd been a fairly recent transplant to the Omaha area would serve to stimulate the good detective's imagination. I mean, coming from the north-east, I was still pretty much of a wild card to a lot of the sensible, well-balanced Midwesterners who so graciously tolerate out-siders. Tolerate that is, until the telltale neuroses so often present in east coast escapees rears its ugly head.

Since my arrival in Omaha, I'd heard many a tale about east coast transplants and their certifiable behavior. From the comments, it wasn't clear if out-of-towners were the only ones to exhibit this behavior, or if acting certifiable was just grist for the mill. I mean, were we easterners really the only insanity Midwesterners saw, or were we just exhibiting an unfamiliar form of insanity? Either way, it appeared as though east coast sanity was on a timer – when it went off, so did we. Perhaps they were beginning to wonder if my insanity timer had sounded, somehow resulting in multiple homicides. Before too much longer I feared they would feel certain of it. It's not as though I could blame Warren; I didn't believe in coincidence either.

"This time you brought our *vic* from your old stomping ground, eh? Were you worried that things might get a little boring for the old Omaha PD," Warren continued.

She's got that cop lingo down too, though I suppose you'd expect that from a police detective, and 'eh?' What was with 'eh?' The good detective must have spent some time in Canada recently – and I was clearly honing my Sherlockian instincts.

The mind tends to wander when serious trouble appears imminent; I think it's a defense mechanism enabling one to escape thinking about the truly terrifying possibilities. And with that realization my nerves ramped up preparing for full-scale paranoia; I could feel my damn menopausal furnace starting to crank up in preparation for a fuel-injected power surge. Menopause has an uncanny ability to smell fear and ensure, by virtue of turning you into a wet dish rag, that you look your worst and seem nervous as hell. Comes in real handy during major campaign presentations and murder in-vestigations. That old ad campaign about "never letting them see you sweat" – ha! And don't even get me started about bloating, weight gain, sleepless nights and so on.... Tough to appear calm and cool even on my best days. But I digress.

Straining to regain focus of the issue at hand, the thought crossed my mind that Warren had a right to be concerned about my involvement. I certainly was. I genuinely hoped that this second murder would not cause her to lose all faith in me and start to believe that, ultimately, I was the cause of all the problems after all. In our last encounter with murder, she'd been surprisingly adept at sifting through the facts and eliminating elements that only circumstantially appeared incriminating. Not once in the entire investigation did she jump to ridiculous conclusions like the clownish TV cops always do. Her assumptions were always that I should be treated as a resource, a distinction that met with my utmost approval and gratitude. I'd have hated for that to change with this untimely second murder cropping up and ensnaring me in what appeared to be a far more damning way. No, I wouldn't have blamed Warren if she turned on me, but it would really suck.

"Detective Warren," I began hesitantly.

"No worries, Leigh," she chimed in before I could get any further. "No one suspects you at this point. We will, however, be needing to debrief you on your knowledge of the *vic* and her recent lifestyle changes. It would also help if you could make a list of all the people you know in Connecticut that *we* should be looking at. We can ask the local constabulary for their help. I don't suppose you've ever solved any murders with them?"

The "at this point" gave me pause, not to mention heart-burn.

"No, sorry, Claire Dockens was my first murder." I suppressed a huge sigh of relief, "I don't know any Connecticut police. Oh well, there was that time when I inadvertently interrupted a sting operation in Fairfield County, but that was just a bizarre fluke, kind of a funny story, really," I rambled nervously."

It was clear from Warren's total silence that my feeble

attempt at humor had not been successful. But true to my nature, I chattered on anyway.

"I was heading home from the office on an otherwise average day, and stopped to gas up at the station I always used. In a million years I never expected to be reaching for the hose – and in the blink of an eye, find myself standing dead center in a circle formed instantaneously by SWAT team trucks and unmarked cars. It was like being in the center of every cop show I'd ever seen, unfortunately it was real and it was happening to me."

"When they all jumped out, fully armed, and started barking questions as to the whereabouts of the station owner, I realized that menopause and its occasional theft of short-term memory, had once again left me with egg on my face."

"The drawn guns instantly shook all the cobwebs free. It dawned on me that by simply doing what I always did, gassing up at my favorite station before jumping on the Merit Parkway for the grueling fifty-nine mile commute, I neglected one rather critical fact. I had known for weeks that the station had been shut down with ominous signs posted everywhere. I'd driven by twice a day swearing at the inconvenience of having to find another place to gas up. Then, on that fateful day, engrossed in thoughts of my late afternoon meeting and plagued by a menopausal memory, I pulled up to the pump without a care in the world, for about a quarter of a second, which was how long it took before law enforcement in the state of Connecticut converged on me in full force."

I shuddered at the memory.

"Let me tell you, it was no easy task convincing those guys I was just an innocent commuter. In retrospect, I could see how they might be reluctant to accept that I was completely oblivious to the multitude of signs, posted on every visible surface on and around the station and its property, which should have tipped me off even if my otherwise engaged brain cells had led me astray. Once the reality of the situation had sunk in, it was crystal clear that the guys on the SWAT team were seriously deflated – and not feeling terribly charitable toward the menopausal. I guess those stakeouts take their toll. They'd been hoping for a spectacular takedown as a payoff for all of their diligence, instead they got a middle-aged east-coast commuter with mush for brains.

"I really lucked out when they believed me and didn't decide to detain me for further questioning. Perhaps this time the inevitable menopausal drenching actually worked in my favor. I'll never really know. Although, I have to admit I've often wondered just what that station owner had gotten — ."

"Leigh," Detective Warren's commanding voice brought me back to the present and away from ruminations of a past encounter with law enforcement, "gotta head out now, but I'd like you to stop by the station at four o'clock today so we can begin our debriefing."

"Sure thing, Detective." I answered quickly. It wouldn't do to annoy her in the least. Plenty of time for that as the investigation progressed.

"Oh, and Leigh," Warren added, "it's pretty clear you've had your share of excitement. I'll get some serious laughs telling your gas station SWAT team story back at the station. Who knows, maybe danger just manages to find you."

Hanging up the phone, I was mentally admonishing my nervous blathering - *man, my mouth could get me into some tight jams*. So much for my sleuthing finesse. Once again, fear trumps finesse!

My business partner, Donny, came sauntering over. As a big guy, Donny worked hard to maintain a fit and trim physique; he usually fell somewhat short of this goal. His usual office uniform consisted of a pair of 'big and tall' jeans and a golf shirt. He worked to fold his awkward oversized frame into a nearby chair. As serious as Donny tried to be when he finally got down to business, the oversized, slightly protruding teeth in his rather long and box-shaped head always made me think of a gigantic gofer. Taking him seriously was tough to do.

"So Donna," he chuckled, unable to keep a straight face; there'd been a lot of cackling going on and I was pretty sure it was all at my expense. "I hear you've got another murder on your hands, and I wanted to thank you."

"Thank me for what, Donny?" I sighed expectantly, sensing a snotty comment on the way.

"Well, you know," he ruminated, "when I moved back here to Omaha, you know from Chicago, I was a little afraid that life outside the big city would be a bit dull for me. But thanks to you, life has become like a constant whodunit, and it never ceases to amuse me."

"Don't you have a proposal to write or something, smart ass?" I offered.

"Oh, now don't get sore, Donna. I don't think I could stand it if you shut me out of your new excellent adventure," he offered through his increasingly annoying bursts of laughter. After this parting comment, Donny made his exit, I would imagine, in search of another victim.

Now I was starting to remember some of the crap I'd taken as we worked our way through Claire's investigation. Funny how well we manage to bury certain unpleasant recollections, until circumstances drag them back with a vengeance.

I had a lot to get done before my four o'clock with Warren. No time to think about BJ. Anyway, thinking about her was threatening to make my head explode. Just as I finished signing expense reports, my other partner bustled in. Wow. Today Liv was in another one of her 'art-as-clothes' vibrant outfits. This one was Kelley green and navy with flowing wavy shapes of solid green, solid navy and intertwined stripes of both, creating a feeling of gentle movement as it flowed over her matching navy slacks and navy and Kelley spiked heels. Pewter jewelry in similar wave patterns embellished her chunky multi-level necklace and the matching dangling earrings and half a dozen coordinating bangle bracelets. I took a minute to take it all in while Liv lost no time in diving in to the topic du jour.

"Again, Donna?" she asked with obvious concern. "How well did you know this one?"

"Donny tell you?" I asked, "He's having just a little too much fun with this whole thing."

"No. I read about the murder on Facebook last night, when I couldn't sleep," Liv offered, "and when I saw that the victim had come from the Connecticut ad community, I figured you must know her."

Amazing. How did she do that? If you set her down on a deserted island, with nothing but Facebook and Twitter, I guarantee she'd know more about what was going on in the world than 80% of us back on the mainland. She had a mind like a steel trap and that made her an awesome business partner. Donny was sharp, too. As a business partner he was often an asset, but he lived for those moments when he could bust my chops, and these damn 'acquaintances' getting murdered were the gifts that just kept right on giving – for Donny!

I spent the next few minutes filling Liv in on what little I knew about the *vic* and her somewhat odd lifestyle. She was as stunned as I that BJ had announced she was moving to Omaha in order to go into business with me.

"I have to ask this, Donna," Liv began hesitantly, "did you encourage the victim to come out here in order to try and convince Donny and me to allow her to buy into Marcel?"

"Liv." I had to admit she'd asked a damn good question. "Liv," I started again, "I'm glad you asked instead of just assuming, and honestly, I would sooner agree to be the lone woman on a Greek freighter than to ever go into business with that FREAKIN' NUT JOB!" I guess I started to raise my voice at the end there, but I could see from her reaction that Liv knew I was leveling with her. Our partnership was too important to ever have her think I'd try anything underhanded like that. I made a mental note to call Donny after we were done to assure him as well. He hadn't asked, but I wanted there to be absolutely no doubt.

Liv and I finished up after I answered a few more questions about Betty Jean.

Then Liv said, "I know this is going to consume the whole agency once again. I'd caution you to keep them out of it, but they all had so much fun watching Claire's investigation unfold, I am sure there'd be no point. I do have to admit, somehow they managed to meet all of their deadlines last time, so I'll just have to assume that this time it will be more of the same."

With that she headed off to a conference call with one of our Kansas City clients to discuss their latest product launch.

I made a quick call to Donny and assured him that I had not made any plans for bringing BJ into our partnership.

"Donna, I never thought you were planning that even for a moment. I know how important ethics are to you, and it's just not something you'd ever do without your partners' prior agreement."

I really appreciated his vote of confidence. He knew me well.

"And besides," Donny chirped. I could almost hear him smiling. *Here* it comes! "If you did I'd enjoy jerking you both around for awhile before bursting your big old self-inflated bubble."

I rolled my eyes as I mentally acknowledged the truth of his statement. Under the circumstances he described, I'd be as vulnerable as a baby mouse in a house full of hungry cats.

That pile of work on my desk wasn't going to do itself. I decided to shoot for a few very productive hours before changing focus to compile my Connecticut suspect list for Warren.

[CHAPTER 3]

The next time I lifted my head up for air was about noon. I figured I'd better get started on that list for Warren before running out to grab a bite. In this business you never knew what would crop up in the course of an afternoon, so that four o'clock appointment at the station was looming large in my mind. I wondered if arriving unprepared at a detective's homicide meeting had any of the same ramifications that it did in school, or with clients. Nonetheless, I was not about to find out.

Let's see... I'd start with my first advertising job and some of the characters who had worked with both BJ and me. The first and most obvious starting point was the owner of the ad agency, Jack Mylar. He definitely qualified as a character. A very suave and debonair gentleman who slept his way through the Connecticut ad community at a time when women had started rising to positions of power. Not a lot of power, mind you; it was the early 80's but they wielded enough power to hold the controls on a company's communication budget. Jack had talent, but his reputation as a "lady killer" rendered other talents unnecessary. All he had to do was flirt in the right direction and the clients beat down our door to get in. I suppose you could say it was women's liberation in its purest form, but it sure didn't look that way when one of his legendary 'rough breakups' ensued.

From what I could see, they were all pretty rough. Probably the most famous of his high drama final acts had occurred just before my arrival on the scene. At the time, he had had a partner in his fledgling business, Gregg McKracken. The love interest in question, Marion Plunkett, had been on their staff. When his love for Marion blossomed, he couldn't do enough for her; he even convinced his partner to put her name on the door with theirs, so the agency was Mylar, Plunkett and McKracken. Sadly, on that fateful day when the pilot light of his burning passion inevitably blew out, all hell broke loose – big time!

Mylar had arranged a covert tryst with his latest conquest, leaving enough clues to ensure being discovered. I guess there is a school of thought that believes a shocking discovery and a volatile scene is preferable to an honest discussion about one's capricious feelings. Well, shocking and volatile it was. Poor Plunkett had to be half-carried/half dragged away as she keened openly over her painful initiation to Mylar's legendary lack of staying power.

By the time I arrived, the only name on the door was Mylar. As folks tell it, McKracken was an upstanding, god-fearing man who couldn't bear to see women treated this way over and over again by his misogynistic partner. During my first few weeks at Mylar, I interacted with a staff of moderately shell-shocked ad folks who were clearly in mourning over losing their moral compass, Gregg McKracken.

Shortly after my arrival, I learned that Mylar without McKracken was a soulless institution that existed primarily to facilitate Jack's sexual escapades. It was Mad Men on crack! Surprisingly, we did some good work too.

Mylar's next major, misguided match-up did not reach quite the same level of highly visible volatility, but it did include a dramatic court scene in which his broken hearted 'secretary turned company VP' tried to convince a jury that she was entitled to half the business. Boy, that sure took me back. We were all holding our breath, especially the women. We all prayed she did not prevail. Had Bettina somehow managed to wrestle control of the company, her first order of business would undoubtedly have been to clear the hallowed halls of Mylar and all of her perceived former competition. In her mind we all qualified. I hadn't been there long before realizing we all qualified in Jack's mind, too!

Thankfully, our luck held out and Bettina was sent packing. From what I heard, the bulk of the fallout consisted of some late night threatening phone calls to her romantic replacement. All in all, a pretty tame experience in 'the life and loves of Jack Mylar'!

I supposed it was necessary to add Jack to the list, but at this point, I doubted he was in any kind of physical condition to travel halfway across the country and commit a murder. Apparently his years of heavy partying, deception, and general debauchery had taken their toll on his aging body. The recent photo of the retired company founder, on their corporate website, in no way resembled the dashing and dapper bon vivant I'd worked for years before. Back then he'd sported gorgeous jet black hair, a handsomely chiseled face and the classic 'Mad Men' playboy physique dressed in outrageously expensive, superbly fitted clothing.

In fact, Mylar's recent photo bore a striking resemblance to the male models in a website we'd just completed for a retirement home. Besides, his usual response to any woman leaving the market was one of relief. No, if Jack had wanted to kill BJ he could have done so during those years when they didn't live half a continent apart.

Furthermore, if my memory was correct, BJ had more of a reason to kill Jack than the other way around. As I recalled, she'd complained about being one of the only two employees he hadn't hit on. Seriously, if you were employed by a notorious lech in the 80's and he didn't hit on you – you became a total laughingstock – and she was.

As long forgotten memories continued flooding back, I also recalled that one of Jack's managers fired BJ shortly after I left; at the time that particular manager had already made significant inroads toward becoming another one of his romantic conquests. Hmmm, I wondered if that could possibly be relevant to the case. It seemed like a stretch.

I was starting to see that I'd end up with a pretty short list if I removed names based on my own assumptions of innocence. Besides, I'd been out of that market for so long I had no way of knowing whether old wounds had been reopened or new wounds had emerged from old relationships. Clearly, I'd be better off supplying the names and the connections I knew and letting the police in Omaha and Connecticut work out the rest. After about forty minutes of diligent concentration I'd completed a two-part list. There were about twenty people who, I believed, knew her enough to want to kill her, and another thirty or so who were acquainted with her on a more peripheral level.

As I finalized the list, I felt puffed up with civic pride. I would save the police a lot of unnecessary footwork. Conversely, it kind of freaked me out that people I disliked were turning up dead at an alarming rate. The fact that both victims had been women in the ad business somehow made it feel even creepier. While two murders may not have established a full-on trend, it was undoubtedly a curiosity. And on top of everything else – I was starting to feel guilty. Don't get me wrong, I didn't kill either one – but if I was being honest, I'd have to admit to harboring thoughts of murdering both of them over the years – a lot. I mean, if it turned out that my occasional psychic forays were developing a telepathic power strong enough to move the forces-of-nature... I shuddered. I would have preferred to use my powers for good instead of aiding evil in its recruitment effort for the Dark Side. Okay, Wonder Woman, I chided myself, my narcissism was getting dangerously close to Clovis-thinking. Man, that thought sobered me up fast!

Clovis Cordoba Seville was a former Marcel employee and the single most self-involved person on earth. If there was one lucky thing about BJ's murder, it was that Clovis could never insert herself into the heart of this case as she had managed to do in Claire's murder investigation.

And that thought proved just how shockingly naïve I could be about the master of self-involvement, namely Clovis.

[CHAPTER 4]

In person, Detective Warren continued to be every bit as reasonable as she'd been during Claire's murder investigation. That helped to lessen my concern that rumors spread by dear, departed pal, BJ, the ones about moving to Omaha to go into business with me, would eventually convince Warren that I'd reconnected with my former colleague and was now lying to protect my vulnerable – and substantial – butt. It was such a relief that she listened intently to every detail of that morning's conversation with Ken and never even shot me any "who're you trying to kid" looks.

As we talked, I started to relax a bit. Warren really did see me as a resource for gaining insights into BJ's persona, as opposed to an easy target for a quick trip to the gas chamber. Okay, that was a bit melodramatic, but hell, we were dealing with murder here; only a fool with my obvious connection to the victim would breathe easily before a suspect was firmly in hand. And wasn't me. I had to figure out how to get more of the details from Warren in order to assess my own vulnerability.

"Uh, Detective, can you remind me of exactly what you saw at the murder scene? The weapon was removed, right?"

"Nice try, Leigh, but since you don't know anything I can't very well remind you, now can I?"

Damn, she was good! Or I was just lame – but let's not go there.

At Warren's prompting, I regaled her with stories of BJ and her interactions with our shared colleagues and acquaintances, constantly reminding myself to keep the humor in check. At times, when reminiscing about some of these early work stories, I'll admit to going a tad overboard for effect. Rarely did I wax poetic in a mere attempt to inform – hell, what was the fun if you couldn't amuse or horrify your listener! What can I say – I'm a ham! On the odd occasion when I did slip into a familiar comedic version of a remembered tale, Warren's raised eyebrow would remind me of my mission and neatly shut it down. Personally, if I were Warren, I'd have preferred the comic rendition, but that's just me.

I related my long and bizarre relationship with BJ from the beginning. I had been hired into an entry-level position at Mylar Advertising, an agency where BJ was the reigning advertising wunderkind. At a mere four years older than I, she had risen to senior planner on our biggest account, Petrovsky Aircraft. BJ reveled at being the 't-shirt and jeans wearing' hero, and she treated me like a poor dumb newbie who could never hope to rival her meteoric rise to stardom.

At first, she was very kind to me in a decidedly patronizing way. Women could be so cruel to other women, and she was the master. Either you were a young superstar from another department, and her colleague, or you were her flunky. I fell into the flunky category and was relegated to performing the less glamorous side of her job.

Initially, if I needed information on the Petrovsky account, BJ would smile indulgently at me and point me to the data I sought. A shift came rather suddenly one day. I poked my head into her office, graced her with my biggest smile and asked for rates on *Aviation Week*, a popular magazine in the aerospace industry.

"What do I look like?" she shrieked at an alarming decibel, "your personal servant? Go find it yourself!"

In my naivety, I deduced that she was having a bad day.

This had never happened before and would not likely happen again – ha! Over the next few weeks that interchange would become the most pleasant of any between us. From that point on, there was no more civility unless others were present to witness.

My initial shock turned to determination. I would go to any lengths to find what I needed without having to bother the diva. BJ had cured me of any laziness, a move that would cost her dearly in time.

After the first year, BJ's *evil-mentor* hold on me had evolved out of her control, resulting in an accelerated rate of deterioration in our already dicey relationship. I'd learned quite a bit about aerospace from the files of the master and the media sales reps, clearly picking up more than she'd anticipated given my *notably limited intelligence* and obvious shortage of world class BJ-esque talents. The diva didn't like my progress.

Adding insult to injury, she had apparently observed my husband, Jon, at a variety of agency functions. That's when she began to resent me for a whole other set of reasons. Being married to a journeyman electrician and an absolutely wonderful guy (poor Ron), she greatly resented my banker husband and his white-collar social amenities.

Apparently, she began to envision me as a threat to her previously uncontested stardom and a threat to her social dominance. The hostility manifested itself in an endless series of backstabbing, sabotage and, at times, full-out assault. During that period, going to the office resembled a precarious walk through a war torn minefield. Stepping on a carefully assembled BJ bomb strengthened her slanderous campaign against me. Any minor misstep elicited a triumphant glisten in those beady little eyes, as she enthusiastically met her objective by announcing throughout the agency that I had again proven myself to be an idiot.

I remembered that time as one of the most trying in my career. It first happened when we got a new account executive on Petrovsky. I was busy in my office and heard BJ greet Jason in the hallway just outside.

"Jason, hi, how are things going?"

"Hello, BJ, is it?" he responded matter-of-factly. Yikes, the diva wouldn't like that! And I was guessing she'd take it out on me.

"That's right, Jason," she crooned in her most charming lilt, "it must be so difficult with everything you have to remember." Yuck, I was starting to wonder if she was going to break out into a southern drawl. Scarlet O'Hara had nothing on her!

"I was wondering if the media discussed in yesterday's meeting had been updated as indicated." This guy had the personality of a doorknob despite BJ's most valiant efforts to enthrall him with her deluded sense of self-appeal.

"It certainly should have," BJ reverted to her most businesslike demeanor, "but let me check for you. Donna!"

Upon hearing her command I promptly hustled to join the conversation.

"Did you finish making those Petrovsky updates?" she demanded brusquely.

Huh? I'm sure I looked as clueless as I felt. There I was between a rock and a hard place – I had no choice but to stick a toe in the water. I cringed and began.

"I'm sorry, BJ, I'm not sure what changes you're talking about."

"Have you lost another memo?" she accused imperiously. She looked at Jason, shook her head piteously and addressed me once again.

"Come on, we'll search your office and see what you've done with it."

After a few minutes of searching it was clear there was no memo. In between ranting about stupidity and carelessness she shared details of the desired changes.

Alone again, in my office, I just wanted to put my head down on the desk and weep.

Two days later, I had occasion to go into BJ's office. I was looking for a particular file I thought she might be using. A cursory glance at her desk caused an involuntary jerk of my head. There, on her desk, and tucked partially under the blotter was a half-finished memo outlining changes to be made to Petrovsky media.

That was only the first of several such instances. There was another instance when I received a public dressing-down for having misplaced yet another memo. Afterward, the others involved came to me explaining that I shouldn't worry, I had not been copied on that memo. This was getting old fast. But what I never knew with certainty was whether any of those incidents were intentional and premeditated, or the result of the beginning of the unraveling of BJ.

One thing to remember when you find yourself in opposition to a sociopath: the truth isn't on anybody's side. In fact, it rarely comes into the equation at all. That said, the next few years were spent learning more, doing more, and dodging landmines at every turn. BJ's maternity leave was the best thing that happened to my early career. It's not like she was going out of her way to teach me anyway. During her absence I stepped up to help and found myself leading the account.

Our department head was a nervous wreck, fearing that our biggest account, Petrovsky, would find itself flailing without the great and glorious BJ. She herself was terrified at the prospect of trying to fill the diva's maternity shoes. Furthermore, as an overzealous new mother, BJ had completely checked out; returning to work could not have been further from her mind, so her guard was down.

Having no interest in the field of aviation, our fearless leader and department head Gabby Joe Dorset was only too happy to turn over the whole responsibility to yours truly. Junior or not, I was all she had and her only "port in a storm" confidence in me paid off for both of us. It didn't pay off as well for BJ.

Gabby Joe was an interesting character. She herself had risen like a meteor from her role as secretary of a small, little known Hartford ad agency to being the department head in one of the two best known ad agencies within the Boston to New York corridor. She was a pretty woman, with a flair for professional, albeit slightly frumpy, fashion. Gabby's light touch of perfume followed her around like a sweet smelling guardian angel. She was a good role model for me in my formative business years. Up to this point, Gabby Joe had herself been held hostage by BJ's firm and furtive grip on the agency's largest account.

When my dreaded nemesis finally returned from maternity leave, she quickly surmised that things had changed. Not surprisingly, BJ genuinely liked the fact that I was doing all of her work. Her legendary laziness allowed her to turn a blind eye to my increased abilities. In fact, the elevated quality of 'our' deliverables had served to bump her status higher still. As expected, she wasn't about to let me share in any of that jealously guarded glory. I was happy to keep my nose to the grindstone and crank out exemplary work and bide my time, while she preened and puffed and accepted accolades. BJ concentrated the bulk of her office hours on showing off her most recent baby pictures, so for the most part she left me alone.

Gabby Joe's 'head in the sand' management style had enabled BJ to create her own set of rules from the very start. Using them, she proceeded to make a mockery of everything that mattered. Instead of working hard to understand aerospace, she had capitalized on her ability to use readily available facts and figures to make herself appear knowledgeable. No one else had bothered to delve deep enough to realize the information had been sitting in the company files the whole time. When, at agency parties, BJ would throw impressive aerospace terms around and Gabby Joe bought her act, hook, line and sinker. She declared BJ the unequivocal hero and no one questioned her – until I came along. It wasn't that I openly challenged the great aerospace rock star – it was just that I picked up the facts, figures and terminology faster and took the time to obtain a greater depth of knowledge. And it showed.

I was breathing down BJ's neck and she couldn't afford to let that happen. Something had to give. That was when the tired old cliché "idle hands are the devil's workshop" came to my rescue in a disheartening, albeit predictable set of circumstances.

After a few months of doing nothing but collecting praise and stabbing me in the back, more out of habit than hostility, BJ started to get bored. The tried and true solution for bored women looking to reaffirm their femininity is? Okay, I don't really know what it is, but I do know that BJ started having an affair. This was not just any affair; it was an affair with a co-worker whose major focus was his legendary stash of illegal substances. It was soon common knowledge that this guy really cared for her; why else would he have shared his mind altering treasures so liberally? And share them he had.

Their twisted and disturbing alliance brought about a number of changes. Oddly enough, as close as I'd been to BJ (she had to keep me close since I was the wizard behind the curtain), I was probably the last person to notice anything. Let's face it; she'd buried me alive under a mountain of planning and paperwork. I'd have been lucky to notice morning from midnight. I finally started to realize that she wasn't climbing all over me at every juncture or using every opportunity to belittle and discredit me. Hell, she was hardly ever in the office; and even when she was there, she was somewhere else.

In many ways I enjoyed this time at Mylar more than any other. However, on those rare occasions when the diva did return to earth for a brief visit, it was duck and cover for everyone in sight. There was no telling how she would react to even the most trivial comment or imagined slight, whether good or bad. Frankly, the prospect of waiting for the other shoe to drop was almost more unnerving than her violent tantrums. I knew this brief respite could not go on forever.

This next part was going to be tough to share with Warren, but I'd vowed that I'd be painfully honest regarding my relationship with BJ, even if the truth pushed me closer to making the suspect list. I proceeded to relate details of the fateful morning when I arrived early and BJ stormed into my office.

"I have an emergency proposal due in two days. You'll have to do it for me," she glared.

"Sorry BJ," I responded forcing myself to appear calm, "I am taking tomorrow off and I can't get out of my plans."

She went berserk! I mean she really flipped out. She called me every vile name I'd ever heard, and then she made up some new ones. I sat unmoving and watched her. Then she stormed out of my office and into the department head's office where I heard her continue to rant for about thirty minutes, while I diligently tried to concentrate on the task at hand.

What I hadn't shared with BJ, during our volatile encounter, was that my plans consisted of a second interview for a very exciting job opportunity. I'd had just about enough of her insane drug-induced behavior and her expectations that I'd cover all of her responsibilities, in addition to my own hefty workload. Even when it appears as though the predator has finally left you in peace, the knowledge that the beast can and will return at any given moment tortures your very existence, leaving you bereft of emotional stamina. I was heading toward burn out. It was time to move on.

Luckily, that was my mindset when our fearful leader called me into her office later that morning, to tell me that she really didn't have a job for me anymore. No surprise. She asked if I wanted to finish my assignment or leave right then and there. I told her I'd be packed up and out the door in twenty minutes. It took me fifteen.

I walked out of those doors feeling more liberated than I ever would have expected, especially since I didn't exactly have a position nailed down yet. Within two hours of being home I received a call from one of the gentlemen with whom I'd just interviewed. I asked him why he'd called me at home when he'd always previously reached me at the office.

"They said you went home sick," he explained.

"They lied," I corrected," I don't work there anymore."

News of my liberation propelled my soon-to-be employers into action, and before the end of the day, I had my next position locked and loaded. I got a three-week paid vacation on Mylar to boot.

I wasn't quite sure that Warren would buy my explanation. The actual events were public record, but my version of exactly how they occurred was not something that could be substantiated. Let's face it; I would have been well within my rights to want to murder BJ for her role in my hasty departure from Mylar. But I genuinely credited her for my lovely three-week vacation. And, in all seriousness, I had been one of the fortunate ones. I had escaped the abuse before my self-confidence had eroded to a point where finding a desirable career-path would be an insurmountable challenge.

As luck would have it, I think Warren believed my version. Besides, this had all occurred over twenty years ago. Navigating this ancient but still emotional story from my youth had escalated my heart rate. I cringed in anticipation of a monumental hot flash, the kind that could make me appear to be lying through my teeth. Thankfully, it never came. The absence of my trademark hot flash could have been the minor miracle that kept me off the prime suspect list, a huge blessing in my current menopausal state. Who says there are no miracles?

[CHAPTER 5]

With our business finished for the time being, Warren graciously offered to walk me out of the station house. Once outside of her office we noticed an inordinate amount of noise and activity, at least Warren thought so. As we moved closer to the commotion, one singular and familiar voice rang out above the rest: Peg? Once again my pulse quickened as both Warren and I broke into a trot. Apparently, she had recognized Peg's commanding tone as well.

Oh lord. We arrived just as paramedics loaded a uniform onto a gurney and were racing out to their waiting ambulance. I frantically searched for Peg and spied her standing calmly next to Babs amidst the throng of cops, clerks, and carnage. I could not begin to imagine what had occurred.

Luckily, Warren found her voice before I did.

"Just what the hell is going on here?" she demanded.

Everyone started talking at once. Except for me, I just stood with my mouth hanging open. It took about twenty minutes, but Warren was finally able to piece together a cogent story. Unfortunately, it did not bode well for any future kind thoughts that the local gendarmes might have for the folks at Marcel. Big surprise.

Apparently, Babs and Peg had become aware that I left the office unexpectedly. Once they had confirmed that I'd been summoned by Warren, their radar leapt into high gear. My ever-faithful protectors were not about to leave me alone to face my accusers. So along they came. As the story goes they were sitting quietly in the waiting area, having been refused access to Warren's office during our interview, when something caught their attention. One of the uniforms had been instructed to grab a ladder and check on a problem with a ceiling tile. There had been a leak, and management wanted a better understanding of the problem before contacting a contractor. Unfortunately for the uniform, he was on his ladder just feet in front of Babs and Peg.

Peg noticed the officer's gaze was fixed on the wrong spot. She was positive her vantage point provided a clear view of the origin of the problem. So, in true Peg fashion, she bellowed that he needed to redirect his search a little higher. He genuinely appreciated the hint and readjusted his stance for a better peak at Peg's discovery. Unfortunately, at about that time, Babs noticed the ladder had some funky piece of wood nailed to the bottom rung. She had visions of the poor guy tripping over the errant piece of wood and plummeting to the hard concrete floor. Just as he was following Peg's advice and adjusting his footing upward, Babs reached out to pull the wood away from the ladder's bottom.

I will spare you the details of the various and sundry injuries; no one wants a blow-by-blow of a uniform cop screaming like a little girl, especially when said uniform is a fairly rugged, burly guy. Once again Warren's beneficence prevailed, as she indicated with a sharp look and a jerk of her head that I should get our little group (Moe, Larry and myself, Curley) out of there before things got ugly.

As embarrassing as it was to have sent yet another police officer to the hospital – it may have occurred once or twice during the investigation of Claire's murder – it was comforting to know those two would always have my back. We were three menopausal colleagues who truly knew the meaning of support. We had bonded over ad-related trials and tribulations years ago. Investigating Claire's murder had served to strengthen that bond as Peg and Babs looked out for me and stuck by my side while I worked my way through the sordid details leading up to the killer's arrest. No task was too mundane or too risky. Their skilled and pragmatic approach to problem solving never ceased to amaze me, whether we were looking to perform the impossible in the office on a daily basis or encountering a hairy situation as we ventured out on the murderer's trail.

Peg and Babs were good people. Together we made quite a motley crew. Babs was my height of 5'7" and Peg was a petite 5'1". Babs had an unruly fluff of medium brown hair, while Peg's short, neat, dirty blonde hair always lay flat on her head with a curtain of straight bangs that hung obediently down her forehead. Both shared my menopausal body type of 'not too heavy' but 'not as thin as we'd like.' Their work uniform consisted of sensible jeans and t-shirts (which switched to sweaters in the cooler months). With my more severe all black wardrobe on most days, we didn't quite look as though we were all going to the same place. I'm told that after some of our more adventuress excursions, during our first foray into investigating murder, we'd become fairly well known among the city's emergency responders. I hoped that wouldn't come back to bite us – at least not any more than it already appeared to be.

Thank God it was the end of the day and we could all slink home and postpone facing our toughest critics, the rest of the gang at Marcel.

[CHAPTER 6]

The next morning came very early. It could have been those two glasses of Kim Crawford Sauvignon Blanc I'd had with dinner. After playing with my bulldogs and eating a gourmet meal prepared by Jon, I collapsed into an exhausted heap, confident in knowing the alarm clock had been set to an ear-shattering decibel.

As I made the serpentine trek around pods and desks to the comfort of my own familiar work area, it became all too clear that our antics of the previous day would be the hot topic at Marcel. I could feel eyes surreptitiously scoping me out as I wound my way around workstations. A glance from me, and those penetrating eyes were magically averted, leaving only the telltale hint of barely discernible head movement and an ill-concealed effort to stifle the mounting laughter. I might have known that Donny's high school cop buddies would lose no time in briefing him on our latest humiliation. Lucky for me, Donny had been there to greet me as I passed through the lobby door, so I hoped the worst was behind me.

"Wow, Donna," he began, "I was worried that this murder wouldn't provide quite as much entertainment as the last one, but I should have known you could turn anything into a three-ring circus."

Now that was uncalled for! I rolled my eyes, gliding past Donny to the perceived safe haven of my desk. As I passed by Kyle's desk, I was feeling the need for a short break from the less than subtle critics surrounding me. Kyle had been in and out of meetings since earlier that morning and wanted to know what Donny had been going on about. Honestly, that man can get on my last nerve. Donny, not Kyle. Kyle was always a welcome sight and a comforting presence. He had a good head and he knew how to work through a problem without creating more havoc than necessary, the latter being a rare trait in our industry. I brought Kyle up to speed on the events of the prior afternoon. I don't know how, but he managed to put a positive spin on the whole ordeal.

"You know, Donna, you were undeniably helping the police," Kyle began, "and I'm sure Detective Warren realized Babs and Peg were in no way responsible for the ceiling problem or that dangerously fragile ladder."

"Really?"

"I'm sure."

I felt better. That's when Kyle adeptly took it up a notch.

"I think I may have a lead on the victim."

"You? But, how?"

"You know the ad community in any city watches over its own, even when the person in question is relatively new to the market. Word gets around."

So true. The ad community in any city was tight knit, and Omaha was no different in that respect. Some industry news was universally known, and there were those who took pride in knowing even the most well-guarded of secrets. Kyle's connections ran the gamut. Naturally, he would hear things connected to something this juicy, the murder of the mysterious out-of-towner. Word on the street was bound to have filtered through. I had a million questions.

"What was she doing here? Who was she working with? Where was she staying? Did she have a permanent home?"

"Whoa, whoa, Donna," Kyle pleaded. "How about you hang

on for just a second and I'll tell you everything I know."

"Yeah, sorry," I agreed, "I guess not knowing anything is making me more nuts than I realized. It was just so frustrating spending all that time with Warren and getting nothing in return. She's damn good at pulling info out of you, and then she doesn't budge an inch. That probably makes her a good cop, but she can be really aggravating."

"I know this whole thing must be freaking you out," Kyle offered. "I mean, when Claire was murdered, we were all prime suspects since she used to work at Marcel, but in this one you're kind of on your own."

"Thanks, Kyle," I grumbled sourly.

I had known I was in a precarious position, but hearing Kyle say it left a lump in my throat. Sometimes it's better dealing with what's in your head than hearing it said. *Hmmm, that was pretty profound. There'd be plenty of time to pat myself on the back for insightful thinking!*

"Sorry Donna, I guess..."

"That's okay, Kyle," I offered, "I'm being too touchy. Let's just hear your update."

"Well, okay," he began again, "do you remember my old colleague, Cindy?"

Did I remember Cindy?

"Wasn't she the one I was coerced into wrestling with, to get some news on Claire's murder? How the hell could I ever forget Cindy?"

"Oh right, sorry to bring that up again, but she called me to ask what I knew about the murder. When I mentioned your connection with the victim - sorry Donna, you know how that information exchange thing goes, quid pro quo and all - she said she actually knew the victim herself."

"Cindy knew BJ?"

"Knew her and interviewed her twice."

"Interviewed her? For what?"

"Apparently, BJ was telling folks that she was willing to do some free-lance media work while you and she were getting the details of your joint business worked out. She needed some extra cash to help her support a new loft apartment in Midtown Crossing and Cindy needed a free-lance media expert."

I needed a few minutes to digest all of this. I knew Warren thought BJ was here to work with me, but it was unnerving to think she'd infiltrated the ranks of the ad community so deeply without my even being aware. I shuddered at the thought of her sharing intricate details of arrangements for a joint venture that existed solely within her own imagination. This hadn't just been some offhanded white lie she'd thrown out on a whim. BJ had clearly thought this through and committed to a new life and a future built on fantasy and subterfuge. My blood suddenly turned cold. Why would someone go to that much trouble to make up an elaborate story – and especially one with so many elaborate ties back to me? There couldn't possibly be any legitimate reason.

It hadn't occurred to me before; BJ's secret and nefarious plan might have been designed for the sole purpose of destroying the life I had worked so hard to build. I knew she had seriously disliked me, but it never dawned on me that she might go to such extreme lengths in order to harm me, especially after all these years. And why stop at harm? Maybe she'd come here to murder me herself for the perceived injustices I had wrought upon her – well, she was nuts, wasn't she? The notion of finding the killer to thank him, or her, seemed reasonable under the circumstances. But speculating about her end goal was pointless with BJ lying dead. It could, however, advance the investigation if we knew more about her intent during the final months of what had been her last misadventure.

Maybe she'd come to set me up for some kind of financial scam. I needed to find out more about what kind of joint venture she'd been talking about, and what, if any, plans she'd put into motion with a direct connection to me. I had to get in touch with my lawyer, Rodney Waters. He would know how to locate any paperwork that might have been fraudulently filed on my behalf. Rodney was impressive. He had a razor-sharp mind and an awesome appreciation of the absurd. I made up my mind to give Rodney a call. But first I had to let Kyle finish his debriefing.

"What else did Cindy have to say?"

"She said her first thoughts in meeting BJ were that a sophisticated media planner would come in handy right about now."

"Hmmfff."

"Cindy is actually pretty savvy. She said by the second meeting she'd come to realize two key factors. First, BJ was all talk with very little to back it up..."

"Smart girl."

"And second, BJ was way too far over the deep end to ever be allowed direct exposure to a client's account. That was a risk even Cindy was not willing to take..."

"Wait, you could tell she had crossed over the deep end?"

"Cindy assured me," Kyle continued, "I've heard some tall tales in my time, but to hear this chick go on about herself, I thought I was looking at Florence Nightingale, Madame Curie and Beyonce, all rolled into one! Not to mention the disturbing little laugh/snort she emitted whenever she thought she was brilliant, funny, urbane – so pretty much the whole time. The odd thing was that the snort kind of seemed natural when you looked closely at her alarmingly equine features."

My impression of Cindy had just risen about a thousand percent. Of course, it had been years since I'd seen BJ. It was possible her "crazy" had gone way past subtle. At this stage it could have been flashing on and off like a strip club marquee, virtually impossible for anyone to miss. Just as the next question came popping into my head, Kyle beat me to the punch.

"She was able to afford the pricey Midtown Crossing apartment because she'd sold her luxuriously appointed home in Farmington, Connecticut. It was right on the border of West Hartford, and probably sold at a substantial premium since she'd been in it for over ten years. But to complicate things further, there were rumors that she packed up in the night and took the entire profit from the sale, without splitting the proceeds with her live-in boyfriend."

I raised an eyebrow. BJ had always been one to land on her feet. A particularly unattractive woman with a decidedly narcissistic approach to life, she always managed to find decent guys who cheerfully bought her expensive homes. Life is not always fair.

Of course, thoughts on narcissistic women always brought one person to mind, Clovis Cordoba Seville, the single most narcissistic person with whom I've ever had the displeasure to be acquainted.

"Well, Kyle, at least Clovis can't get in the middle of this one," I asserted, trying to find a reason to be positive.

"Actually, Donna," Kyle began.

"NO, Kyle."

"I'm afraid so, she called right before I saw you."

"And said what?" I asked with dread and more than a little morbid curiosity.

"Steel yourself," Kyle continued, "Clovis is sure that the solution to this murder will occur only when those relationships between you and she, and the ones between BJ and she, have been examined. It is her belief that she is even a more integral part of this investigation than she was in that of Claire's murder."

I groaned. This meant that, actual connection or not, we were sure to get a daily helping of Clovis Crazy until the murder was solved. Although I was extremely disturbed at the prospect of frequent contact with Clovis, I had to concede that listening to her might prove fruitful. As loathe as I was to admit it to myself, Clovis' protestations that she was the center of the whole Claire murder mystery actually, sort of, turned out to be true. As convinced as we'd all been that her self-involved yammering was merely the ranting refrain of a narcissistic lunatic, Clovis had been integral to the solution of Claire's murder. I don't know if that is more indicative of the fact that Clovis' Romanian gypsy background did, in fact, enable her to 'know' things, or that crazy people tend to hang out with other crazy people, who are generally more likely to murder than your average run of the mill individual.

I returned from my reverie to hear Kyle finish his briefing.

"So, she wants you to call her immediately," Kyle finished.

For once, I was actually anxious to talk to Clovis. I couldn't wait to hear what was on her mind. Perhaps I should stop and take my temperature before making that call. Curiosity or not, it was just not normal for me to want to call Clovis.

[CHAPTER 7]

There was no point in wasting time. I knew what had to be done. Grabbing the nearest available conference room for privacy, I proceeded to make the call to Clovis.

"Well, Donna, what took you so long," she managed to whine and shriek at the same time.

Note to self: always take two Motrin before calling Clovis. I decided to ignore the first jibe and get right down to business.

"Clovis," I barked, "tell me what you know about BJ."

"Well, hello to you too, Donna," she squawked. "All this time and you can't even inquire after my well being?"

"Well, Clovis," I fed the beast, "your profile is high enough around here that I really don't need to ask."

It was nauseating, but facts were facts: an appeased Clovis is actually less annoying than an agitated one. I was groping for any chance I might have of surviving this interaction without permanent scarring.

"Oh I suppose that is true," she preened. "I should try not to forget that. Well, Donna, BJ and I became quite close in the short time we had together. It seems as though she sought me out as one of the key players in the Omaha market. She was smart enough to know that you'll always fare best when you start at the top."

Maybe four Motrin.

"I will say one key thing that I learned from our recently deceased colleague," she continued. "You certainly did some exaggerating about your career back east, Miss Northeast Expert. I mean, BJ thought the world of you, don't get me wrong, but I could tell that she was trying not to bare her soul and admit that you accomplished very few of the things you claim to have done back there."

"So, in other words, she backed up everything I've said about my career in the northeast?" I asked.

"Well, yes, that is true, but I could tell that it was an effort hiding the real truth so carefully. No need to be ashamed with me, Donna. I have kept enough secrets about your shortcomings since your arrival in Omaha. You should know that you can trust me implicitly."

I knew that six Motrin would start to bother my empty stomach.

"Right, Clovis, you're a saint. Maybe now would be a good time for you to tell me about your short but impactful relationship with our latest murder victim."

"Oh right, we probably should get back to the business at hand. Well, BJ says she met me at the Ad Club luncheon, by chance, but I happen to know that she tracked me down in order to introduce herself. We chatted for a bit and I could see that the poor thing needed guidance. I mean, she'd been in town for over a week, and had some ridiculous notion of going into business with you. I don't mind telling you that I lost no time in informing her of what a dismal proposition that would be. To her credit, in short order she began to realize that her misplaced loyalty to you would be disastrous without my wisdom and counsel – as we've certainly seen on numerous occasions!"

"Gee, thanks Clovis. I know I can always count on you to look out for my best interests."

"Don't mention it; you know I've always got your back."

That she did; wasn't the back the easiest angle from which to stick a knife?

"Tell me a little more about her description of our relationship, Clovis. How did she explain our supposed decision to work together out here?"

"I wouldn't know. I just don't have that much of an interest in such things. You know I've never been a nosey parker."

Had I actually wasted a phone call on this? I had learned nothing except for the exact date of BJ's arrival in Omaha. With the conversation not entirely focused on Clovis, her only acceptable course of action was to disengage, of course. How would I get to the bottom of this puzzle without a solid resource, one who had more than a passing interest in events that did not revolve solely around her? Just as I was about to start the long and torturous process of ending my call with Clovis, it was easier getting out of a confessional after admitting you'd murdered your rich old aunt - not that I would know, actually - when Clovis came forth with an unexpected golden nugget.

"Of course, she did ask me not to mention our few brief meetings to you."

"Why would she ask that?"

"Oh, she said that you and she had always talked about starting a company together when you worked together so closely back East. According to BJ, she knew you would be delighted to have her here, but she didn't want to get your hopes up until she had settled in. She was afraid your nerves would be too much for you, what with all of your fretting and fussing, never truly believing that she would ever really consider moving to a backwards area like the Midwest. She was certain that you realized it would be a challenging adjustment for a bright lights, big city girl like Betty Jean to make.

Backwards area, indeed. If I recall, some of my annoying early conversations with Betty Jean, virtually everywhere on

47

earth – short of Manhattan itself - was a "backwards area." How the poor thing suffered so. It must have been utterly excruciating being the only true urbanite enduring endless exposure to one hick town after another. Funny thing about it was, she laid claim to being the chic sophisticate without ever having lived or worked anywhere near an urban center. What a tragedy. How unfair that we, the backwoods hicks, were holding her back so shamelessly.

I couldn't deny that sounded exactly like something BJ would say. I'd forgotten just how much our murder victim could be a self-involved, self-aggrandizing diva herself. In fact, she and Clovis would have been twins separated at birth from a personality standpoint. From the neck up, no two looked less alike. Clovis was a bleached out frizzle-haired blonde with a cherubic face, resembling Barbie's little sister Scooter after accidentally sticking her finger into a light socket. Her curveless physique was custom-made for off-the-rack clothing, however, Clovis made two critical mistakes in her attire. For some reason she always chose garments that were one or two sizes too large. That, coupled with the fact that she wore the highest possible spiked heels made – ones that a circus stilt-walker would find challenging - created a phenomenon that was odd – to say the least. A walking Clovis was Frankenstein's bride come to life in miniature, replete with frizzled-hair, long flowing garments and a walk almost as sturdy as an infant first time out. Naturally, Clovis read the constant stares of those around her as open admiration.

BJ, on the other hand, sported a dark brown mane of snarly, kinky hair and distinctly equine facial features adorned with a beak that, I'm told, was used as the model for Elphaba's nose in *Wicked*; her face could stop a freight train. From the neck down both appeared startlingly thin to the point of emaciation with one marked exception: BJ was nearly six feet tall, while Clovis was teeny tiny, barely clearing five foot. Both believed that their appearance was envied by women pining for model-perfect physiques and desired by men with lust in their hearts.

Both couldn't have been more wrong, sort of.

Although neither was the femme fatale and fashion icon they deluded themselves into believing they were, both had a mystifying ability to attract men that seemed willing to risk all for them.

In an age where the educated and intelligent are emphatic about looks not counting – enlightened folks know that's not entirely true. I am embarrassed to admit that I, along with virtually everyone else who knew either of them, had occasion to wonder why any male would be attracted to those hot messes. The sum total of my wisdom has only ever been able to come up with one old cliché, *to each his own.*

From a totally pragmatic (i.e. selfish) standpoint, it did interest me that BJ had made it a point to tell Clovis I was not yet aware of her presence in the market. I wondered to how many others she'd made that same request. It appeared as though I'd have some witnesses to corroborate my ignorance of BJ's presence in Omaha, a fact that could come in very handy should some sudden turn of events place suspicion on me.

I managed to extricate myself from the call with Clovis just in time for my ten o'clock client meeting. Maybe a few hours of normalcy would help to eradicate the murderous impulse that a conversation with Clovis always elicited.

Our meeting ran long, so we invited our client to lunch. Blue Sushi seemed like an excellent choice since we were all hoping for something light.

By the time we returned to the office, it was almost two.

There were some phone calls I needed to return. Once on my own, I began to revisit my recent conversation with Clovis, causing me to wonder if Cindy had also been asked to keep BJ's presence a secret from me. I'd have to remember to check with Kyle on that since it would be so instrumental in cementing my innocence. I know, I know; Warren was consistently forthright in declaring her belief in my innocence, but if you hail from New Jersey, good luck letting go of paranoia – it's not like I don't try. It also occurred to me that the more I learned of BJ's life just prior to her death, the more intricately she and I appeared to be linked. One couldn't be too careful.

After dutifully returning all of the phone calls, I still had time to get in a few more tasks before calling it a day. I started by checking Marcel's Facebook page to contemplate my next entry. Once logged in, I noticed an odd comment on my last entry, which consisted of photos of our 'Friday's at four' office party from the prior week. Someone with an indistinguishable picture and the name Dakota had commented, "having murder as a hobby can be a deadly business." Okay, someone was obviously trying to rattle me, but threats on Facebook? That is just not cool! Cool or not, it did manage to make the hairs on the back of my neck stand out, so I'm sure it served its intended purpose.

I had to find Kyle and share the first scary event related to our latest adventure, aside from the actual murder itself, of course. Unfortunately, Kyle was in a client meeting. I decided to call it a night and get home to the safety of Jon and the bulldogs. Heading out, I was sure I resembled a startled hoot owl as my head swiveled from side to side on the lookout for danger lying in wait. I hated the victimized feeling that came whenever a threat hung over your head, real or perceived.

[CHAPTER 8]

Jon and the dogs were comforting; they formed a protective barrier around me all evening. Once in bed, my protective dog detail, plus Jon, lulled me into a contented and restful slumber. Getting that elusive night's sleep is always a challenge to a menopausal woman, even when she isn't being threatened by a murderer, well, most likely a murderer.

Before falling asleep, Jon made it a point to mention that he had not yet been able to solve BJ's murder. He needed a bit more time.

Jon has an amazing ability to solve a mystery within minutes of hearing the circumstances. Of course, in our thirty-plus year marriage, most of the mysteries he'd solved had been presented to us as entertainment rather than headlines taken from the local news. However, with the advent of Claire's death, Jon had proven that real or fictional, his problem solving-skills were unparalleled. It was impossible to watch an Agatha Christie movie with the man – he had it figured out within the first five minutes. Over the years, I'd learned to read the murder mysteries first, before Jon, thus eliminating the four thousand times he'd ask me "well, have you figured it out yet?"

I smiled thinking about how lucky I was; I had married my baby-faced best friend all those years ago. Today I could think of no one I'd rather have as my constant companion. The baby-face transformed into a very attractive looking guy with a kind heart and a quick wit – sometimes too quick!

The next morning dawned bright and sunny. Jon decided to forego sleeping in so that he could join me for a quick cup of coffee before I headed to the office. After the bulldogs finished their breakfast and gobbled their post breakfast treats, Jon poured his coffee and grabbed the morning's *World Herald*. He opened the paper to begin his daily ritual and turned toward me with a simple question.

"Now that you've prepared your list of Connecticut suspects for Warren, who jumps out as most likely?"

I just looked at him. I'd been so busy strolling down memory lane and digging through my recollections of 'old times' that I hadn't even considered who I felt would really want to kill her. Sure, I had twenty names on my 'more likely' list, but that was just because they had a longer, closer relationship with BJ than the others.

"Good question."

Clearly, I wasn't a complete natural at this detective stuff. Jon just shrugged and turned toward his paper. I knew that Warren would rather I continue to assist her in this very factual manner. She would far prefer that my information be offered without conjecture or conclusions. Conjecture and conclusions had propelled me into action during the investigation of Claire's murder, which, for some inexplicable reason, Warren never viewed as positive. Unfortunately, my highly competitive psyche could not help but turn Jon's simple question into a challenge too irresistible to ignore.

As I reviewed the characters on my list, they began to fall into an order of their own. Someone like Jack Mylar had certainly known BJ for a number of years, but would she have been important enough in his life to generate the kind of passion that would make him kill her? I seriously doubted it.

Even her first ex-husband, Ron, who certainly fit the prime suspect profile by virtue of being her ex, seemed unlikely as a real suspect. In fact, divorce was probably the nicest thing

BJ ever did for him. Even when you factor in the humiliation that she caused Ron by her blatant drug-induced dalliances, it was still difficult to view him as a likely suspect. From everything I'd heard, Ron was able to make a very nice life for himself with a lovely woman who absolutely adored him. Of course, it was certainly possible that BJ had managed to find some new way to torture her long-suffering ex during the years I had not been around to hear about it. Perhaps that was where I needed to begin my questioning.

By the time Jon finished his coffee, my short list of actual suspects was complete.

"Okay, Jon, I can answer your question now," I offered.

He peeked at me out of the corner of his eye. I knew what that meant. He had moved on from the mild curiosity which prompted him to ask his suspect question. His main goal now was to remain uninterrupted in order to finish reading the paper.

Jon tried valiantly to convince me he hadn't realized I was addressing him, hoping I'd give up and head for the shower. I could feel his tension.

"Nice try, pal," I continued, dashing all hopes that he might escape from the conversation his seemingly innocent question had generated. "You didn't really think you could throw me into 'detective mode' and then pull an ostrich move when things started to percolate, did you?"

I could see from his face that he was ready to cut his losses.

"You'd think after all these years you'd know the drill. If you can't stand the heat, get out of the kitchen."

I had meant that figuratively, but, in this case, he'd literally have to remove himself from the kitchen to escape my ire. Jon rolled his eyes.

"Okay," I started again, "your question made me think. At

first, I didn't really see a way of differentiating any of the folks on my primary list, but then I started to remember the rules of murder investigation – according to all the best TV detectives – follow the money and the romantic connections. By analyzing BJ's life in light of those guidelines, the short list was kind of a no-brainer. The way I see it, if she was killed by one of her Connecticut relations it would most likely be Rick WyCliff, the Mylar colleague with whom she had the ill-fated affair that broke up her marriage and who she later married after her divorce from Ron. To cement his motive, I've heard she left WyCliff after a business deal with a third partner went south and she needed a fall guy to take the blame for their questionable activity. Yeah, she set him up pretty good...not that he was a choirboy himself.

Next on my list was Porter Enzo, a media salesman she was rumored to have dumped in order to take up with WyCliff. Sales reps are the folks who sell time and space to advertising agencies on behalf of their clients. There are print reps and broadcast reps; in fact there are sales reps for every type of media from digital display ads running online to signage at sports arenas. I worked with Enzo long before the advent of digital advertising, the phenomenon that altered the balance of media forever. Back then Enzo sold ad space, or ad pages in a trade journal. There was speculation that BJ had awarded more business to him than was justifiable, that is, up until she dumped him. I remembered that particular interlude; he had been undeniably glum and cranky, not at all his usual perky self. Sales reps generally never exposed negativity unless they missed out on a buy; at all other times they were often too delightful and charming to be believed. Enzo's behavior had been a dead giveaway that rumors we'd heard were not just rumors.

The final suspect on my most likely list was another media sales rep by the name of Lou Cavrola. For some strange reason, BJ and Cavrola had formed an unholy alliance, the one that spawned the business deal for which I'd heard WyCliff ultimately took the fall. When she and WyCliff married, they also formed a business partnership with Cavrola, purchasing small apartment buildings in ghetto neighborhoods. They would purchase the apartment building, fix it up just enough so that inspectors would let it get by, and rent it to poverty stricken tenants who had no resources for anything better.

Once the buildings were 75% occupied, they would unload them on unsuspecting, neophyte investors looking for a healthy return, and typically a quick and unrealistically lucrative turnaround. From what I'd heard, BJ and WyCliff would take on the role of seller, and Cavrola, who was also a seller, would take on the role of a potential buyer bidding against their pigeon for the building in question. Word had it that their close rate was surprisingly high. Typically, within a year of being sold, the apartment building itself would fall apart just enough to put the unsuspecting buyers into serious debt. The extent of the deterioration often resulted in scaring away any other potential buyers who could conceivably bail them out and save them from their inevitable fate of ending up dead broke.

BJ and Cavrola had a lot of big ideas. In addition to their crooked real estate scam, at one time they had intended to open their own sales rep firm, making commissions from the sale of magazine pages. I found this out when Cavrola made a routine sales call on me one day that rocked my very world. Little did I suspect, a sales meeting with an old business acquaintance became BJ's first attempt to lure me into a business partnership.

At the time, I was aware that Cavrola and BJ had formed some sort of unlikely business connection, but I knew none of the details. Cavrola was working for a well-respected, albeit not overly successful trade magazine that he was desperately trying to get me to buy for some of my industrial clients at Maxwell and Mulberry, the New Haven agency I moved to after Mylar. Once seated comfortably in the conference room he began his monologue in a direction that caught me totally by surprise. Instead of extolling the virtues of his employer's product, he blurted out a statement that stunned me into total silence – quite possibly for the first time.

"BJ and I are thinking of starting our own rep firm and we'd like you to be our partner."

I had nothing. For a long time.

"She knows that she treated you horribly all those years ago, and she feels terrible about it now," he continued as though my brain were actually processing what he'd said.

While I'd like to be able to report that I smiled graciously and declined with savoir faire, in reality, the shock rendered both my brain and my speech unintelligible, so the best I could do was an awkwardly stammered, "uh, uh, uh." Not cool.

Then, all I could do was stare mutely. Had BJ been fully cognizant of all the horrors she'd inflicted upon me? I couldn't fathom the degree of depravity that would cause one person to so knowingly abuse another. The only reason I hadn't run her over in the parking lot years ago was the belief that she couldn't possibly realize just how miserable she was making me. Knowing now that her actions had been conscious and quite possibly deliberate made my finger start to itch for those car keys.

Sadly, I now knew that true evil did exist on this earth. The ability to doubt absolute evil had been a key factor in my peace of mind up to this point. From here on, I would be performing without a net; it was an important yet unwelcome lesson to learn. And there sat Cavrola, calmly awaiting my response.

I can honestly say that I have no recollection of the exact words I used to turn down the most absurd offer of my career. I do believe that I was gracious, but the actual conversation is a blank in my mind. Cavrola, being the consummate salesman, took it as a maybe and insisted that the door remain open. He went on to pitch the merits of his current magazine as though it were any other of the hundreds of sales pitches he'd made to me over the years. And, if truth be told, I probably didn't listen much less than usual.

I had tried to put that unpleasantness behind me years ago. Dredging it up only served to get my brain and my indignation all stirred up again. Perhaps one of the most challenging aspects of this case was that BJ had always been an enigma for me. The pieces of the puzzle just never seemed to fit.

The fact that she detested me was irrefutable, so why on earth would she seek me out and want to go into business together all those years ago? That was the true irony here. To folks in Omaha, it seemed perfectly natural that two former colleagues would hook up years later in a joint business. And so it would be, if the two were any other than BJ and I. All these years later my resolve had not weakened.

What kind of lunatic would knowingly go into a business with someone who hated and emotionally abused her?

After sharing my observations, and a few side tracks, with Jon, I sat and awaited his proclamation.

"Interesting," he declared.

"Yeah, and?"

"No and."

"What do you mean, no and?" I grumbled. "Don't you think I've created a very plausible list of suspects?"

"Sure," he countered, "but it's early yet. And don't forget all of these things happened over fifteen years ago. It's far more probable that her murder was a result of recent events than a dredging up of past history, don't you think?"

"Well, if that's what you think, why did you have me go to all this trouble sorting through my list for the most likely candidates?" I snarled.

"I didn't 'have you' do anything," he replied patiently, "I merely asked what I thought was an obvious question. A simple "no" would have sufficed."

I shot him a glacial glare before heading up to shower and dress for work.

[CHAPTER 9]

Traffic was light that morning so I breezed in a few minutes early. As I approached Donny's little alcove on the way to my desk, I could see that he was in full form, enlightening a handful of Marcel staffers on what was evidently a fascinating topic, judging from their rapt attention. Just as I moved past the intense little gathering, Peg spotted me and motioned for me to join them.

"Hey," she whispered, "he's got some inside info on your buddy's murder from Frick and Frack."

Frick and Frack, as we lovingly referred to them, were Donny's high school buddies-turned-Omaha cops. We'd gotten to know them fairly well during the investigation of Claire's murder. In fact, at one point after the threats started, they were part of a detail that was assigned to guard me. Their real names were Riley and O'Dowd, and they were actually pretty sharp police investigators, although our early sense of them was that they were another set of Donny's groupies just happy to tag around behind him and absorb his self-declared greatness. That was the thing about Donny. Having grown up in Omaha, he had connections like no other. There was virtually nothing that occurred in the entire city that could be hidden from his discerning appraisal. This murder was no exception.

I had to admit I was damn curious for details of the case. Up to this point the whole thing felt like a bizarre dream, the kind that shakes you and leaves you off balance until you can slough it off the next day. I knew that once I had some concrete facts, the whole thing would seem more real to me. Farley hadn't known any specifics, and Warren wasn't giving any away. I was well overdue for something salient, something that would enable me to envision this murder and accept it as real. Donny didn't disappoint.

"Oh hey, Donna," he'd finally noticed me, "you'll probably want to be briefed on some of the facts surrounding the murder, right?"

"I thought you'd never ask."

"Well, what do you say we head over to Aroma's? We've got about forty-five minutes before our first meeting."

He didn't have to ask twice. Aroma's was the coffee shop directly behind our office. It had a comfortable, Bohemian, student-friendly vibe and some very nice coffee blends. The downside of Aroma's Coffee Shop was that, tucked in the front corner, was an incredible smelling, tiny little bakery called Bliss. It was aptly named. The smells emanating from that space were a constant challenge to my willpower. Curse you, vile diet!

With coffee in hand, Donny and I selected a table in the corner so that he could brief me without fear of leaking sensitive information to the rest of the coffee dependent public.

"So," Donny started, "you knew that she was renting a place at Midtown Crossing, right?"

"Yeah, I knew."

"The jury's still out as to whether or not she could afford the place, actually. My buddies tell me there's some real funny stuff with her financial situation. It will be a challenge to get it all sorted out. In fact, I've agreed to consult for them. They're convinced the sooner the money gets sorted out, the closer they'll be to a solution. And I think they're probably right."

It was convenient for Frick and Frack that their high school buddy also happened to be a CPA. That fact had also come in extremely handy for us, at Marcel, over the years.

"So where did the murder actually take place, Donny?"

"The papers reference something about an empty office building in NoDo."

NoDo was the area to the north of the downtown business district that was the last remaining holdout for refurbishment. Since the new T.D. Ameritrade stadium, housing the Men's College World Series, had been built, NoDo real estate was suddenly in great demand by developers in search of old abandoned office space just begging for a cool, hip transformation.

"What was she doing in an empty office building in NoDo?"

Hadn't Farley made mention of a NoDo office?

"Decorating the office for your new business," he grinned mischievously.

Give me strength. How was I going to get through this entire investigation without making it to the top of the suspect list at least once? It's bad enough I'm the only one who knew BJ prior to her arrival in Omaha, combined with the fact that she'd told everyone she met that her move here was in order for us to go into business together. The fact that she was murdered in the suite of an office building she'd ostensibly leased as our new office space together was more than I could tolerate. There was no escaping this steam roller. I could see that now. Even in death the woman plagued me. I began to wonder if Warren was just playing me for a fool, pretending to need my assistance in order to keep me close by so she wouldn't have to look very far when it was time for an arrest. Was I just kidding myself? Hey look, I'm serious about people from New Jersey: we see hidden motives everywhere. It's part of our charm!

Donny could see that things were starting to get to me. The telltale twitch in my left eye had made an appearance – that always scared the crap out of him. At least I had that going for me! Poor guy had to move into supportive mode and abandon all the tacky, tasteless jokes he'd planned to share in the 'torture Donna over coffee' portion of our agenda.

"Hey, Donna, take it easy," he soothed. "It's not as bad as you're thinking."

"How do you know what I'm thinking?"

"You're thinking that every detail of this investigation has a major connection directly back to you," he offered, "and that, even if they want to believe in you, eventually they will have to acknowledge that the overwhelming common thread is – you. You're thinking it will be tough to justify why they haven't arrested you, since you seem to be the only common thread."

"Impressive. I guess you can read my mind, or is it just so obvious that no one with a brain could miss it?"

"No," he continued gently, "extremely intelligent people know that things are not often as they seem."

"Wow, that was deep," I had to admit. "Do you really believe that? Better yet, do you really think Warren believes that? Frankly, I wasn't expecting a lesson in philosophy from you of all people."

"First of all," he responded, "I absolutely think Warren is smart enough to know that. She has good instincts and her instincts tell her you're a straight shooter. She's also gathered enough damning evidence about the murder victim to know BJ was capable of getting herself mixed up in any number of nefarious situations, with or without help from you. Don't think that doesn't factor into Warren's analysis of the case. Second of all, it's not that I'm unfamiliar with the various philosophies available to help us cope with certain of life's phenomena. It's just that I find the candy-ass, sappy situations that typically call for this type of mollycoddling and hand holding to be nauseating beyond words. The fact that I have chosen to make an exception in this instance should in no way influence your sense of me as a hard-ass. It's just that, as any highly intelligent and evolved individual, I am capable of extreme flexibility when the situation warrants it."

Surprisingly, I actually felt much better. Donny was a smart guy. His argument made a great deal of sense. I would take author Echkart Tolle's advice and "live in the now" instead of conjuring up a variety of scenarios in which justice failed me and all hope was gone. Put simply, why buy trouble? Also, I couldn't help but feel honored that Donny had broken one of his hard and fast rules and displayed genuine empathy to help allay my fears. That could not have been easy. I think the facial twitch was even starting to subside.

"Thanks, Donny," I offered appreciatively, "for pulling me back off the ledge. Don't worry, your secret is safe with me."

Satisfied that his rare gesture of kindness did not fall on deaf ears, Donny moved on with his briefing.

"The murder weapon is a bit of a puzzler," he shared. "Even my guys aren't saying until there's confirmation, but Riley says it's the damndest thing. Says there was one clean hole the size of a 22-caliber bullet dead center of her forehead, but no bullet anywhere to be found."

"You mean the killer dug the bullet out of her head before he left?" I asked as I pictured the grisly possibility with horror.

"No," Donny added. "That wouldn't have been possible without really messing her up. Something really strange happened here. I could tell by the weird vibes I was getting off Riley and O'Dowd when we started talking about the murder weapon. Whatever it was, it was seriously unusual."

I took a moment to will my breakfast to stay put while fighting to keep my mind from envisioning the results of

Donny's "messed up" remark. It occurred to me that my constitution might not be strong enough to get me through this case. I was kind of glad it was time to get back for our 9:15 meeting.

[CHAPTER 10]

Our meeting ended at noon. As I returned to my desk, Peg scooted over with a unique request.

"Let's grab a quick lunch and check out the murder scene," she urged.

Something in my head told me this would be the dumbest thing we could do.

"Okay," I replied eagerly. "Will Babs join us?"

Peg, Babs, and I. That had been the recipe for certain disaster throughout the investigation of Claire's murder. And our recent foray to visit Warren indicated things hadn't changed all that much. We grabbed a quick bite at The Diner and headed north toward the nearly refurbished NoDo office building that held the crime scene. I knew there was little chance that we'd get in. Police would have the place locked up tighter than a drum. There would probably be crime scene tape as far as the eye could see, and I wasn't overly anxious to stumble upon anything that might have been left after what had to be a violent and deadly encounter. My stomach is just not that strong. I have to admit to being curious, to see the outside at least.

We got there and found a parking spot on the street nearby. You could see that the police had been busy at work securing the building, leaving little chance of gaining entrance. I took a moment to reflect on the place in which my former colleague and foe had breathed her last. In that brief contemplative moment, I failed to see Babs disappear out of sight. Turning to Peg for an explanation, I watched as she disappeared around a corner.

I was starting to get a bad feeling. I waited a few minutes, fighting my rising frustration level. If I returned to the office without Babs and Peg, Liv would kick my butt! Where the hell were those two? Just as I was about to let loose with a primal scream, Peg scurried back around the building and beckoned me to follow her.

As I turned the corner of the building, I saw an identical building. Babs was already inside, and Peg was urging me to follow her in as well. At first glance my instincts cried "get the hell out of here before someone gets hurt." The place was a disaster, dust and dirt everywhere, and everywhere the eye could see, walls were crumbling.

"Hey Babs," I yelled, "could this place be condemned?"

"Nah," she responded from God knew where. "I've been in way worse before."

Somehow her comment failed to soothe my nerves.

"Come on, Donna, we're up here," Babs and Peg shouted in unison.

"Where's here?" I barked.

"Come around the corner to your right and you'll see a make-shift stairway up to the next floor," Peg replied.

"You mean this rickety scaffolding type thing?" I asked hesitantly.

"That's the one," acknowledged Babs. "Now just grab on and start climbing."

"You can't be serious. Have you seem my shoes? I will break my freakin' neck if I try to climb on that thing!"

"Well, leave your shoes there and hoist yourself up here," countered Babs.

"No!" Peg bellowed. "Did you see all the nails and jagged boards on that floor? We don't have time to take her to the emergency room! Donna, you stay right where you are. We'll check things out up here and fill you in."

"Actually guys, I'd feel a lot better if you just came down right now," I urged, "because, you know I'm—." That's as far as I got with my rebuttal when I heard a loud bang followed by a series of smaller bangs.

"Oh God, what was that," I said, not really wanting the answer.

"I'm alright," Babs croaked.

"Peg, what's—"

"It's okay, Donna," Peg assured me, "Babs found the window that looks across the courtyard and in through the murder window. She just piled up a few crates so she could climb up and get a better look is all."

"No, not all, Peg, based on what I just heard-"

"I'm sure it sounded worse than it really was, you'll see when she comes down. Babs just had the wind knocked out of her, no visible marks or bruises," Peg assured.

"Yeah, Donna," Babs chimed in. "Nothin' worse than when I get the bug to paint my whole house in a weekend. You've seen me come in after those marathons looking way worse than I do right now."

I rolled my eyes.

"Will you get down here now?" I pleaded.

"Not yet. I saw something interesting and I need to get a better look," replied Babs.

Against my better judgment, I climbed the scaffolding to offer my support. If truth be told, now I was really curious. Surprisingly, the spiked heels provided me with the perfect hook to secure one foot on a rung as the next one began its ascent. Who knew?

As I climbed from the scaffolding to the plywood floor above, I took a deep breath and looked around. Babs and Peg were right; there was a clear view into the office where the murder had been committed. You could see crime scene tape all over the place. Unfortunately, from where we stood, it was impossible to see the floor and the object that had gotten Babs' attention.

Then I looked at Babs. Holy God she was a mess! She was covered from head to toe in a thick grayish brown dust that made her appear to have had a full makeover from hair color to eye shadow and lipstick. The knee of her jeans was ripped and her knee was bleeding. At least I think it was blood. Mixed with that grayish brown dust it looked more like roast beef gravy.

"Holy crap, Babs! We've got to get that cut cleaned up or you'll end up with an infection," I urged.

"Plenty of time for that, Donna. Let's just reconfigure these crates to get one more look," Babs instructed.

She was in her element now. There was a job to get done and, like the U.S. mailman, neither rain nor snow nor sleet nor disgusting filthy construction dirt in her mouth, would distract Babs from her appointed task. Looking over at Peg, I could see the same look of determination. Those two were unstoppable, and that's what we all loved about them. I looked down at my black high heels. Much like the lower half of my dress black slacks, they were enveloped in dust. I just shrugged.

We restacked the crates being careful to check each layer for its stability. Once satisfied there would not be a recurrence of Babs' death defying spill, or as Peg had begun referring to it: "cirque de so wrong." We were ready to test our handiwork. Peg and I realized at about the same time that Babs was getting into climbing position.

"NO!" we both yelled.

Babs was startled but regained her footing. That's when

Peg took over.

"You do not think we are going to let you climb up onto that thing again, do you?" said Peg in a voice that had me trembling a little.

"Why not?" Babs wanted to know.

"You're kidding, right?" I shook my head.

"Well, guys," Babs retorted, "Donna can't do it with those shoes, and Peg has developed a fear of heights that seems to get worse each time we see someone tumble from a ladder, which is surprisingly often lately."

Peg and I looked at one another. We knew what had to be done. While Peg swept the area around the mountain of crates with a stray piece of cardboard, I took off my shoes. With the help of Peg and Babs, I made my second shaky climb of the day. Once at the top, I took a minute to test the stability of the dubious looking structure. It seemed okay. I positioned myself toward the building across the courtyard and got my first full glimpse of the murder scene. The chalk outline of BJ's body was the focal point of what appeared to be a very chic and contemporary workspace. Most chalk outlines, you know the ones on TV and in the movies, clearly show the torso along with two arms and two legs. BJ's outline was not as clear, leading me to believe that she'd sort of crumpled into a heap. There was no way of knowing if she'd been face up or face down.

It hit me harder than I'd expected. First there was a lump in my throat, and then I could feel my eyes begin to well up with tears. Was I just an incredibly compassionate person who had finally been confronted with the grisly murder scene of a former colleague, or were my menopausal hormones messing with me again? Note to self re hormones: get a blood test!

I took a moment to compose myself. You never want colleagues to see you looking all teary-eyed, even if they are incredibly compassionate and understanding people themselves. It's just not cool.

"Okay, guys, let's roll," I uttered, swallowing the lump in my throat.

"Sure," Peg patiently responded. "Just not literally, please!"

Babs chuckled, "Yeah, that would be bad."

"Whatever." I rolled my eyes.

And that was when I noticed it. It was in the far right hand corner of the room, as Babs had said. But what was it? I took a closer look. It was a smushed-up lump of neon orange about the size of a bread box. As I strained my eyes to try and make out more details, it appeared as though there was an insignia repeated evenly over the entire surface. I was pretty sure it was made of a leather-like material. Very strange.

"Well," Babs urged, "what is it? It's driving me crazy."

"Can you describe it?" Peg asked. "Tell us what you're seeing."

"Hmmmm," was all that came out.

I attempted to describe my discovery.

"Oh," said Babs. "I didn't get the insignia and the leather part. That's very interesting."

"But what the hell could it be?" Peg pressed, "Come on, guys, you've seen it. Now what is it?"

I looked at Babs and she shrugged. Shaking my head I felt around for the right position to begin my descent.

"Oh well," I shrugged, "you can't win them-" And then I stopped abruptly. Unfortunately, both mouth and feet stopped at the same time. Had it not been for quick action on the part of my compatriots, I would have emerged from that building looking like Babs' twin. I swayed dangerously far forward, and then veered around to the right. With Peg and Babs holding onto both me and the house of crates I was standing on, I was able to survive the shift in weight load without crashing into a mangled heap on the filthy plywood floor. Whew, that was close! I took a moment to compose myself. Then I remembered what had jolted me in the first place.

"Hey guys, I know!" I cried.

"Donna, are you alright? I didn't see her hit her head."

Peg turned to Babs with a puzzled expression. "What the heck is she yammering about?"

"No, I don't think it's a head injury; I'm pretty sure we kept that from happening," Babs countered.

They both looked at me with concern, as though my near fall had caused my brains to slide out my ear.

"Give me a break," I groaned. "I'm fine and I'm pretty sure I've figured out what the lump is."

Satisfied with the possibility that I might still be lucid and capable of thought, they turned anxiously in search of the answer to this frustrating riddle.

"Armani," I offered.

"Armani who?" Peg responded.

"It's an Armani handbag, well, actually a knock-off," I clarified.

"Oh yeah, I can see that," Babs concurred, "that makes perfect sense."

"Not really," Peg interjected. "Sorry to burst your bubble, but the police would not have left a designer, I mean knock-off designer, handbag in the middle of a crime scene."

Babs looked at me with a dejected frown.

"She's right," I admitted. "There's no way they'd have left it there."

"Maybe they didn't," Babs declared.

That made us all stop and think. Had someone been in the room and left a bright orange Armani calling card, after the police had finished examining the crime scene?

Following an animated discussion of the facts before us, we all came to the same unshakable conclusion: the bag was put there after the police examination, and there was a strong likelihood that it was left by the murderer returning to the scene. Upon arriving at that conclusion we experienced a collective shudder. Then we looked at one another with a shared thought. *Let's get the hell out of here, now!*

If anyone were to ask me I would be unable to provide details of our departure. I can say with no little amount of wonder, we all made it down without further incident. And I'm pretty sure we broke a land speed record in our scramble for the car.

[CHAPTER 11]

Heading back to the office, we discussed our civic responsibility with increasing volume. Did it include informing Warren about the bag? Peg insisted it did.

As you can imagine, I was none too thrilled at the thought of alerting Warren to our little snooping expedition. It would be bad enough to admit that I was actively involved in the investigation after her strenuous recommendation that I sit this one out. Having to admit that we'd kind of tampered with the murder scene would not make me a likely candidate for homecoming queen at the next policeman's ball. I was pondering my limited options when Babs chimed in.

"No, Peg," she countered, "the police will be back in there for something or other, and I'm sure it will be soon. No point getting Donna in hot water with Warren unnecessarily."

That's my girl, Babs; I should have trusted that she would have my back. See, Peg isn't always right, and Babs may be the only person who can tell her that and live. I breathed a sigh of relief assuming I'd dodged a bullet. Seems I was getting ahead of myself.

"Forget it, Babs," Peg's continued. "You know very well that the earlier they find every piece of valuable evidence, the higher their percentage of ever solving this thing will be. A conspicuous designer bag...."

I shot her a look.

"I mean, knock-off designer bag at the murder scene is without question a valuable piece of evidence. Hell, for all we know the murderer has placed a signed confession right in that very bag."

Although Peg undoubtedly realized she'd gone a tad too far with her 'confession in the bag' theory, she knew she had us. It was too big a risk. If this evidence turned out to be critical to the case, we were already tampering with the investigation for not having reported it earlier.

Peg parked the car while I contemplated the best way to break the news to Warren. It was tricky because, valuable though the information was, the fact that it came from me could prompt Warren to put a lid on my sleuthing, forcing me to tow the line for the rest of the investigation. That would be truly unfortunate since I was just getting warmed up. I decided to try and find Kyle for some advice on the best approach with Warren. He was always so good at communicating tricky subject matter.

Walking through the lobby door we came face to face with Donny on the way to his next meeting.

"Damn it," he complained.

"What's wrong?" we responded in unison.

"I'm late for this meeting, so I can only spend a few minutes laughing my ass off while you explain what the hell you did to make you look like you just came from the great Dust Bowl," he chortled. "This is gonna be good!"

"I have absolutely no idea what you mean," I pronounced imperiously as I pushed past Donny with my girls in tow. Babs opened her mouth to reply to Donny, but a swift shot to the back from Peg propelled her forward rendering her temporarily mute. I did not need that right now!

I passed Kyle's desk on the way to my own. He was nowhere in sight so I checked his calendar. If his meeting didn't run long, he should be finishing up shortly. Nothing appeared to be scheduled for the next hour, so I grabbed that time for our Warren discussion and spent the next twenty minutes catching up on e-mails and phone calls. A quick check of Facebook revealed a cryptic message from Dakota, "Still haven't learned?" An icy chill shot up my spine. Would anyone believe this was a genuine threat aimed at me? Did I believe it? I tried my damnedest to convince myself it wasn't.

Kyle's meeting ran a bit long, but nothing like the marathons that so many meetings turn into. Once finished, he grabbed a coffee before tackling his next subject. With Diet Orange Sunkist and notebook in hand, I headed into our smallest meeting room to wait for Kyle; getting away from my computer, and Facebook, seemed to be helping. Within minutes I could hear his approach. It's not that his shoes are noisy, it's just that the poor guy can never make it across the room without being stopped by question after question. As he made his way from the kitchen, I tracked his progress by the voices that waylaid him on his journey.

"Hey Kyle," Babs asked as he rounded the corner near her desk, "do you want to see the roughs from the TV campaign we just shot?"

"Sure Babs, just throw a meeting on my calendar, I'd love to see them," Kyle responded.

"Oh, Kyle," Shelly blurted as she saw him pass her desk. "When can we talk about NQR?"

"Check my calendar, Shelly, whatever time slot's open," Kyle directed.

God bless him, though. He was single-minded in his determination to reach our meeting without further delay. He kept walking and getting stopped, but he remained undeterred. After three more inquiries – on the fly – Kyle finally breezed into our meeting room with coffee, notebook, and calendar in hand. Once safely inside with the door closed, he sighed, shook his head and sat down to face the next all-consuming task.

I felt a little guilty. The poor guy never got a moment's rest, and here I was using up his precious time to help me with my extracurricular adventure. I said as much but Kyle was quick to reassure me. Big surprise. I had to remember to keep my Facebook worries to myself! That would only make things worse.

Determined not to tie him up any more than was necessary, I rapidly briefed him on the challenge at hand.

As usual, he had some good thoughts on approaching Warren with sensitive information in a way that would prevent me from plunging myself into hot water.

"Warren's pretty sharp, as you know," he began, "but murder makes everything hypersensitive. It's not an everyday occurrence, so normal is kind of out the window."

I wasn't exactly sure where he was going with this, but Kyle was quick in getting to the point.

"Warren may know that you didn't have a great love for BJ, but she was once a colleague of yours," he continued. "I don't think the good detective would think it so unusual that you'd find yourself drawn to the murder scene because of your unmistakable, albeit unwelcome, spiritual connection with BJ."

I must have looked somewhat skeptical. To be honest, I was feeling very skeptical because I felt my loathing of BJ had been fairly widely known. How could he be so sure that Warren wouldn't just assume I was the murderer characteristically returning to the crime scene? Sensing my hesitation, Kyle pushed on more aggressively.

"Look, Donna, you're gonna have to sell it," he pressed. "It's Academy Award time. I know you want to keep things on the up-and-up with Detective Warren, but you messed up. You should have stayed away from the murder scene. If there's no way out of this corner you boxed yourself into, you could soon be on the outside of the investigation and on the outside of Warren's trust. That could end up costing you a much higher price than you're prepared to pay considering your questionable relationship with the murder victim."

I had to admit, he had an extremely valid point. Maybe I could make this work, but I would need to cover more of the bases before I was ready to face Warren.

"Let's say I convince Warren that it's perfectly normal for me to feel compelled to check out the murder scene, that's still a far cry from getting her to accept my trespassing in an abandoned building, just to poke my nose into the area that had been cordoned off by the police?" You're right as usual, I did go a bit too far.

"That's easy," Kyle replied smugly. "Warren knows you well enough to realize that once you were there, you wouldn't be able to walk away without having seen everything. Then you'll want to emphasize the fact that you did not actually invade the area cordoned off by the police. You did not breach the crime scene tape out of respect to Warren and her team. Don't lay it on too thick or she'll smell a rat. Like you said, Warren is a smart lady."

I was starting to like this approach more. It's not as though I had much of a choice. Warren had to be told about the new evidence.

"One last thing," Kyle cautioned, "your focus should be on the new information and the fact that you made sure to get it into Warren's investigation as soon as possible. It's the subtle distinctions that will save you from exile. You're not lying, you are placing the focus where it works best for you, and luckily, you have new information that should grab their attention in a big way."

Okay, that was settled. I thanked Kyle and checked my watch. It was 4:15 and I had to be home before six to freshen up for our wine tasting at Le Voltaire. I decided to head over to the police station and brief Detective Warren in person.

As I walked toward the station Warren was rushing out with Frick and Frack.

"Detective Warren," I began, "I have some new information, related to the murder, that you'll want to know about."

All three police officers stopped for a second.

"Sorry, Donna," Warren apologized, "we got an anonymous tip on some new evidence at the crime scene. The caller suggested that it could lead us to the murder weapon. Can your news wait until tomorrow?"

It took me a moment to recover. Oh, man, this was my lucky day! What were the odds that someone else would get this information to Warren only a few minutes before I was about to risk so much by confessing my little indiscretion? Who says we don't have guardian angels.

"Donna?" Warren ventured with an odd look on her face, "You hear me?"

"Oh, sorry detective, yes, of course I heard you."

Perhaps unnecessarily, I offered an explanation for my momentary lapse through Alice's looking glass. "It just surprised me to hear there was more evidence at the crime scene. I mean it's cordoned off, right?"

"Very true," Warren confirmed. "In fact, we've never had a breach of a murder scene before. So you can see why we're in such a rush to check it out. It appears as though our perp is pretty cocky and can't stay away from the scene. This could be the break we've been hoping for, so if there are no further questions-"

I cringed inwardly at her reference to the perp returning

78

to the scene.

"Oh no, no, Detective, I wouldn't dream of holding you up any further," I replied. "Any chance of getting the details on what it is that you find?"

I knew I was pushing a good thing, but you can probably tell by now that I almost never know when to quit. Thankfully, Warren took it in her stride.

"We'll see," she offered vaguely.

I knew that was the best she could do. After Warren and her team moved on, I checked my watch to find that it was already 4:45. Time to head home and get a jump on preparations for the wine tasting. I was really looking forward to a relaxing evening with gourmet food, fine wines, and a number of our closest friends. Throughout the course of the year we attended many functions at Le Voltaire; the food was always great and the wines carefully selected for their ability to compliment each meal to perfection. On this particular night I hoped to be transported to France by an unparalleled sensory experience, one that would enable me to escape the self-induced pressure of BJ's murder investigation. I knew my friends were likely to have questions about the murder – and maybe even suggestions – but most of them were intuitive enough to understand the value of being able to decompress when life starts getting too demanding, with the possible exception of Ed.

If I made decent time I'd gain an extra few minutes, which would give me a chance to play with my bulldogs. Not that it would help all that much. If I had the nerve to turn around and leave "my girls" soon after arriving home from the office, I'd find the couch pillows strewn across the floor upon my arrival home. That's how my bulldogs show their annoyance when we foolishly abandon them for an evening. One thing about bulldogs, you always know where you stand.

As I headed back to my car, I had a sudden flash of awareness. Of course! I knew precisely where that anonymous tip came from. Babs and Peg, my two guardian angels, had called it in. Had to be! I could have wrung both of their necks, and I wanted to give them a huge hug at the same time. I knew they had stuck their necks out to save mine, but I also knew it could easily have blown up in all of our faces. God love them, they would be the death of me one of these days; maybe literally if we all weren't more careful! I started wondering how strong tonight's wine would be.

[CHAPTER 12]

We arrived at Le Voltaire just in time for the first pour. This was a fairly large gathering, but half of the attendees were good friends and fellow wine (and food) aficionados. As usual, the tasting was in the back room. Insulated from the dinner crowd, it's comforting yellowy-gold faux stucco walls enveloped inhabitants in a warm and sultry Provencal caress.

There were no outer windows, but a large alcove behind the room housed the formidable wine cellar, visible through a massive interior plate glass window which acted as sentry for all the vine-ripened pleasures safely ensconced within. One glance through the glass brought the most discerning wine connoisseur to his – or her – knees.

Jane and Cal Fiesty and Fleur and Francois Boulevardier sat together at one of the rustic tables for four placed strategically against the window. A quick wave from Jane confirmed she'd spotted me, and they all flashed welcoming smiles of acknowledgement.

After exchanging the requisite double cheek kisses, Jane looked me straight in the eye. "Donna, we were just talking about that terrible NoDo murder. One of the nurses where I work said that you knew this victim, too."

Oh here we go. I realized at this point the odds of escaping the whole murder thing for an evening were down to zero. Figures.

Jane continued as though reading my mind, "You don't have to talk about this if you don't want to. But I have to admit, we are a bit curious."

"No, that's okay, I'd want the dirt if I were in your shoes."

At that moment, Ed arrived at my side with an empty glass and a bottle of champagne.

"Care to try our aperitif?" he offered, "I think you'll find it very pleasing. It's Ruinart R. Brut, a special request from our host, Olivier. He felt it would be the perfect entrée to an elegant and relaxing evening. It is the most charming blend of Chardonnay, Pinot Meunier and Pinot Noir, which is a kissing cousin of Dom Perignon."

Two gentlemen with whom I was unfamiliar sidled over to Ed and his bottle, looking for an aperitif for themselves and their dates. Ed grabbed some glasses and, smiling, began to describe the delightful nectar as he poured. As I moved away to give him a chance to help the new guests, Ed leaned toward me and spoke in a conspiratorial voice, "Remind me to tell you about our visit to the house of Ruinart, starting with a VIP dining experience and private tour of the galleries, and ending with an exclusive wine tasting."

I nodded and smiled as I stood to the side giving Ed a chance to finish his duties. A total immersion in the world of fine dining was my best shot at escaping the relentless reminders of this murder and all the stress it entailed.

Ed von Hapsburg was a good friend and a wine distributor. He and his wife Eva were always a lot of fun to have at a party. Ed was also one of the few people I'd met, since moving to the heartland, who really seemed to have my number. Or more accurately, he was one of the few who openly admitted to having my number. Ed and Olivier, our host for the evening, had worked hand-in-hand together for a number of years. Their food and wine kinship was long standing and widely traveled.

"Kill or maim any annoying sales people this week, Donna?" Ed casually queried as he walked back toward me with the barest hint of a shit-eating grin. He'd clearly forgotten his promise to regale me with tales of his visit to Ruinart. Judging from his smart-ass remarks, the anticipated story of his visit to Reims and the oldest house of Champagne would have to wait until later. "I could use a good laugh tonight."

So much for elegant and relaxing!

"Ed!" Jane intervened, "you do know that Donna is in the middle of that whole NoDo murder, don't you? Do you honestly think she wants to hear your twisted humor laced with violent imagery right now?"

"Oh geez, Donna," Ed started, "I honestly had no idea you were involved in another murder. Oops."

Eva appeared at my side. "That is so typically Ed," she offered, "foot in mouth before the first course; it's like a sixth sense, he always zeroes in on the hottest of the hot buttons."

At this point Ed's face turned a bit red. I couldn't be sure if it was embarrassment – it was hard to embarrass Ed – or a healthy flush at the thought of a fun evening dissecting a murder investigation and me.

"You're wrong, Eva." Ed replied, "My foot is definitely not in my mouth. The only thing going into my mouth is this epic feast! And now that Donna's providing the entertainment, it's all good!"

Clearly embarrassment was not the cause of Ed's red face. Figures. Eva shook her head and moved on to chat with Fleur and Francois. They had just come back from a three-month holiday at their charming and elegant Paris apartment. Eva, a dedicated Francophile and world traveler, had numerous detailed questions on which restaurants were worthy of adding to her next Parisian itinerary.

Eva and Ed made a cute couple. He was a big guy, like football player big. He sported a reddish brown, regular guy haircut with a shock of thick, shaggy bangs and a matching bushy mustache. The wire-rimmed glasses perched atop his nose were not bold enough to steal attention from the big blue eyes that hid behind them. Ed's dress consisted of chino-like slacks and short-sleeved button down shirts in casual patterns such as large plaids. His clothing almost always tended to be light in color, in sharp contrast to my 'all black all the time' basic rule of thumb. Eva, on the other hand, was a diminutive beauty with a curly reddish mane that appeared to have a mind of its own. The amazing thing about Eva was that, from the top of her head to the tip of her toes, she was unconsciously trendy chic. When you looked at her you saw what other women labored hours to achieve. But still, you could tell as you watched her and spoke with her that it had all sort of just happened.

I envied that kind of style sense. She could mix fabrics and patterns that would unquestionably baffle the ordinary woman, though she barely seemed to notice that she had, yet again, pulled off a perfect blend of cool, right down to her very stylish dark red-framed glasses. It hardly seemed fair that I would sometimes have to spend an hour or more trying to decide which black slacks to wear with which black blouse. Seems as though it should be easy, right? If you said yes, I can only hope you are not in any way associated with the fashion industry.

"You know, Ed," Jane offered, "give him a gourmet repast and a few cheap laughs – that will be engraved on his tomb-stone." Jane and Cal were a welcome addition at any gathering, and Jane was never one to hold back when some-thing needed to be said. Cal was another big guy with grayish white hair and silver wire rimmed glasses. His wardrobe frequently gave the feeling of an affluent tourist visiting the Hawaiian Islands. By his side, Jane was an attractive blonde with an expensive casual wardrobe that reflected her mood of the moment with just the right compliment of 'jewelry as art' bling. One never knew what styles, shapes or colors Jane would be wearing, but they were always cool and very put together.

As I looked around the room, I could see a few more of our usual crew. Stealing a first sip of champagne, I watched as the glamorous Fortesques entered the room. Olivier and Desiree Fortesque were the owners of Le Voltaire and something of an international power couple in their own right. Olivier was a talented chef who was born, raised, and professionally trained in France. We typically saw him in some form of professional chef's clothing, although with his GQ looks he could pretty much pull off any fashion statement. His wife, Desiree, was a local girl, born and bred; although as a first generation U.S. citizen, her upbringing was a mix of Midwest values and European sensibilities. As a young woman, Desiree walked her way through Europe and the Far East on fashion runways. Although her fashion career had been a number of years earlier, the beauty that made her runway worthy was still very much in evidence.

"Are you enjoying the aperitif?" Olivier asked in his charming French accent.

Before I had a chance to answer, Ed was at our side with glasses for Desiree and Olivier.

As he poured, Ed informed the Fortesques that the evening's entertainment would consist of a spirited discussion on the recent murder and the odds of my ending up behind bars. As he finished pouring and chuckling, Ed stood back with a grin to await Olivier's response.

"All right, all right, Ed," Olivier winked. "You know very well that we have a responsibility to our guests. If we do not curtail some of this joking around, we run the risk of compromising the ambience of the elegant wine tasting that they will expect this evening. There are more important things to discover here, no?"

Ed was looking a tad sheepish at this point. Who did he think he was kidding feigning a conscience anyway?

"Have you shared with our guests the interesting details from our incredible trip to Reims to tour the oldest champagne house in Champagne?" Olivier asked. "And if I were to ask Cal which is that oldest of champagne houses, would he know that it is the producer of this evening's aperitif, Ruinart?" Olivier shook his head doubtfully, although his eyes sparkled with amusement.

"Not only have I told him all of those things," Ed countered, "but with my expertly honed descriptive abilities, I am confident that Cal would be able to conduct the tour through the underground chalk galleries himself using tidbits shared from my natural gift for narrative. Olivier, you know how serious I am about wine. Given a choice I'd pass on even the really big laughs before screwing up an evening of this caliber!"

"Then you've done well, my friend," Olivier replied with a smile and a playful pat on Ed's shoulder. "I am pleased to hear you say that. Now let's get serious and review what we have left to get done. We'll need to be moving along if we're going to keep everything running smoothly."

As he and Ed embarked on a run through of the wines and whether or not any of them required decanting Desiree and I had a chance to catch up. In addition to working side-by-side with Olivier to promote their restaurant brand, after leaving the catwalk, Desiree had earned her MBA and become a seasoned business consultant in her own right. She had a good head on her shoulders and I always welcomed her suggestions.

"You knew the victim," Desiree stated matter-of-factly.

"Lucky me," I replied grudgingly.

"You'll want to review the facts and theorize about the most likely scenarios," she continued.

"I've kind of already started," I admitted.

"There's really no alternative," Desiree cautioned, "from what I've gathered it would be foolish to wait around until the police are able to fit the pieces of evidence together. Given your relationship with the victim, it is likely that you would end up being a prime suspect at some point during the investigation. After all, you are the easy solution." I was starting to think this wine tasting would not help me relax and forget the stress surrounding the murder.

"Well, Desiree." Before I got further she interjected, "Listen Donna, the cost of hiring a good defense attorney just to prove your innocence could prove devastating to your bank account. Unfortunately, they don't reimburse for unnecessary defense expenses. But I brought all of this up for a reason, and it was not just to make you feel paranoid. During my studies I had occasion to participate in some mock trial procedures. Some were criminal cases. I'd like to offer my help to piece together the available information in the hope of finding either the actual killer, or enough evidence to assure the police of your innocence." Her generous offer made me feel much better. Desiree knew her stuff. She found practical solutions that enabled her business-consulting clients to improve their companies appreciably.

I felt certain that Desiree's business sense would provide me with a process to help navigate this daunting challenge. With her help I might even be able to crack this case before I was forced to coordinate all of my other accessories with handcuffs. Handcuffs, damn! That thought caused me to chug my champagne. At the rate I was going, I'd never know if this vintner had indeed coaxed this wine into displaying the subtle properties Ed suggested. I don't think I tasted a thing. Too bad; I guess murder and wine tasting don't mix. I made a mental note to avoid wine tastings during future murder investigations. What the hell was wrong with me, future murders? Suddenly all of my thoughts revolved around murder. I needed a break – and a lot more wine. Onto the next bottle!

I made my way over to the hors d'oeuvres table to sample the delectable foie gras en torchon topped with fleur de sel, over brioche grille, and gelee de raisins blanc. Olivier's head chef had prepared this delicacy to compliment our first wine, a lovely Gewurztraminer with just the right amount of sweetness to pair perfectly with the foie gras. I figured I'd hazard another quick pour of champagne before accepting a taste of the Domaine Ostertag Fronholz, a unique bottle which was qualified by the French descriptor, Vendange Tardive. As Ed approached with the bottle, I was just savoring my last sip of the Brut. I took a deep breath and nodded for Ed to pour. The foie gras would go a long way toward keeping the sweet wine from shocking my palette. Glancing up, the twinkle in Ed's eyes propelled my first taste from a sip to more of a gulp. Just as Ed was preparing for his next wisecrack I bolted, once more, for the foie gras and safety.

While helping myself to foie gras and slices of brioche, I listened as Olivier explained that Vendage Tardive stands for late harvest. Wine connoisseurs understand that a late harvest Gewürztraminer will be particularly sweet, because the grapes have been left on the vine for an extended period, even as late as the first snow or frost, in order to allow them to reach the highest level of sugar. As I took my first bite of foie gras, I detected a more pungent flavor than expected. My second bite confirmed that our chef had marinated the foie gras in a lovely cognac, creating a delightful contrast to the sweetness of the syrupy French wine, which hinted at a distinctly German influence.

I acknowledged the wonderful effect of the complementary and contrasting flavors and simultaneously noticed that Marie Louise and Dave Campanella had sneaked in. They lingered near the entrance sipping champagne and chatting with Phillippe and Jeannie LaPlage.

I smiled and waved, I'd catch up with them later.

Marie Louise was outfitted in her traditional ensemble of casual academia; when you looked at her you saw an instructor and academician. Occasionally Marie Louise threw caution to the wind and sported some serious bling in her ears.

Jeannie was much more of an enigma: sometimes it was Land's End, sometimes a bit of academia. Then there were all the other times, when she was either a rhinestone cowgirl, or just a lady with soft, drapey fabrics and well-placed bling. Many of us were predictably unpredictable, Jeannie was just unpredictable.

Once pleasantries had been exchanged, Marie Louise leaned in and murmured in a low voice, "how're you holding up, Donna? I can only imagine the stress you must be under considering your connection to this murder victim."

"I know. I couldn't believe my eyes when I read that this latest victim had just moved out here after working for over twenty-five years in the ad business in Connecticut," Jeannie jumped in. "Naturally, my thoughts leapt immediately to you, Donna, which I'm guessing was the same reaction the police had."

"Oh well," I began.

"The police know Donna to be a resource, and not a

murderer," asserted Marie Louise.

The rest of the group weakly murmured their agreement with ML's assessment. I got the feeling not everyone was as convinced that my worries were for naught. That made their obvious determination to stick by my side come what may seem almost heroic. I sat quietly for a moment, feeling just a tad choked up. Or maybe that was the champagne.

As I stood quietly, struggling to maintain my decorum, Phillippe drew near and discreetly shared an observation.

"You know something, Donna? I think you have nothing to fear from the police. Just based on what I have read in the papers and heard on the news, I believe this woman was killed by someone much closer than a business acquaintance. I have a hunch her murderer was in the family."

As Phillippe moved on to sample more of the aperitif, I pondered his comment. Did he have a special insight into the behavior patterns of BJ's familiars, or was he just demonstrating his ever present French chivalry with a damsel in distress? I supposed only time would tell, but I took comfort in his words.

As I let Phillippe's words sink in, I realized it was time to sit down for our first course. The heavenly scent of vichyssoise de poireaux avec pomme de terre de Noirmoutier, otherwise known as potato leek soup, now had our full attention. A vichyssoise is always served chilled, and is a thick white concoction of amazing flavors. My first spoonful confirmed rumors suggesting that the presence of the Noirmoutier potato was an unparalleled gastronomic treat. Savoring the subtle leek flavor, I glanced at the other diners and their obvious appreciation of the remarkable blend of flavors, nearly as intoxicating as the wine itself. Sophisticated food and wine pairings afforded the kitchen staff an opportunity to prepare many of the delicacies, such as leek, that had not yet made it completely into the accepted American dining sensibility. Olivier and his staff quickly filled our glasses with Brouilly from Domaine de Chateau de la Valette. The Brouilly was a 2010 issue named Cuvee Prestige. Olivier enlightened us on the dichotomy that was the Beaujolais region of France. Those of us who enjoyed the study of wine, and frequented tastings, were painfully aware that Le Beaujolais Nouveau was a mediocre experience at best; unfortunately, the rapidly growing awareness of this disappointing effort was responsible for an unwarranted lack of respect for Beaujolais' other stellar offerings. The frequently ignored Brouilly was a classic example of a delightful Cru made from the Gamay grape. Luckily our hosts were extremely well-versed in wines that were often overlooked by the less discerning aficionado.

Between groans of ecstasy over the pairing of potato leek and superior Cru, Marie Louise managed to utter a well-informed question regarding BJ's murder.

"So Donna," she began, "this latest murder victim was a former colleague with a delusional idea that you welcomed her into your life and your business, yes?"

"Well put, Marie Louise, I couldn't have said it better myself, and trust me I've tried," I rejoined.

"I don't mean to drag you back into an unpleasant place in the middle of this lovely escape," she lamented. "I'm just incredibly curious about this odd woman and concerned about how it could affect you."

"Same here," I agreed. "I would like nothing better than to explain what the hell she was up to. Unfortunately, I have never been able to understand that woman, and her recent strange behavior is even more bizarre than anything I witnessed all those years ago. I'm without a clue. Sadly, if I were a police officer investigating the case, I don't think I'd believe me."

"Don't worry," Marie Louise consoled, "we'll get you through this."

Ed walked by and interjected his own brand of support. "Yeah, I'll bake you pies when you're in prison," he finished with a hearty guffaw.

Before I had a chance to respond, I was momentarily diverted by the sight of my glass being filled with Chablis Premier Cru and the arrival of my dorade grille au thyme de Provence et confit de fenouil. Murder would have to take a back seat to the call of the sea.

As I sipped Jean Marie Brocard's Fourchaume, and experienced the scent of grilled sea bream with a soupcon of fennel, I was transported to the coast of France. All thoughts of this perplexing murder were obliterated from my consciousness. It was amazing. I was further transported by Olivier's story of the visit he and his father made to the Brocard vineyards and the royal treatment they were given. A lovely flavorful and delightfully light Mediterranean fish delicacy finished off with lemon, herbs and olive oil and served with an exceptional chardonnay – does it get any better than that?

Right about then my glass was filled with a lovely and dense red liquid that was identified as Vacqueyras. Olivier described this Rhone wine as a cousin of Chateauneuf de Pape and Gigandas. Ed jumped in to clarify that the Reserve Saint Dominique in our glasses was, in fact, predominately Grenache and Syrah. I did detect a marked similarity to the Chateauneuf de Pape that we enjoyed so frequently. Engaged in the nuances of this deceiving wine, the arrival of my filet d'agneau en crout feuillettee and the accompanying julienne de ratatouille came as an extremely pleasant surprise. Lamb has always been my favorite of all the meats, and the light and flaky puff pastry provided a fitting accompaniment to the savory and flavorful lamb. It just kept getting better.

I had had my fill of superbly prepared food matched perfectly with a sophisticated array of Europe's most overlooked wines. Rather than risk overindulging, it would make sense for me to do the smart thing and forego the final pairing of the night. That wasn't going to happen.

Sensing that overindulgence prevailed, Olivier wisely held the final course until he detected a subtle shift, which signified a willingness to eat once again. In the meantime, I made the rounds of the room, chatting with everyone. It was probably for the best since every single person there had a theory or a shared rumor relating to BJ's murder. They would not be satisfied until they were assured that I was not missing any key information. This evening was doing more than providing a brief respite...it was bolstering my courage with each friend that vowed undying support!

Comments poured in from virtually every angle. They waxed philosophic on whether I'd murdered her in cold blood or I'd been her unsuspecting dupe in a complex plot against me. As I made my way from table to table, hearing a variety of murder related speculation it was heartwarming to realize the common theme was a desire to help me. In all my years in the Northeast, I never had this sense of unflagging support and caring. Was that a tear starting to well up in my eye? How embarrassing. Of course it didn't hurt that tonight's wine had been extraordinary as well as plentiful. There was one incontrovertible fact: I was growing sappier by the minute. I was even starting to slur my thoughts. At any rate I was feeling fortunate – and more than a little sleepy. Hic.

If I felt lucky then, I would begin to feel like visiting royalty when I realized what we had in store for dessert.

Simultaneously, a champagne Ruinart Brut Rose and a soufflé de chocolat au Grand Marnier with crème fleurette appeared in front of me. At that moment I was the only one in the place. I had a vague sense that someone was laboring to get my attention; they were not destined to succeed. This was the positively perfect finish to a decadently delicious meal.

All in all, the night had been filled with disparate remarks, some that stung and fed the paranoia and some that confirmed an unbeatable support network that made me feel invincible. Either way, I'd take my breaks any way I could get them.

I was surprised at how much everyone already knew about the details of the murder that were yet to be released. Omaha was a close-knit community. We didn't need six degrees of separation as in the Kevin Bacon game – the game that coincidentally originated in Omaha – for us it was rarely more than one degree. As a transplanted Northeasterner, I never failed to marvel at the smooth way in which the lines of communication hummed. It was tough to surprise anyone. Sometimes that was a good thing.

As I passed by Dave Campanella on my way out the door he said, "You seem overwhelmed right now. Just remember that your friends will work this puzzle until the truth surfaces."

I did feel that an enormous brain trust was at my disposal, and I would put it to good use.

Winding down for bed, I continued to replay many of the conversations of the evening in my head. Although I'd written the evening off as a break from the stress, there was something niggling at the back of my consciousness that suggested an important piece of information had come up over our gourmet feast. But I'd be damned if I could remember what it was, or even who said it. That was just so annoying! I'd have to check with Jon, he was always so good at recognizing those critical insights at the moment they cropped up. In my case, I'd be wracking my brain for days for the tiniest of hints.

[CHAPTER 13]

The next morning dawned early, and while I was grateful to have behaved somewhat sensibly in my food and wine consumption the night before, I wouldn't be running any marathons. With any luck it would be a quiet day.

My next thought was that by wishing for quiet, I'd probably jinxed any chance I had at realizing it? Yeah, that's how it goes.

I hadn't made it halfway across the office when Peg barked, "You're here. We'll need to get you in the middle of this project, too!"

All eyes shifted to me as I tried to look nonchalant while trekking across the last thirty feet of weathered old wooden flooring on the way to my desk. This was right about when I usually tripped. Thankfully, luck was with me that day, and I made a graceful traverse across the rest of the office. I dumped all my stuff, started my computer, and took a quick peek at any e-mails that might tip me off as to what project had suddenly erupted into an 'all hands on deck' emergency. I didn't get far before Peg was standing at my desk, holding a pile of papers and fidgeting with impatience.

"So what's up, Peg?"

I'm proofing this and it needs editing," she declared. "I told you I don't edit."

"Yes, sure, I'll be happy to take a shot at it."

This was something I could handle and even enjoy. Until Peg's next proclamation.

"Okay, then, you've got forty-five minutes before it needs to be back in proofing. It goes on press at noon."

Great. There was nothing fun about forcing yourself to rewrite someone else's work with a gun to your head. Especially since I was not a 'copywriter.' I graduated college as an English major and taught high school English before jumping over to the exciting world of advertising, where I spent years as a media director before morphing into an operations/HR/research/'whatever no one else can or will do' specialist – I guess that's how they define ownership.

Hardly the right field experience for a writing-on-the-run assignment like this. I looked over at Peg; she shot me a withering look. Message received. Stop feeling sorry for yourself and get it done! I put my head down and began to read the copy in question.

Once into the spirit of the assignment, it became evident that a slight misplacement of words had been the culprit. It didn't take much to get it all sorted out and back on Peg's desk for the next round of proofing. I had to admit, there was something energizing about jumping in to help fix something with a tight deadline pushing up against your back, and getting it done. Before having a chance to bask in the reflection of my own self-acknowledged glory my phone began to ring.

"Hey Donna," Kyle began eagerly, "I went to my DMA (Direct Marketing Association) meeting last night and saw a former colleague from my days at FDT, Maria Mantino."

"Yeah?" I couldn't really see where this was going.

"Turns out her brother had started dating Betty Jean when she first arrived in Omaha." Kyle finished.

"Okay, now you've got my attention," I pushed, "what did you learn?"

"I learned that we're going to lunch with Maria and her brother today!"

"Really?" I asked. "Does the brother know anything about

me and my relationship to his dead girlfriend?"

"As a matter of fact, Maria called him after the meeting. His name is Mario..."

"Maria and Mario?" I rolled my eyes.

"I know, I know, their Mom didn't do them any favors. They're twins too. At any rate, when Mario heard that I knew you, he was the one who insisted we meet as soon as possible. In fact, he was pushing for breakfast this morning. I held out for lunch since I knew you'd probably be getting a slower start than usual after your wine tasting last night. So how was it?"

Kyle never ceases to amaze me. Most other people forget you told them you're going on a two-week vacation and rant about where the hell you are the minute they need you for something. They're always so shocked to learn that you're out of the office and not at their beck and call. But not Kyle; he remembers everything down to the most minute detail. You definitely get the feeling that he's always listening; he cares enough to remember. As someone who forgets pretty much everything, I am stunned at his ability to retain the details of his own life and those of the key people in his world.

I have a theory that one of the biggest frustrations in most people's lives is the feeling that they are virtually invisible to those around them. No one listens; no one remembers what you say. Everyone has earplugs to block out the world unless you do something stupid, and then everyone hears and remembers – and if they should forget, there's always Facebook! When Kyle is around there's an ever-present sense of hope that someone is listening, someone remembers and someone is there to offer support when you begin to lose hope. He really has a compelling gift. I would go so far as to envy him, but I'm not as crazy about most people as he is. You could say I'm part of the problem, but I digress.

"Well, Donna?" Kyle urged.

"Oh sure, yeah, wouldn't miss it," I forced myself back to the conversation at hand. "Just let me know when you're ready to go."

After I hung up the phone, I noticed that the message light was blinking. It was a message from Ken Farley, the guy who'd first brought me the news of Betty Jean's demise. Ken suggested I call him tout suite. He had picked up an interesting tidbit after running into BJ's second husband at an Ad Club event in Hartford. In his voicemail message, Ken suggested that this could be the big break I'd been looking for. It might even crack the case wide open.

As I listened, I could tell Farley had been watching too many episodes of CSI. It was fairly evident he was feeling envy over my proximity to the case. I thought about Ken, all safe and beyond suspicion back in his Connecticut haven, and then I compared his situation to mine. Once again, I was in the limelight waiting to make the suspect list for a murder I did not commit, just because of my dubious relationship with the victim. There he was, far from the threat of danger which pervaded my every waking moment – okay, maybe I was getting a bit melodramatic, but my butt was on the line – and he was safely enjoying his little dalliance with intrigue. It was starting to piss me off. As curious as I was about his 'breaking news' I would make him wait until after lunch before finally calling him back. Was I cutting off my own nose to spite my face? No doubt, but it would bug him more than it did me, and that made it worth a little face spiting. Besides, I looked over at Kyle's desk just in time for him to give me the high sign. It was time to head out for lunch. It had been a most productive morning.

[CHAPTER 14]

Kyle had chosen a quiet little lunch bistro downtown for our meeting with Mario and Maria. They were an interesting pair. Although twins, Mario was tall and bean pole skinny, while Maria was short and almost as wide. But their faces were almost identical. They both had beautiful Mediterranean coloring and movie star quality features. Knowing BJ's preference in men, I could have picked Mario out of a crowd. He looked just like a clotheshorse with a face pretty enough for GQ. Without a doubt he was BJ's perfect man.

One thing did seem out of sync though; ironically, he looked nothing like either of her two husbands. I hadn't thought about it before, but as vocal as BJ was about her preferences, she'd never been with a guy who'd even come close to fitting them before, at least not to my knowledge. Now you could say that only a shallow person would be with someone based on looks alone, and if you did, you'd be describing the BJ that I knew. Hence my confusion.

Her first husband was big and hulky, like Paul Bunyan. Her second husband was smaller, round, and menschy like an urban 'Cousin It' from the Addams family. And, oh yes, he had long silky hair and a moderately long beard, which BJ had shorn like a prize shearling after the county fair the minute they were officially a couple. Even with shorter and more kempt head and facial hair, the 'Cousin It' image was first in my mind whenever I thought of poor old WyCliff.

Looking over at Maria as she spoke animatedly to Kyle, I could see that she was a true beauty. Granted, she could stand to lose a few pounds, but her face was radiant and lovely with sculptured cheekbones that a runway model would envy. Her chestnut hair was thick and luxuriant falling in loose curls that gently caressed her shoulders. Maria wore just enough make-up to enhance her features without masking them. While Mario was dressed in expensive but casual attire, Maria was sporting a chic business suit with a pair of Christian Louboutin heels that were to die for! For a moment, I thought about sitting on my feet and hiding my DSW specials so that people walking by the table couldn't make the obvious comparison between our footwear. Sure, Van Eli's could usually hold their own, but not at this level of competition!

As I glanced across the table, I could see that Maria and Kyle were ready to bring Mario and me into the conversation. Too bad I had no idea of what had been said up to this point. I'd really have to start paying attention if I hoped to pick up on any subtle nuances. Good thing Kyle was so expert at gently guiding a conversation along. I could use some gentle guiding right about now.

"So Donna," Maria started, "Kyle tells me you worked with BJ when you lived back east."

"I had that unfortunate distinction, yes," I answered before thinking to myself, oh crap, how would Mario take that comment? First sentence of the day and I'd already stuffed my DSW Van Elis into my mouth.

"Relax," cooed Mario in a wonderfully rich and soothing voice, and did I detect a hint of an Italian accent, or was that just wishful thinking on my part?

"I-" I blurted.

"No, it is okay," he offered, "I know that you and BJ had some differences and you are entitled to your opinion. In fact, I have a great regard for honesty at almost any cost."

As I gazed at Mario's kind smiling face, I wondered what it was about BJ that had ever attracted someone this wonderful. But before I had a chance to ponder the possibilities, Mario continued.

"Actually," he went on in a soft, almost conspiratorial voice, "my own involvement with BJ has me feeling extremely troubled and vulnerable. Things were not usual with us."

"Mario's nervous," Maria jumped in to spare poor vulnerable Mario, "He knows that the police always look to the partner first when a murder of passion has been committed."

"A murder of passion?" I interjected, "What makes you say a murder of passion?"

"Well, based on the murder weapon, there doesn't seem to be any doubt that the murder was not pre-meditated," Maria finished.

"Murder weapon? What was the murder weapon?" I demanded, feeling angry and embarrassed that a couple of amateurs had a lock on the most important piece of evidence when I had zip. Okay so I'm an amateur, too, but an amateur with some serious street creds. Whether deserved or not, I was given credit by most everyone for solving Claire's murder, and I was tight with the lead detective and her team. Apparently not as tight as I'd thought.

"Hey Donna," Kyle reasoned, "Why don't we focus on what's important here. No matter the source, we want details on the murder weapon, right?"

"Of course, you're right, Kyle," I agreed, "I tend to get a bit carried away when I'm in the middle of a murder investigation. Please forgive me and continue with what you were saying."

"Donna," Mario jumped back in, "Perhaps it would be better if we did not share the gruesome details. It might be more than you are ready to handle at this point."

I rolled my eyes. Who did they think they were dealing with here? I'd been down this road before and I can take it! Save your soothing charm for someone who'll fall for it, Romeo, I was thinking. But I said, "Evidently you're not aware that I have solved other murders..."

"Oh, I am well aware of your involvement in the Dockens murder investigation," Mario assured me. "In fact, that is why I was so anxious to meet you for lunch today. But if you are sure that these details will not..."

"I assure you, Mario," I responded, "Nothing you could say would trouble me in the least."

"Well, if you're sure," Maria jumped in.

"I am quite—"

Before I had a chance to finish, Maria blurted: "Her Christian Louboutin."

"What about her—"

"She was murdered with her own Christian Louboutin spiked heel," Maria finished.

"How, I mean, what—"

"The killer made a perfect hole, right in the middle of her forehead, with her brand new, red, snake skinned Christian Louboutin four-inch heels," Maria pronounced.

I was stunned speechless. I looked to Kyle; he appeared to be a troubling shade of green. I looked to the twins and they were maudlin. I felt my bread and butter start to make its way back toward the light of day. I did a quick visual check and then bolted for the ladies' room. Something about the thought of a brand new pair of fashion forward pumps being used to slice through brain tissue just did not sit well with my constitution.

Once I was sure there was no more bread left to eject I made my way back to the table, mindful of the humility I had clearly abandoned earlier. I felt like a complete fool. What must these people think of me, bragging about my big time murder solving experience, and then falling apart like a little girl when the details were too much to handle. I should have known they'd be charming and understanding. In a way, that almost made me feel worse! I wish they'd called me a pathetic loser so we could all move on with our lives. Where's Donny when you need him? With that thought my brain reverted right back to Aroma's and Donny's speculation on the cause of the hole in BJ's head. Things were fitting together in an incredibly grisly way. Oh God, I was getting woozy again.

Much to my dismay, the twins were more charming and understanding than before. Their concern for my wellbeing was beginning to border on obsessive as they fussed and fretted over making me ill. Kyle's face was still morphing its way back from Elphaba green (straight from the stage of *Wicked*) so he was laying low for the moment. Someone had to drive this caravan forward, and it was time for me to suck it up and start the engine.

"I'm okay guys, really," I insisted, "you can relax. In fact, now that I've humbled myself (and none too soon if you recall my earlier luncheon demeanor) by praying to the gods of porcelain, maybe we can finally move on and get into more issues that are salient to this case. Thank you for sharing the details of the murder weapon...."

This final comment was met with a repeat performance of fussing and concern over having caused such extreme discomfort. If I wasn't mistaken, I thought I observed Kyle's face heading back into the deeper green family. This was hardly productive.

"Look," I continued, "Your concern is very touching, but I needed to know about the murder weapon. It's not your fault that I'm not as tough as I'd like to think."

"I find this vulnerability to be enchanting," Mario crooned with a slightly heavier Italian accent.

I hoped they didn't notice my unavoidable eye roll. This was no time for faux Euro-charm; there was work to be done! Although there are days... never mind! Back to work!

"Let me ask you a few questions," I attempted to divert their attention from the nurture-fest that was currently underway. "Tell me about your relationship with BJ, Mario."

I asked this question with trepidation. Prying into the intimate relationship of anyone, much less someone I disliked palpably, not to mention someone who was recently deceased, was just creepy. But it had to be done if we were to learn anything of value from this meeting.

"Ah," Mario began, "that was a strange thing. I met this woman, BJ, while sitting at the bar in M's Pub. You know how it is there, constant activity with an electric atmosphere and no chance to really think. We shared a brief conversation, and then it was time for me to meet my sister Maria and some friends at her apartment. So I said my good-byes. Apparently, that meeting occurred during BJ's first week in town. I never saw her again until a week or two before her death."

"Wait, are you saying?"

"I am saying that I heard through many sources that I was her boyfriend. I have no first-hand knowledge of this relationship," he concluded.

I looked over at Maria and she appeared to be close to tears. Personally, my head was spinning for the second time in one lunch meeting. I wasn't really sure what to say next. Luckily, Kyle had just about regained his equilibrium and was ready for some sleuthing.

"Mario," Kyle began skeptically, "Are you telling us that BJ invented her whole relationship with you? Why would anyone fabricate an entire relationship like that? Are you sure you're not trying to distance yourself from a messy situation by exaggerating—"

"Whoa, Kyle, back up," I jumped to Mario's rescue as I observed both he and Maria beginning to tense up and look indignant.

"Remember, Kyle," I gently chided, "this is the same woman who has made up a colossal amount of bullshit about yours truly."

As I saw the dawn begin to break through Kyle's intense scrutiny, Mario spoke up.

"Thank you, Donna," he remarked quietly. "I know this is difficult to believe, but it is the truth."

"Mario has found this whole experience to be so disturbing," Maria chimed in. "He feels very strongly about respecting women, and it goes completely against his every fiber to call a murdered woman a liar."

"I have not known what to do, Donna," Mario continued for himself, "I was very anxious to meet you because I had heard wonderful things about your crime-solving ability."

There it was again. Where was all this hype about my crime-solving ability coming from? I had never actually solved a crime; yet I seemed to get full credit every time Claire's murder was discussed. It's not actually solving the crime when the murderer confronts you, because in his paranoia he is convinced you're onto him even though you're not, and the entire city of Omaha (okay maybe it just seemed like the entire city) leaps into the fray to save you from this maniac. Yet the more I protested, the more I was honored for my brilliant investigative work. I do like to think of my work as brilliant; but in all honesty, I have to admit that I'd never solved anything. The really strange thing was that the police acted as though I'd been Sherlock to Detective Warren's LeStrade. That was a flagrantly unfair assessment of the good detective's capabilities. Was I the only one who saw things as they really were? And yet, if truth be told, I was occasionally known to leave reality in the rearview mirror and believe my own hype.

"Mario, I—"

"Now Donna," Maria jibed, "Kyle warned us that you always behave in an extremely humble manner when your fans overtly praise you."

My fans? I had fans? This was news to me. I looked at Kyle and he shrugged. It was getting late, and we really had to be getting back to the office. So I did what any self-respecting falsely touted hero would do – I threw him a line.

"Sure Mario, I'll keep an eye open for evidence that supports your assertion. I don't see how you would make the suspect list under the circumstances."

Kyle and I departed to exclamations of lifelong gratitude and adoration. The twins insisted on paying for lunch and pushed for another meeting later that week. They were anxious for an update on Mario's status. Ironically, they had been the ones to supply all of the information to us this time. I was still somewhat baffled at the serious lack of information making its way to me. Time to talk to Donny and his cop cohorts.

[CHAPTER 15]

Kyle and I breezed back into the office and were immediately engulfed in a sea of phone messages and e-mails. Some things never change. After forty-five minutes of calling and writing I glanced at my watch. I had twenty minutes until my next meeting, just enough time to give Farley a quick ring.

As I looked up Ken's phone number, I began to recall my thoughts after hearing his message earlier. I was such a bitch! The poor guy called me from halfway across the country to give me some information he knew I'd want to have, and what did I do? I decided to keep him waiting because he was getting on my nerves. Talk about shooting the messenger! Of course he'd be curious about the murder. Who wouldn't under the circumstances? I really had to gain control of this overblown ego before it threatened to make a jackass out of me – publicly. I'd already been a jerk at least two times today; I hoped to avoid a third. I dialed Ken's number.

"Hey Donna, glad you called!" he answered.

That didn't go a long way toward making me feel any better about myself.

"Ken!" I tried to borrow his perky delivery, "What's going on?"

"I picked up a little piece of gossip that I thought might help you unravel BJ's bizarre grand plan."

Ken's comment certainly rang true. In my book, BJ's behavior was always bizarre, but in recent months she had taken things beyond her generally twisted norm straight into the Twilight Zone. The problem was that in her diabolical way she'd taken me with her. I had met some strange characters in my time, and BJ was certainly one of the strangest.

Right now, though, I realized the biggest problem I faced was that even with all the awesome folks doing everything possible to assist and support me during this challenging time, I was being a big knothead. What the hell was wrong with me? I needed all of these people and all the help they could offer. They say your second murder is the hardest, and I was beginning to see why. Even though I hadn't exactly joined the ranks of Agatha Christie's finest, I was acting as though I had. I took a deep cleansing (and hopefully IQ raising) breath and responded to Ken.

"Fantastic, Ken, I really appreciate everything you've done to keep me informed!"

Now I held my breath, hoping that I'd be able to deliver my response with the right amount of zeal and still sound sincere.

"Well hell, Donna," Ken rejoined, "After all we've been through together over the years, I can't imagine not jumping in with both feet to see that you come out of this okay!"

That did it! I was officially a shit and Ken was an angel! At least I knew where we stood, and apparently Ken didn't because he seemed to buy my forced sincerity. I'd work on summoning some real sincerity and get myself back in the game.

"Well, here's the thing," Ken continued, "bet you didn't know that BJ got fired from that fancy position she landed at the firearms company, did you?"

"They dumped her at Jones & Mazzola?"

"Six months ago," Ken went on. "But you know her, she pulled out all the street 'creds' to get the big job, and then immediately started looking for someone else to actually do the work. I guess at Jones & Mazzola they have no tolerance for goldbricking."

Goldbricking? Had he been watching old movies? Worse yet, I knew precisely what he meant, which made me feel as though I'd popped out of an old movie myself.

"Yeah," Ken continued, "I have it on good authority that she was escorted from the building by not one, but two armed guards, and they searched her car before letting her drive away!"

"You're kidding" was all I could summon.

"Not at all," Ken assured me.

It's always a rush when one is able to locate that perfect nugget of information that will both amaze and delight an associate. This was unquestionably one of those times and Ken knew it.

"So she was running away after another failure?" I mused.

"Sure seems that way to me," Ken agreed, "and that lends a good bit of strength to your claim that she didn't rush to Omaha because you were poised and anxiously awaiting her arrival. She had about burned all of the bridges left to burn in Connecticut. This last failure would have been way too humiliating to bear without the story of a better opportunity calling her name."

"And I'm guessing that the story she told her confidants as she packed her bags to move to Omaha, did not include a part where she was dismissed from Jones & Mazzola?" I speculated.

"Right again. In her version, she walked out because they expected her to compromise her ethics. Turns out it was all for the best since you had been pleading with her to move out to Omaha and join you in a lucrative business partnership."

What she lacked in brains, she more than made up for in sheer gall. Jones & Mazzola trying to compromise ethics? How could she possibly hope to pull that off? I had to hand it to her. That she would even attempt to tarnish a revered American institution, a brand with unimpeachable credentials took guts. Trying to convince her contemporaries that Jones & Mazzola had questionable ethics was like suggesting that Mother Theresa wasn't overly fond of kids.

I just shook my head. Was there no end to that woman's ability to reinvent the details of her life, twisting them into an enchanted and even enviable fable for her eager onlookers? She was clearly willing to take her fabrications to ridiculous extremes. The real puzzle was how she managed to have so many of the trappings of great success scattered throughout the various aspects of her life that she could generally convince any doubters. I mean, rarely were her feet shod in anything less than Louboutin (I shuddered at my recollection of their latest use), and her gangly stick-like body was clothed in nothing but a fashionista's dream wardrobe. To look at her would be to believe any story of how she'd made it to greatness. Who would doubt someone so clearly dressed for success? I guess in her world there was no need to work hard and save your money, because you would just invent all of your extraordinary triumphs and discredit your critics anyway.

Apparently I had been fortunate that my lack of notoriety kept her annihilation of my character contained within the walls of Mylar. It also occurred to me that BJ was able to get away with her fabulous tales, because the average person could not even begin to comprehend the level of deceit that went into even a small portion of her yarn spinning. That meant either the average person was basically honest or hopelessly naïve; even the realist in me was rooting for the former. Either way, one thing was clear: Ken had done me a huge favor by calling with this information so early in the investigation.

As I thought about my friendship with Ken over the years, I realized that his loyalty should come as no surprise. Ken had always been a good friend. A good friend in business is not quite the same as a good friend in one's personal life. In my business dealings with Ken, there had often been opportunities to throw each other under the bus, and neither of us had ever taken that cold and ruthless option to further our own careers at the expense of the other. I guess that was about as good a description of a true friend as any. You could go as far as to say that my business relationship with Ken was the opposite of the one I had with BJ. Not only did BJ go out of her way to throw me under the bus at every opportunity, she often created the opportunities herself. Yes, Ken had been a good friend, and being separated by half a continent did not appear to have changed that at all.

I thought about the implications of what Ken had told me. It all started to make sense when you examined the facts surrounding BJ's shockingly unethical behavior and combined that with her understandable desire to beat a hasty retreat from a market where it was unlikely she'd find any safe haven. Under those circumstances, leaving seemed like the logical choice. Thankfully, the fact that she'd left a trail of lies that could easily be disproven made my protestations over her Omaha yarns appear far more credible. In fact, it would seem that both Mario and I should be able to breathe easier as Warren continued to make progress in her investigation.

I thanked Ken profusely, perhaps going a tad overboard, but I felt it necessary to acknowledge my appreciation of his friendship.

It was time for my 2:30 meeting, so I tried to put the day's findings to rest and concentrate on my client's new product offering. It promised to be a very exciting launch, which made it easy to focus on the challenge.

After an extremely productive meeting and the realization

that our timeline would be tight getting to market, I hurried to catch up with Donny to see if he'd learned anything new.

I caught him on his way into a late meeting. We agreed to meet at Aroma's first thing in the morning. That gave me the rest of the afternoon to catch up on some phone calls and respond to all the comments on the latest post on my menopause blog.

As I headed home that evening, I mentally recanted the main events of the day. The lunch with Mario and Maria had been a real eye-opener for me. I learned the identity of an extremely important piece of evidence (the murder weapon) from virtual strangers who were not expected to be in the know. I had also learned that I wasn't as tough as I gave myself credit for being. Embarrassing as that lesson was, it was still one worth experiencing. The humility gained from my fifty-yard dash to the ladies' room might save my life one day. It was enough of a wake-up call that it might just prevent me from taking too much risk should things get dicey at any point during the investigation. The key was to keep it from making me too paranoid to function. As with the myriad minefields and stumbling blocks in the world of business, finding the right balance between pushing the envelope and sticking your neck out too far was always a challenge.

By the time I had finished reviewing my conversation with Ken, I was home. My bulldogs greeted me at the door with their usual enthusiasm, and from the amazing aroma it was clear that Jon was in the kitchen concocting more of his culinary magic.

After Jon served an extremely healthy and surprisingly tasty chicken and vegetable dinner, found in the pages of *Cooking Light*, it was time to take the bulldogs around the block. We watched an old movie on Netflix and went to bed early as Donny and I had planned an early morning tetè-a-tetè at the coffee house.

[CHAPTER 16]

By the time I reached the coffee shop the next morning, Donny was already there and sipping from his first cup. I grabbed a small Nicaraguan blend, lightened it with milk, and plunked myself down on the cracked leather sofa by the exposed brick wall. Donny was seated just opposite; his six-foot-three frame more than filled the space on the matching cracked leather overstuffed chair. What a great way to ease into the day.

Donny spent the first fifteen minutes briefing me on some new business issues that we would probably need to discuss within the next week or so. Once up-to-speed on marketing and advertising issues, it was time to begin our rundown of the murder investigation.

"So what's with your buddies?" I started, "They're the last ones to know about the murder weapon?"

"They know about it," Donny countered, "but Warren issued strict orders to keep it under wraps until she gave the green light. I was going to fill you in this morning, but clearly that won't be necessary."

I shared details of my lunch with Mario and Maria, possibly downplaying my undignified dash to the john. Why ask for abuse? Then Donny revealed the official assumptions passed on by his cop buddies.

"The guys said that, considering the murder weapon, all of the women on the suspect list have just jumped to the top. I'm kinda wondering if a woman would have the strength to drive that—"

"Yeah, thanks, no need to paint the whole gruesome picture once again."

Donny gave me a quirky smile. Something told me he knew precisely how I'd reacted to Maria's description of the murder weapon and how it was applied to BJ's forehead at yesterday's lunch. Just great, that would undoubtedly haunt me for the rest of my days!

"Although physics was never my strong suit," I began, "I think the width and shape of the spiked heel, if the killer's arm were pulled way back and thrust forward at a rapid rate, and assuming she was holding the shoe by the toe, would give a woman the necessary inertia to get the job done."

I could tell Donny was significantly impressed by my vast scientific knowledge. In all honesty, although physics was hardly my forte, I was raised by a Dad who was a mechanical engineer, and these things did come up more frequently than you might imagine when conversing with him. You'd think I'd have aced physics. Well, not if you met my high school physics teacher. He adopted an 'all students are delinquents until proven innocent repeatedly and under duress' attitude. And man, he could sure apply the duress. Who says the teacher doesn't have a major impact on the student's outcome? A fact I held as sacrosanct during my own years of teaching English.

"Mmm," he grunted, clearly envisioning the physical principles necessary to overwhelmingly increase a given woman's strength.

Mmm was high praise coming from Donny. I could tell he was ready to move on.

"Yeah so, anyway," he continued, "the first eight or ten suspects are now women."

I thought about the implications of so many women as

potential murderers, and I couldn't help but wonder if I'd made the list.

"You're not on it," he stated casually, as though he had just read my precise thoughts.

"You sure?"

"What do you think?" he asked. I felt his tone could have been less acerbic.

How dare I doubt his information! What could I have been thinking? A smidge of euphoria crept into my psyche. There were eight or ten women who hated her enough to kill her; they must have hated her more than I did? That might be hard to swallow given a normal human being, but with BJ it really wasn't much of a stretch. It was a huge relief that Warren and her crew had been so thorough they'd managed to ferret out obscure background on the victim. They could have jumped on the easy solution considering I was a known sitting duck, right here for the plucking. I was feeling really good about things. On the other hand, I couldn't help but wonder how I'd had the dubious distinction of meeting so many larger-than-life nut jobs in my career, the type who managed to push people far enough that they'd gotten themselves killed. Ah well, I suppose that's what comes with an industry as chock full of characters as the ad industry. Most times we were proud that few of us were average or predictable – but sometimes it was a distinct disadvantage. You didn't read about a lot of insurance executives getting whacked!

Far be it from me to look a gift horse in the mouth. At least I wasn't on the suspect list. That's when I starting wondering who was, and that's when Donny launched his next shot.

"Yeah, and the women at the top of the suspect list are the ones deemed most likely to have handled Louboutin's before," he finished with an evil grin.

Damn him! He hands me an official reprieve from paranoia only to follow up with a shot about my lack of haute couture savvy and my legendary frugal (okay cheap!) shopping habits. That really hurt! There was a reason I didn't start more days having coffee with Donny. He could be a real smart-ass. I knew damn well that having handled Louboutin's before was not a prerequisite in making it onto the suspect list. Well played, my Machiavellian friend, well played!

It felt like a good time to pack up and head over to the office, but a glance at Donny revealed that he was clearly not finished with our discussion.

"You know, this murder isn't nearly as fun as the last one," he lamented. "It's so much harder to dive in when you don't know the victim or very many people she knew."

I could see his point. When Claire was murdered, we all knew her and everything about her. Helpful memories popped into virtually everyone's head from time to time. With BJ things were quite different; I was the main conduit to her personality, her past, and people she knew in her past. For me, the big neon question mark was in relation to the short time she'd been in Omaha. I was just starting to learn who she'd interacted with and I still didn't have a clue as to what she was really doing here. There was so much we didn't know.

"So," Donny continued, "Liv and I have been talking about having another competition to solve the murder. I know she felt bad about losing to me in the contest over Claire's murder."

Losing to Donny? Liv didn't lose to Donny. We had pretty much all agreed that everyone had tied except for my husband Jon, who had written the murderer's name down on paper and given it to me days before anyone else had any idea. The rest of us all pretty much found out at the same time, when the murderer damn near caused me to join Claire in the great beyond. I guessed if she and I ever did meet over there we wouldn't bond any better than we did here. If I played my cards right and kept out of the direct path of murderers, I had reason to believe it would be a long time before I'd get a chance to find out.

"You have an interesting memory, Donny," I started.

"Yeah, whatever. Look, we don't really have time to rehash that whole thing." He quickly moved on, "I just wanted to fill you in on the competition and let you know that we'll be scheduling a time when you can answer some basic questions about the victim, probably later today."

I readily agreed to help the teams. They had undoubtedly made a positive contribution last time. Since this case was proving to be a greater challenge, I hoped they could help get things moving. It's sometimes worthwhile to put smart thinkers in competition with one another; they're usually at their best when pushed to the mat.

At that, Donny and I headed toward the office to get the workday underway. Once we got to the doorway I waved Donny ahead. Something was bugging me and I needed to think it through. I replayed our conversation in my head over and over. Every time I came to the part where the most likely suspect was a very strong woman only one name came to mind – Cindy.

Had my admiration for her rapid dismissal of BJ masked a deeper issue between those two? I couldn't get it out of my head. Perhaps a brief detour to Cindy's office and a few carefully worded questions would put my concerns to rest.

I changed course for the parking lot. Normally, I wouldn't attempt to interview a suspect without some back up, but I was pretty sure that Cindy could not possibly have committed this gruesome murder – I just needed to be absolutely sure.

Cindy graciously accepted my early morning interruption

and greeted me warmly.

"Hey Donna, how are things going with BJ's investigation?"

"So far things just keep getting more and more bizarre," I replied. "I recently learned that the murder weapon was a deified fashion icon."

"A Louboutin, I know, they're my favorites."

Really? Does everyone in Omaha wear Louboutin's but me? I would have to sit down and give my budget a good going over–"

"Horrible, right?"

Cindy was obviously still talking, but she'd lost me to Louboutin envy.

"Hey Cindy, how do you know the murder weapon? The police haven't officially released that information yet."

"Oh, come on, Donna, you know how choice details rocket through this city," she replied, with a hint of an edge to her voice.

Uh oh, had Cindy picked up on a tone in my voice? Guess I wasn't as subtle as I thought.

"Donna, why did you come over here, anyway?"

There was definitely more of that edge now. My brain was racing but getting nowhere fast. I did not want this perfect physical specimen pissed off at me! It's possible I had thought of that too late.

"If you think that you have the right to come over here and start treating me like a suspect—

"Oh, come on, Cindy! Don't you think you're being slightly overdramatic?"

"I'm what!? Donna, you'd better haul your ass out of here before I do something that will make BJ's murder look like a Campfire Girl initiation!"

And I believed her too, since she was lunging toward me

with a menacing scowl on her face.

Once back in my car, I reviewed the bad choices that had landed me here without a second to spare. Hadn't I known Cindy was really sharp? What made me think my stupid, amateurish questions would escape her radar? Clearly, I needed to think things through more carefully, before taking action. And no more road trips without my posse.

As I drove back to the office, I reflected further on my nearly fatal conversation with Cindy. Was her instant, volatile reaction normal for someone who had no guilty conscience, or had I been right about her deeper involvement with BJ? Was she the murderer? Was she merely an innocent person, incensed by my implied accusations? Or had I just witnessed the classic response of a body pumped up on steroids?

I returned to the office, no wiser for my troubles.

[CHAPTER 17]

The first person I saw upon entering our loft space was Peg. She was charging toward me with an intent look on her face.

"Good thing you're here," she practically slammed into me, "you've heard about the murder weapon, I suppose?"

Had everyone heard about the murder weapon at this point? Had it been on Omaha.com?

"Clovis called," declared Peg, reading my mind.

Of course, undoubtedly Clovis would know. She would make it her point to know every single detail surrounding the murder so that she could determine how to be the center of the entire investigation. As much as I was relieved not to have made the suspect list, Clovis would be offended and horrified if her name did not head the list. After all, this kind of genuine drama did not come along every day. She was not about to miss out on being the central focus. Who cared about the victim, as with everything else this murder would revolve around Clovis!

During the investigation of Claire's murder, I learned not to sell Clovis short. It hadn't occurred to me that someone who was not the victim, nor the murderer, could be the central character in a murder investigation. But Clovis was no amateur at stealing the show! She took center stage fairly early on and managed to have all of us working to keep her there. The fact that she distracted everyone with her attention-getting antics, and wasted a colossal amount of time, did not deter her one iota. You had to give the devil her due.

Perhaps Clovis developed the need to be center stage while growing up in her Romanian gypsy family caravan. So much about Clovis was a puzzle. How she emerged from her nomadic and often disturbing gypsy childhood to become a communications professional remained a mystery. In all honesty, how she stayed a communications professional, when there was documented proof that she never actually did any work herself, was tough to fathom. Her most impressive talent was an uncanny ability to pass her tasks on to those around her with a multitude of excuses; the most believable of which stretched the imagination beyond all reason-able boundaries.

Those issues merely scratched the surface. Everything about Clovis was cloaked in not so much mystery as the bizarre Clovis-centric romanticized version she created to showcase herself. One did not think of Clovis as the enviable, romantic yet pragmatic female lead in a Jane Austin novel, or even one of Charles Dickens' downtrodden heroines. She was far more like Jane Lynch's evil depiction of a female gym teacher and glee club saboteur in Glee, without Jane's talent or sense of humor.

Any contact from Clovis raised the fine hairs on the back of my neck. But as I recall, she claimed to be closely acquainted with our victim. It would be necessary to debrief her. Knowing her as I did, I was probably in the best position to get her to cough up some semblance of the truth. Of course that was predicated on the fact that she had actually had a relationship with BJ and that her fond memories were not more examples of her imaginary adventures.

"She wants to meet you for lunch," Peg continued cautiously, knowing that my reaction would not be joyful. "So I thought Babs and I could accompany you and run interference. How about it?"

Having Peg and Babs around was possibly the only way I would consider having lunch with Clovis. They were about the only two who could stop that freight train in her tracks and prevent a derailment. Although I had a sinking feeling about this meeting. Of course any meeting with Clovis would elicit that response from me. It was time to suck-it-up for the cause.

"Sure, why not?" I responded with a notable lack of enthusiasm, which Peg knew was in no way related to the prospect of spending time with she and Babs, "should we see if Kyle would like to accompany us?"

"Uh, actually, it was Kyle who got the call from Clovis," Peg offered, "I think he made his excuse before Clovis finished her first sentence. In fact, all I really got from him was a garbled 'Clovis, lunch, Donna, can't, really, really can't, not today'."

Peg shrugged but I could see that Kyle's disjointed monologue had concerned her.

"It's okay, Peg," I assured her, "it's a very common syndrome among those exposed to Clovis. He will actually be able to communicate in a normal fashion once his brain has registered a successful escape from the 'jaws of absurdity'."

Peg was visibly mollified. She nodded and I could see that she was remembering past Clovis encounters, so I continued. "Let's get this clambake nailed down before I join Kyle in the land of the babbling zombies. Oh and Peg, let's try to find a restaurant that will afford us some degree of privacy to avoid an audience, and an easy escape route when our audience avoidance strategy blows up in our faces."

"I'm on it," Peg assured me.

[CHAPTER 18]

Babs and Peg decided that our best bet for an isolated lunch would be at Spaghetti Works. Nothing with the name spaghetti-anything was high on my list these days (pasta consumption signaled the death of most diets), but I knew I would be able to get a salad so I could make it work. Once there, we were escorted to an out-of-the-way booth where there were no other diners within sight. With luck, that would really cut down on the histrionics from Clovis. I mean why expend all that energy with a limited audience who already knew your full range? Besides, Clovis would be a tad more circumspect around Peg since her bad behavior had incurred Peg's wrath in the past, and that was something no one ever wanted to do.

I looked around at the kitchy, honky tonk décor that surrounded us. We were probably also safe from running into the town movers and shakers as well. That would be a good thing.

Clovis arrived within moments of our being seated. I could tell from the look on her face that we were in for a bumpy ride. Well, what were the odds that things would go smoothly? As Clovis clip clopped across the old wooden floors on five-inch stilettos, causing her to wobble dangerously close to falling over, she appeared to be lugging the weight of the world along with her. The tiny, blond, waif-like creature had barely enough bulk to be held to earth by gravity. Her business clothing, dark gray tailored slacks and a white button-down blouse with a big white ruffle down the front, appeared to be about two sizes too big for her. I guess when you were that petite off-the-rack stuff was just not a great option. Combined with the aforementioned five-inch gray spiked pumps, she looked like a five-year-old playing dress up in Mommy's clothes.

The look on her face was clearly one of pain, evidence of the great burden she could no longer bear. She managed to mix that extremely negative combination with a touch of insider smugness topped off by a smidgeon of high drama. It was actually disturbing to behold. I struggled to keep my eyes on her and appear polite, despite powerful instincts desperately struggling to avert my gaze.

"Hello there, ladies," Clovis brayed in a low, husky voice sounding nothing like the high, squeaky, little girl voice we had all come to know and dread. "Thank you for agreeing to meet with me on such short notice."

"It's not like you left us much choice, Clovis," Peg countered, "and what happened to your voice?"

Peg and Clovis could not have been more different. Although both were diminutive, Peg was as solid and sturdy as the rock of Gibraltar. Everything about her was sensible, from her cute pixy haircut to her tan dockers and white button-down work shirt. Peg looked sensible, talked sensible, and acted sensible. Tolerating someone as nonsensical as Clovis had to be the hardest thing for Peg to do; yet she took great pride in her ability to handle people, and she would not be defeated by Clovis.

Babs stood by in her ever-vigilant support of Peg. Together, they were unstoppable, and it wasn't as though Clovis hadn't tried.

"What do you mean?" questioned Clovis in a voice closer to the one we had come to know and dread. "My voice is fine."

Peg looked at me with a 'get me out of this' expression. "Have it your way, Clovis."

"So Clovis," I dove in like a lamb to the slaughter. "What's going on?"

"Well," Clovis began her chronicle, "As I'm sure you're aware, I have landed myself smack in the middle of BJ's murder investigation?"

"Yes, you mentioned that you and BJ were acquainted."

"Acquainted?!" Clovis bellowed, "I hardly think the word for it is acquainted! Why, I may be the one person who knew her best. I'm certain I knew her far better than you!"

"Sure, Clovis, I only knew her for twelve years, and you knew her for – what – six weeks? I can see why you could think that."

"Go ahead, use your sarcasm as you always do. That's one of your main problems, your baseless blanket assumptions. Do you think just because you've known someone for years that you could possibly know them better than someone with whom they've formed a close knit bond, a sisterhood?"

"You know, I'm not going to argue with you over who knew BJ better. That is a distinction I will gladly concede because frankly, I wish I'd never known her!"

"I really don't see how you can say that, Donna, when she moved all the way out here to save your career by going into business with you. It seems terribly ungrateful if you ask me," Clovis finished with a regal snap of her fluffy blonde head as she emphasized her disgust by theatrically turning away from me.

"You do recall that I was unaware of any of this, Clovis?" I responded.

"I know you've been telling people that," Clovis' retort came as a slap in the face, "but I am not convinced."

I narrowed my eyes and gave her my best Clint Eastwood imitation, knowing on some level that Clovis was notorious for never picking up on subtleties of any kind.

"In fact, before she was so tragically killed, BJ was able to convince me that you were fully aware of her plans and anxiously awaiting a long overdue reunion."

This was more than I could bear. Wasn't Clovis the one who'd informed me of BJ's admission that she didn't want me to know what was going on? I'd have commented but words would not have come out. Luckily, Peg was not quite as tongue tied as I.

"All right Clovis, now it's time to put up or shut up," growled Peg. "What's your proof?"

"It's simple, Peg. BJ confided in me that Donna here had been anxious to go into business with me for quite some time, but she'd been too shy to ask. That's why BJ made it a point to look me up, because Donna told her once they teamed up, it would be critical to bring me into the partnership. The veracity of her statement was immediately evident to me. How else would someone new to town know of my stellar business reputation and Donna's constant attempts to ride my successful coattails? No, Donna may not have been in on all of the recent plans, but she certainly knew that a partnership between the three of us was imminent. How could she not?"

"And furthermore, Clovis continued, "I believe that Donna's feeble attempts at distorting the truth, regardless of my attempts to set things straight, may have resulted in my current position at the top of the suspect list," she finished with a mournful groan. And did I detect the faintest of fleeting smiles?

I didn't know whether to laugh or blow a gasket. I had to give BJ credit. Telling Clovis I was desperate to be in business with her was the perfect way to convince Clovis of absolutely anything else – it would cement BJ's credibility! Once BJ realized the power of playing on that enormously overblown ego the little Romanian gypsy would be putty in her hands.

Now I had to face the sobering fact that this lunatic had undoubtedly been out there since BJ's murder regaling everyone with tales of our mythical business partnership and close bond. That was all I needed. I was working hard to keep myself out of jail, and this narcissistic, self-deluded nut-job claimed to have proof positive that I'd been lying all along. At this point I must have instinctively reached across the table to grab her by the throat.

When Peg spotted me, she attempted an interception. I'm not exactly sure what happened at this point, but I believe it went something like this: Babs saw Peg lunge for me and decided to grab on for added ballast. In order to ensure her solid footing, Babs leaned her upper body backward and put one foot on the banquette to brace herself against our combined weight.

Unfortunately, as she leaned back, Babs knocked into the larger-than-life cigar store Indian behind our table. Apparently, the Indian had sustained a slight mishap a few weeks earlier and was not on solid footing himself, so he began to topple over. Peg abandoned all hope of helping Clovis and dove for the plummeting statue. She succeeded in tackling him so he wouldn't smash on the floor. Regrettably he landed smack in the middle of Omaha's largest salad bar with a resounding crash.

The aftermath was surreal. Diners within a twenty-foot radius were covered in lettuce and fixins. Glass plates and salad dressings were shattered and intermingled on a wide expanse of floor making walking virtually impossible. Which explains why the ten or so waiters, who came running at the sound of the crash, all began a bizarre and frenetic dance as, one by one, they hit the slippery, olive oil coated floor and started to slide.

All told there were fewer injuries than you might guess. The ambulance was only necessary for four of the brave wait staff. Unfortunately, the Indian did not survive his dive into the salad bar, nor did the salad bar survive. Peg, Babs, Clovis, and I were unceremoniously escorted out before we'd even sampled our breadsticks.

As dazed as we were walking out of the restaurant, Clovis managed to turn to me with one last parting shot.

"You know, Donna, I'm not sure I'll ever be able to forgive you for getting BJ out here to plan a business for the three of us to run together, and then getting BJ killed before we even had a chance to toast our future success!"

And with that she stormed off. I probably don't need to mention that Peg and Babs were each hanging on to one of my arms – and they each had a leg of their own wrapped around the wooden bench outside of Spaghetti Works.

The walk back to the office was a bit of a blur. Once back, Babs and Peg fussed over me, and forced me to drink several cups of strong tea. It seemed as though I'd drunk about a gallon before finally convincing them I'd survived the latest Clovis onslaught. Clearly my tolerance of the woman had reached an all-time low. Even carefully controlled meetings surrounded by sympathetic colleagues were not enough of a barrier against the infuriating revisionist and frighteningly delusional concoctions of Clovis, and what they could elicit from you. Her ability to push buttons was second to none, not even NASA technicians launching a space shuttle. Sadly, it was the effect her egotistical ramblings had on my temper that concerned me the most.

I glanced at my monitor and learned that Donny had scheduled a short briefing session for four-thirty, which gave me two hours to finish up some research and make one or two necessary phone calls. I'd have to hustle.

[CHAPTER 19]

"I just have a few items that need clarification, but before jumping into my questions, I want to be sure everyone knows about our newest division," Donny began.

What the hell was he talking about?

"Yes," Donny continued, "I'm referring to the one we'll create to handle the inevitable demand for our specialized restaurant design skills in the aftermath of Donna's latest restaurant remodeling work."

I rolled my eyes. After the next several minutes of totally un-PC Indian war whoops, accompanied by raucous laughter that seemed to border on hysteria finally died down (apparently these folks had some pent up crazy to release), Donny jumped into his briefing.

It appeared he'd gathered his old team and was anxious to get the competition started. He knew Liv would waste no time getting her team in gear. Frick and Frack sat opposite each other with Donny at the nearby helm surveying his posse.

Aside from Frick and Frack, Donny's team was limited. It consisted of Sam Knight, our Director of Social Influence and a man who thought more outside the box than virtually anyone else I'd ever encountered, which made his humor bizarre and worthy of Seinfeld fame, and Clarke Holmes, a creative mind with a penchant for the ultimate truth. It occurred to me that in Clarke's truth, reality might not be the most compelling factor. In other words, Clarke could discover the actual murderer, and then determine, in the grand scheme of things, that the person who wielded the murder weapon did not meet his criteria and must therefore be eliminated regardless of incontrovertible evidence.

In this case, where the spiked heel ultimately caused BJ's death, if the person holding the heel at the time of her murder did not meet his intellectualized assessment of the criteria for this particular murder, the evidence should be overlooked and a more suitable candidate fitting the murderer's perceived profile should be sought. It was an ethereal approach to problem solving. Things were not always what they seemed, so physical evidence be damned! In Clarke's world alibis were not such a big deal – it was more about fitting the profile.

You know what they say: If I'm smart and I think it through, I'll come up with the right answer. Wait is that what they say? – Oh well. At any rate, even at the risk of Clarke's unmitigated disdain, the police repeatedly allowed the existing physical evidence to lead them to the killer – probable or not. Poor misguided slugs. One thing you could count on from Clarke, he would make you think. Usually until your head hurt!

As Donny's team came to order, he began the debriefing process with a very thorough list of questions regarding the victim and her past history. It was clear from the nature of some of his questions that he had the benefit of some prior knowledge of my relationship with BJ. About a third of the way into his questions, Donny felt the need to challenge my credibility.

"Donna," he began, "it's pretty clear that BJ was not your favorite person."

"Really? That comes as *such* a surprise to me!" I countered.

"See, that's what I'm talking about," Donny pressed, "your credibility is in question when each response about BJ is cloaked in barely concealed hostility."

"She made the beginning of my career a nightmare, and then when I was sure I had escaped her evil presence permanently, she turned up halfway across the country, in my new home, and managed to implicate me in her highly visible murder. Why would you ever think I would bear any hostility toward her? I was getting ready to renew my vows and make her my matron of honor."

"Geez, Donna," Donny whined, "Could you tone down the drama just a tad? You're starting to sound a lot like Clovis."
Okay, that was going too far! I sounded like Clovis? I had to take several deep breaths before I could even respond to such an accusation. Damn that Donny. After a few big gulps and some deep breathing I found my voice again.

"You smug, son-of-a—"

"Donna, Donna," Donny interjected, as the realization hit that in this instance he needed me more than I needed him if he was to continue to play OPD homicide consultant with his buddies. "I'm sorry. I knew that crack was going too far when I said it."

Wow. An apology from Donny? That never happened. I was nonplussed. Hearing his apology went a long way toward returning my voice to its normal range, several octaves lower than the screeching howler monkey decibel the Clovis crack had elicited. It's not like I was naïve enough to think his contrition was sincere, it was just good to have the upper hand now and then.

"Really, Donny, you'll have to do better than that if you want any information from me."

"I know, I know," he admitted.

This new placating demeanor was so uncharacteristic. It was awesome! He was practically groveling at my feet. It was about time! Clearly, there was nothing he wouldn't do to gain the edge in a competition. I intended to take full advantage of his ass-kissing strategy while it lasted. God knows I'd probably never see it again.

"You may continue," I offered.

I was nothing if not gracious. The relief was clearly visible on Donny's face. It felt good to be holding the cards. It might behoove me to hold them as close to the vest for as long as possible. I had to admit my reasons were twofold: first to retain the power, that was always a challenge with our partnership, and second to frustrate the hell out of Donny, and that was just for fun! Well, it's not like I pretend to be perfect – right?

We managed to make it through a few less impertinent questions before he slipped back into annoying the crap out of me. Unfortunately, my card-holding moments proved to be jarringly short lived. As Donny regained his equilibrium, his snot-nosed attitude came back with a vengeance.

"Guess that lunch with Clovis was too much for you to handle. Give me a minute and I'll get a strait jacket to keep you from hurting yourself and others."

The man did not know when to quit. We adjourned the meeting having accomplished little. Lunch with Clovis had pushed my stress level to the breaking point. Then, insult was added to injury when it was followed by Donny's questionable choice of meeting ice-breakers; he just loves to keep poking the bear. You'd think when he was finally close to compiling a complete picture and needed my information to fill in a few crucial gaps, he'd back off. Rather than using his intuitive skills and being a little flexible under the circumstances he chose to push every one of my buttons, I think he even hit a few snaps. Oh well. His loss.

After our frustrating attempt at communicating, I was anxious to get home. The extra commute and the highway traffic were a huge pain on a night like this when I was feeling bone weary. Although it wasn't a bad commute, I had been spoiled by the three-mile distance home from our former office building.

The easy travel of the past twelve years had felt like a reward for having survived the insanely intense road time of my last position in the Northeast. Before making the big move to Omaha, I'd managed to turn myself into an extreme east coast commuter, driving an hour and a half each way to get to work. At the time, taking that position had seemed like a stellar career move. In retrospect, a decent quality of life should have taken precedent. Oh well, live and learn.

When the opportunity of a move to Omaha and an executive position at Marcel materialized, it just felt right. With a home based business he had operated successfully from literally anywhere we'd travelled, Jon's greatest concern in accompanying me on this move west was his fear of not being able to get Yankee games on TV. I have hung out in lift lines in Utah and museum lobbies in Salzburg waiting for Jon to get off one of his famous "anytime/anywhere" conference calls, conducting his business in some of the least likely places. We used to joke that he could operate his business wherever there was a phone and a computer, and that's even more applicable today. He's about as portable as it gets, so when it became my turn for the big career move, Jon readily packed up his traveling office and moved to Omaha.

As I drove down Pacific Street nearing home, I wondered what I'd find there to greet me. Would Jon have sensed my elevated stress level and prepared one of his amazing gourmet meals? I was betting on it. Rounding the last bend, I hit the button for the garage door. As I maneuvered the car into what Jon refers to as 'the world's smallest three-car garage,' I realized immediately that my wonderful evening of pampering was not to be. Jon's car was gone. Rats!

I gathered my paraphernalia and trudged into the front hallway. It was tough to hold onto my disappointment when Jasmine, Roxi, and Sweet Pea were clearly so thrilled to see me. I fussed and petted and watched my beautiful bulldogs prance around the house in sheer delight – what could top a greeting like this? I stowed my bags and jacket on the banister, out of harm's way. Then I saw the note on the counter.

"Early game tonight. Fed and walked the girls. Would have made you something – but knew you ate out for lunch and figured you'd want to eat light tonight."

Shit. Softball. I forgot again. Oh well, maybe I'd feel better after a glass of Kim Crawford.

Relaxing on the floor of the family room with my glass of wine and bulldogs at my side afforded me an opportunity to think through the events of the past few days. Unquestionably, I was still experiencing some level of shock over the bizarre information I'd been forced to jam into my overloaded brain. I suppose it was inevitable I'd start comparing my role in identifying Claire's murderer with my role in BJ's murder now. A lack of patience had me in a constant state of nervous energy. I'd been methodically working through details and evidence in a disjointed process, trying to fit facts together in a way that would result in answers. To a large extent, it was this process which still enabled me to feel some semblance of control when so much felt out of control.

It dawned on me that even though I'd prepared a comprehensive list of east coast suspects for Detective Warren, I was primarily spending my time defending myself against the fantasy story that BJ had concocted around me rather than taking a proactive role in searching for and examining critical details. If I was going to be totally honest with myself (and what the hell, I should be open to trying new things) there was no reason for my defensiveness since there hadn't been any accusations leveled at me. It was as though I expected to be doubted by everyone so I had to work full time to dispel the doubts. I was getting caught in my own shorts. Even with the positive reaction I'd received from Warren and the team, I knew two things that made it impossible for me to abandon my paranoia. First, they could change their minds about me at any moment, and second, if they did it's possible they would not let on immediately. My New Jersey origins would serve to make me wary, fueling the paranoia when others were satisfied to let down their guard.

By my second glass of Crawford, I was determined to turn things around. No longer would I focus on defending myself. It was time to move on. I ran that thinking past my girls; they didn't seem to find any holes in it. That's the great thing about bulldogs; they love you unconditionally though they are very demanding companions, but in an intellectual discussion they are almost always behind you one-thousand percent! I sat down to a light supper after distributing liver treats to my supportive companions. After supper we all settled down to watch House Hunters International, eager for Jon's return.

[CHAPTER 20]

The next day, I was still resolved to be proactive. I gave some serious thought as to how I could be most helpful in the investigation. Considering my connection to BJ, it seemed that ferreting information out of some likely suspects could be worthwhile. At Warren's request I had compiled a list of Connecticut suspects early on. But according to Donny, the police investigators had altered it considerably, adding non-Connecticut suspects and ranking it in favor of a female killer. Eight women were now leading the pack. I imagined that the majority of them were Omaha residents since my Connecticut list had only featured two women, total. It would be a challenge getting my hands on the suspect list; I couldn't see Warren's team just handing it over. The obvious short-term solution would be for me to compile my own female dominant list and try to work it for information. Even if I was unable to correctly identify all eight of the suspects, I was pretty sure I'd be able to figure most of them out. Then I could gather some information on each one and make my own analysis.

It dawned on me with a sinking feeling. Clovis was probably my best resource for people who BJ knew in Omaha. Crap. Oh well, I'm nothing if not realistic. Since nothing positive emerged from our Spaghetti Works fiasco, I still had a ton of unanswered questions. If I had to find a way to debrief the "Diva of Darkness," debrief her I would. Rest assured, if I could take another tack I would, but avoiding Clovis was looking unlikely.

I spent the next fifteen minutes outlining action steps for Phase I of "getting the hell out of my own head and into the game." My outline broke out into two main parts: first, likely female suspects in Connecticut, and second, in Omaha. I figured it might actually be best to start with my Connecticut contacts because they'd known her longer and better so there was more chance that one of them had been pushed too far and killed her. Hell, maybe she moved to Omaha to flee from someone who was getting close to that point, and I was nothing more than a convenient beard.

Of course, the obvious benefit of starting with Connecticut folks was that it provided the opportunity to avoid Clovis initially. Who knew, if my work on the Connecticut suspects proved fruitful I might never have to address the Omaha side. Self-preservation would have me hitting that Connecticut side hard!

I figured I'd start with Porter Enzo. He had always been an excellent source of information; he also had the dubious distinction of being a former BJ intimate. But first I would make a few calls and find out if he and BJ had had any sort of contact over the past decade. If not, he'd be easy to eliminate as a suspect. In the meantime, even given the female angle assumed by the police, there was no solid evidence the killer was a woman. Everyone was still under suspicion.

My next step was to find someone to fill me in on Enzo's whereabouts and interactions over the past decade. On top of the list was his number one competitor: Ben Stickley.

I caught Ben on his way to an early lunch; why could I never remember that the east coast was an hour ahead of us? Ben seemed genuinely pleased to hear from me after all this time. We spent a few minutes getting up to speed on each other's lives and then Ben beat me to the topic of murder.

"Hey Donna," he offered, "Did anyone tell you about the murder of your former colleague?"

"As a matter of fact, Ben, that's actually why I'm calling today," I confessed. "I was hoping you could shed some light on a few things."

"I'll answer anything I can," Ben replied, "But wouldn't you get more by talking to some of your former colleagues at Mylar? I mean, I didn't exactly see that much of her. You know her close relationship with Porter Enzo kind of made me persona non grata with "the diva." And now that I'm thinking about it, I kind of recall she was not exactly your favorite person either. So, why such interest?"

"Ben, were you aware that BJ had moved out to Omaha a few months ago? Did you know that she was murdered out here?" I answered his question with my own questions.

"Oh god, Donna, I never made the connection," he replied. "I had heard that she'd moved to the Midwest somewhere, but to be honest, I wasn't really sure where you were. So it never even occurred to me."

"Understandable," I acknowledged. "I wouldn't expect you to know, why would you?"

"Wow, was it just a huge coincidence that she ended up in the same city as you?" he pressed. "Or have you two developed an affinity since you moved away?"

"Actually Ben, neither," I replied.

"Oh, sounds complicated," he said.

"Yeah, complicated."

I filled Ben in on my bizarre tale and he was duly creeped out.

"Jesus, I do recall she had started getting a little 'stalky' with you while you were still out here. Sounds as though she finally flipped her nut completely. I hate to think of what she had planned for you!"

That was it. Ben hit the nail on the head. In that one

sentence he had clarified the basis of my obsession with BJ's murder. When you reviewed the facts, sure BJ moving to my city and telling everyone – except me – we were going into business together was kind of psycho. That, added to the fact that she'd been murdered in a highly visible and extremely dramatic manner, made it completely bizarre. But, for me, the most pressing mystery of all was the part of her plan that seemed to center directly on me. What had she planned on doing? It explained why this whole thing had me so crazed!

You may think me self-centered to the point of hysteria, but the undeniable fact that she had concocted an elaborate plan, leading back to me at every juncture, suggested a sinister outcome where I was the hapless victim and not just some pawn to help move her toward her goal. I shuddered. Had I narrowly escaped becoming a casualty in another of BJ's amoral plots? I couldn't help but wonder if her efforts had been focused on taking me out. Had it been sheer luck that someone murdered her before her dastardly plans for me had been realized. That only applied if the police didn't decide that I had the most to gain by her death. Wasn't that a sobering irony? Someone may have done me a big favor by murdering her, but it would hardly feel like a favor if it landed me on death row!

No wonder I'd been so distracted since hearing from Farley. At the risk of sounding like Clovis, this whole thing really did appear to revolve around me. Now solving her murder would be secondary for me. I wanted to know what the hell that bitch had been plotting to do to me.

I wondered how I could have been so blind. Passively content to sit on the sidelines and help the police peripherally when all the while I played a pathetic marionette to a twisted puppeteer from the other side of the grave. It was time to take control back and get in the game. It was time to wake up and face facts.

In retrospect, I didn't think Stickley would be central to my renewed efforts. Had I realized that earlier I doubt I'd have called him at all and his insights had proven to be invaluable. Knowing my true objective felt very liberating even though, viewed through this light, it was far more terrifying: to think that someone could be nuts enough to plot such an elaborate ruse in order to mess me up! I felt as though I'd dodged a huge bullet.

"Donna," Ben began tentatively, "Are you all right?"

"Oh sorry, Ben. Your last statement really caught me off guard." I admitted, "It hadn't occurred to me in quite that way before, but thanks to you I think I've finally found the focus I've been missing. I've got some rethinking to do.

"Well, regardless of your approach, if you unravel part of the mystery, I would guess the other answers would fall into place," Ben reasoned.

He had a point. It was likely that these objectives were inextricably bound. I should continue on my quest to identify the killer. At any rate, considering the perception BJ had created about our level of involvement, the murderer could potentially be quite a threat to me, even if the police weren't. That's something I wouldn't fully comprehend until BJ's plans for me were unmasked, nevertheless, I wanted him/her behind bars tout suite.

"When did you get so wise?" I asked, only half kidding.

"Donna, Donna, Donna, I was always this wise," Ben replied, "You media planners never could bring yourselves to give media reps the credit due us."

Well, he had that right. Actually, sales reps were a fascinating group of folks. They were either, really smart and extremely helpful, just plain pushy or empty vessels that bought the company propaganda and wouldn't know the truth if they fell over it. Ben had been an unusual combination of all three. He was really smart and could be helpful, but he bought his company propaganda to the point where he couldn't always see reality. And man, could he be pushy. You never really knew what to expect when you called Ben. Luckily for me, this time brains won out, and Ben gave me the shove I needed.

I would search for answers to what BJ had planned for me, and secondarily, I'd work to put her murderer behind bars. It occurred to me that my search would be far more centered on her east coast contemporaries since it was doubtful she'd revealed her true intentions to brand new acquaintances; nor was it likely that these new folks had had a chance to see through the BS yet. I didn't really hold much hope that she'd blatantly revealed her evil scheme to even her closest Connecticut connections, but there was more of a chance that they would have seen though her thinly veiled fabrications.

I would set aside my investigation of Enzo and focus a little closer to home. The challenge would be finding someone close to BJ who would be willing to talk to me. I figured her first husband, Ron, would be the best place to start. As much as he would have liked to expunge her from his life, the fact that they shared a son together forced an inextricable bond. Ron might know some inside information and he probably liked me better than BJ these days anyway. What the hell, it was worth a shot.

[CHAPTER 21]

I played around online until I found Ron's phone number. This was going to require some delicacy; I mean it's not like I ever had more than a nodding acquaintance with Ron. Calling him up out of the blue might seem odd, although I supposed a condolence call wouldn't be totally out of place. Come to think of it, that might also help me with husband number two. Although I knew WyCliff far better than Ron, having worked with him for several years, a call to him would activate his enormously suspicious nature. WyCliff had firsthand knowledge of the animosity that existed between BJ and me, whereas Ron may only have known that she hated my guts and thought I was a moron. He may not have been aware that I considered her to be the devil incarnate.

I steeled my nerve, took a deep breath, and dialed Ron's number. After a few rings someone answered.

"Hello," said a sweet but sturdy female voice. Oh crap, would the new wife even let me talk to Ron if she knew this was about the horrific she-devil who had undoubtedly made their lives a living hell just for sport? I proceeded to introduce myself and explain that I wanted to extend my condolences to Ron.

"Oh yes, wasn't that tragic?" she replied. "How nice of you to think of Ron at such a sad time. I'll go get him, he's out back chopping some wood. Oh and by the way, my name is Sheila. Ron and I have been married for ten years now. As you can imagine, he's not exactly grief stricken about losing his 'less than charming' former wife." Clearly Ron's taste in women had improved with age – or experience. "But he is extremely concerned over the effect it will have on their son, Mickey. Well, hang on, dear, I'll just give Ron a yell."

Hmmm. Naturally, I knew about Mickey. He was the wunderkind son she'd had when we worked together years ago. He would have to be close to thirty now. Hmmff, I hadn't really given much thought to Mickey at all. That was really sad. I mean with all of her grotesque and destructive behaviors she did have one redeeming quality. I remember she loved her son with a white-hot intensity. In fact, based on many of her comments about him, her love for him was absolutely obsessive, even for a mother.

The thought of her cherished baby as a grown-up was difficult to assimilate. In my mind, he remained an infant or a toddler. Any way you looked at it, losing his mother would be a genuine tragedy. Well, here it was. I was finally going to feel something more than shock, surprise and dread. Maybe I wasn't the cold-hearted shrew I was thinking I'd become. I was beginning to feel a deep sadness for Mickey and his tragic loss, which meant there was hope for me yet. Damn, that could cost me my objectivity! I was hoping to avoid an emotional investment altogether. I should have known better; just the anticipation of witnessing overwhelming grief will melt a steely resolve faster than a hot flame will melt butter. As I was ruminating about Mickey facing life without his Mom, Ron finally came to the phone.

"Donna?" he began tentatively, "it's been awhile."

"Hi Ron, how are things?" I made my first chess move. "I'm truly sorry for your loss."

"Yeah," he responded, "that was something, huh?"

Hmmm. Not sure where to go with that. It seemed like an odd response to the murder of someone close, even if it was your ex-wife. Oh well, might as well just jump right in with both feet.

"How is Mickey handling things?" I asked in what I hoped was a sympathetic tone.

"Mickey's a trooper," he answered, "but it's been strange, I'll say that."

This wasn't getting any easier. Ron's responses were not at all enlightening. Was he sad or was he celebrating? I honestly couldn't tell. Would this end up being a total waste of time? I should have remembered that tall, bulky and rugged Ron was a man of few words. There might be a way to draw him out, but I sure as hell didn't know him well enough to know what it was. We could be on the phone until next spring and I still might not get anything definitive at this rate. Turns out I had nothing to worry about. My mental meandering actually did me a favor for once. Apparently, we'd been experiencing a pregnant pause, which makes folks uncomfortable according to all the cop shows. I guess Ron was no exception. Anything but silence!

"Now that we're talking," Ron continued, "I have to ask you a question."

Was that really Ron initiating a topic? I was encouraged. That may have been the longest sentence I'd ever heard him utter. Better jump in there to keep the momentum going if he's on a roll.

"Shoot," I responded.

"If my memory's not playing tricks on me, I didn't think you and BJ got along so well."

Oh crap, was he getting ready to hang up on me? Luckily, he wasn't finished.

"If I'm right, what happened that made you want to go into business with her? I mean she didn't exactly have a great track record," he finished.

"Ron, I have to know, what did she tell you about our going into business together? Because honestly, we hadn't been planning anything. I had no idea she'd moved out to Omaha, and I have to admit to being more than a little freaked out at what I've been hearing since her murder."

"Oh, man," Ron continued in an odd voice, "I was kind of afraid of that."

"Afraid of what?"

"Well," he sighed and hesitated.

Just as I was about to jump in with full bore paranoia, he continued.

"Things hadn't been good for her here, not for a while," Ron shared. "You remember she had a pretty high opinion of herself. She kind of thought of herself as a star, in fact."
Ron took a short breather, and I was too stunned to comment. So I just waited.

"You know how she always thought she was the big success with the big career and all the material perks and advantages that come with it, right?"

Clearly that was a rhetorical comment, so I awaited his next declaration. Good old Ron was proving to be a whole lot sharper than his harpy first wife ever gave him credit for.

"She'd pretty much hit the point where even she, with her ability to spin anything to her advantage, had to admit that she'd hit rock bottom. All that was left for her was to find a real job and make a few bucks in order to get by. And by that I mean just a regular job, not some fancy, glamorous 'position.' Those opportunities just weren't coming her way, hadn't been for a long time. She was getting downright desperate. There was no savings and no alimony from her second divorce. But as destitute as she was, it was not enough to get her to be realistic about what had to happen."

"Oh god." It was the best I could do.

"It was pretty hard on Mickey. He's married with a small daughter, you know."

"I didn't know that. Wow! And, I guess, congratulations, you're a grandfather...and that means..."

"Yeah, BJ was a grandmother," Ron finished my sentence. "And that did not sit well with her at all. I mean the combination of the perfect storm of hitting the skids, losing her whole sense of being a superstar, and making a hard landing into 'grandparenthood' was too much for her to handle. She started getting weird – I mean more weird than usual. Mickey doesn't know it, but Sheila and I had been paying her hefty mortgage and providing her with a small amount of cash for the past year."

I was stunned speechless. Stone cold speechless.

"Mickey was so proud of his wife and baby, and BJ rejected all three of them. She and Mickey hadn't spoken in months. Well, at least not until right near the end."

Now the wheels in my head kicked in and started spinning again. That explained why BJ would consider moving out of the Northeast, her playground. In retrospect it shouldn't have been all that surprising. From the beginning, BJ had been a minor talent in a mid-sized New England ad agency. When they landed Petrovsky Aircraft, a huge account that did not interest the media director, Tony Lou was happy to palm all the planning off on one of her direct reports, and BJ knew an opportunity when she saw one. As the Petrofsky Aircraft account continued to grow, so did BJ's reputation within the agency. That's when things started happening for her. During my early days at Mylar, vague reminders of that simple and humble girl who could barely believe her good fortune still existed. But not for long.

And again, I was reminded of the one thing that never ceased to amaze me. Just a little hard work on her part would have enabled her to genuinely evaluate aerospace and military publications with either a U.S. or global audience. She could have developed brilliant strategies engineered to positively impact the clients' business. But BJ just took the prior media list and ran ads where and when the client indicated. To her credit, she kept track of an extensive media schedule and she made sure the ads ran right. But that was about it. Hers was not the first meteoric rise to stardom built less on her media acumen and brilliant thinking than on doing as she was told and keeping it organized.

She was left to her own devices since no one else in the media department had any interest in the world of helicopters. It had a lot to do with being in the right place at the right time, and it changed her life forever. I guess it was no wonder that after I'd been around for a bit and displayed an interest in actually understanding the media in order to carve out a clear strategic direction, she decided she'd have to take me out. That seems to be about the time her proverbial train permanently jumped the track and the word normal ceased to apply to anything pertaining to BJ.

It occurred to me that much of her self-aggrandized self-image came from her own depiction of herself as a hot, young business genius/fashionista. Being a grandma would certainly have put a crimp in her style. It was no wonder that her selfish dream kept Mickey permanently frozen in adolescence. How horrible that must have been for her poor son; if he couldn't freeze time and stay a child, his own mother would want no part of him.

"Ron." I shook my head trying to bring it back to the present. "That's unbelievable."

"I know. In all the wild things I've seen her do I would never, in a million years, have thought she would hurt Mickey in this way. He was crushed and stunned. I have to admit I had been unable to stop BJ from spoiling him shamelessly as he was growing up. That made her rejection even more impossible to comprehend. It hasn't been good," Ron finished, with the understatement of the century.

"Wow Ron, incredible!" This dialogue was not advancing my reputation as a brilliant conversationalist. I was doing the best I could under the circumstances.

"Sheila and I were trying so hard to be parents and grandparents to Mickey and his family. We were determined to make up for the hole in his life that was created by losing his Mom's affection. He was so excited about the birth of his first child and anticipating that BJ would be thrilled to have his precious baby to dote on and spoil. It never dawned on him that the blessed event would backfire and shake the foundation of everything he's ever known."

"Sheila is clearly a saint. It was so wise of you to try to fill the void that Mickey must have been feeling. How was that going?" I asked. "It may have been a great idea, but it would be difficult to pull off."

"Actually, things were going better than I could have hoped, if only."

Oh, right. BJ's death changed everything.

"After BJ's first trip to Omaha, she'd found a place to rent and was ready to begin her 'fresh start'. I guess a little time away made her forget that Mickey had been responsible for making her a grandmother. She called him when she got back into town. Mickey was nervous thinking she'd want to get together. He was worried about her erratic feelings in close proximity to the baby or his wife. He didn't have to worry.

BJ merely wanted him to rent a U Haul and lug her furniture out to Omaha.

The timing was bad. Here was a guy who had never been away from home, and now with a wife and a new baby, his mom was asking him to drive halfway across the country and hang around with her for a while. Sad thing was, Mickey was so lost without his mother's love and affection he happily agreed, much to the frustration of his poor wife. So Mickey packed his bag and left."

"Well, she always did have a hell of a lot of nerve. Oops, sorry Ron." I had to remember who I was talking to here.

"It's okay," Ron went on. "You know Mickey was out there at the time of the murder?"

"Oh God, no, I didn't know that."

"Yeah, he was able to escort her body back to Connecticut for the burial," Ron continued. "And here's the worst thing."

"There's something worse than being rejected, used by the mother you adore, and then being nearby as she is brutally murdered?" I asked quizzically.

"Yeah, actually there is," Ron kept going. "After he got back home, Mickey noticed something funny about his bank account. Turns out the bank account he'd been using for all of his family expenses was the very same bank account we opened when he started college. Stupid kid, he didn't see a need to open a new account when he still had a perfectly good one already, so he didn't. Only problem was, we'd opened that account the way parents usually do, with the kid as a signer and one of the parents as a signer."

I was afraid of where this was going. Please tell me even BJ wasn't capable of...

"The money was gone. All of it. Mickey had saved up quite a nest egg. With the small amount left over from his college days combined with the money he'd saved since graduation, Mickey had had almost seventy-five thousand dollars in that account. And she took it," Ron finished with a slight tremor in his voice. "And that's how she was able to pay for her 'fresh start'."

What could I say? What amazed me most was that with all of the terrible things she had done, and was undoubtedly planning to do, to me, she had managed to do far worse to the son that she loved so dearly. I think that verifies her mental illness.

[CHAPTER 22]

After my call with Ron, I felt drained. Ron's heart wrenching story caused all of the emotions I had so successfully been repressing to cascade down on me. I couldn't help but be reminded of Phillippe's comment about a family member being the murderer. Could he be right? It just didn't seem likely, even given all the drama BJ had created for them. As I sat staring out the window, the world slowly began to right itself. Little by little the fog in my brain dissipated. I knew what had to be done.

Clearly the series of circumstances that had brought BJ out to the heartland had been incubated and hatched back East in a more convoluted, even psychotic, scheme than I could ever have imagined. Time to book a flight to Connecticut and confront the key players face-to-face. It stood to reason that, if BJ was perpetrating horrible injustices against her son and his family, she must also have been deceiving and cheating others as well. Perhaps one of them had discovered her shameful little secrets and extracted their revenge against this raging sociopath. Had I been on a jury, I would have found it difficult to convict anyone of lashing out at her.

I called Jon to share my travel plans. He insisted that we would head back east together and make it a joint investigation/family visit. When I objected to his barely-concealed plan to tag along as my babysitter, he quickly reminded me that without a cadre of babysitters during my feeble attempt at investigating Claire's murder, my fate could well have mirrored hers. He'd made his point. It was time for a long distance road trip (i.e., a sky trip)!

Once calendars had been checked and travel plans made, it turned out I would fly out on my own after all, and Jon would follow in two days. That would give me a full five days of face-to-face time with the folks who really knew BJ and her deepest darkest secrets. The thought of uncovering those pearls of macabre wisdom brought a lump to my throat. I wasn't really sure I was ready for a full on plunge into the dark side, but there wasn't much choice.

My flight was booked for the next morning at 11:00 A.M. Since I could ill afford any additional time away from the office, it was determined that I would work for as long as possible and bum a ride to the airport from my peeps, Babs and Peg.

At 9:20 A.M. the next morning, Peg was busy loading my bag into her enormous SUV, while Babs was scouting the area for any other items earmarked for the trip. I would fly into Bradley Field and stay at my mom's house in Somers. Mom was excited about the prospect of a visit, but in reality, I think she was more excited about getting into the middle of the investigation. As a lifelong devotee of Agatha Christie and Sherlock Holmes, investigating a real murder had long been her dream. There was a time when I felt that way, but when the opportunity presented itself with Claire's murder I was forced to realize just how ill-prepared I was to face genuine danger. It's not all it's cracked up to be!

A minor adjustment to my schedule, and there was virtually nothing I couldn't handle from my remote site at Mom's. Thank God for e-mail, voicemail, and teleconferencing. Before the advent of these conveniences, a last minute trip like this would have been difficult to impossible without an act of Congress, or God. These days it was possible to be virtually present in the office no matter where in the world you were, literally. Now, instead of being out-of-touch when traveling, an iPad and a smart phone meant you never even had to get behind in your correspondence. Thinking back on earlier times, it was amazing that we ever got out of the office at all. Oh well, necessity is the mother of invention. Peg caught my eye with the "let's roll" facial gesture followed by the beckoning wave. I was ready.

Good thing the airport was barely a stone's throw from our office. The entire trip consisted of Peg lecturing me on possible dangers during my investigation, while Babs pointed out immediate areas of concern.

"Hey Peg, that guy on the bike has the right of way," and "Do you see that car to your right?" In between traffic safety outbursts, Babs occasionally interjected a cautionary note for emphasis during Peg's steady stream of "keeping Donna safe without us 101."

After passing Gallup University, we noticed there was road construction ahead. Groaning in unison, we saw a detour sign directing us off the main drag and onto some back road none of us had ever noticed before. God bless Peg, though, her diatribe never faltered. She had one chance to brief me as a captive audience and she wasn't about to waste a precious minute in driving minutiae.

As we continued along, I murmured an occasional acknowledgement of Peg's discourse and Babs' roadside color commentary. Suddenly I noticed a shift in Babs' tone. Was I mistaken, or did I detect fear? Perhaps actually listening to Babs might shed some light on her shifting demeanor. So I did, sort of.

"Peg, I don't know, none of this is familiar," Babs cautioned.

Well, that should be no surprise. None of us ever came this way. As I scanned the road ahead, for the first time, it occurred to me that the typical detour signs, the ones telling you how to get back to the main drag, did not appear anywhere in sight. That meant one of two things: either the city of Omaha was falling short of their usual thorough job of marking detours, or we were going the wrong way. As I thought about it, it was unlikely the city had erred, unlike life in the Northeast, where detours in highly complex driving situations never even pretend to tell anyone how to navigate around the commotion. Omaha respected our drivers. Diverted drivers in the Northeast are left to fend for themselves in crazy over-congested roads unfamiliar to them, and oftentimes more than a little hazardous.

As my ruminations drew to a close, it occurred to me that the intensity of Bab's nervous chatter had escalated to borderline hysteria. I had a bad feeling. Peg, on the other hand, never missed a beat; she was still regaling me with dire warnings and predictions of disaster. It was hardly a calming experience.

Suddenly Babs let out a shriek which succeeded in commanding our full attention, "Shit, Peg, we're on the runway!"

All eyes were ahead as the taxiing 727 came barreling toward us with intent.

I'm not exactly sure what happened after that. Flashing red lights and bullhorn warnings prevailed. The plane managed to stop as Peg swerved furiously to extricate us from its path. We skidded off the edge of the runway on two wheels. I don't know what frightened me more, the thought of rolling Peg's SUV and being thrown through the air like a rag doll, or being decapitated by the wing of a frantically braking jet. They say your life passes before you at a time like this, but I merely experienced a bone chilling, icy terror.

As all parties struggled for optimum damage control, time seemed to stand still. I was told afterward that the whole thing took about three minutes. It felt like three days. Either way, it definitely felt shorter than the time we spent in airport security before being transported to the police station for booking. I guess I never realized there were charges involved in stopping a plane during takeoff. I know now.

Once through processing, I was able to rebook on a later flight. Warren was kind enough to give me a ride to the airport. Funny thing, that detour was actually pretty simple, if you paid attention.

Warren used our time together to brief me on the ways in which I could be helpful to the ongoing investigation, along with a healthy dose of jarringly real threats for doing anything stupid. I assured her that I would not even consider doing anything to proactively endanger myself. The look I got reminded me that being proactive was not the prevailing concern – 'being' was enough to worry her. She had a point.

As she dropped me off in front of the airport, Warren shared one last thought, "I will make it my business to locate officers in every town you plan to visit. You'll have my list before nightfall. Enter it into your cell phone and do not hesitate to use it if you have even a mild concern during your sleuthing process."

Oh great. I could just picture myself as the 'guest of honor' at a little tea party hosted by statewide Connecticut police investigators. I was sure they would welcome me with open arms. It was far more likely that just one call would result in threats and a possible ejection from the state.

Warren must have been reading my thoughts because she ended her debriefing with, "this kind of arrangement is highly unorthodox and would normally be rejected outright. What makes it unique is the fact that it's a murder investigation, and they will err on the side of going overboard to help me out no matter how strange the request. I will brief them on your help and cooperation during the Dockens murder; it will give you some standing with the troops. Just one thing, though."

"What?"

"Don't push your luck!"

Personally, I think that goes without saying, but what do I know? I thanked Warren for the ride and the help and dashed into the airport. I wasn't taking any chances on missing this flight.

[CHAPTER 23]

It was a huge relief to finally touch down at Bradley Field. Aside from the harrowing ride to Eppley, changing planes in O'Hare was always an unnerving crapshoot. That was one of the few challenges of living in Omaha; there weren't a whole lot of direct flights anywhere. That fact alone kept Omaha from growing into the booming metropolis it was poised and ready to become. There was no doubt that with direct flights to all major metros, Omaha, with all of its surprising amenities, would be unstoppable both as a place to live as well as a tourist destination. We were central to everything – smack in the middle of the country.

As I headed down to the baggage carousels, I saw Mom eyeing new arrivals with an anxious expression on her face. She spotted me and waved. We shared a quick hug and proceeded out to the parking lot. No need to wait for luggage; the brevity of the trip enabled me to jam everything into a carry-on.

It was a twenty-minute drive back to Mom's house. A drive rich with nostalgic landmarks from as far back as my junior high years. We passed through Windsor Locks, Suffield, and Enfield before reaching Somers, where Mom had been living for the past twenty years.

It was always great coming back to Mom's. She'd created a lovely warm and comfortable home in the fashion of an upscale resort, including gourmet fare cooked by the great lady herself. She loved nothing more than to pamper her two daughters, their husbands, her two granddaughters, their partners and a whole slew of granddogs. Of course, Mom's idea of pampering was to provide ample food and booze; for everything else you were on your own. In lieu of a hotel bill, she managed to find long unattended chores for each of us to tackle.

Once inside and shed of my baggage (the kind on wheels, the baggage in my head was going nowhere fast) we chucked our shoes for slippers and sat down with a cocktail in her two-storied family room to discuss the game plan for the next few days. It always felt great to be in this remarkable room with its floor-to-ceiling windows overlooking the bucolic, rolling countryside. Not only was I safe from the demands of the outside world, I was also afforded a spectacular view of Hartford, Connecticut to the left and Springfield, Massachusetts to the right. On one side of the 30-foot wall of windows stood an equally impressive fireplace built of natural stone that reached all the way to the ceiling; on the other side was a fully stocked wet bar garnished with black granite and African rosewood cabinetry, equipped with a refrigerator and sink. Next to the bar was the short flight of steps up into the kitchen and its fragrant promise of the delectable dinner to come. Mom had a casserole in the oven and would pop up to check it periodically. During one such diligent trek, she bellowed to me from the kitchen.

"Dahw, will you get the large chafing dish from the butler's pantry?"

Dahw was her nickname for me. It was an odd Jersey-style pronunciation, short for Donna. She denied both the pronunciation and its origin. People who weren't used to it were always puzzled that I responded to this unusual sound that seemed to fall somewhere between a yawn and an angry cat's complaint. When she didn't call me that, she called me Peachy. I preferred Peachy.

I called her Ma, and it sounded like Ma.

"Yeah, Ma," I responded, as I left my comfortable spot on the white leather sofa and trudged up the steps through the kitchen into the dining room. "Anything else while I'm in here?" I shouted.

"Not right now, thanks, but I'm ready for another half a drink. How about you?"

"Yeah, okay."

I would have offered to fix her a new drink, but we didn't do that in our family. We were very serious about our drinking. We knew what we liked and didn't exactly trust each other to get it right. So everyone made their own drinks. It made for a far more convivial gathering when we weren't looking at each other and wondering, "why did he make this so strong?" or "didn't she put any alcohol in this at all?" And few had peeled my mother's lemon rind to the precise thickness – too thick and the bitterness of the pulpy white within marred the perfection of her martini, too thin and it did not hold its delicate shape while floating in a sea of vodka. I guess everyone has that unconquerable challenge; mine was to achieve the perfect lemon peel. Based on past performance, there wasn't much hope I'd reach that lofty goal. I so preferred those days when she chose two enormous green olives over her usual lemon peel garnish. Olives don't require skill.

We had a delicious and relaxing dinner. By the time the dishes were in the dishwasher, I was really starting to feel the results of a day of travel, followed by a couple of stiff drinks. The savory meal that followed was the straw that broke this camel's back. I could easily have gone to bed, but it was only nine o'clock and Mom wanted to relax with some cable news. I knew she would have understood, but I just didn't feel right deserting her so early on my first night in town. I plunked myself back on the enormous white leather sectional, which Mom had designed to fill the room with a glove-like fit, and focused my attention on the newscaster. Twenty minutes later I awoke as I slid off the couch and onto a Persian rug.

"Oh sweetie, why don't you just go on up to bed. I know how tired you must be," Mom crooned.

"It's okay, Mom. I feel refreshed now," I yawned.

I don't think I was kidding either of us, and rather than kiss the rug for a second time, I packed it in and said goodnight. Mom's parting comment was something to the effect of "I love to see you relax like this. I know you don't get the opportunity very often." Oh well, at least Mom felt pride over helping me relax enough to lose my last vestige of dignity. Does anybody ever really feel like a grown up when they're back at Mom's house?

The next morning I was up by seven and grabbed a quick breakfast. I made some notes on the best means of reaching the folks most likely to have answers to some of my burning questions. My list was pretty short. I wanted to talk to the people who'd been closest to BJ just prior to her move west, but first I had to find out who they were. It had been well over a decade since I'd had any knowledge of her existence at all. My first task was going to be locating some of the folks who'd known her best when we worked together; I'd try to determine if they'd remained close. It was going to be somewhat of an uphill battle. First, I had to find folks who knew her. Then I had to find a way to make them spill their guts to me.

It occurred to me that this initial phase of flushing out my prey might have best been done long distance rather than to waste valuable time phoning around from within the state of Connecticut. Yes, perhaps that was true, but something about being back here was helping me slip into the mindset that would yield the best results. I guess from Omaha the whole thing had a surreal quality, which rendered me unable to act or even care very much about what happened to BJ. I only hoped I'd see some results rather quickly. It would be a shame for this trip to be a waste.

As I lamented my haste in hopping on a plane before organizing the investigation, Mom came out of her bedroom. Seeing her in an elegant, fluffy robe made me realize that no trip out here could ever really be a waste of time. Spending time with Mom always fed my soul.

It was at that point when I realized that coming out here was only partially about getting to the bottom of BJ's ludicrous plan; it was as much about needing my Mom to help make everything all right. I smiled with the satisfaction of knowing that at least one of my goals would be successfully achieved on this mission.

"What?" Mom asked quizzically.

"What, what?" I retorted.

"What's putting that smile on your face? It wasn't there when I first came into the room," she nudged.

"Guess I'm just happy to see you."

"Well, isn't that nice? I couldn't be more thrilled to have you here, Peachy. Have you had your breakfast? I've got some beautiful melons in the fridge."

I smiled.

"It's good to be here, Mom."

One quick cup of coffee with Mom and I pushed myself to get upstairs and into her office where I could begin making calls. I was tempted to skip the investigation altogether, hang out with Mom, and swim in her pool. I knew I'd regret that decision when I arrived back in Omaha, most likely none the wiser about Ms. Thornton's master plan. It didn't feel great to know you could so easily picture yourself leading the suspect list in a grisly murder case. Anything I could do to keep that from happening would help put my mind at rest when the police felt ready to make an arrest.

Thoughts of police and arrest proved to be excellent motivators to get me up and moving. My first call was to a woman who had been BJ's closest friend during our days at Mylar: Ann Marie Plante.

Ann Marie had been such an unlikely friend to the slithery-tongued BJ even back in the days when the bulk of her negative energy had been focused only on making select co-workers miserable. Those were the days before she graduated to proactively attempting to destroy careers, and later still when she created a fantasy world for herself and her familiars. A scenario that rarely intersected with the mundane existence offered by reality. I had genuinely liked Ann Marie. Being trained by her as a new employee had had its good and bad points.

Having passed her rigorous requirements for each and every task, there was little chance of ever getting lazy or lackadaisical on the job. The mental image of her pointy toed boot figuratively kicking your sorry ass relentlessly until you fixed whatever imperfection you'd let slip through – no matter how minor – was permanently ingrained in my psyche. This tiny little woman could strike fear into the hearts of any who crossed her path, and she was always so surprised that she'd had any effect at all. Talk about presence. There was no room for error, and there were no gray areas in Ann Marie's world.

Once trained by her, I carried my zest for perfection like a well-polished badge; I retain her excruciatingly high demand for perfection to this day. The hard part was getting to that level of understanding without having your head ripped off along the way. But get there I did, and I've often credited her with unleashing the unrelenting work ethic, which has served me well.

Ann Marie was nothing if not a straight shooter. She put up with no bullshit, whatsoever. Countless times I'd been in the room when a sales rep who'd received one of her insertion orders or media placement orders had called to ask a question after assuming that an important piece of information had been left out. She would listen calmly as the rep explained that she had not specified 'if the page ad should be placed on the right or left side.' Once the question had been asked there would be a second or two of silence followed by Ann Marie's inevitable razor sharp response: "Can you read?"

"What?"

"I said, can you read?" she'd repeat.

"Well, what, I'm not sure I....oh," would come the final tiny little sound.

At this point the doomed sales rep usually realized that the great Ann Marie had left nothing out of her order; the rep had failed to read the entire page. Some fast and apologetic ramblings would precede a click that ended the call. Ann Marie would turn to me with her signature epithet: "Idiots!"

It paid to be on your toes around Ann Marie. After Googling both she and the Mylar staff, I obtained her phone number and steeled myself for a blast into the past.

[CHAPTER 24]

Talking to Ann Marie took me back twenty years. She seemed genuinely pleased to hear from me. It took a lot to please Ann Marie. We got the big stuff out of the way in about ten minutes, and then I frankly outlined my reason for contacting her. Knowing Ann Marie as I did, being anything less than completely forthright would only blow up in my face, wasting both of our time. 'Know your audience' is an adage by which we live and die in the ad business; it holds true when communicating via mass media or in a one-on-one dialogue.

We agreed that our discussion of BJ would be more productive in person. I offered to treat for lunch, dinner, a drink, or whatever worked best. Although I'd gladly have shared any of these occasions with Ann Marie, I knew full well that her structured and rigid lifestyle was well planned in advance and not given to shifting without a matter of urgency. Spur of the moment she was not. To my surprise, she took me up on my offer of a glass of wine after work.

"Yes, Bernard will be late this evening. That should give me enough time for a quick glass of wine." So typically Ann Marie, hearth and home above all. I had to respect that. Her priorities never wavered.

Before she rang off, she offered one word of caution.

"Although I have kept in touch with BJ over the years," she began, "I can't honestly state with any certainty that the scenario she laid out for me regarding her move to Omaha was much more than a ruse to prevent my interfering and discouraging her. I have no illusions that she was at all transparent in her maneuverings – especially within the past five years or so."

Hmmphhhh, unfortunately that was an excellent point. Given the extent of BJ's delusions, I wondered if any living individual would really be able to give me an accurate snapshot into this complex and twisted psyche and an understanding of her intentions. For what it was worth, I wasn't even sure that BJ herself would have been able to identify reality from 180 degrees away from reality – pure fantasy. This would be a time when instinct would rule. Unless there were clear facts supporting each and every step of her plan there would be no way to arrive at the whole truth. It would be hell to sort through the details if the stories I gathered in my fact-finding trip east were not in sync, and I was not optimistic given BJ's penchant for falsehoods. It was encouraging, however, that someone who knew her as well as Ann Marie was convinced that her recent behavior seemed dubious. I shuddered to think that it might be possible, but I was certain Ann Marie would make an excellent witness for my defense should that ever – God forbid – become necessary.

My next task was to track down the most recent ex. That would prove to be somewhat more challenging given that Rick WyCliff had moved around a bit in the years since we'd worked together. Rumor had it he was running a small ad shop from his home, and I had no idea where that might be. Thank goodness for Google.

After a leisurely lunch with Mom and a visit with her friend, Lauralei, I was finally ready to get down to the task at hand. Lauralei was but one of Mom's vast legion of friends. They'd been a huge part of my socialization from a very young age; I was a bit of an old soul and found these women and views on life fascinating. My sister, on the other hand, would typically go into hiding when one of Mom's "girlfriends" was around.

A boatload of searches and a few dead-end phone calls finally yielded the details I needed to track Rick down. Once I had the number I found myself stalling, which was really irritating. I was a grown woman, a former contemporary of this clown, and I owned my own business. Why should I care about his reaction, even if he suspected I had a role in his ex-wife's murder? I mean I never cared what he thought when we were working together. I couldn't understand why I was feeling intimidated at the prospect of contacting a former co-worker who I hadn't seen in a decade. Did this kind of thing happen to everyone? Or was the recent removal of testosterone in my hormone compound taking its toll on my normally fearless demeanor?

Menopausal women are very much at the mercy of their hormone specialist. With bio-identical hormones they test to determine which of the levels are low, and then they prescribe the precise amount. The interpretation of those results and necessary supplementation tends to be somewhat subjective. Not every doctor/specialist agrees that any testosterone replacement is ever advisable for a woman. Articles on the subject caution about potential weight gain, hair loss, and acne from an excess of testosterone; conversely, too little could discernibly soften that useful aggressive edge and replace it with timidity and self-doubt. It was a delicate balance.

Before entering peri-menopause, my testosterone level had been inordinately high. That was my natural chemical make-up. Now that my hormones had to be artificially administered, I was occasionally nervous that testosterone levels lower than my norm were taking the edge off my steel resolve (I've been accused of having steel balls on more than one occasion) and turning it into more of a soft and fluffy demeanor. Soft and fluffy was so not me. I could ill afford a weaker resolve, and recent events were making me wonder. My doctor had recently removed the testosterone from my hormone mix entirely; that made me nervous. I wasn't con-vinced the switch was as much for my sake as it was to satisfy a personal belief of hers, but I was willing to give it a try in the event that things would improve. So far they hadn't.

It was time to bite the bullet and call Rick. How bad could it be? After much soul searching and other stalling techniques, I took a deep breath and dialed. Rick picked up on the third ring. I greeted him and explained that I was back east for a visit. Then I went on to extend my sympathies to him on his recent loss.

"Bull," Rick replied.

"Bull?" I echoed.

"Yeah, bull, Leigh. You're full of it."

"Go on," I pressed calmly. How could I have been so nervous at the thought of calling this example of the modern Cro-Magnon man? He could barely function in polite society. Ironically, of BJ's two husbands, he was the educated professional and the boorish clod. I couldn't imagine anyone leaving that wonderful, sweet man, Ron, for this slope-headed, knuckle-dragging goon. I was feeling crabbier by the second.

"You think I don't remember how you left BJ and me out of the massive party you threw after we were married?" he accosted.

Oh my God! The man was unbelievable! Twenty years earlier I had had a house party for about ninety of my closest friends. I invited Ann Marie and a date, because I genuinely liked her. I had not invited BJ and Rick, because we had been out of touch for years, not to mention that she and I disliked each other intensely. Actually, he wasn't exactly my favorite person at that particular time either. Why on earth would I have invited them?

When I ran into Rick at an Ad Club event a few weeks after the party in question, he launched into a dramatic verbal assault condemning my grievous indiscretion. His public attack offered more amusement than concern as he confirmed that my failure to invite them had caused BJ such intense angst she was unable to function for some weeks. It was with great difficulty that I managed to forestall the uncontrollable laughter threatening to erupt at any moment of his nonsensical tirade. I was trying my damnedest to affect a duly concerned demeanor as I stood there listening to sound and fury clearly signifying nothing. I sincerely hoped he did not suspect my dilemma as he droned on indignantly.

He was such a schlub. He really believed she would appreciate his indignant (and public) verbal assault, which blatantly revealed her obsessive and manic ravings over being excluded from my party. There he was: the hero, vindicating his wronged lady and securing the ultimate victory. Man, was he in for a rude awakening! He painted a surprisingly accurate picture of her angry rants, though; had there been any doubt that he was exaggerating the level of her lunacy. The precise description of a behavior pattern I'd witnessed many times over assured me of his credibility.

Not only was I greatly amused at her distress, I was also imagining how she would kick his ass from here to the west coast and back for admitting it to me. At that point I actually had to bite my tongue to keep from laughing in his smug, self-righteous face. He was probably already imagining the rich rewards his heroism would earn him upon arriving home. The man clearly knew nothing about women – particularly certifiable women. Wouldn't he be shocked and dismayed when the proud depiction of his self perceived heroism elicited an unrelenting onslaught of abuse. Sadly, he would probably never know what hit him.

After Rick had finished his rant, and heard what he believed to be my abject apology – in reality all I had said was, "it was never my intension to make anyone feel left out" – he sternly acknowledged the appropriateness of my contrition, but stormed off indignantly nonetheless. Once he was out of sight I cracked up. It was awesome! Not only had I hosted a wonderfully successful party, I had also managed to royally piss off a woman I would happily watch being run over by a freight train - repeatedly. Talk about a win/win. I should have sent WyCliff a thank you note for confirming what I had only previously suspected.

In the present, I was having trouble believing my ears; how on earth could he still be harping on that stupid slight after more than twenty years? Jesus buddy, get a life! "I'm sorry, Rick," I feigned ignorance. "I've been living in Omaha for the past twelve years. To what party are you referring?" I couldn't help but rub salt into his open, suppurating wound. Hell, he was asking for it.

"Come on, Donna, don't pretend you don't remember," he barked indignantly.

"Oh Rick," I continued. This was actually kind of fun. What the hell, I'm from New Jersey, we're known for our slightly warped sense of humor. "You can't possibly be referring to some social event I hosted over a decade ago, can you?" God, he was one of those East coast boneheads who were such fun to mess with. They thought they were so slick, but you could typically drive a truck through the holes in their self-involved, manic rants. It was outbursts like these that gave those of us from the Northeast a bad reputation.

He started to back-peddle when he realized he was making himself look like a giant loser. "What I was starting to say was that I've never thought of you as someone with a lot of compassion for BJ. "I held my eye roll in check unnecessarily as he futilely attempted to gain the upper hand. "That's why I'm not buying your phony kind words," he finished.

I had to get myself under control. Fulfilling a desire to 'take him out' would ultimately make me the loser since it would be unlikely I'd get any kind of valuable information from him. What the hell? Like I said, I'm from New Jersey! I was itching to go for it! I cleared my throat in an effort to reorient my head and focus on the prize.

"I won't lie to you, Rick," I replied. It's often best to announce what you're not going to do just prior to doing it. What were a few white lies in the interest of justice? Another useful technique is to start your sentence with a truth to catch them slightly off guard in their assumption that you're most likely going to lie.

"I was not overly fond of BJ." that was the truth – pause – now for the whopper – "but it shook me more than I could ever have expected when I heard she'd been murdered."

Another pause. A sigh morphing into a groan from Rick. "Oh Donna, how could this have happened?"

Score! Then, wait for it...

"I never stopped loving her," he cried. I mean, really cried. He was blubbering like a baby now.

With all of the unpleasant history between BJ and me, I had really never had a beef with WyCliff. Sure, he had been an arrogant prick, but that described half the men in advertising in the Northeast back then. I genuinely liked Rick when we worked together. Sadly, he had chosen to go over to the dark side when he married the shrew, but we all make mistakes. I just didn't feel right sitting here listening to him cry. It was pathetic. Worse yet, listening to him was making me want to cry.

"It had to be just awful for you," I offered.

"Still is," he sniffed in an attempt to get himself under control.

"I really am sorry about that, Rick. You don't deserve this." I threw out another gratuity to help him pull it together. Maybe now it was time to go full tilt.

"I'm sure you'll feel better once they know what happened and the murderer is found," I ventured.

"I don't know, it's not like it will bring her back," he whined, which was preferable to the tears.

"That's true, but closure is important in helping loved ones move on."

"I suppose," Rick agreed. "Is that why you're calling?"

"Well, sort of." Would my admission put him back on his guard?

"I heard some rumors that you were into solving murders now," he mused. "Do you have any thoughts of solving BJ's murder?"

This is normally where I would deny any significant involvement in solving Claire's murder, but humility wouldn't get me anywhere with WyCliff. If I showed even a scintilla of doubt in my detecting abilities he would brush me off unceremoniously. It was time to break out my best BS and sell it with confidence.

"Well, I will admit to a modicum of success in that area," I began. "As a matter of fact, the OPD has come to rely on me for most of the murders that remain unsolved these days." Okay, so I was stretching the truth to a point that was not even barely recognizable, but I was fairly confident of being safe from discovery.

"OPD?" he asked curiously.

"Omaha Police Department."

"Oh, sure, I get it," he replied.

Some people could not bring themselves to get interested in anything occurring more than a handful of miles away from where they lived and worked. Die hard Easterners were often a prime example of that! Time to get focused here. I could tell I was starting to lose him.

"Yes Rick, I must admit that the initial shock after hearing about BJ brought me back to a time when she and I worked closely together and helped each other. A time before competitive struggles became the core of our relationship. I have to admit that fond memories of our early friendship, few though they were, are responsible for my growing obsession to bring this horrible, murdering creature to justice. But I can certainly see why you would rather I not get involved."

"Please," Rick begged, "Help them bring this unbearable situation to an end."

I started to feel a little creepy. I mean my motives were pure – well, sort of – but I was really manipulating this poor guy, and he was starting to seem more pathetic with every utterance. Man, having a conscience could really be a curse! I took a deep breath and resolved to lead the conversation to a more rapid conclusion for both of our sakes. "I've been gone so long that I don't know enough about what has been happening in her life, and I certainly don't know what prompted her to pick up and move to Omaha."

"I have to admit it myself," he said. "The more I learn, the more I realize there's a lot I don't know. But if it helps, let's meet and I'll answer any questions you have. Just say where and when."

I hadn't expected to get this far. It caught me off guard. It took a minute to decide when and where to meet. The thought of seeing him at night, over a drink, was less than appealing. I didn't really see WyCliff as a lunch guy.

"How about breakfast tomorrow?" I blurted before giving myself a chance to think further. "We can meet at that little place on the main street of West Hartford," I threw that out knowing it would be a convenient location for him and hoping it would help me end this interminable call.

"Sure," he replied tentatively. "Can we make it nine o'clock? I've been having some trouble sleeping and it helps to have some extra time in the morning."

"That's fine," I agreed. "I'll see you at nine then."

"Thanks, Leigh," he replied before hanging up.

As I allowed my mind to revisit some of our conversation, I shook my head at the thought of Rick being such a wuss about a few sleep-deprived nights. It wasn't like I wasn't hoping for a little R & R on this visit myself, but I was mindful of all the menopausal women living sleep-deprived lives. Rarely were we afforded the luxury of adjusting our schedules to accommodate our insomnia. Oh well, it wasn't his fault; maybe I need to work on being a little less of a hard ass.

[CHAPTER 25]

I sat back to think about all I had learned and what I still needed to learn after talking with Rick. A picture of BJ's life in the years since I'd moved to Omaha was beginning to emerge and there was a clear theme. I first met BJ when she was the Mylar Advertising wunderkind. In her daily wardrobe of designer jeans and t-shirt, sans bra – which in her case was sort of a non-issue – she handled all the planning for Mylar's Petrovsky single handedly, thus taking the advertising world by storm. This unremarkable young woman was being touted as one of the savviest media planners in both aerospace and the military.

It was still a time when women were typically seen as support staff to the men at an ad agency – or any company for that matter. The few women who did make an impact in the world of business tended to be frumpy, older crones with nasty and unbending personalities who dressed in thick wool business suits – skirts, never slacks. They were generally reminiscent of Hitler in a dress – and most of them had enough of a mustache to pass muster. Yet here was this thin young slip of a girl and she could out-plan anyone in areas where no woman had dared to tread before. Yes, in retrospect, when I started my advertising career at Mylar I was walking in behind the permed tresses of self-promoted greatness. I just didn't know it.

At that particular point in time, media departments had flipped from being all male domains to being virtually all female – outside of the New York broadcast community. Media was considered clerical, kind of an extension of the secretarial pool, which made it an ideal breeding ground for the careers of women with aspirations. What that meant in lay terms was that no one knew anything about aerospace and military because they were two areas that held no interest for most women. Anyone who was willing to jump in and handle one of these accounts was looked upon with awe, and BJ was no exception.

Arriving when I did, I spent a great deal of time assisting BJ in handling the overflow of this very large piece of business. At first, I too was in awe of the young female genius. How did she know so much about helicopters, an area shunned by most women? Over time, as I developed a comfort level with magazines like *Aviation Week* and *Armed Forces Journal*, I came to realize they weren't as foreign and intimidating as I'd imagined.

Once the agency 'darling' went on maternity leave and my media director became a deer in the headlights, it was only natural for me to jump in and attempt to fill the great one's shoes. I then became the creator of this mystical media plan. I started by reading old plans and reviewing media kits for each magazine. I met with the sales reps and began to realize that military and aerospace media planning was really no different from planning media in any other industry. I even became somewhat of an expert in identifying the more obscure global publications. More importantly, what I learned permitted me to unearth the secret that had enabled BJ to appear extraordinary. When I realized she had merely done what others hadn't bothered to do; overcome her natural intimidation of and lack of interest in the subject, to become the leading expert, I had the keys to the kingdom.

To her credit, BJ had doggedly persevered enough to achieve a basic understanding of the helicopter industry, which was all she needed in order to make some obvious recommendations. Even though the information was there at her fingertips, she never bothered to master any depth of knowledge within the rotor and wing arena. But back then I was the only one who knew her secret. To everyone else she was a true phenomenon.

No one else saw what seemed so obvious. She took the simple route at virtually every turn. When BJ wanted to reach pilots, she used *Professional Pilot Magazine*; when she wanted her message to be read by army personnel, it was *Army Aviation*, and she didn't bother to venture much beyond that in the guise of strategic direction. She didn't have to, those around her were in awe.

The problem was, when she returned from maternity leave those same people were already starting to wonder how I had been able to take over her role and continue to run the account without a glitch – and without ever having to call and ask her any questions. Once she realized her idyllic world was being threatened, that's when the full crazy came out and pointed its heat seeking-missile directly between my eyes.

From that point on and for the rest of my days at Mylar our already abusive relationship deteriorated even further. I virtually felt that bulls-eye perched on my head. Though they'd begun to question, the majority of her followers remained loyal; however, a small, insignificant group of us began to see this deified prodigy begin to unravel in a most unsettling way. As the unraveling progressed our group grew in significance. At least I was no longer alone.

Now according to her Connecticut acquaintances, crazy had taken over the show. It was oddly gratifying. Yet I couldn't help but feel that life would have been a whole lot easier had I not been the one chosen by fate to unveil her secret. The price for that role had been high.

I had learned a lot from the few conversations I'd had. I felt certain that my meetings with Ann Marie and Rick would fill in even more of the gaps and detail her descent into publicly documented functional psychoses, but would any of these things direct us to the killer? So far, it wasn't looking all that promising.

I checked my watch and saw that I still had about an hour before leaving for drinks with Ann Marie. It would be a good time to check with the office and find out what more they'd learned about the murder.

It took fifteen minutes to make the rounds of folks with questions for me before I was able to get transferred to Donny for late breaking news.

"Hey, Sherlock," he started. Would I be better off just hanging up and e-mailing him apologies for a bad connection? I closed my eyes and took a deep breath as he continued. "Some of us have kept our ears to the pavement for real clues that could wrap this case up, while others have chosen to visit Chez Mom's resort and wander aimlessly down memory lane."

Despite the shot, I couldn't help but smile at the image of Donny with his head down on the pavement like a modern day Indian scout. The sentiment passed quickly and I became impatient. Was he merely amusing himself or did he have something worthwhile?

"Good one, Donny, now shake the pebbles out of your ear and tell me what you've got!"

"Met my boys for a beer last night," he began. "They said they've collected a bunch of evidence indicating the vic had lots of company from back East in the two weeks preceding her murder. They already knew her son had flown back out after he'd already been out once with the moving truck, but it was looking like at least one other Northeasterner had made their way out by car, which made it harder to collect corroborating evidence. They're almost finished contacting all of the gas stations and hotels on the route from Hartford to Omaha. They're pretty sure one of the visitors, besides her son, was male, and if they confirm their suspicions that there was at least one female, we could even be looking at a Murder on the Orient Express scenario."

"Do they really think she could have been killed by more than one person?"

"No. But my boys speculated that the more East coast folks who were visiting at the time of the murder, the greater the percentage that she was killed by one of them and not by anyone out here," he concluded.

"I guess that's good, but do they put me in the "anyone out here" category or am I in the "East coast folks" category?"

"They know you're one of us."

Wow, I didn't see that coming. That was a bit of a shock. It's just possible that was the nicest thing Donny had ever said to me. I wasn't quite sure how to respond. As it turned out that wasn't a problem.

"And don't take that as a compliment. We're just not like those New England snot noses who can never accept anyone that wasn't born into the fold. We Midwesterners are a more welcoming people."

"Relax," I assured him. "The world never has to know that you came so close to making a really nice gesture toward me."

"How can you say that, Donna, I'm always nice to you! You know you really need to quit being so overly sensitive about everything...."

"Yeah, right, Donny, *I'm* overly sensitive! Well, if there's nothing else, I need to run to meet an old friend for drinks."

Realizing he'd been prattling on and I hadn't been listening,

Donny brought his focus back to the conversation. "Not really, there's not really anything else yet. The guys said they're anxious for your update on her East coast connections."

For a moment, neither of us knew what to say. Had Donny just admitted that information I obtained would be pivotal to the investigation his police buddies were working on?" I smiled, just a bit, at the thought of his self-derision over the compliment he'd let slip.

Donny abruptly moved on to the next order of business.

"So when are you back in the office? I want to schedule a meeting to review projections."

"First thing on Monday."

We hung up, and I rushed into the guestroom for a quick change of wardrobe before heading out for drinks. But I couldn't get Donny's comments out of my head. I'd almost forgotten my fashion rule of dressing with the person you're meeting in mind. It's not about being someone other than who I am. I would just make slight alterations in my normal dress designed to offer them a feeling of familiarity, and thus comfort, in order to put them more at ease. Conversely, if I were planning a meeting where intimidating the other person could be of benefit, I would dress in a way that I thought would put them more on edge.

In the case of Ann Marie, she liked a casual jean or flowery skirt with a casual/feminine top. She was not big on jackets or accessories. Although I wore my signature black, the skirt was a casual chino material and the top was a little softer than usual. I kept the bling to a minimum with my standard rings and a pair of simple earrings that were not overly dramatic. The outfit was totally me, only slightly oriented to appeal to her sensibilities. I wasn't about to go to floral skirts for anybody; there is a limit to what the human imagination can process. No one who'd ever met me would expect a floral skirt. Dressing for your audience only worked if you didn't go too far and lose what was genuine; a flowing floral skirt would be far less believable on me than seeing a ballet dancer perform a pirouette en dedans across the stage in farmer jeans and shit kickers. If you ever want to really shake things up, dress in a way that is not at all you. You'd be amazed at how off-putting it will be to those around you. Once in a while, it can be kind of fun.

[CHAPTER 26]

Ann Marie and I had agreed to meet at a bar in West Hartford. That made the trip a little shorter for me. I'd also have the option to go highway all the way, or take a little detour on secondary roads. I opted for secondary roads since it was the only real way to soak in a little of the local color. I gave myself some extra time just in case memory failed me and it took longer to find my way. We were scheduled to meet at the original Max on Main gourmet burger place at 6:00 P.M. Max's was trendy when we lived in Connecticut a decade ago, and apparently its appeal had not diminished; the owner had recently opened another location in Springfield, Mass.

With my Garmin set for Main Street, West Hartford, I set out. After twenty minutes or so, I had ventured into familiar territory that elicited pangs of homesickness with its un-mistakable New England feel. Everything else in the area was either nouveau New England or flat out modern looking. As the road wound around, gradually curving, I emerged on a vaguely familiar section, though it was not exactly like any place I'd ever been. It was reminiscent of areas I'd seen skirting the reservoir. That would make sense, because there was definitely a reservoir in the vicinity. Fresh out of college and ensconced in entry-level jobs in Farmington, my old roommate and I would meet there with our sandwiches for a leisurely lunch.

It was attractive in its appointment, yet more austere than the larger surrounding area; a characteristic that was also indicative of being near the reservoir. Although there was nothing sinister about this stretch of road, I'd started to feel somewhat unsettled. The area looked completely deserted, not at all normal for this overpopulated part of the state. As I was surveying the vicinity for something to jog my memory, my Bluetooth rang.

It was Peg, God bless her. Had her intuitive powers warned her of my discomfort? It wouldn't surprise me.

I glanced around frantically for a place to pull over. Luckily, there was a 'scenic lookout' that was wide enough for a few cars, so I pulled in and put the car in park before answering. I wasn't sure of the 'cell phone and distracted driving' laws in Connecticut, but I wasn't about to take any chances.

"Donna," Peg's voice blasted through my speaker, "How's home?"

"Good to hear your voice, Peg," I responded, no longer feeling so alone.

"Babs and I wanted to update you on some new aspects of the investigation," she went on as Babs yelled her greeting into the receiver.

"Hi, Donna, we're glad we caught you."

Peg and Babs proceeded to share the news they'd picked up from Tim, our favorite printer. He'd been in earlier that day with news from his brother who was apparently on Detective Warren's investigation team. It was actually pretty big news. Apparently Porter Enzo had been one of the mysterious visitors from Connecticut during the weeks before BJ's murder. That shocked me. Clearly, none of her East coast connections, at least not the ones I'd spoken with, had been aware of Enzo's recent pilgrimage west.

As we chatted and shared questions and answers, I became aware of another car driving through the lookout. It was an older, beat-up model driven by a grungy looking guy. As I watched, the car pulled in and rolled to a stop slightly ahead of my rental. Hmmm. I wondered what was happening here.

"Donna, hey Donna," Peg urged, "Have we lost you, Hon?"

"Uh, sort of, some weird looking guy's up to something. I need to keep an eye on him, but I can still listen."

The creepy guy turned toward me and was motioning with a moderately intimidating gesture. He was beckoning with his hand and scowling maliciously with his face. I couldn't be sure what he was trying to tell me, and I couldn't be sure if I should feel threatened. Peering inside his wreck of a car I could only see his head. He was a weasely looking guy with an uneven new growth beard and a head full of grimy looking, unkempt hair. I watched for a few more seconds, wondering if my assessment of his gesture had been accurate or just my active imagination. Shame on me if I was letting his unkempt appearance convince me that he was a dangerous thug. Just as I was beginning to convince myself that his aggression had been my own fanciful notion, the ferocity of his movements ramped up to a level I'd have to describe as frenetic. His wild gesticulating, with harsh, erratic movements that no longer seemed beckoning, enabled me to make out a tattered and unclean blue work shirt. I still hadn't a clue as to what he was trying to communicate to me; I just knew I hadn't seen that level of physical animosity since my last visit back East to the 'coast of no patience.' It was amazing what you could ascertain from non-verbal communication.

I didn't know what to do, and Peg and Babs could sense my trepidation. Their valiant attempt to put me at ease did serve to give me more confidence than I felt. Thank goodness, because at that moment the scumbag started to get out of his car and walk straight toward me. If he had any interest in communicating in a civilized manner, his body language was doing him a grave disservice. Whatever his mission, I couldn't allow myself to be a sitting duck, particularly when he was so obviously agitated.

"Guys, he's coming over," I whispered as though his hearing me would be the problem. "What should I do?"

"Donna," Babs jumped in, "You get yourself out of there – now!"

"Yeah, Donna," Peg interjected, "Forget us and gun it!"

By now he was closing in on my hood. I saw him raise his arms above his head in a gesture that appeared almost triumphant – oh shit, was he closing in for the kill? I jammed the car into reverse and bolted backward just as his joined hands were coming down on the space where the hood had been moments before. With the intensity of his blow he would surely have made an enormous dent in the car – had it been there. His body pin-wheeled forward and he flipped over like a Russian gymnast practicing for the Olympics. The remainder of his attire, grungy, ripped work pants and running shoes that had seen better days, was a perfect match for his upper body ensemble. He landed hard. Ouch! That must have hurt!

I knew I should get the hell out of there, but as with a train wreck, I was having difficulty pulling myself away. Besides, for the moment, this guy was down. I clicked the lock mechanism to ensure that all doors were secure and settled in to watch.

"Donna," Peg urged, "What's going on?"

"Oh, Peg," I chuckled, "You should see this guy. He wiped himself out, big time!"

As I finished my sentence, the scumbag was finally picking himself up. He stumbled, shook himself off and began to search for me. Once his menacing eyes locked onto my rental he charged; I was pretty sure I could hear the deep guttural bellow of a war cry as he progressed. It took me a second to break free of my terror-induced paralysis and hit the road. Just as he reached the door handle, I jammed the pedal to the metal and bolted backward. My slimy friend hung on for about seven seconds before he lost his grip and flew backward. Although I didn't actually see it, I heard a loud crash. By the sound of it my pursuer had made it back into his own vehicle in record time – through the windshield.

I was out of that seemingly bucolic little lookout and speeding toward the town center with a vengeance. Within ten minutes I was in a more familiar, more populated business district and finally allowed myself to exhale. After another five minutes or so I heard an odd sound.

"Uh, Donna," Peg whispered. "Is everything okay?"

Oh God, I had completely forgotten that Babs and Peg were still on the phone. I looked around and pulled into a bustling parking lot in front of an upscale strip mall. I parked the rental and gave some thought to calling Warren's contact. Since I couldn't be sure how culpable he would find me in this whole circus act, I chose to forego that option. Before talking I looked around for signs of unwanted company.

"Hi, guys," I finally responded. "That was just bizarre."

"My god, Donna," Babs replied, "That must have been so frightening. Fill us in on the details."

"Unbelievable," Peg proclaimed when I'd finally finished describing the entire incident. "And you still have no idea what his deal was?"

"None," I acknowledged. "I guess now I'll never know," I finished, feeling extremely bewildered.

"Count your blessings," Peg said. "I've never heard of anything like that."

"I wish I could say the same," I countered, "But in the Northeast you do occasionally hear about these random acts of senseless violence. Aggression just seems to be closer to the surface out here, and I think being on the road tends to exacerbate the hostility. I just wish I knew if that guy was okay. Maybe I should put a call into 911? Even if he was an escaped lunatic, I can't stand the thought of leaving him lying there."

"Being around people like that would make me constantly paranoid!" Babs asserted. "Donna, let us call the emergency crew. You go ahead and get out of there. Better not take any chances!"

She was right. I shouldn't hang around too long just in case. Although living in the Heartland did have its own set of challenges and bizarre occurrences, it was just that blatant hostility against another human being, for whatever reason, did not materialize nearly as rapidly or as easily as it did here in the Northeast.

I remembered that it was often a quick trip to violent with some of the nut jobs that crossed your path. And, if truth be told, the closer you got to New York City, the higher and faster the escalation of hostility. I could almost never make a trip back to New York without getting yelled at by someone I'd never met before. I can't even remember a time when anything like that had happened to me since living in the Midwest. My tolerance for volatile behavior had diminished significantly since moving to the Heartland. I could take it for short periods of time, but I was sure as hell not drawn to it! So many Northeasterners accepted it as second nature. Escaping that fate had been one of the most welcome perks of moving west.

I finished my conversation with Peg and Babs and turned to my Garmin to find the restaurant and the drink with Ann Marie.

[CHAPTER 27]

Ann Marie beat me to the restaurant by about fifteen minutes. At a glance I could see the years had changed very little about her. A few more wrinkles around the eyes and mouth and an updated hair-do was about it. I'm pretty sure I recognized the colorful, flowing skirt reaching well below her knees and the coordinating top that still fit her as it had all those years ago. Although she hadn't seen me in over a decade, Ann Marie knew instantly that something was wrong. And here I thought I'd masked my agitation so well.

"What happened?" Ann Marie began.

Although I was loathe to waste our precious investigative time recanting recent unpleasantness, I couldn't resist the urge to spill my guts. What can I say? Talking has always been therapeutic for me. I started at the beginning and filled her in on the whole bizarre story; she listened with classic Ann Marie stoicism.

"Do you want to go back?" Ann Marie asked.

"What do you mean, go back?"

"I'll find out what that SOB was up to, just give me two minutes with him," she continued. Her own agitation was palpable.

I had forgotten about that East coast in-your-face fearlessness whenever one of our contemporaries has been compromised. Although significantly smaller than I, she could always make me feel safe. I couldn't imagine anyone who would risk incurring her wrath – even someone carrying a gun.

Before I had a chance to respond to her magnanimous

offer, I became aware of two uniformed policemen marching determinedly across the crowded bar. I felt a brief moment of panic before realizing they couldn't possibly be here because of me. There's no way they would have known I'd been in that turnaround and inadvertently caused that creep to pinwheel ass over tea kettle. I doubted he'd be quick to tell them considering I was merely defending myself against his vicious attack. I couldn't have been more wrong.

"Ms. Leigh?" the first officer asked. "Are you Ms. Donna Leigh?"

"Who me? Yes, officer, what can I do for you?"

"Well ma'am, we received a call from a Detective Warren from Omaha, Nebraska," he explained. "She said she'd been contacted by some colleagues of yours who told her you were in our neck of the woods, and that you'd been approached by an aggressive stranger in a nearby tourist lookout. She asked if we'd check things out and make sure you were all right – and she knew precisely where you'd be right about now."

I have to admit, knowing that my girls still had my back, even 1,500 miles from home, really warmed my heart. Even Warren was looking out for me with the local cops; she was reaching out from the heartland to keep me safe. A closer look at my visiting gendarme revealed a pair of matching blue uniforms, but that was where the resemblance ended. The speaker was a stout gentleman who looked a few short years of retirement age. He was rugged and balding, standing about five foot ten. His partner, on the other hand, was movie star handsome with sparkling blue eyes and hair so dark brown it appeared almost black. Clearly his free time was spent working out at the gym. I figured he was late twenties, early thirties at the latest. It was hard to feel intimidated by a police presence with those blue eyes looking down at me from his six foot two vantage point.

"I guess you know about my close call at the 'lookout' earlier this evening, then," I ventured.

"Yes, ma'am," the cute cop finally spoke, and even his voice was appealing, "but we'd like to review the details with you if you don't mind."

"Sure, I guess so." I wasn't all that thrilled about reliving the unpleasant experience yet again, but I didn't think that was quite as voluntary as it had sounded.

Once I'd finished retelling my story, the senior cop jumped in to get me up to speed on the procedure that was already underway.

"We've got an APB out on this guy," he assured me. "He shouldn't be too difficult to find with the description we've got."

"Do you know anything about him at this point? Did the emergency crew pick him up when they were notified?"

"Based on the description we do have some thoughts on his identity. It shouldn't be too long now before we bring him in for a lengthy debriefing," he reassured me. "By the time the emergency crew got there nothing was left but a couple of divots in the turf and some tire marks."

As he said this his cell phone rang. He excused himself and took the call. My feelings were very mixed. I was greatly relieved that my attacker had not been found in a semi-conscious state, but the thought that he was still running around out there, still crazy, and still not thrilled with me was not reassuring.

"They've got him," he shared. "We'll get to the bottom of this in no time. Thanks for the specifics; that should help us pin him down faster."

"We'll head down to the station now to question him," tall, dark and smiling joined in. "Are you planning on being here for much longer?"

"We'll be here for as long as you need us to," Ann Marie had found her voice, clearly embroiled in the intrigue of the moment, not to mention the lure of those baby blues – guess she was more human than I'd given her credit for!

[CHAPTER 28]

An hour and a half and two glasses of Sauvignon Blanc later, my cell phone rang. It was the older of the two cops, I later found out his name was Officer Stavic. He asked if I would mind heading over to the station so they could ask me some more questions and fill me in on my attacker's situation. Since I had no idea of how to get there, ten years and a number of road improvements – or road 'reorientation' was playing hell with my navigational skills, which were shaky at best. Stavic made sure Ann Marie had directions. Although I protested strenuously, she insisted on accompanying me to the station. I had to admit it was comforting to know I wouldn't be out on the road alone, at least not initially. Having Ann Marie's fearless persona to scare off any hidden attackers on the way to the police station was a welcome bonus right about now. Funny thing, I'd always taken pride in my own "fearless" reputation, but in the aftermath of a very real assault (make that attempted assault) it was amazing how fast bravado took a hike.

We arrived at the station and were placed in an interview room. I'd seen so many of them throughout my years of watching cop shows, it kind of felt like home. From the look on her face, Ann Marie appeared to be having a similar experience; we exchanged knowing glances and settled in to wait. A few minutes later, Stavic and his easy-on-the-eyes partner, who turned out to be Officer Benson, came in to join us.

"Thanks for helping us expedite this matter, ladies," began Stavic. "This shouldn't take long."

Benson remained silent. That was just fine.

"After interviewing the suspect and making a few corroborating phone calls we are, at least, able to give you a motive of sorts," he continued, "although I'll admit, it's a tough one to swallow." He sniffed and then snorted. I leaned in to give his monologue my complete attention as he continued, "Bollmoor, that's his name. He's a prominent businessman who really enjoys his gardening. They tell me that normally he looks a whole lot better than when you saw him. Dresses in Saville Row suits, heard that's a fancy men's store though I'm a Gentlemen's Warehouse kinda guy myself. I don't think you can go wrong with 'Gentlemen' in the name. Anyway, the guy drives a beamer. In fact, he's the CEO of a large multi-national corporation headquartered in Stamford. Some European sounding name; I think they said digital media content, or something. The guy's worth millions."

"That guy?" I choked. "That disgusting slob of a guy is usually Mr. GQ hotshot executive?"

"So they say," he shrugged. "You saw him after a whole day of gardening for the town beautification counsel. Seems he really throws himself into the cause on these volunteer planting marathons. Today he must have overdone it with the digging and the heat. When he drove by the 'lookout' he mistook you for a woman he'd been arguing with that morning. In fact, they had had their argument right in that very 'lookout' where you were pulled over."

"Really?" I asked. "He had a fight that morning with a woman in the same 'lookout'? And the woman resembled me?"

"Not exactly like you, but there's some resemblance, we downloaded her picture from Facebook." He pulled out a photo of a woman who bore only the slightest resemblance to me. She was clearly much heavier and not nearly as stylish from a hair, clothing, make-up and jewelry standpoint. And she looked at least a decade older than I do.

"She looks nothing like me," I insisted, "no one could mistake me for her."

"That may be, ma'am, but we believe your attacker did just that." I moved to protest but the officer raised his hand indicating he wanted to finish his story. "Maybe it was over-exposure to the sun, maybe his eyesight's no good. The fact remains, we believe his claim that he thought he saw Mary Beth Leander in that car in the 'lookout' for the second time that day. After their argument this morning, seeing her there really teed him off because they'd been arguing heatedly over which planting would work best in that particular spot. Apparently Bollmoor fancied himself a master horticulturist and did not handle it well when a 'lady who lunches' wealthy and bored housewife challenged his expertise."

"So he wanted tulips and she preferred azaleas and that made him behave like a homicidal maniac toward me?" I growled. "I'm afraid I'm just not buying this bizarre tale of society gardening gone wrong."

"Actually," he continued now quoting from his notes, "he wanted myrtle and flocks with a scattering of Mountain laurel to provide a more natural plant-scape, indigenous to the area. She, on the other hand, felt that a brighter splash of color would lend some much needed life to an otherwise dreary roadside visage. It wasn't until she suggested bright pink begonias that he finally blew his cork. I guess the fight got pretty heated according to one or two of the other volunteer gardeners, Ms. Leander was even heard to threaten that Bollmoor could 'plant any damn thing he wanted, she'd just circle back and rip up every plant he'd sweat his butt off planting.' To add insult to injury, it seems Ms. Leander was incensed that Bollmoor would even suggest planting a 'protected' bloom like Mountain Laurel in a place too accessible to the ignorant public; she made clear her intention to rip out every Mountain Laurel he planted and whisk it away to safety." He finished reading from his notes. Gearing up to laugh in the kind officer's face, I noticed that Ann Marie was speaking for the first time.

"Seriously, Donna," she insisted, "I've been reading about these garden volunteer attacks. They've been occurring with more and more frequency in the more affluent townships all around the state." I just looked at her shaking my head in disbelief.

"Only in Connecticut could town beautification volunteers turn rogue and start attacking one another, "I just laughed, "and just my luck, I get caught in the middle of a Mexican plant-off (which is not unlike a Mexican stand-off only with the added benefit of horticulture) between two over privileged, self-involved do-gooders. So he thought I was Leander making good on my promise to rip out all his hard work?"

"That's about the size of it, Ma'am," Stavic acknowledged." Then, when you refused to acknowledge his signals, he went off the deep end. Thoroughly agitated, he jumped out of his vehicle to ensure the precious plantings were safe, that's when he tripped and appeared to be charging you."

"Well, good intentioned volunteer planter and international businessman or not, this guy is off his freakin' nut and should be institutionalized," I declared. "I mean, if looks could kill, I'd be dead right now." I wasn't shy about letting them see my anger at this ridiculous turn of events, but in reality, I had to admit that the age-old Mountain Laurel story had really brought back some long forgotten memories. The instant they mentioned Mountain Laurel was at the center of this acrimonious debate, it became crystal clear that Bollmoor's ludicrous story was likely to be true. I remembered that stupid 'state flowering bush' debate from my earliest years in Connecticut. These people just did not have enough to occupy their time! Somehow, the introduction of the age-old Mountain Laurel debate had instantly drained all the terror out of this recent, potentially lethal, adventure; at this point my biggest fear was the probability that Bollmoor would not be the only one to come out of this looking ridiculous. Does that make me selfish? Depends who you're asking!

"Actually, that's the other side of the equation," Stavic went on to explain. "According to Bollmoor, the look you saw and the velocity and trajectory of his attack were, in fact, the result of his tripping over a watering can someone must have left behind."

"What are you saying?" I asked more perplexed than ever.

"Well, ma'am." I was starting to genuinely dislike that sentence starter. "Bollmoor tells us he was po'd but he just wanted to talk to Ms. Leander. He would never have hurt her. It's just that when he tripped it scared the bejesus out of him. He never leapt at you and he thinks the ferocious expression you saw – was stark terror at the thought of his inevitable brutal landing, which became considerably more brutal when you moved your car."

"Oh, but what about when he dove and grabbed my car handle?" was all I could muster.

"Says he grabbed for anything in a desperate attempt to find his balance," Benson chimed in. Of course he did; just where were those Good Samaritans when you needed them? Was I wrong in feeling that all eyes were on me? Hey, when you're from New Jersey – you swing first and ask questions later! It doesn't make me a bad person.

After several moments of contemplative thought I offered, "But, when he got up it really looked like he was coming at me.

recollection of a huge mystery involving BJ's older sister, Rosie, shortly after I started at Mylar. I never did learn the details of the sister's fate. I did, however, learn that as a result of her unfortunate experience, BJ felt an undying affection for the group of lawyers who played a prominent role in the sister's journey. I felt an inkling of the old curiosity that had enveloped me during those early days. My curiosity was more easily held in check now so ironically, the long awaited details finally came spilling out after I had ceased to really care.

Ann Marie filled me in on Rosie's entire twisted story. Apparently, as a youth, she had gotten mixed up with an unsavory crowd. She went from minor infractions in her adolescence, shop-lifting, joy riding, to more serious crime as she matured. By the time BJ was in college, Rosie was into some pretty serious fraud and petty larceny. The younger sister, BJ, had placed her big sis on the highest of pedestals; she saw Rosie as a folk hero and had every intention of following in those haloed footsteps. Luckily for BJ, she was too young to join her sister in anything more than petty larceny and some playful scamming of fellow classmates.

Her sister's final bust, the one that ended Rosie's career in crime occurred just before I joined the Mylar staff. It also ended BJ's aspirations of a full time criminal career and relegated her to a small time crook. It seems that Rosie, who had never committed a selfless act in her life, had forced a promise from her baby sis never to live on the spoils of her crime. BJ was forced to seek honest work, so her scams and hustling became more of a hobby.

Wow, I had no idea; that explained so much. God, that sibling thing had a major impact on people. Then I asked Ann Marie if Rosie was still behind bars, and she hit me with the biggest shock of the evening. Rosie had died in prison.

Holy crap, it was getting easier to understand BJ's bizarre and erratic behavior! I had to be careful not to become too sympathetic toward her though; it would only get in the way of this investigation. Besides, dead or not, she was still an evil bitch!

By our second glass of wine, I had absorbed this shocking disclosure enough to ask a few questions. The one that loomed above others was this: if BJ had systematically alienated all of her friends, family and colleagues, why was it that so many of the men with whom she had been involved were still carrying a torch for her? I mean, I get that looks aren't everything, and God knows her looks could have stopped a freight train, but what was it? Why did so many of them seem to have trouble letting go?

Ann Marie's confession that she had wondered the same thing was my second big shock of the night. When the two were together at Mylar; it seemed as though Ann Marie would do anything for BJ. It never dawned on me that she could be remotely cognizant of BJ's many failings. Apparently I'd been wrong.

The rest of Ann Marie's story centered on a theory she had about BJ's men. She believed, after BJ had made the choice to move on from her first husband, Ron, her subsequent relationships were more like charity projects. She began to prey on men who had fantastically high aspirations of success, yet little or no hope of realizing their goals. It was easy for BJ to move in with her promises of grandeur, these self-deluded men believed in their superiority.

She acted as a female Svengali, promising to transform them completely. Her ministrations would make these men wealthy and successful beyond their wildest dreams, and she was convincing. Ann Marie was quick to assure me that physical attraction was not essential in such a relationship. BJ could have been 'Victoria's Secret model' beautiful or downright two-bag homely and it wouldn't have mattered. These guys were too self-involved to care about how anyone else looked, they just needed some serious money to live "the good life." That's where BJ came in.

[CHAPTER 29]

Deeply engrossed in thought, Mom's street came along sooner than expected. Learning the details of BJ's mystery from so many years ago had been fascinating, and helped me to understand why BJ had been destined for an illegal and even amoral way of life. Entertaining as it had been, I didn't feel my visit with Ann Marie brought me closer to finding the killer. Sure I'd found reasons why folks would want to kill her, but with BJ that was hardly something new. In fact, after reviewing everything we'd discussed I was pretty sure Warren would prefer I keep it to myself. Had this trip to Connecticut been a waste of time, at least from a murder solving standpoint? I was so sure I could help the investigation along; I felt disillusioned. Maybe a late dinner with Mom would help me feel better about things in general.

God bless her, Mom had dinner warming and the glasses chilled by the time I hit her driveway. We relaxed over a drink before helping ourselves to hearty bowls of beef barley soup with sourdough bread. Somehow, after eating, things didn't seem as dire. Mom convinced me that it's not unusual for mysteries to get most confusing right before they became crystal clear. How did she put it? "It's always darkest before the dawn."

We finished our meal with coffee and munched on freshly picked fruit. After eating, we found an old murder mystery to watch until bedtime. I was even starting to feel glamorous and sophisticated after a few hours of watching Nick and Nora effortlessly and elegantly uncover a treasonous plot to aid the Germans in World War II. At least my stumbling aimlessly around in search of BJ's murderer did not endanger the free world!

As the movie ended my yawning reached epic proportions, thus signaling the end of yet another enjoyable evening. Climbing the stairs to the guest suite I was mentally organizing plans for the morning and preparing for breakfast with my old colleague, BJ's latest ex. I think I was sleeping before my head hit the pillow, and it's unlikely that I moved a muscle until morning. That never happens at home where I share a bed with a husband and three generously built bulldogs.

* * *

The next morning as I was showering and dressing for the meeting with WyCliff, I pushed myself to land on the best approach. It was great to reconnect with old acquaintances, but if I wasn't moving the investigation forward I was just wasting everyone's time. I knew Mom was hoping I'd find enough intrigue to keep me in Connecticut for a while, but I hadn't made any critical discoveries yet – at least that I was aware of. Maybe a professional detective could piece some of this information together and use it productively, but I sure couldn't. I made up my mind to call Warren after my infamous breakfast with WyCliff. If she felt I was making progress I'd stay, at least a few more days. Otherwise it was time to cut my losses and head on back. Just as I was deciding on the cutoff the phone rang. Jon wasn't going to make it east after all. Our dog sitter had the flu. That made me more determined than ever to wrap things up one way or another.

I pulled out of the driveway, waving good-bye to Mom. Even though WyCliff had been living in West Hartford for a while, he texted that we should meet closer to our old stomping ground near Mylar. Frankly, that was kind of a relief. Although I didn't feel tragically scarred by my violent interlude of the preceding evening, the thought of retracing my steps through West Hartford so soon afterward was not appealing. In fact the thought alone made me shiver just thinking of what could have happened. I shook my head trying to free myself of the remaining vestiges of fear, the ones that had burrowed into my subconscious since late yesterday. I couldn't afford to allow fear to enter the equation if I expected to be productive. It was stupid, I knew. The night before I'd been able to put the whole thing behind me. I even laughed it off – in reality I'd have to admit it had hit me harder than I thought. It was damned hard being human!

I decided to focus on the drive itself and my face-to-face conversation with WyCliff. Would I be able to pull off the demeanor that would enable me to extract anything useful from my former colleague? Based on our short conversation the day before, I sensed he'd need a seriously heavy dose of Rick-centric sympathy. Especially since I'd learned through my tireless digging, that BJ had dumped him and left him to take the fall on a failed, fraudulent business venture with our buddy Cavrola. That kind of acting, the kind virtually dripping with empathy, was a lot easier to fake over the phone. Oh well, there was only one way I'd find out. That was right about when I pulled into the familiar parking lot for The Farm Shop.

I spotted WyCliff immediately. He was in a big, overstuffed booth in the corner, quietly sipping a cup of coffee. I didn't think he saw me right away, so I took a moment to check out what a dozen years had done to change my old acquaintance. From what I could see, he'd lost a few pounds and trimmed his hair into a fashionable short style. In years past, his hair had fluctuated from long and unkempt to not quite as long and unkempt, you know that Cousin IT look. The short hair was a pleasant surprise. He looked better than I remembered. WyCliff sported a well-manicured beard which was a vast improvement over his former Duck Dynasty style beard. The clothes were trendy and flattering. One thing about BJ: she knew how to make her men dress. As I gazed at Rick I realized that he bore a slight resemblance to Richard Lewis, my favorite 'I'm so put upon' comic, and based on our recent chat it occurred to me that the look really fit. I reached Rick's booth and slid into the seat across from him. He nodded his head. "Donna," he said, acknowledging my presence.

"Hey, Rick." We were beyond pretending to be thrilled at our unexpected reunion.

"Coffee?" he mumbled, pointing to a pot on the table. I poured myself a cup and waited for him to set the pace of our tete-a-tete.

"You don't look so bad," he offered. A classic Rick remark transporting me back to the days when we worked together at Mylar.

"You, either," I countered, not about to lay it on thick and appear insincere this early in our visit. In fact, I was starting to think there might be an unexpected benefit to having this meeting in person. I'd been so focused on WyCliff as BJ's pathetic ex that I'd sort of forgotten about our shared history as coworkers. Prior to his ill-fated hook up with Medusa, I used to genuinely enjoy hanging out with Rick. The realization kind of caught me by surprise.

We settled into a comfortable conversation about "stuff" that really took me back. What I'd always appreciated about Rick was the fact that he would never bullshit. He never pretended to care about stuff he didn't – so you always knew where you stood. I liked that. When the waitress finally made it over to our table, she broke us out of our easy patter. We ordered quickly, apparently both realizing there was work to be done, so we got down to it.

I filled WyCliff in on the details of the actual murder and the pieces I'd been able to put together about BJ's life in Omaha. As I finished my overview, I noticed that he was looking a bit pale and somewhat green around the gills.

"Hey, Rick, I'm sorry if I'm being too blunt."

"No, Donna, it's okay," he sighed. "I guess I just didn't realize how far from reality BJ had begun to stray. It's so hard to fathom that she would focus on you after all these years, and even move her whole life out to Omaha on the basis of a total illusion. I always knew BJ had a disturbed mind, but I never thought she was really certifiable. The woman who was running around Omaha with all those stories about you was a card-carrying lunatic."

"That sums it up pretty well. And when you put it that way, I wonder why I'm breaking my neck looking for the trail of logic that brought her to Omaha when, in fact, it would be more like a trail of illogic."

That's when our yogurt and granola topped with fresh fruit arrived. Rick and I took a moment to refill our coffee and quietly munch on breakfast. Apparently we both needed a break to digest the implications of what could possibly have happened to BJ to make her travel fifteen hundred miles from home, and a lot further from sanity.

"Ya know," I started, "you're right about something. This whole situation is crazy for so many reasons. We will never come to any really helpful insights unless we drop all pretense of polite society and really get down to basics, so I'm going to jump right in and be as blunt as I need to be. If you can't handle it, I'll understand."

"It's worth a shot," he gave me a green light – kind of pale and sickly green but green nonetheless. So I took it.

"I have always wondered what it was about BJ that attracted you in the first place. I mean, she wasn't exactly easy on the eyes, and frankly she had a disposition to match. I feel as though understanding her attraction to men could be helpful."

"Wow, that was a direct hit!" He was evidently feeling a bit shell shocked already. Oh shit – did I blow it? It was just that we didn't have much time.

"I'm sorry to be so blatant, but the woman was hardly a beauty queen and a charmer," I continued, aware that this whole conversation could end abruptly. It was still unclear as to whether or not WyCliff could handle my grilling of his most personal feelings.

Rick smiled, sort of. It was an odd expression – possibly an "I'm just getting ready to fire off my Uzi" face. I waited patiently.

"I really missed that about you, Donna," he started. "I'd forgotten just how harsh you can be."

It felt like old times. I could ask the outrageous questions and Rick could decide whether or not to share. Only thing was, these questions were a lot more personal than ones I'd asked in years past, and it had to enter his mind that the last thing BJ would ever want would be for him to reveal any intimate secrets to me. I felt a twinge and hoped sincerely that my questions had come 100% from a need to gather information and 0% from my own morbid curiosity. But then, nothing he could tell me would be able to hurt her anymore. Rick must have arrived at the same conclusion because he finally started to answer my question.

"That's really a tough question. I have to give it some thought."

"Take your time. Guessing will only be counterproductive."

He nodded his agreement and took a long sip of coffee. Then I heard another long sigh. I held my breath hoping this was the sigh before sharing.

"Whew, what was it about her that appealed to me? I don't think I've ever really given that consideration before. And so much has happened between now and then. Well, okay, I'll give it a try."

At this point I was starting to doubt I'd ever get anything useful. And I was starting to get bored. Note to self: never ask a man what attracted him to his ex, now murdered, wife – it just takes too long!

"Okay Donna, I think I've got this. Let me see if I can articulate my thoughts in a way that won't make me seem like a jerk."

"Rick, don't worry about what I think," I urged, hoping to speed things up even slightly.

"That's easy for you to say, but after everything I've been through, I don't want to come across as shallow in my feelings of devotion. I don't want you to think that the initial attraction was the only feeling I had for the woman I married."

Wow, he cared about what I thought of him. That caught me off guard. He had tried too hard, through the years, to make me think he cared nothing about my opinion on his relationships, or for that matter any other part of his life. And now to find that he was reluctant to talk because he feared I'd think him shallow. Will wonders never cease?

"Rick, just get started," I suggested.

"I had worked with BJ for several years," he eased into his monologue. "During that time I divorced my first wife and was separated from my kids. I guess it was no real secret I was trying to be a swinging single guy, but I didn't exactly fit the profile."

Interesting. I had been aware of all that, I just never expected he'd realized it as well.

"I guess I'd have to say I saw two things in BJ initially. She was acting wild, like she wanted trouble. There was something appealing about that. I could supply trouble. But there was also a vulnerability that was equally as appealing. She was broken; could I fix her? I'm going to say that this was the initial appeal."

Having known both of them as these events had unfolded, I could see it. What he'd said really rang true, I couldn't help but wonder, though, what turned it into more than a cheap affair – what made it a marriage? No need to wonder; Rick was preparing to enlighten me.

"Once we were together, BJ never lost an opportunity to let me know that she could make me better than I was. Not in a way that put me down, but in a way that made me think I was so close to awesome that with a little tweaking from her I would realize my full potential. She made me over inside and out. I knew I looked better, and she said she could make me successful in every other way, too. I had been slaving away in the business world and hadn't been feeling the appreciation and success that seemed appropriate. Maybe I couldn't get there on my own. Maybe I needed her to help me reach my ultimate destination. She could help me attain the success I so rightly deserved. I believed in her because she believed in me."

BJ as a female Svengali. That was Ann Marie's theory and it explained so much. All of these men had fully believed they were destined for greatness, but they were able to get only part of the way on their own. With BJ they would make it all the way. Or so they believed.

"So," I pressed further, "it wasn't her looks you fell for?"

As soon as it came out of my mouth I felt like crap. What an awful thing to say to a man about his recently murdered ex-wife. I was scum. It would serve me right if WyCliff told me to go 'hmmph' myself. I really could be a jerk sometimes. That might have been my obsessive curiosity.

"Hmmph," Rick started.

Here it comes, I thought, and I deserve every bit of it!

"When we first worked together, I knew BJ as Ron's wife. I was in no way impressed by anything about her. There was no physical appeal. I didn't even think she was hot like some of the other women that came to work at Mylar."

"Interesting," I replied thoughtfully. This was confirming one of my personal theories about flings in the workplace. I didn't think they were usually about physical attraction – at least not alone. Based on some things I'd read and quite a few things I'd observed, I thought they were more about getting attention and being thought of as interesting and appealing. "So, then, when did things start to percolate for the two of you?"

"I guess it was at an agency party shortly after my wife and I split. I was feeling like a failure. I felt I had failed to be the man my wife needed or the ideal father for our kids. I was feeling pretty sorry for myself. BJ had said things were frustrating for her too, so we decided to go out back and tap into some coke I'd scored the weekend before. After that we talked for hours. BJ was frustrated because she wanted to be the woman behind a great man, and Ron would never be destined for greatness. She said she thought my wife was a jerk to let someone as amazing as me go. It all seemed to make sense. She'd been listening to me for hours, and the more she listened, the more impressed she seemed to get. I was feeling good about myself for the first time in a long time. When BJ started to flirt it just seemed natural. She thought I was a great man and she found that overwhelmingly appealing. I know I found it appealing."

Rick took a moment to refill his coffee. He took a few long sips and seemed to be a million miles away. I thought better of interrupting his reflection – so I just waited. After a few minutes he continued his narrative.

"After that, we were just together. She treated me like a VIP and molded me into something I could see was better."

I had to agree. I remembered that time. Rick had started looking better in every way, and he'd started acting less goofy too. Before then he was like a big dumb walrus running from client meeting to client meeting. After that he started to look pretty good. No one at the agency had failed to take note of his magical transformation. I just wondered, if BJ knew how to make someone look that good, why hadn't she applied some of that knowledge to herself? Granted, nature hadn't exactly done her any favors, but with the right hair and make-up she could have improved by a fairly large percentage – and she never did. Her clothing was okay; she usually wore jeans and a t-shirt that fit her fairly well. But then, once she decided she was fashion model material and started wearing designer clothes, she never failed to select the most ludicrous of outfits, a lot like Edina in Ab Fab. Never understated, she always drew enormous attention, which, in my humble opinion, was not ideal for someone who would have been better off wearing cammo and hiding in the nearest bush.

[CHAPTER 30]

"So what attracted her to you?" I asked.

"Gee, thanks Donna."

"Oh God, sorry, Rick. That was rude too!"

"It's okay," he assured me. "I get what you're asking. Well, let me think."

What a putz! Why did I keep doing that? Had I lost my inner compass entirely?

"Hmmm, I guess I was attractive to her because of her mean streak."

"Huh?" Now I was confused.

"I know I don't have to tell you that BJ had a gigantic penchant for cruelty."

"No, that's true, having been the brunt of that 'penchant' for longer than I care to recall, I'm well aware of BJ's proclivity for torturing others. I'm just wondering how it applies here."

"Unfortunately, it's simple. She was in the mood to make Ron suffer, and she felt I'd be an easy conquest. Which I was," he finished as his face gradually reddened.

"Well, Rick, anyone could see..." I started.

"No point in making excuses for me now. I was easy pickins for the black widow, and we both know it. Besides, even in my pre-BJ lifestyle I was doing more fun and exciting things than she'd done with Ron in the entire time she knew him. I was going to discos and concerts, going to gourmet restaurants. About the most gourmet experience she'd had with Ron was at Taco Bell; even then he ate the simplest thing they offered. Hell, compared to Ron I was Indiana Jones with a decent stash of coke."

"Did you ever love each other?" Cripes, I was starting to feel as though I'd been possessed! I mean what else could account for this rampant case of runaway mouth?

"We thought we were madly in love. At least I did. We laughed about being the envy of everyone around us – everyone who had a dull and boring existence while we led a life of glamour and excitement. In retrospect, I think we were each a little more in love with ourselves, and we were probably never really in love with each other. Coke can go a long way toward making you feel 'in love' too. So with the combination of getting what we wanted – or needed – and with a butt-load of coke that we went through during that time period, we thought the rest of the world wished they were us!"

"In fact," he continued, "I vaguely remember a day when BJ was mad that you were hot for me."

"*Me*?!" I barked, "She thought I was hot for *you*?!"

"Calm down. We were trying to get out of the agency to spend some alone time and you were determined to talk to me before we left."

"I probably had a deadline..."

"You did, but you see my point here, don't you? We were not behaving rationally regarding anything, and that's how a lot of our relationship was."

"Yeah, I guess," I admitted reluctantly, "I can sort of see your point."

"Well, you got really lucky that day, anyway."

"How do you mean?"

"Oh, BJ was in rare form. She was going to pound your head in and leave you for dead in the parking lot," he recalled fondly.

"Oh, I'd like to have seen her..."

"Well, just be glad she settled on making fun of you all through our intimate little lunch date instead," he offered. "She gave you some serious bruises, but none of them were physical. In fact, if I'm not mistaken, once she gave it some more thought, she laughed at herself. Yeah, now I remember, she said the fact that you had no looks, no brains, no style and no personality – meant no one need ever be jealous of you!" Now he was laughing.

"Why, that no good..."

"Maybe it's time to move on to something more productive." It would have sounded much more professional had he said it without the hysterical laughter. So happy to provide comic relief.

Rick was right. All of this was interesting – and some of it was damned annoying – but now that I'd heard it, it didn't seem productive in helping us find BJ's murderer. Although at the moment my interest in solving the case had more to do with wanting to shake her murderer's hand rather than see him or her behind bars!

Rick looked pensive. "There is something I'm debating telling you."

"You're kidding, right? I thought we'd managed to cut through the layers of time and revert back to when we had a close working relationship. Am I kidding myself?" I asked. Actually, I whined.

"Yeah, this is different, though,"

"How different?"

I wondered if this was something I'd wish I could "un-know" after I knew it?

Silence.

Long silence.

"All right Rick," I started reluctantly, "you might as well

spill it."

"Donna, I'd have to have your absolute word that you would not share this with police, here or in Omaha," he replied conspiratorially.

"You have it."

"You're sure?" No, but how could I walk away from what had to be a critical piece of information? The scary thing was that if this was really critical information, it would make me an accessory by not reporting it to Warren immediately. So far, in my brief but volatile crime solving career, I had never knowingly and deliberately been on the wrong side of the law – well, at least not in a major way.

"Let's hear it," I urged.

"Donna, you may have heard that some of BJ's East coast familiars were in Omaha at the time of her murder," he paused for effect.

"Is that it, Rick? Because you're right, I do already know that. I thought you were going to give me something new here. What's the big deal about my mentioning that to the police?" I was feeling somewhat letdown after all of Rick's build up.

"Right, but I'm not finished yet." That's when he dropped his bomb. "I was one of them. In fact there were six of us out there at the time of the murder. I know everyone who was there, and I'm pretty sure I know why, at least in most cases."

That really was big. I had the immediate urge to call Warren and report every bit of this news. But I couldn't. I had to really consider what Rick had just revealed. Would I be able to keep my mouth shut? Honestly, I wasn't so sure.

"Six of you? Including her son?" I asked. "Because the police already know Mickey was out there."

"Yeah, Mickey and a companion, me and three others. The cops know that Mickey was out there to help her move. I doubt they know that he went back out just before the murder and they don't know about the other five of us yet either. And now you can't be the one to enlighten them," he reminded me even more obnoxiously.

"I know, I know," I agreed. Now we were slipping back into that old pattern of animosity that had sometimes defined our working relationship. If I recalled correctly, that never netted me the information I needed to get the job done way back when. I didn't see this as being any different from those annoying occasions years ago. I continued trying to pull the tone back to the 'amicable teammate' mode from earlier in our breakfast. Besides, Rick wasn't 100% right about what the cops knew, and I didn't see a need to enlighten him. Payback's a bitch!

"So Rick," I asked, "Why were all of you out there?"

"I'll tell you why I was out there. During the course of my marriage to BJ, I became fairly close to Mickey. You know my first ex had moved the kids to the west coast. I'm still their Dad, but we're just not close. Mickey became very important to me; he was almost like my own son. He was very aware that my feelings for him and his mom were genuine, albeit somewhat misguided based on his mom's capricious nature. Even more than that, I became Mickey's confidante as time went on. He was close to his dad, but he also knew that many of the issues he was forced to deal with because of his mother's behavior would end up tearing Ron apart making him feel guilty. There was virtually nothing he couldn't share with me. When he told me about his mom's ultimate betrayal and how he found out he was determined to head back, show up on her doorstep, and confront her with the sordid details. Knowing him as I did, I knew talking him out of it would have been futile. I figured the best thing I could do would be to follow him out there and be around to help pick up the pieces after she disemboweled him and left him broken and bleeding."

"Geez, Rick, that was an amazing thing for you to do," I acknowledged, impressed by his caring and selflessness. Apparently Rick had grown as a person since I'd known him years ago. "So what did he do when he realized you were out there?"

"He never knew. She was murdered before he and I connected."

"What about the others?"

"You know I'm going to have to be heading out now. Why don't we agree to chat next week some time."

I started to sputter and mutter. He couldn't leave me hanging like this! But before I could put my objection into words, Rick cut me off at the knees.

"That's all I'm prepared to share until I see how well you're able to handle your part of the bargain. A week or so should give me a chance to be sure that you have honored our agreement."

I couldn't really argue with any of his logic. He had every right to control his information. I was free to explore the four mysterious people myself; whatever I figured out on my own was fair game – I could tell Warren if I so chose. Maybe that was for the best. Rick and I exchanged contact information and said our good-byes. I made sure he knew that it was likely I'd be back in Omaha before our next conversation.

On the drive back to Mom's, I made two decisions based on my sense that the answers really did reside in Omaha. I would book my flight home for the next day, and I would call Kyle and run all of this by him. I guess I needed a companion in my role of accessory.

[CHAPTER 31]

Back at Mom's, I was thrilled to learn that my sister, Melissa, though we called her Lissa, had taken a couple of vacation days. She was, at that moment, driving down from her home in upstate Vermont to join us for the end of my stay. What a great surprise! It really helped to postpone the sad realization that my family visit was coming to an end. I rushed off to make flight plans since I'd be heading out the next night at 5:00 P.M. Then I invited Mom to select a dinner restaurant for the three of us, my treat. It was the least I could do considering they'd both done so much for me. I headed to Mom's home office and settled in to call Kyle in the hopes that I could catch him before my sister's arrival.

Kyle was on a conference call, so I left a message and changed for a quick dip before lunch. I had no sooner submerged – which isn't all that impressive considering Mom keeps her pool at a balmy eighty-two degrees – when my sister came running out onto the upper patio. She called down and waved indicating she'd change and join me. The only problem was, when the two of us got anywhere near a pool together we reverted right back to childhood. Mom would never get us to abandon the pool for a lunch table. Our Mother is smart though; she anticipated the insurmountable challenge and opted to bring a tray of goodies down for a decadent poolside feast. It was awesome!

During the course of the afternoon, my travel plans came up. Mom was clearly disappointed I'd be leaving so soon, even though we'd be seeing each other within a month or so. For the sake of our idyllic afternoon, she did her best to push any negative thoughts aside and enjoy the magnificent day with her girls. We made our plans for a fabulous gastronomic experience that evening; we had one night so we were going all out to ensure it would be memorable. After an afternoon of paradise, swimming and sunshine, gabbing and laughing, and let's not forget eating, we were more than ready to head into the showers when the late afternoon shadows began to cast themselves over more and more of the pool. After showering, I threw on some terry cloth shorts and a sleeveless top and started going through the remainder of my clean wardrobe trying to decide on the best outfit for our big night. That's when the phone rang, and it was Kyle.

"Hey, Donna, how's it going out there? I hope you're enjoying some of the beautiful weather poolside!" Kyle enthused. "It must be just gorgeous!"

"Gorgeous, yes, it really is gorgeous." Sometimes, when I get into a singularly-focused mindset, I have a tendency to block everything else out. Kyle was not about to let me do that; he was right. He knew it would take some coaxing to get me to take a breath and fully enjoy my surroundings. He wanted details!

Once past the obligatory 'life is good when you're on vacation' banter, I launched into my breakfast conversation with WyCliff. Whenever there was an issue that hugged the edge of moral/ethical, I always felt better after talking to Kyle. His moral compass was unsurpassable and I could rest easy if my actions met with his approval. I was nervous he would tell me to ignore my promise to Rick because a police matter trumps a promise to a former colleague. The truly amazing thing about Kyle's advice, it always makes you feel better; I should have known this time would be no different.

"Donna, I can see your dilemma," he acknowledged. "You've made an outright promise to Rick, but you have an allegiance to Warren since you have, in effect, made a promise to share any pertinent information you pick up on your trip east."

"Exactly, Kyle, I feel as though I've made two promises and they are diametrically opposed, so what do I do?"

"At this point you keep your promise to Rick," he advised. "You can always choose to share with Warren if the opportunity presents itself, but that may never be necessary."

"But Kyle-"

"What I'm saying is..." Kyle persisted, but in the nicest possible way, "for all you know Warren may already have this information; she doesn't share everything with you." Good point – that thought had not occurred to me. "And even if she doesn't know already, there's a good chance she will soon enough. I mean, people who travel leave a trail – you have to know she's checking hotels/motels, gas stations, restaurants and any other venues that someone from Connecticut, or somewhere in the northeast, visited during the time of the murder. So it's only a matter of time. From what you're telling me, you don't even know the identity of all BJ's East coast visitors yet. Can you even be certain that you know the real reason Mickey and Rick, or any of them for that matter, were here? When you break it down like that, what do you really have to share?"

Wow, he was so right. I didn't have much information at all, did I? And the police definitely knew some of this already. That thought was a huge relief, but also kind of disappointing. My big scoop amounted to not much of anything. Once again, he had delivered and taken the pressure off of my already overloaded brain. Everything always seemed better after a conversation with Kyle. How did he do that?

"Thanks, that's just what I needed to hear," I sighed. "Now out of there, and have yourself a fabulous, relaxing dinner and don't give me another thought."

"Wish I could," he said. "Still haven't had lunch today."

Now I really felt like a jerk. Here he was running around so much that he couldn't take time out for lunch, and I had insisted he call and put my mind at ease.

"Kyle, you know better than to skip meals," I scolded. "You need to go home and scrounge up some food even if it means leaving a few things on your desk for tomorrow; I'm sorry I distracted you on such a crazy day."

"Actually, I will have to leave my food plans on hold in order to get down to the police station and bail Peg and Babs out of the pokey."

What? I must have heard him wrong.

"You heard me right, Donna." He was back in my head again.

"But."

"After they spoke with you last night the guilt started to set in; with you back East they had completely ignored the investigation and gotten back to life as usual. After hearing of your close call, they decided to take some action to save you from dealing with it yourself once you're back."

"They are so awesome." Now I was feeling very wary of this latest indignity and growing increasingly curious.

"Yes, good friends and the best people," he added. 'They wanted to do a little poking around in the victim's fancy new digs so they perpetrated a little B&E.

"And they got busted! Oooh, bad timing, huh?"

"Not at all." Now I was puzzled.

"They didn't get busted when they broke in?" I asked,

knowing I would regret it.

"No, they didn't. Once they were inside they could see that the bathtub drain was plugged and the faucet was leaking at such a rate that the floor would have been flooded within the hour. Left unchecked, they knew the water would eventually make its way down to the lower floors and do a ton of damage on its way – so they called and reported it. And then they got arrested for Breaking & Entering."

"You can't be serious! They saved the property owners from enormous inconvenience and potentially huge repair bills and they *still* got busted for the same B&E that enabled them to offer that help?" I was outraged.

"I know, but when I asked those same questions I was told that there were too many parties involved to be able to discount the legal implications entirely. An arrest had to be made. Thankfully, the arresting officers have shared that any judge will take the entire scenario into account, along with the fact that they were actively involved in helping solve Claire's murder, and let them off the hook. Right now it's about going through the motions. No one's expecting the charges to stick."

"Still, that makes me nervous."

"Getting those two thinking a little more cautiously is not necessarily the worst thing," he countered.

"I guess, as long as that's the worst that happens," I agreed. "Just one more thing, Kyle. Do they think the murderer broke in to flood the apartment?"

"No, actually, they're pretty sure the building janitor was selling tours of the murder victim's home to make a little cash on the side. Apparently, that day there had been a particularly large group with some rowdy kids in the bunch. They must have broken from the pack and messed with the plumbing for kicks. Well, as you can imagine, there will be one unemployed janitor in Omaha pretty soon."

"Unbelievable."

Knowing where Kyle was headed, we brought our call to a rapid close – a little fear was one thing, but enough is enough! Before he rang off I made Kyle promise to keep me posted on Peg and Babs. He assured me he'd get them out before the end of the day, but couldn't promise any information on their release.

[CHAPTER 32]

We had a great time at Mom's favorite tapas restaurant. There was a lot of laughter, and I shared information I had learned about BJ at breakfast. We also decided to permit ourselves one more day of poolside paradise before Mom drove me to the airport.

The next day was spectacular! Brilliant sunshine made the crystal clear pool water appear to sparkle like blue diamonds, reflecting the perfect azure sky. The rolling hills, baked in warmth and tranquility created the ideal, bucolic setting, and the cloudless sky afforded us views revealing both the Hartford and Springfield skylines. It was breathtaking.

Mid-morning I headed inside to call Farley. I was feeling guilty about making the trip out and not making time for him. It was probably just as well he was rehearsing for an important presentation later in the week, and had no time for more than a quick update. I filled him in on my trip and assuaged my Farley-based guilt. Back to the pool!

We spent the rest of our day talking, swimming, joking and ultimately solving the major problems of the world in our spare moments. We snacked on healthy fruits and vegetables, and managed to sneak a bit of comfort food into the mix with a lunch of Genoa salami on rye and German potato salad on the side.

By the time we had to pack up and head out we'd all had enough water and sun.

* * *

Getting home felt good. The dogs were jumping and barking and squeaking. They pushed each other out of the way as each fought to get close enough for big kisses and some long-awaited attention. They damn near knocked me over a few times, but Jon finally came to my rescue.

Jon was fully briefed on the intelligence I'd garnered from my whirlwind visit east. He agreed with Kyle's advice about keeping Rick's secret – for now.

We wound down the evening with a glass of wine; he sipped on a full-bodied cab from California and I savored a glass of my favorite, Kim Crawford Sauvignon Blanc. I was exhausted and ready for a good night's sleep. We explained to the dogs that tonight was not the night to wake us up unless something serious happened – hell, it was worth a shot, right?

The next morning came so early. Why had I been in such an all-fired rush to get home and back to my normal routine? Maybe if I closed my eyes for just a moment I'd wake up to one more poolside day – yeah, right! Time to get up and get things going, since that was kind of my only choice.

If the alarm clock was my first rude awakening, the drive downtown was a close second. Had I forgotten how to drive? Or was every bad driver in Omaha out this morning to welcome me home? By the time I reached the office, I realized that an attitude adjustment would be necessary if I planned on surviving the day!

It took about an hour to respond to all of the welcoming rituals, read all the new e-mails, and listen to phone messages. I had just about finished when it was time for the first meeting of the day, which lasted until 12:30. Rushing out of the conference room, I found Peg and Babs still hard at work at their desks.

"Come on, you two, I'll buy you lunch and you can fill me in on your latest escapade," I offered, more as an appeasement than an information gathering forum; I just couldn't help feeling guilty that they'd put themselves in an untenable situation on my account so it was the least I could do.

In her usual command and control manner, Peg informed me that neither of them had time for lunch out, but if it made me feel better I could treat them to something they could eat at their desks. Then she smiled without looking up from her work. She knew me too well. I set out to find a luncheon feast for my "partners in crime." In truth, the thought of a lunch out so soon after our 'Indian in the salad bar' experience had me feeling a little nervous anyhow.

After considering the options, I headed over to Patrick's Market to see what delicacies I could dig up for the dynamic duo. I settled on an "in office" picnic of fried chicken, home-style potato salad, three bean salad, and some homemade lemonade to wash it all down. For dessert I picked up some Ben & Jerry's ice cream treats on a stick. I felt the need to go all out on this treat. We ended up heading out front to the crate-styled benches built by our design crew – with Marcel green cushions – for a genuine outdoor picnic lunch; sometimes, greasy chicken is the tie that binds.

Our lunch break gave us a chance to catch up. I was incredibly relieved when Babs and Peg confided that a circuit court judge had made it a point to stop by and tell them they had nothing to fear. He considered them to be model citizens. Not only were they trying to help solve a gruesome murder, but they had also put themselves at risk in order to help others avoid an unpleasant problem. He also told them to keep his comments 'close to the vest' since technically they should be prosecuted to the fullest extent of the law. Although he acknowledged that judges at his level did have a fair amount of leeway, he still had to tow the line this close to an election. Personally, I felt that his chances of reappointment would improve if people knew that he went out of his way to apply realism to his adjudication, but he was the expert. Far be it from me to impose common sense on any aspect of politics.

The afternoon was much more pleasant once the looming fear of what might happen to Peg and Babs was erased. I was free to move on to other aspects of the investigation and, oh yeah, to get caught up on work. I was kind of stumped as to where to go next until Liv stopped by my desk mid-afternoon to mention that she'd run into Kyle's former colleague Cindy while I'd been back east. Cindy had indicated she had information to impart regarding some of BJ's activities since moving to Omaha. That was all I needed. The game was afoot – again! Liv agreed to set up a coffee date with Cindy for first thing in the morning. I was less than thrilled when I realized that our "early meeting" meant 7:30 A.M. My fervent suggestion to make it at a later time was rejected when Liv explained that her first client meeting was set for 8:30 – later was not going to work. Oh well, there are worse things in life – I think.

I finished out the day with a short internal meeting and a brief chat with Donny.

"My boys tell me the suspect list has grown since you headed East."

"I definitely came to that conclusion when I was out there."

"And," he continued, "they've rethought the 'it's most likely a woman' theory. Now they're looking at men and women."

"Really?" I asked. "I came to that conclusion based on some of the conversations I had back east. I guess great minds do think alike."

"Yeah, that's just what I was about to say," replied Donny with an impossible to miss roll of the eyes. "Thing is, they're back to square one. Instead of eliminating suspects, the list keeps growing. That's not making them happy down at the station, and I guess the Mayor is putting the pressure on the Chief. We do our best to attract new people into the area, especially entrepreneurial new people (now it was my turn to roll my eyes, BJ an entrepreneur? Indeed!) and word is starting to spread that once we bring 'em in – we kill 'em!"

"Oh for Pete's sake!" I cried. "Where is that word starting to spread?"

"I think in the Mayor's head," Donny smiled, "but that's enough to get him out sniffing around and rattling some cages." I nodded my agreement; I could definitely see that happening. Too bad, Warren and her crew didn't need any more pressure, but I guess that's public service!

I thanked Donny for the update and headed back to my desk to pack things up for the night. As I was shutting off my computer, I noticed the blinking red message light on my phone. There was one message, and it was a strange one. In a voice that was both muffled and garbled, an unidentified caller said, "Look into the Facebook threats; that will lead you to BJ's killer." At least that's what I think the caller said. It actually sounded more like "look into the tailhook jets that will feed you to V.K.'s pillar," but I was pretty sure that wasn't right. On my way toward the door I spotted Donny heading out. I called and asked him to hang back so I could share my latest tidbit. Donny was very interested in learning the caller's identity so we headed back to my desk and I replayed the message for him. Still nothing. That caller did not want to be identified.

Donny made me promise to keep the message saved because he'd be seeing Frick and Frack at tonight's soccer game, and he'd make sure to get them up to speed. Really? Did he think I was born yesterday? Like I would go and erase police evidence on a murder case. He then informed me that it was likely the police would want to make a copy of the message to see if they could enhance the voice quality and make a positive ID on the caller. Oh please, what sort of TV neophyte does he take me for? The majority of U.S. citizens know more about police procedure on identifying the voice on a message with a tip on a murder investigation than how many feet they should leave between themselves and the car driving in front of them. Homicide law is so much more compelling than vehicular law.

"Roger that, Captain," I interrupted his instructions, perhaps with the slightest hint of sarcasm as I grabbed my stuff and headed for the door. There was that eye roll again. Whatever.

Once home, I spent an action-packed few minutes watching each dog try to one-up the other for my full attention, while Jon explained that we'd been invited to the back deck of our friends, and neighbors, Mary Louise and Dave Campanella for a glass of wine. We arrived to find half the adults in our neighborhood sipping wine and offering food dishes in order to turn the evening into a full-fledged impromptu barbeque. Our neighborhood was so great – and fattening!

[CHAPTER 33]

The worst thing about neighborhood cookouts is they never end early. The second worst thing is they always seem to mysteriously appear on nights before an early meeting. Oh well, I had one thing going for me; at least our meeting didn't entail my having to make an important presentation. I just had to sit, sip coffee, listen, and respond with a baseline of intelligence; with some luck I might be able to accomplish that.

Predictably the next morning found me dragging my sorry tail, though I was the first to arrive at the coffee shop. Just as well, I could get my coffee and find the most comfortable seat in the room. The more I pampered myself today the less I'd regret the night before. Once settled into a big overstuffed leather chair in a seating group near the front window, it dawned on me that I was still the only member of our little party to have arrived. I knew I hadn't gotten there a second too early and yet I'd had time to order my coffee, pay for and prepare it, and scout around for the perfect place to plunk down.

I had to have been there for fifteen minutes already (maybe, in reality, more like five – but time weighed heavily this morning). Why were they so late? I glanced down at my watch – actually, I glanced down at where my watch would have been had I indulged in coffee before getting dressed. I looked around for a clock – and there were none. Of course, if this place relied on being the ultimate coffee experience, they didn't want ticking clocks around to remind patrons of the pressures of the outside world.

Just as I had convinced myself I'd gotten the details of this meeting wrong, Cindy breezed in all apologies and hello's. She asked if I needed anything else as she headed over to order her coffee. I took a deep breath, feeling a bit foolish. My coffee was still too hot to drink, so how long could I really have waited? As Cindy was ordering coffee, Liv sauntered in and Cindy was able to kill two birds – and a bran muffin – with one stone. Liv and I barely had time to acknowledge each other when Cindy hovered over us carefully placing her purchases and scoping out her descent into leather heaven. Even though it was mid-summer, the fire in the fieldstone fireplace made for a very cozy morning venue when added to the brown and beige, leather and fieldstone, high-end ambiance surrounding us.

"So Cindy," I jumped right in to get things going, "Liv tells me you have something you'd like to discuss related to BJ's murder."

"True, Donna, that's true," Cindy responded, "but before we get into that whole can o' worms I've got a question for you. Do you think there's any chance I can talk Blondie into a rematch?"

"None," I glared, to Liv's great amusement.

"Now Donna," Liv smirked, "Personally, I would give ANYTHING for a front row seat...."

I shot her my best "if you want to live beyond today you'll drop it" look – nothing. She and Cindy were chatting and laughing like a pair of old buddies. It was really annoying. Oh well, at least Cindy wasn't still pissed off about my recent visit.

"Look," I stood up. "If you got me down here at this ungodly hour to discuss--"

"No, Donna, I swear," Cindy assured me, "I really do have something I want to share that's connected to the murder. I'm sorry, I just could not help trying one more time; that YouTube video was great for business!"

Yeah, not for MY business!

The "rematch" Cindy suggested referenced an earlier humiliating episode. On one particularly black day during Claire's murder investigation, Kyle, Peg, Babs and I stopped into Cindy's gym to ask a few questions. Once we finished our little interview, Babs requested that one of us have a chance to wrestle Cindy. If hell froze over I would never forgive Babs for that little indiscretion. Apparently one cannot wrestle unless one is attired correctly, and that day I was the only one who looked to be the right size for the available costume. Under great duress I was forced to "suit-up" before being unceremoniously thrown into a ring where Cindy is some kind of wrestling phenomenon.

Needless to say, my time as a punching bag was short-lived. I folded like a worthless hand in gin rummy and was carted back to the agency after a brief attempt to stem some of the more prolific bleeding. As if the pain to my psyche weren't traumatic enough, I returned to the office to find the entire staff viewing my foray into 'guts and glory,' which was in my case more like 'guts and gory' on YouTube. It was not one of my finer moments, certainly not a moment I ever intended on repeating! Oh, the indignities!

At this point, both Liv and Cindy were staring at me with obvious apprehension, as well they should. I viewed them through my narrowed eye slits and wondered if I'd ever be able to focus on anything else under the circumstances. Liv's phone rang and she walked outside to take the call. That left the two of us, and Cindy was scared.

"I, I swear, Donna, I'll never bring it up again," Cindy promised.

"I suggest we move along to our next subject before we run out of time and I run out of patience," I responded. I figured I deserved a little imperiousness, all things considered.

By the time Liv returned from her call, Cindy and I were in the middle of our conversation about BJ. She'd started with the details of their initial meeting.

"I went to the Ad Club luncheon and there she was, working the room," Cindy began, "and she was pretty smooth. I never put two and two together that she was scouting for information about you."

"Really, Cindy," I probed, "She was asking about me and you didn't realize she was asking about me? Granted I haven't had a full cup of coffee yet, but I'm having trouble imagining how anyone could manage that."

"I know," she acknowledged. "You'd think it would've been obvious, but she asked a million questions about advertising in Omaha. In retrospect the questions that connected to you, either directly or indirectly, were the areas where she dug the deepest. In all honesty, though, she mixed things up enough that I don't think anyone was the wiser."

"I guess I see how that could happen, especially since you hadn't started second guessing anything about her yet."

"Yeah, we were just excited there was new blood moving into the area. We were more interested in where she was from and what she'd done."

"And telling you she was from Connecticut didn't set off any alarms?" I pursued.

"I'm pretty sure she said she was from the Northeast," Cindy pondered. "I don't believe she ever mentioned Connecticut per se; that would have been a dead giveaway – oooh, sorry – If she'd mentioned Connecticut, people would have started asking her if she knew you."

Liv walked in and signaled that we'd have to wrap up sooner than we'd hoped.

"Gotta go put out a fire, guys," Liv apologized. "Sorry to have to break up this little briefing so soon. But you know how it is. And Donna, I'll need you on this too, so chop, chop!"

"I'll give you the Reader's Digest version," Cindy offered, "so you can be on your way. BJ asked me to lunch to help her get acclimated in the community. That lunch was when she hit me with her big news. She said the two of you had always talked about going into business together, and that you'd really been pushing for it recently."

"What's this?" Liv interjected. "Really, Donna, you're mad at a dead woman?"

Apparently Liv had noticed that my face had turned red and was looking strangely contorted. After her comment, Cindy stopped her story, staring at me with trepidation.

"Get a hold of yourself," Liv continued. "If you can't deal with it, let's just go."

It was extremely disconcerting to hear of BJ's claim that having her move West was not only with my knowledge, but at my urging. Somehow that made it all seem even worse. But just like with any other train wreck, I wouldn't look away.

"No, no, I'm sorry, keep going. I really want to hear the highlights. Do you think you could really speed things up? I'll keep it together."

Cindy looked at me and then Liv. Liv nodded her head. I took a few deep breaths. Cindy steeled herself and started in again, only faster.

"Okay, well, she asked me not to say anything to anyone because she had come out here without your knowledge."

"Yes, right! That's what I've been telling everyone!"

"Give it a rest, Donna, or she'll never get through this story," Liv warned. "I'm running out of time!"

"All right, all right. Keep going, Cindy."

"She said she was going to surprise you by settling in and finding the perfect office space for your new business," Cindy explained. "I even asked her if it was wise to commit to office space without your approval, but she said you two had discussed it so much that she knew exactly what you wanted. She even said she could decorate the whole thing so that when you walked in you'd be thrilled."

That explained a lot. Not only was BJ claiming that she would be shopping for our new office without my knowledge, she was also saying she planned to decorate the whole thing behind my back. How else could she have been here for a couple of months telling people about our business plans without my ever hearing a thing? This actually made sense in an insane sort of way.

And all this time I had been so nervous fearing the police would never believe me. Hell, I had even started to think I was losing it. I mean, how could no one have mentioned anything to me? At one point I even convinced myself that I had been told, and had suffered a blackout memory lapse. It was more amazing than ever that the police genuinely seemed to be in my corner. I was having trouble believing my own claims.

Ultimately, talking to Cindy provided some helpful insight. Pieces of the puzzle were starting to fall into place. At this point, Liv was seriously antsy about getting back to the office. I knew we had to head out so I took one last shot at getting something really helpful.

"So Cindy, what made you decide to share this information now?" I began. "And can you tell me what part of it stands out most in your mind?"

"Oh yeah," Cindy nodded. "When she told me her ex-boyfriend came out to help her get settled into her new apartment. He wanted her back and he wanted to go into business with the two of you. Oh, and one other thing just dawned on me, I had to excuse myself and respond to a text when we were together. Once it was sent, I realized she'd been mumbling to herself. She murmured something about not caring about the expense since she's be getting plenty of money from you."

Incredible, I did not expect that!

"Yeah, and then she went on to say she told the boyfriend she never loved him and she never respected him as a professional in the ad industry – man, she could be harsh – he just blew."

"I want to hear every detail."

"No, Donna, I've got to go now!" Liv protested. "Right now!" She grabbed my arm, waved good-bye to Cindy and dragged me open-mouthed out the door and to my car.

Once back at my desk, and after resolving Liv's crisis, I realized I had forgotten to ask which ex-boyfriend. I called Cindy and left a message on her voicemail. Damn her, why couldn't she be at her desk! This would drive me nuts; it had to be Porter Enzo, right? And what else had she said about getting money from me! Just at that point, Kyle swung by my desk so I filled him in on our coffee meeting. He was as intrigued as I'd been. He guessed it must be Porter, too. And he was equally intrigued about the money comment. Maybe we were finally starting to get to BJ's real agenda regarding me.

This second interrogation of Cindy had yielded so much more than the first. Relief or not, I was starting to seriously doubt my detecting ability. I could have gotten all of this in the first visit if I'd asked the right questions. Instead, I wasted a lot of time trying to figure out some of these things on my own. It was discouraging, especially when I still didn't have all the puzzle pieces from Cindy. Of course, some of this could be blamed on Liv's emergency and her insanely tight schedule –

we often found ourselves running out of one meeting so she wouldn't be late for the next one.

After sharing Cindy's latest revelation with Kyle, I sat back and took a breath. I barely had a chance to exhale before Kyle shared his own scoop. Apparently two or three of her exes ran into each other, out here, about three weeks ago. A major altercation ensued and BJ was nowhere in sight.

"How did you find out about this?" This was good stuff!

"It was the strangest thing," he offered, "I was taking our new client out for dinner and I ran into Warren and a date."

"And she told you important details of the investigation?"

"No, actually, she wanted to know if I'd heard anything," he hastened to correct me, "and when she realized I had no idea what she was talking about, she asked me to put a few feelers out and see what I could come up with. So I started to poke around a little on my own."

"Uh oh."

"No, its fine," Kyle assured me. "I've just started to piece some of the details together. Apparently the men in her life all find Dèlice irresistible, you know, since she lives right there at Midtown Crossing it's so convenient for anyone visiting her."

"You mean they had a fight right there in between coffee and scones?" I pressed.

"Kind of," Kevin admitted. "I mean, it's not like they started throwing punches or anything. Things did get a bit loud from what I've heard."

"So wait a minute, did you say two or three of her exes?" Was it two or three?"

"Well, that's the thing," he mused, "We're not exactly sure."

"What do you mean we're 'not exactly sure'? Did some people say two and some say three?"

"Not exactly. There were three guys, but since we're not

sure exactly who they all were, we don't know if it was two exes and one was with a buddy, or if all three were her exes. We are pretty sure WyCliff was one of them, but that's about as much as we know. We still don't know the cause of the fight or whether or not any of them ended up angry at the victim. There's still a lot we need to figure out."

Oh, great, so my dear close friend, WyCliff had been holding even more back than he'd let on at our marathon breakfast/ revelation session. It was disappointing to think he wouldn't share something that big, especially since it was so likely I'd find out at some point. And I thought he really wanted to help me find BJ's killer.

Breakfast had been the perfect opportunity for him to unburden himself. One thing was becoming clear about these murder investigations: now that I'm an experienced detective with one solved murder under my belt (not that I'm trying to grab the glory for solving Claire's murder, but I was intimately involved in the process), I'm starting to see an annoying trend. Just when you think you're starting to work things out, something will always come and throw a monkey wrench in the works.

As Kyle moved on to his pre-lunch meeting, I settled in to return a few e-mails and phone calls. Thankfully a lot can get done when you really focus. By the time lunch rolled around I had finalized two tricky negotiations, confirmed that my changes on a pending contract had been approved by corporate attorneys, reviewed three potential candidates for a job opening – found one great possibility in the bunch – and wrote a blog post for our company blog. I was feeling completely self-satisfied; the way you do when you've accomplished a great deal in a short time and have beaten every one of your self-imposed goals. A session like this would always go a long way toward ameliorating the frustration over the 'moving forward/moving backward' roller coaster that seemed to be the norm in a murder investigation. I was feeling a whole lot better and far more optimistic about things.

Just as my thoughts turned to lunch – alright let's face it, my thoughts are never really far from food at any time – the phone rang. It was Maria, the twin sister of BJ's purported love interest. She wanted to know if I would be able to meet her for lunch; she had a few things she wanted to discuss with me, in private. I could feel the hairs on the back of my neck stand up. Could this be the break I'd been looking for? I agreed to meet Maria at Pitch, the gourmet pizza place in Dundee. Maria didn't want to be anywhere near MidTown Crossing or the Old Market; she really wanted this meeting to be hush, hush.

Trying not to get my hopes up too much, I grabbed my purse, fished out my car keys and sunglasses, and bolted out the door and into my car. There really wasn't much traffic to speak of, and I pulled into the cramped parking lot next to Pitch within ten minutes. Once there, it dawned on me that we could easily be spotted by any number of people Maria would prefer to avoid. Being such an easy city to get around made Omaha a very desirable place to live. It also made hiding tough to accomplish. Even I, a fairly recent transplant from the Northeast, was starting to run into people I knew frequently when I was out and about. Oh well, we'd just have to take our chances; short of buying a bag lunch and heading to one of our houses, this was our safest bet.

[CHAPTER 34]

By the time I got to Pitch, Maria was already snuggled into a half-booth against the wall, contentedly sipping an iced tea. She perked up when she saw me. I had to remind myself that, despite her eagerness to communicate, this could still be a dead end. Maria looked lovely in a pale cream colored suit with an eggplant tee-top and cream colored wedge sandals. Her chunky jewelry, a mix of gold and eggplant, managed to set off both the cream and the eggplant while adding just a touch of sparkle. The woman looked sensational. I made a mental note to review my wardrobe and figure out what I needed to add in order to spiff things up and pull off this kind of casual yet elegantly sophisticated look. There would have to be quite a few wardrobe adjustments!

Maria sat on an upholstered bench seat against the west wall. I sat on the chair opposite. Pitch was a very cool blend of modern steel and concrete treatments set within the framework of an old garage. The garage doors were updated and modernized to become the perfect disappearing wall on those spectacular al fresco dining days that we so often enjoy in Omaha.

"Hey Maria, how's it going," I started on a light note.

"I'm so glad you could make it on such short notice, Donna," she replied. "This is kind of bugging me and I think discussing it with you will help my anxiety."

"Okay, Maria, lay it on me."

"Well, here's the thing, I've been starting to hear rumors about BJ's men from Connecticut."

"Yeah?"

"From what I've been hearing, more than one of her past exes was actually in Omaha during the time of the murder."

"Based on what I've heard recently that seems to be accurate," I acknowledged. Disappointment started to crush my idealistic optimism. I was mentally writing-off Maria's declaration as nothing more than a repeat of what I already knew. Luckily I was listening with one ear or I would have missed the important part.

"So Mario had stopped in to Dèlice for a quick espresso when three men, one who'd been sitting and sipping coffee, one who'd been standing at the counter, scrutinizing all of the delicacies in the display case, and a third who sauntered in fifteen or twenty minutes after Mario had sat down with his espresso, became aware of each other and things got tense. Now she had my full attention, Mario had witnessed the altercation at Dèlice, and Maria was going to give me a blow-by-blow of the whole thing! This alone was worth the drive into Dundee! She continued with her narrative.

"The guy who walked in recognized the guy at the counter immediately. They were clearly shocked to see each other and exchanged strained greetings. Mario said it was really awkward. They were having trouble meeting eye-to-eye, when, at just about the same moment, they both noticed the third guy sitting near the window drinking coffee. That must have been too much for Mr. Counter to bear. He cried out in frustration, which got Mr. Coffee drinker to join their little gathering. Mario said that, at first, all three seemed startled and confused; then, as the implications sunk in the lid blew off the pressure cooker!"

"Was it a jealousy thing?" I asked, riveted to Maria's every word.

"Mario didn't think so, at least not at first. With three guys talking at once it wasn't very easy to follow, Mario thought two of them were worried that BJ was being stalked by the third guy. There was more of a protective aspect to some of the comments Mario heard."

"Sure, she probably told those guys plenty of stuff to make them suspicious, even hostile toward each other. That sounds like something she would do. It's not like the truth meant anything to her. Did Mario ever find out who they were?"

"Someone called the guy drinking coffee, WyCliff," Maria responded. "I think the counter guy was Don or Ron or something."

Ron? Oh my God, could that have been Ron? Geez, that's all I needed, did every man in BJ's life take delight in lying to me? If that was Ron in Dèlice then Ron lied to me during our heartfelt conversation, too. He certainly never mentioned this encounter or even that he'd ever been to Omaha. I was starting to feel like a complete moron. Everyone I'd spoken to in this whole investigation had in some way lied to me.

I mentally reviewed my conversation with Ann Marie. She was not one to lie, but I hadn't thought Ron was lying to me either. This was very demoralizing. For the first time in either murder investigation, I was feeling as though I wanted to take my ball and go home! I mean, in a way, even Ron's new wife, Sheila, had been sort of lying to me. I mean, she didn't come right out and say, "Ron's never been to Omaha," but you'd have thought that she might offer the information knowing, as she did, that I was calling from Omaha and that the murder had occurred out here.

As I brooded about my naiveté, more like stupidity, in believing that these people had totally opened up to me, I was clearly starting to wallow in self-pity. It was so disheartening to realize that I was just not credible as the great detective after all. At the end of each one of those conversations, I was certain

I'd obtained every relevant piece of information. How wrong I'd been! Every one of them had played me for a fool – even the really nice ones.

As I contemplated these feelings another discouraging thought occurred to me. I had really focused my trip back East as a means of uncovering BJ's motives for involving me in the bizarre and twisted plot that had gotten her killed. Not only had I failed to identify her killer, I had come up empty on all fronts! I didn't find one person who claimed to understand her Omaha scam – the one that involved me, in spades. Things were looking worse than I'd imagined. Luckily, Maria could see that I had mentally checked out, and she wasn't about to waste her breath yammering on with no one listening; she was a lady with a clear agenda.

"Hey, Donna, you in there," Maria bellowed. With no immediate response from me; she banged her fist down on the table three times. "Yo, Donna, look alive. Are you listening to me?" Maria demanded.

"Oh, yeah, sorry Maria, I guess my mind wandered for a minute there," I admitted.

"I guess." Guess I wasn't getting any slack from her either. "So as I was saying, Mario said one of the guys was called Elmo, do you know an Elmo?"

"You mean Enzo? Could it be Enzo? I'd heard he was in Omaha."

"Yeah, that works, it was probably Enzo," Maria concluded.

"Wow, so now we're sure that BJ's first husband, her second husband, and her broken-hearted boyfriend were all in Omaha at the time of BJ's murder? And they all knew about each other?"

"I guess that's what I'm telling you, Donna," Maria conceded, "not that it means all that much to me."

"Oh, this is huge!" I assured her. I could feel my voice getting higher and screechier with each word. "So then what happened?"

"Mario wasn't really sure what happened next. The coffee drinker suddenly blew up at the newest arrival; you know, counter-guy. Mario thought that might have been a combination of protectiveness with a generous hint of jealousy."

"That would make sense. BJ's relationship with Enzo was her first step toward deserting Ron, and then Enzo just couldn't let go. Even throughout her whole marriage to WyCliff, Enzo hovered around embodying a silent threat to any kind of screw up from WyCliff. That's a lot of pressure. Then, once BJ and WyCliff split, she briefly returned to Enzo as her transitional guy. I always suspected that WyCliff had to use real self-restraint in not punching Enzo's lights out at some point."

Before Maria had a chance to comment my phone beeped with a text message. I grabbed the phone to discreetly check on the level of urgency. One look and I was ready to bolt. The text was from Peg. It said Clovis had been calling for me since I'd left the office. In her usual psycho approach, when she was told I was at lunch, rather than wait she continued to call back on different lines until she reached an unsuspecting intern who innocently told her where my lunch meeting was being held. According to Peg, Clovis was between five to ten minutes away from bursting in on my lunch with Maria.

I started apologizing to Maria and pulling money out of my wallet. I figured if I threw enough money on the table to pay for lunch while simultaneously making my excuses to Maria, I might have a chance of escaping before Clovis rolled in. As I moved into warp speed, Maria was looking at me warily. I could see that she was worried I'd suddenly flipped my nut. She should only know Clovis! Maria began the standard post-luncheon "oh no, why don't I pay for lunch" dialogue. This would never work if I was going to avoid a Clovis encounter.

"Maria," I whined, "there's no time. Clovis will be here any second now." I was reluctant to admit the real reason for my haste. For people who didn't know Clovis, my comment would undoubtedly seem bizarre and even cruel. From the look in Maria's eyes, I could tell the hasty departure I so desperately wanted was probably not to be. I couldn't very well walk out leaving Maria convinced I'd blown a gasket. I would have to bite the bullet and accept my punishment. I sighed and settled back down.

As I contemplated the best way to explain my freakish behavior to Maria, Clovis blasted into the restaurant in a flurry of activity. For a petite and waifish looking blonde who seemed so fragile that a mild breeze could blow her away, Clovis could sure make a thundering entrance. As diminutive as she was, her deliberate effort to clothe herself in business-fashion garb just a tad too loose once again made her appear hopelessly lost in her own clothing. Her fluff of blond, frizzed-out hair, the very feature she thought made her a blonde bombshell, actually made her look washed out and even less substantial. For something that small and seemingly insignificant, she had a decided capacity for volume.

"Donna, there you are!" she charged right in. "How many days have you been back from that waste-of-time-excursion East without calling to check in with me? Do you really think you're going to find any valuable leads without help from me? Honestly, I don't know why I bother trying to help you! Now, probably the most important clue has revealed itself and you were nowhere to be found! Why does that not surprise me?"

She took a breath, so I jumped in. "Clovis, have you met..."

I glanced at Maria as she began shaking her head violently

from side to side, her fear filled eyes darted around. She was looking very much like a rat trapped in the back of the food cupboard. Suddenly, Maria popped up yelling "gotta go." And ran out the door so fast I thought whiplash might result. As she ran, I think I heard Maria utter something like "sorry Donna, now I get it." Clovis had struck again. In fact, I think the time from zero to sixty in Maria's enlightenment set a new land-speed record.

I wasn't sure whether to be relieved that Maria realized I wasn't nasty and psychotic, or to be afraid that I was stuck here with Clovis and no buffer of any kind. Clovis spoke again. I chose fear.

"Clovis," I interrupted her ranting diatribe. "Is there something you want to tell me?" I asked as calmly as I was able.

"Well," she resumed, and then went on to regale me with her version of all the indignities that had befallen her since I'd left for my trip east. Attempting to stay focused, I pushed aside the sweet self-preserving daydreams offering temporary escape. I had no doubt that a blessed escape now would only mean having to live through Clovis' delivery of the information for a second time.

I concentrated on filtering out the screechy and frenetic voice patterns and the narcissistic ramblings in a desperate attempt to identify a point – any point. I picked up "Warren" and "suspect," then there was "me," "me," "me," well, you get the gist. She finished with "and so I figure you owe it to me since your trip east is what caused Warren's team to lose their focus in the first place. Honestly, Donna, you could have waited to plan your visit at a time when other people wouldn't be so inconvenienced. But then, look who I'm talking to; no matter how I try to help you grow personally, that over-whelming self-centeredness of yours always rears its ugly head

– and at the very worst of times."

There. I could tell she was finished because of her tendency to end on a statement addressing my inadequacies, specifically in this instance, a rant on my self-centeredness. Hoping to take a moment in order to sift through the total garbage from the 'demand for action' garbage, I could see that thinking would only give 'Her Nibbs' the opportunity to breathe deeply and jump into the second round of her own mind-numbing narcissism so I did the unthinkable; I gave her the "just a minute" finger. Observing her stunned and indignant demeanor, it occurred to me that there would be a price to pay for that little indulgence. On the other hand, it did serve to shut her up for a glorious few seconds, giving me the chance to filter and replay her monologue in my head for the remotest hint of anything factual. Before Clovis had a chance to recover her composure, I was set to launch into my response.

"So, you want me to talk to Warren on your behalf because you have been removed from the suspect list?" I questioned – and no question has ever been more rhetorical than this! So typically Clovis. If she was off the suspect list she would cease to be at the center of the attention. That just wouldn't do.

As usual, Clovis had a way of suggesting action steps for me that I would undoubtedly be taking. As was often the case I did find myself taking her advice, but for a completely different reason than the one suiting her purpose. She was right; I needed to talk to Warren now. Not, of course, about anything having to do with the psychotic little princess in front of me and her desperate ploys for attention, but about numerous other things. To expedite my escape, I readily agreed that I would call Warren immediately upon my arrival back at the office. No need to mention that Clovis' name would probably never enter into the conversation.

Temporarily appeased by the thought that she would once again top the suspect list, Clovis wound down, enabling me to finish paying the bill. With Clovis somewhat subdued, we took our leave of Pitch and headed toward the parking lot in miraculous silence.

As we reached the sidewalk adjacent to the parking lot, a familiar SUV came blazing up the street carrying my emergency rescue crew, Peg and Babs. The moment I spotted them I knew why they were here. Being all too familiar with Clovis' style, they assumed I would need help in making my escape. God bless those two, did I mention they always had my back!

Before I had the chance to signal that things were actually under control and winding down, a series of unfortunate circumstances began to unfold. Peg had angled her enormous SUV close to the curb in order to initiate whatever ploy they had chosen to extricate me from my volatile companion. Apparently, said companion had failed to notice the sizeable vehicle barreling towards her from behind. What happened next was sure to give me nightmares for many a week to come. As the SUV neared us, Clovis realized suddenly she wasn't parked in the lot next to Pitch, but rather, directly across the street. She pivoted unexpectedly and stepped into the street, and directly into the path of Peg's approaching vehicle.

In my nightmares it always happens like this: Peg and Clovis lock eyes and realization hits them both at the same time. Clovis leaps backward, landing on our esteemed mayoral candidate, who had apparently been lunching at Pitch with potential campaign donors and had chosen that unfortunate moment to exit the building. Peg pulls her wheel slightly to the left, far enough to keep from running Clovis down, but without the necessary reduction of speed causing her vehicle to barrel directly into the nearest fire hydrant. Of course the hydrant is dislodged, unleashing a geyser of water and soaking everything within a twenty foot radius.

Not being one to sit idly by during a crisis, Babs had also sprung into action. Having realized the catastrophic potential seconds earlier than either Peg or Clovis, Babs had frantically sought a buffer between tiny little Clovis and the steel tough SUV. She chose the only solution available, bags of "stuff" in the back that Peg had picked up for a photo shoot later in the week. Grabbing every bag she could reach with a speed normally reserved for super heroes, Babs threw one after the other at Clovis and the candidate in an attempt to soften the blow.

Quick thinking on everyone's part kept our post-lunch adventure from being the tragedy it could so easily have become. Somehow that was no consolation for Clovis, who was in the process of extricating her soaking wet self from the soaking wet mayoral candidate. Making matters worse, the contents of the "buffer bags" thrown by Babs were fluttering all around having been freed from their plastic prisons upon impact. Apparently our upcoming photo shoot required mountains of feathers stuck to every visible surface, which was why they'd been treated with a light coating of dried glue. Need I describe the effect of those mountains of feathers as they landed on the soaking wet Clovis and her barely conscious political victim?

Being the kind and considerate person I am, I waited a bit before picking off the handful of feathers that had stuck to my slightly damp shoulder. I'd been fortunate, I'd managed to move away before the water and glue-covered feathers descended – and the fallen had regained their footing. My own amusement promised to outlast the new mayor's term should he manage to overcome the fallout from a 'tar and feathering' and actually get elected; and I was in good company based on a scan of the immediate area. It seems as though the only two who were not reduced to hysteria by our little encounter were Clovis and the candidate. While he was working hard to regain full consciousness and keep from choking on a face-full of feathers, Clovis had launched into an animated and vitriolic diatribe that gave her the appearance of an Indian shaman in full rain dance regalia. Unfortunately, her ire did little to quell the infectious hilarity all around. The heartier we laughed, the higher and more ear-piercing she shrieked. Our ears may have hurt, but we were unable to gain control of ourselves. In retrospect, it wasn't terribly unlike other agency events featuring livestock and funky props, and we had more of those than you might think. In fact, compared to a recent zombie photo-shoot, this was pretty tame. We worked hard in the ad biz and deserved every bit of the comic relief that so often seemed to seek us out. We could usually keep the casualties to a minimum.

Once the firefighters made the necessary repairs to the hydrant and helped clear the area of laughter and feathers, there was no point in hanging around, so we headed back. As Peg, Babs and I stepped through our small but chic lobby into the main room of the agency, Donny's head popped out of the first conference room. How does he do that, anyway?

"Hi guys," he said with a smile from ear to ear, "Wait, Donna, I'd like to shake your hand."

"Why do I think I will be sorry for asking? Why do you want to shake my hand, Donny?"

"I would shake the hand of anyone who tarred and feathered Clovis," he explained, "not to mention using her to take out that dumb-as-dirt politician in the process; that was just brilliant! Even his detractors are spreading reports that his IQ has improved by at least ten points since lunchtime. The fact that he's done anything at all is a sign that there is an IQ – don't laugh, there was doubt! I'd have to say as enjoyable as that must have been, I'd have killed to have been in the board room for his 2:00 P.M. meeting. A little bird told me he was meeting with an uber-sophisticated and elitist entertainment company from New York. He was sure that convincing them to open their next operation in Omaha would make him a shoe-in for the mayoral election."

With a focus on our unusually rich offering of chef-owned restaurants as the basis of his argument for our unexpected sophistication, he managed to persuade them that Omaha offered the best of both worlds, a surprisingly urbane population at an amazingly reasonable cost per square foot. No one could argue that a market of our size would never normally have the extraordinary dining opportunities found here. His dinner soirees had gone a long way toward impressing the self-satisfied Gotham magnates and he was expected to close the deal at today's meeting.

My contact was able to record some damning phone footage of a table full of sharks in their six-thousand dollar Saville Row suits expecting to hear from the worldly executive they had come to know as our candidate. Needless to say, aforementioned sophisticated parties were stunned to see a pseudo-sophisticated farm boy picking feathers out of pockets and shoelaces throughout his decidedly less than suave closing statement. Check it out on YouTube. It was painful to observe. I had to see it for myself to believe that the New Yorkers were all looking around for hidden cameras – convinced they'd been punk'd!

[CHAPTER 35]

After viewing the 'chicken plucking' meeting on YouTube nine or ten times, I placed a call in to Warren. She suggested we meet at a coffee shop at the end of the day to get caught up.

Peg ran over and hustled me into a conference room before my call had disconnected. We reviewed the timeline on a new business proposal currently in-play. It would require some hustle to finish on time, but what else was new?

She could see from my demeanor that I was in a rush to head out the door, so Peg used that to her advantage and assigned me three additional sections of the proposal before taking pity and releasing me.

* * *

We ordered our coffees, and then Warren apologized.

"I don't know about you, but I'd prefer a nice chardonnay right about now. Unfortunately, I have a firm rule about imbibing in any alcohol while I'm on the taxpayers' dime." Warren was looking particularly fit and fashionable in her sleek and simple dark slacks and boots with coordinating dark tailored blouse. Her long and luxurious dark hair completed the illusion of easy elegance.

"Oh please," I assured her, "don't give it another thought. Perception versus reality is the demon created by assumption and misinterpretation, then exacerbated by the reality that every phone has become a media conduit. Big Brother is here; he just came through the back door."

"Wow, that's pretty profound," Warren offered. "Who said that?"

"I guess I just did," I answered, surprised at the force of my own observation. In truth, Warren had my sympathy. I remember how careful I'd been years ago, as a high school English teacher. I would never go to dinner or out for a drink with friends in the town where I taught. I could ill afford to have students make extreme assumptions about my social life and morality. Poor Warren wasn't just limited to avoiding one small town; she had to watch herself wherever and whenever. And with the advent of social media – we were all under constant surveillance. I had to admit: lately I found myself increasingly annoyed each time I'd innocently check into Facebook only to find myself in yet another unflattering party photo that I sure as hell wouldn't have posted myself!

Deep in thought, we sipped our coffee and mentally switched gears to the present and a murder that wouldn't solve itself. Warren's focus shifted and she was ready to get down to work.

"What's new?"

With those two words the spotlight was on me. I wasn't sure I had anything that wouldn't prove to be a total waste of her time.

"Not much," I admitted. "I honestly don't know if I have anything worthwhile."

I went on to share my conversations with BJ's friends and family. Then I filled her in on my lunch with Maria and the growing realization that I'd probably make a lousy detective since evidently everyone felt compelled to lie to me; and they did it effortlessly. That thought made me wonder, had Clovis been hitting close to home in her grousing about my self-centeredness? While I was on a roll I took the opportunity to share my unfulfilled desire to find out how I fit into BJ's final "plan" and what she'd intended as my fate. Warren listened with the patience of a saint as I finished a tale of ineffectual detecting and personal frustration that reinforced my feelings of failure.

"Don't be so hard on yourself," she admonished. "Real detectives follow a path they do not control. You don't create the story behind a murder like so much of what you do in *your* world; you uncover it. And you don't uncover it on your time; the facts reveal themselves as they do. That's probably the greatest frustration for any investigator. We don't control much in our journey to the truth."

"You're nice to give me a pep talk. But I have seldom invested so much time in a project that left me feeling as though I'd accomplished nothing. You know, ironically, as much as the threatening notes I received while investigating Claire's murder scared the ever-living crap out of me, I would almost prefer the fear they evoked to these feelings of worth-lessness; at least my fear was accompanied by a sense of pride that I was making the killer nervous. At this point I'd take almost anything; I'm not even counting those stupid cryptic messages that keep cropping up – it's not even clear they're connected to the murder! "

"You say that now," Warren replied, "but trust me, the professionals don't always have much more than you do at this stage of the game. We just keep our heads down and continue collecting data until we catch a break. If I remember correctly, the threatening notes did not give you a feeling of validity so much as a feeling of victimization. Given the choice between that kind of validity or feeling frustrated that you're not filling Miss Marple's shoes – I think you're better off where you are. Besides, now that I've heard your update, I don't completely agree that your detecting has been inadequate."

"Yeah, I guess you're right," I acknowledged. "Now that you remind me, that whole victimization thing is not something I ever hope to relive, it's also possible those stupid, cryptic messages are more real than I'm willing to admit to myself."

With so many disparate details floating around it was tough to feel any sense of control. I didn't know how Warren did it. She seemed unfazed by her apparent lack of progress and was coaching me to follow suit. Maybe someday, but right now I craved validation of some sort.

"All right, what's your assessment of my snooping?" I asked against my better judgment.

"I think you got some valuable insights into a few of her closest relationships. That will help us fit pieces of the puzzle together. Sure they all lied to you about being in Omaha, did you ever stop to think the lies were more about themselves then about making you look stupid? Why would any of them want to admit they were clearly more invested in BJ than she was in any of them? They were probably embarrassed, trying to come across as caring but tough guys, ruled by logic. How much tough guy logic do you think was in a decision to run halfway across the country because they cared so much? Not to mention that a public admission of being in Omaha at the time of the murder could absolutely get someone on the suspect list when they'd clearly want to avoid that altogether. Now let me ask you, did you ask Ron if he was in Omaha at the time of the murder?"

"No."

"And did you ask WyCliff if he knew of any altercations between her visitors?"

"No."

"So they didn't lie. They took the standard path of most folks with close ties to a murder victim – the less said the better.

Your contribution was to fill in relationship details so we can get inside their heads, and your report of the coffee shop tussle helped complete the picture. In my book, you have no reason to apologize."

"Yeah, you think?" I wanted to believe her, but after feeling so gullible it was hard to accept reassurances that easily. One thing was starting to sink in, however. I could be far more productive if I took myself out of the equation. None of this was about me.

After that Warren filled me in on the odds and ends that the police had uncovered since my last "official" update. Although they were taking a much harder look at some of BJ's male friends and exes, they still believed that a female perp was most likely. I guess I was still having trouble with this theory; frankly, I just couldn't see it. Guess that's why my status is still amateur. Warren admitted that it was an unorthodox suspect list. Highest ranking suspects were, as yet, unknown, while the male suspects were all identified lower down on the list.

It felt good to get home that night. The dogs must have sensed my disquiet because they grouped around as if protecting me from a predator. Jon and I talked quietly over a glass of wine and a light dinner. He agreed with all of Warren's observations, so I resolved to reorient my focus and have the patience that professionals themselves need in order to move forward in these investigations. Was I flattering my-self by comparing my sleuthing skills to that of a professional? Most likely.

[CHAPTER 36]

I got into the office early the next day, with the thought that if I focused my mind on work and let my subconscious loose on the murder, it might help me filter through some of the known facts and sort things out. It didn't take me long to get into the groove; how long had it been since my entire focus had been on "normal" things? It felt good.

Jon Skyped me mid-morning. "I know" was all it said.

I know? What the hell...Oh no. Dammit, he solved the murder – again.

I responded. "You know who killed BJ?"

"Yes. I wrote it down and put it in a Tom Clancy novel."

Here we go again. "What took you so long?" Yeah, I know I can be a bitch!

I toyed with the idea of bugging Jon for the name, but history had taught me that he wouldn't give it up until the murder was solved. People always asked why Jon would choose to keep the information to himself rather than give me a heads-up to watch out for an individual he knew to be dangerous. Frankly, although I knew it to be flawless, Jon's murder solving prowess was not yet fully accepted by police investigators. I guessed that would take at least a few more murders – God, I really hoped it wouldn't get to that.

At any rate, Jon knew that if he gave me the name and a dire warning to steer clear of the individual in question I would find myself drawn to the murderer much as the moth is drawn to flame. Based on my history, Jon kept the name safely out of my universe as the only means of keeping me safe. I know, I know, that makes me rival for 'nut job of the year' along with some of my most distinguished but flaky colleagues; what can I say?

As my subconscious continued to work on the problem, two issues rose to the surface as hot: if the known suspect list was so male-heavy, and the police still felt fairly certain that the murderer was a woman, which of these men had been closest to the murderer? And, what had BJ planned for me? No, I couldn't completely let go of that enigma. Had those plans been a catalyst in her murder?

We knew a lot more about the whereabouts and actions of the men from BJ's Connecticut life now than we had when the possibility of a female murderer first surfaced, however, we knew virtually nothing more about the objectives behind her plan for me. Although we did know, even if she had no sinister motive for involving me in her scheme, she had more than enough reason to need an excuse for leaving Connecticut having burned more bridges than *Engineering News-Record* features in a decade.

But back to the issue at hand, had I merely been a convenient excuse after all? Perhaps, but my gut told me that was not the case. Of course, my gut rarely ever tells me I'm anything BUT integral to pretty much everything – okay, so we all have a little Clovis in us now and then; at least I have the guts to admit it! Clearly facts were going to be necessary since my instincts would prove to be somewhat less than reliable under the circumstances.

The more I thought about it, the more I thought my next action steps should focus on those issues. I would have to completely revamp my lists. Well what did you expect – gunplay? Lists and talking to people were my best shot at helping without inviting grievous bodily harm – which I fully intended on avoiding! The first list would be of the men from BJ's east coast life followed by the women they knew who had impacted her life. A refinement of the list I'd already created. I called Desiree to get some tips on how best to approach the compilation of each list. Her suggestions would save time and make me look a lot more organized. I was kind of excited to see the end product.

As I worked my way through the most recent intelligence, I would also attempt to identify the sixth guy once and for all. I felt as though things were finally starting to take shape. Instead of random lists of people who knew BJ, these lists would be comprised of real suspects, people who had exhibited unusual behavior toward BJ near the time of her death.

The second list would be a compilation of those who might know how I had fit into BJ's recent plans, if any existed. Most of the people I knew, the ones who'd been closest to her, were clueless regarding any intentions toward me. Perhaps it was time to search out some of her more recent familiars, ones I didn't know or hadn't been in touch with recently. Sure, it would be harder. They might even feel animosity toward me; that was a chance I'd just have to take. There was one addition to that second list I would resist contacting: Clovis had alluded to the fact that she knew the back story, but was not about to enlighten little old undeserving me. I found it hard to believe that BJ would have spilled her guts to Omaha's 'oracle of insanity,' but that may have been wishful thinking on my part. In retrospect, if BJ figured out that handing Clovis ammunition of such magnitude would undoubtedly cause me grief, it would be reason enough.

One might surmise that this line of thought was a waste of time, in as much as Clovis had already refused to share the alleged story with me. Those of us who knew Clovis, had a secret weapon. I'd add Clovis to the list; if I reached the point where continuing other lines of pursuit seemed futile, and it seemed that Clovis' knowledge could actually prove useful, I had merely to invite her out and get her stinking drunk. As painful as that prospect might seem, in reality it would only take about forty-five minutes before every secret I ever wanted to know – and several that I didn't – came gushing out like water from an open fire hydrant on a hot New York day! The most difficult part would be trying to forget over 70% of what did come gushing out – where is that *Men in Black* taser when you need it? Then there was the unpleasant task of seeing her safely back home without being trapped indefinitely. Should I find myself heading down that road, I would be up to the challenge!

Time to get down to work, then I'd grab a quick lunch and focus on creating my lists. Once the lists were in hand I could formulate action steps for each person I'd been able to identify.

By the time lunch rolled around, I was ready for a break. Having written a handful of answers for three different new business RFPs (request for proposal), I could no longer tell one from the other. When you get to that point, it's always best to take an enforced rest break. You never want to get confused and inadvertently respond to the RFP for an aerospace account with a complete overview of your ability to promote rock musicians. For some reason prospects frequently failed to see any similarities or relevance between themselves and your experience with anyone else – and that much of a stretch would certainly work against us! It really helped when prospects had some imagination.

I chose my favorite out-of-the-way diner and decided to stroll over since the weather was magnificent. Usually summer days in Omaha were sunny and sweltering. Not today. The temperature was in the high seventies and the humidity low.

Once outside, my mind raced through the chances of being able to stay here indefinitely. I didn't have any meetings scheduled for the afternoon. Maybe I could drag my computer out to our lounge area. The site of our recent fried chicken outing. I was getting way ahead of myself, time to grab a quick lunch and set pen to paper.

The diner was about a seven-minute walk through the old market, during which I passed a dozen or so restaurants and their al fresco diners. Figures I'd selected one of the only old market restaurants without al fresco dining – but today's lunch was more about productivity than communing with nature. With luck there'd be time for that later.

I ordered my diet plate and Diet Pepsi. Then I settled down and got busy. The first potential suspect list consisted of the core men in BJ's life. Included were her first ex-Ron, her son Mickey and his friend, her second ex-WyCliff, her ex-boyfriend and transition lover, Porter Enzo. I had a sneaking feeling Lou Cavrola should also be on the list, but we'd need further evidence to know for sure. I gave some thought to how we'd pin that down. I was pretty sure Warren and her crew would know in due time even without help from me. Why not let Warren do her job and stay clear? Man, that was hard for a control freak with no patience and a firm hold on paranoia, like me!

As I considered my options, I realized Cavrola was probably on my second list, too. This lunch was proving to be tons more productive than I'd even hoped. By randomly juxtaposing the two lists, my subconscious had cris-crossed the subject matter I'd been thinking of as separate and largely unrelated; I may have inadvertently stumbled upon an important resource for BJ's deepest darkest plans. Who better than Cavrola would be privy to any destructive or potentially damaging subplots concocted by BJ? Wasn't he the guy who helped her devise all of those crooked money-making (more like money stealing) schemes they'd shared during their partnership? Clearly BJ had not openly shared her amoral side with the majority of her friends and acquaintances. I had to get to Cavrola!

Once my mind was set it all seemed so clear. Climbing into the dark side of her mind would mean communicating with the business partner of her 'dark side.' It felt right and suddenly I felt brilliant. Before allowing myself to head back to the office so I could strut my overinflated head around in front of an audience, I was determined to finish the first list and capture the women with close ties to these men I'd listed.

This part of the list would be more difficult. After spending a large portion of the morning on WyCliff, I still had no women to add to the list near his name. Just for the hell of it I added his first wife, what's her name, although I didn't for a moment believe that she was relevant to anything. I had to forcibly prevent myself from editing out some names before feeling certain I'd even captured the majority of them. I really had no way of knowing BJ's relationship with WyCliff's ex. For all I knew they could have had a history of violence against each other. I'd always had the sense that his ex was a bit unfeeling, but that she was a smart lady and a good mom. As for BJ, that alone could be enough to make her hate the woman; her hostility was anything but rational.

I took another fifteen minutes to list the obvious women: son Mickey's rejected wife, ex hubby Ron's lovely new wife, Sheila. I didn't think any of Mickey or Ron's former girlfriends would be relevant. It would make sense to find out about women in Enzo's and WyCliff's lives. I needed to know more about Mickey's buddy and any women in his world, and while I was grilling Cavrola about nefarious schemes I would try to scope out any women in his life. That would finish list 1; I would work my way through and Cavrola would be my first stop.

The best part of that was, even though there hadn't been time to create list two during lunch, Cavrola would probably end up being the most important person on the list anyway, so talking to him would kill two major birds with one stone.

I rushed back to the office with a renewed sense of purpose. Spending the afternoon out front while answering yet another batch of RFP questions turned out to be relatively painless, except, of course, for one gust of wind that blew some pages of the aerospace RFP around the side of the building. My amusement over the fact that this RFP had taken flight provided enough relief from the tension to enable me to buckle down and get the remaining questions answered. When I shared my hilarious aerospace observation with Liv, she pursed her lips and rolled her eyes. Guess she'd had enough of answering RFP's too.

[CHAPTER 37]

By the end of the day I was feeling invigorated. The fact that I hadn't previously considered Cavrola as a key source of information probably meant I was too close to this thing to be effective; luckily, I was pretty sure I could make up for lost time now that I'd zeroed in on my source. I'd go home, pour a glass of Kim Crawford and begin to compile a list of questions to ask Cavrola, while I waited for Jon to prepare our dinner (I was pretty sure Jon would be on board with this plan). As anxious as I was to move forward and debrief Cavrola, I was also a bit reluctant. If I rushed into our conversation and came up empty, it would be a major letdown. The longer I stalled and dragged this out, the more time I had to believe the solution was just around the corner. Hell, I own an ad agency; I dream big!

The drive home went by in a flash. I even forgot to call Jon and fill him in on my pre-dinner plans. Not a problem, though; once past the bulldog greeters it took less than a minute to get Jon up to speed on my proposed agenda.

He got to cooking. I poured wine and sat down with my iPad. It wasn't easy to concentrate; Jon's impromptu meal smelled like heaven. This was my favorite kind of evening at home, sipping a lovely wine with Jon, in anticipation of a gourmet feast while wrestling with an interesting puzzle, all the while surrounded by my precious bulldogs. I was so very content. That's when the phone rang. Jon and I exchanged looks. His said, it's probably a telephone marketer, but would you check to be sure? Mine said, we both know this is nothing, but I have to make sure. I abandoned my seat at the kitchen counter and grabbed the phone on the desk next to the wine fridge.

A quick glance suggested we were both wrong. The caller ID indicated it was a Connecticut caller whose number I didn't recognize on sight. That meant it could be a business call for Jon. He still maintains many of his business contacts in the Northeast; in fact they're a fairly significant part of his commercial finance business. Although normally I wouldn't answer one of Jon's business calls, the hour meant either it wasn't for his business or it was some sort of problem – either way, best to get it.

"Hi, Donna? Donna Leigh?" began a tentative, youngish male voice that was completely unfamiliar to me. "This is Mickey Thornton." A moment passed (I don't know, it could have been an hour) while I worked to slow my rapid breathing.

"Donna, are you there?"

"Oh, yes, sorry, Mickey, you just caught me off guard," I replied.

"Yeah, I figured hearing from me would be kind of shocking for you," he admitted. "I just couldn't think of a better way to introduce myself in order to lessen the shock factor, and I needed to talk to you."

"Oh no, Mickey," I assured him, "I'll be fine. It was just that initial surprise."

I know you can't judge a book by its cover, but I thought Mickey seemed like a really nice guy. Stupid, huh? Making that kind of assumption based on so little. It was just something about the way he sounded, and I realized that surprised me. Why? I guess because BJ had been so unlikeable and Ron had been so likeable that I must have assumed there was at least a 50/50 chance Mickey took after his overbearing Mom. Before we even got into the reason for his call, I already felt guilty.

The poor guy had just lost his mother, a mother who had turned on him and treated him badly in her last few months. On top of everything I didn't like her, which made me feel even guiltier. Again, stupid. But you can't help how you feel. Maybe I was less ready for this conversation than I thought. No point in speculating; my curiosity would never allow me to postpone hearing what BJ's son had to say!

"I called you for a few reasons," he began more sure of himself now. "I'm just gonna be blunt if that's okay. I'm afraid some of this will seem really bizarre; I don't want to freak you out."

"Mickey, after everything I've seen and heard over the past year or so, I'm having a harder time believing the things that don't sound bizarre. Does that make any sense?"

"Ya know, it really does," countered Mickey, "that makes me feel as though calling you out of the blue might not have been a stupid move. Thanks for helping put me at ease; you certainly don't owe me, or anyone in my family for that matter."

He ended on a note that sounded decidedly bitter. I felt a pang for him. Man, this guy had really been through it.

"Mickey," I responded, "if there is anything I can do to help you and your family, please know that it would give me great pleasure."

"God, Donna. I really didn't know what to expect when I called, but it sure as hell wasn't this. Thank you."

"What can I do for you, Mickey?"

He took a moment and cleared his throat, "I want to start by apologizing...."

"Mickey, no, no need to–" I interrupted.

"Donna," he cut me off compassionately, "please let me say this."

"Of course, Mickey." I didn't need an apology, but maybe he did.

"I want to apologize for my mother's strange behavior in the months before her death. I will probably never truly understand so many of the bizarre decisions that she made in those days. Why she chose to involve you is a mystery to me, but I may be one of the few people with even a small insight into that particular choice."

He knew something about how I fit into her plan. With any luck, if we combined what he knew with my own knowledge of her character and our history, we'd pin this sucker down! I was excited at the prospect of finally getting some answers! Now I just had to be patient and let Mickey finish his commentary. It would be a mistake to rush him no matter how impatient I was feeling.

"There's more to apologize for." I waited.

"I didn't know until after Mom died how crappy she was to you years ago. You probably knew she was pretty unbalanced. I never really got how messed up she was until just a few months before she died. I guess she did her best to keep me away from all that crazy stuff she did. You probably won't believe it but she seemed to set her sights on you most of all. I couldn't tell you why."

"I'm not really sure how to respond to that," I said.

"I can imagine, it must be so weird to be the victim of seemingly random hostility. As far as I've been able to figure, it's not like you did anything to warrant her wrath," he added.

"Wow, I'm impressed, Mickey. I wouldn't think most people would take the time to figure out whether or not I had any culpability. You're an amazing guy. So much of that stuff happened before you were old enough for nursery school; in fact some of it was even before you were born. You certainly have nothing to apologize for."

"Now that's where you're wrong," Mickey countered.

"Granted, it should be Mom herself apologizing to you, but since that's not possible, it falls on my shoulders. I'm not about to shirk my responsibilities, especially since, on some level, I've been aware, but blissfully feigning ignorance, of my Mom's path of destruction through the years."

So far this conversation had been both surprising and enlightening. If I'd thought I liked Mickey when he first called, I was sure now. I was, however, starting to wonder if restitution would be the extent of my enlightenment from this conversation. It was difficult to suppress the urge to push him into jumping ahead. He would get there in his own time; patience. Maybe it would be foolish to push him at this point, but I could at least participate in the conversation.

"Where did this information about my history with your mom come from anyway?" I asked.

"Everywhere," he responded to my surprise. "As the details of her move to Omaha began to unfold there were versions that included plans with, and for, you. Once your name came up, it was a field day. Apparently many colleagues from your days at Mylar had remembered her atrocious treatment of you. Even Dad knew some of it. People weren't afraid to share the sordid details with me because it had been fairly common knowledge that she and I had had some serious problems. Ironically, I think a lot of the people who shared details of your early relationship with Mom were openly sharing them with me so I could feel better about my own bad treatment. As odd as that might seem, it did result in my feeling something of an affinity toward you; that's the other part of the reason I'm calling."

This was definitely getting interesting. I wasn't sure how I felt about it yet. Talk about mixed emotions! I would have to chew on this for a while in order to sort it all out. But no matter where my thoughts ultimately landed, they would not deter my feelings of admiration for Mickey. The guy had guts! Suddenly I wasn't feeling so impatient. Letting Mickey work his way through his agenda would be just fine. We'd get there eventually.

"I guess that probably seems odd to you," he continued, "the fact that I could develop an affinity for someone I really don't know at all."

"No, actually it doesn't, Mickey," I volunteered. "As long as we're being so candid with each other, I'll admit that I'm amazed at how well you seem to be doing, considering what your upbringing must have been like."

"Yeah, true," he sighed, "very true."

"I'd like to help if I can, Mickey."

"Thanks. I'll get back to that after I share what little I know about her thoughts on you and the relationship you had."

I sighed. He continued.

"As I was growing up, my mom would mention you occasionally," he shared. "Sometimes she would paint a picture of you as an incompetent moron who needed her help and guidance in order to remain employed. During those times she would complain bitterly of the amount of her time wasted in protecting and guiding you in muddling through your re-sponsibilities." Now I was getting pissed off! Goddamn that bitch! One thing was clear, she and Clovis had far more in common than I'd realized. Before my thoughts catapulted me into a full-fledged tantrum, Mickey continued.

"The other times were almost more bizarre. I'm talking about the times when she would mention you as a lost friend, or close relative; someone she missed almost desperately. You're probably thinking that the disparity in her feelings for you should have alerted me that she was hardly 'cooking on all four burners'. Well, I can't dispute that. But I can say I thought of her as a woman who had a close colleague she sometimes remembered for the challenges, and other times for the positive aspects of their association. Did I think of her as moody and even capricious? Hell yes! But from my vantage point, that didn't appear all that unusual when I thought about the changing nature of most close relationships between people."

"Of course, you're right," I acknowledged, shaking my head at my own ability to forget human nature and its capriciousness. "But Mickey, do you know anything about my involvement in her move to Omaha?"

"I was just getting to that, I thought it would help to fill you in on how she vacillated regarding your relationship over the years." I nodded my head in agreement (it was irrelevant that he was unable to see my reaction through the phone – apparently he knew what was in my head). "I really believe that part of her decision to move to Omaha was because she had a delusional idea that you really needed and wanted her out here. At times she seemed to feel that you were her only hope at success and any chance of security. I think that was when she was at her most delusional."

"Really?" was all I could get out. Legendary conversationalist, I!

"Then there were the other times," he confessed, "and those times were considerably darker."

"There was a good side and a bad side?" I recapped in my typically brilliant deductive style.

"Yeah, Donna. There were times when her intentions were clearly geared toward hurting you, in some way. It was very much like Jekyll and Hyde. She was going to 'get you'. I just never found out how."

I gulped. Then I gulped again.

"Of course you are aware that leaving Connecticut made perfect sense under the circumstances. The wolf was unquestionably at her door. Her lies and deceit were coming to light and many of us would be looking for retribution. If only she'd made an arbitrary decision to move to Omaha, or any market, and not try to tie it to you based purely on delusion – whether positive or negative."

"Hmph." More brilliant conversation!

"Donna?" he asked tentatively.

"Still here, Mickey, sorry that was a lot to digest," I admitted, "but I really appreciate your sharing this information with me. Now tell me what I can do to help you."

"Really, you still want to help me after all that?" he asked.

"More than ever," I shared as my voice and my resolve strengthened.

"Well, if you really mean that, I'd appreciate the opportunity to talk some things out with you," he ventured.

"Mickey, I can honestly say that I would be honored to be your sounding board if there are things you'd like to discuss." I was floored! I took it as a huge compliment under the circumstances.

"Thank you. I've taken up enough of your time tonight, but I sure appreciate the opportunity to call you back another time and just talk a bit. I know that sounds crazy, all things considered, but I think it could be good for both of us."

"You're probably right," I agreed. It would really be cathartic to talk things out with someone who knew BJ so well. There was virtually no one else who really knew her with whom I could talk openly. No one in Omaha knew her – not even the 'great and wonderful' Clovis knew her all that well, despite her claims to the contrary. The folks in Connecticut who knew her might not be thrilled to hear some of the things I'd have to say about BJ. Ironically, her son was the only person I was sure really got it, and it made me feel I could let my hair down without having to worry about tripping over myself in the process.

"You know, it's not that I don't have anyone to talk to," Mickey started to make excuses. "I have a great wife and a wonderful step-mom who will talk through anything with me. They're just too close to this whole thing."

"Well, that's certainly understandable," I offered.

"Yeah, I think they're too close to all of the drama with Mom," he added. "Now that sounds silly too. No one was closer to this mess than you were, but I don't get the feeling that you've been affected by everything as obviously as they have."

"Thanks, I'll take that as a compliment," I chimed in. "I always like to think things don't get to me; more times than not I come out on the short end of that, though. I can see why your wife would have trouble removing herself enough to be objective. You two have been through so much, and at a time when your parents should be congratulating and helping you with your new little one. As far as your stepmom goes, based on some of your dad's comments, it sounds as though Sheila was incredibly charitable toward your mom."

"Oh sure, on the whole, Sheila is truly one of the nicest people I've ever met. She has been wonderful to me; she really filled a hole in my life when my own mom wasn't there for me. But lately things have started getting to Sheila."

"How so?" Jeez, I hadn't caught a hint of that from either Ron or Sheila when we spoke. I was really losing my touch. I found it hard to believe they were both such consummate actors they could fool me so easily, yet the facts were the facts!

"I guess it started when mom had one of those 'switch to negative' moods with Sheila. You know, like she had with you when I was growing up. She started bad-mouthing Sheila to anyone who would listen. Some of the stuff was pretty bad.

When Sheila was asked to leave her church group it was quite a shock. After a little bit of detective work, they were able to figure out that the request was a result of some rumors Mom had spread about Sheila's past. Seems she told her hairdresser that Sheila had been an au pair for some wealthy families, which was true. What Mom also told her was that there'd been several instances of household theft during each of Sheila's au pair gigs, and worse yet, she insisted that Sheila had broken up the marriage of every one of the couples. Both allegations were untrue, but enough of the couples were divorced to make it seem plausible. What we're not sure of is if Mom knew that her hairdresser's mom was in Sheila's church group."

"Oh Jesus, that really sucks. She could really do some damage, damn her!"

"No Kidding! I'm guessing you've only seen the tip of the iceberg. I hate to say it, but you're lucky someone put an end to Mom before she got to you."

Wow, that poor guy. My heart really broke for him. It must be awful to know that you have some of those genes – and so does your precious new baby.

"Anyway, that was a wake-up call for Sheila. Not everyone is good down deep. In retrospect, she was fine with being out of the group since they'd proved how small minded they were when they booted her out. The whole thing changed her though, killed some of her irrepressible love for mankind. That was sad to see. Then, when Dad suggested they start paying some of Mom's expenses, I don't think he realized just how heavy a blow he'd dealt Sheila. Oh she acted like she loved the idea 'cause she believed it was a wonderful and generous gesture on behalf of my dad. She never wanted to discourage his caring and kindness, but seeing their hard earned money go to Mom was a bitter pill to swallow. I don't think Dad even noticed, but for the first time since I've known Sheila, I've heard her make some derogatory comments, and they've sounded bitter. I know, too, that Sheila had been counting on remodeling their kitchen. The money that went to Mom put those plans on hold indefinitely. Sheila's such a great person she'd never complain to Dad."

"Sheila's a freakin' saint!" I agreed, "Oh gee, Mickey, I'm sorry, that was so rude!"

"No, that's a lot of the reason why I'm looking forward to our conversations, I've been told you don't hold back. I need that!"

Mickey and I said good-bye after scheduling our next conversation. I would really look forward to it. Mickey was awesome.

Once back in the kitchen, I realized I'd been on the phone with Mickey for about an hour and a half. I tracked down Jon and the dogs and apologized for interrupting our evening, an evening for which Jon had worked hard to prepare a sensational meal. In typical Jon fashion, he announced he'd fed the dogs and put our dinner on warm so it would be ready when I was. We poured another glass of wine and sat down to a feast – just what I needed! As I filled him in on my call with Mickey, I realized I'd neglected to ask about a million key questions. Oh, well, better to wait until next time anyway. There was already plenty going on in our conversation without my interrupting to interject a bunch of questions. Undoubtedly there'd be other opportunities for that.

[CHAPTER 38]

It was Friday. I was looking forward to the weekend. If today turned out to be a little slower than the rest of the week, I'd try to get to Le Voltaire for the weekly Friday lunch and wine tasting. It's such a rare treat for me. Lunch goes from about 1:00 to 3:00; everyone brings a bottle of wine they think will be interesting to share – and we sample. Even if you go with the intention of holding back, everyone is so gracious and generous that if your glass sits empty for a moment, and you blink, the next time you look it will magically have refilled, and we all concur that wasting good wine is unthinkable! The opportunity to sample impressive wine with the world-class food that is always featured is very much like dining in Europe. After a hectic week, the prospect of that escape was very appealing. I would gratefully leave the nine-to-five world in my rearview mirror.

I ate my breakfast and fed the bulldogs. After showering, I dressed in black jeans and t-shirt, topped off with a black tailored jacket. Black shoes and simple black and silver accessories completed my ensemble. I was ready for Friday.

Traffic was light. Omaha was ready for the weekend. It had rained overnight, but I could tell the sky would clear by ten and it would be another magnificent day. That's one thing I love about Omaha. You can wake up to pouring rain and be looking out the window at blinding sunshine before 10:30. That never happened back East. Out there when you woke up to rain your only thought was "please make this rain last for today only."

Since moving here I have often theorized about why so

many folks back East were quick to snap. Even though I have not found scientific data to support my theory, I believe that the sun shines more in Omaha; the sky is sunny most of the time – hardly ever cloudy and gloomy. I know, for a fact, the nice weather lasts longer here, it starts early to mid-April and goes through mid-to late October compared to back East where the warm weather is from May through early to mid-September. Weather conditions and lifestyle benefits (such as, you can really have a life) make Omaha a place that just plain feels better. Ironically, friends back East have noted my sunnier personality, but are clinging to their East coast gloomy skies nonetheless.

Arriving at the office, I hustled to get through all of the "hotter" issues on my plate. I was anxious to track down Cavrola, and still manage to escape for that much needed break with good friends. Maybe I was expecting too much. Time would tell.

Once Peg was satisfied I had completed all my mandatory tasks, I sat down to finish some correspondence and put out a few fires. Pressing issues were resolved in time for our Executive Committee meeting. We raced through our agenda in under two hours – that might be a record – and were adjourned by noon. Now I had to make a decision. Should I try to reach Cavrola or back burner my curiosity and head to lunch? Ah hell, Cavrola was probably at a client lunch; besides, he'd be there later. I bolted for Le Voltaire!

That gave me another thirty minutes to clear up questions that had arisen since the Exec Committee meeting. Miraculously, I breezed through questions on HR policy, parking dilemmas and the action plan for the leak over Pope's workstation in record time, so I grabbed my purse and headed for the door. As I drove down Thirteenth Street for the trip west, I started to mentally replay last night's conversation with Mickey. BJ had clearly become more delusional than the folks around her realized. It helped me come to terms with the total fabrication involving me, and the one that revolved around her dating Mario.

I had to remember to call Mario and let him know the authorities were unlikely to doubt him once they knew of Mickey's observations and concerns. And then there was Mickey. I found myself feeling very maternal toward him. That was a bizarre place to be. As a woman who's never had kids, the majority of my maternal potential was used up on dogs. Being someone who very much wanted to "give back," any maternal sensibilities were generally geared toward rescue dogs. Having maternal feelings for a human was alien to me. It's not like I never had them, I had nieces and nephews and friends and neighbors, but it didn't come naturally. Having maternal feelings toward a grown man who was also the son of the women I disliked probably more than anyone else in the world – felt weird.

If I separated Mickey from his background and birth family, it seemed like the most natural thing in the world. There it was. I'd go with that. Looking at it from that angle actually made it feel right.

By the time I resolved my maternal awkwardness I had arrived at 156th Street. A luncheon escape would help get my head back on straight.

Walking through the door I spotted the group immediately. Tessa greeted me and the group began to take notice, one by one. Their initial surprise at my arrival immediately turned to a heartfelt greeting – I felt more popular than Norm walking into *Cheers*!

The group was on the small side today; sometimes it was

best that way. I started at the head of the table and worked my way down, greeting everyone. I greeted the French folks with the customary bisous to each cheek, or the double bisous depending on their preference, and the Americans with anything from a nod, a handshake, a hug, a buss on the cheek or a slap on the back. As I finished the rounds I looked up to find Belinda steering toward an empty seat. It was great to see Belinda Mountblanc and Jules LePlage (Phillippe's son) since they didn't always make it to lunch, either. They were renovating their house, which took most of their free time. That and their beautiful dogs. They had a few lovely large dogs and were very good canine parents. Those dogs were treated like royalty. You know, the way all dogs should be treated!

Jules' dad, Phillippe, sat at the other end of the table with Olivier's mom, Suzette. They chatted away in French while Jeannie proudly followed their dialogue. At one point, Suzette turned to ask Jeannie's opinion during a particularly animated part of the conversation.

"Oh, thanks Suzette," Jeannie mumbled in English, "I have to concentrate on listening when you go this fast, don't ask me to respond, too." Suzette and Phillippe smiled and continued on with their banter; they were proud of Jeannie's progress and would let her join in at her own pace.

Although Desiree's work schedule had prohibited her from breaking free to attend this week's Friday lunch, that didn't deter her mom, Annabelle, who sat next to Belinda and regaled her with stories of her own DIY renovations as a long-time landlord and home owner. I may have been mistaken, but it appeared that a particularly nasty rendition of an overflowing toilet, one that had to be broken in order to be replaced, was making Belinda a little green around the gills. As if he sensed her discomfort, Olivier appeared at just that moment carrying a platter of lamb sausage. I picked the right day to come; lamb sausage *Merguez* was a rare treat for me. Ironically, Phillippe and Olivier were just a tad embarrassed whenever the Americans made such a fuss over the rare delicacy.

"We eat *Merguez* like Americans eat hot dogs," they told the crowd. "It's no big deal."

Ah, but it was a big deal. I'm not saying that I don't crave a really good hot dog once in a while; you know, one heaped with sautéed onions and peppers or sauerkraut and...okay you get my drift, but these lamb sausages were "to die for." No hot dog was ever quite that good, not even the all-beef Kosher ones!

As we simultaneously decided on our first pour and sampled the lamb treats, we settled into conversation with the people closest around us. At first, the seat next to me was empty, but it quickly filled with a new arrival, Pascal. Pascal is a very handsome, very fit Frenchman with an ex-wife and a daughter in France and an ex-wife and a son here in the U.S. He's a wonderful and loving father who works very hard, spends time with his kids and spends a great deal of time keeping himself fit. Pascal is also the perfect dinner party guest. He dresses impeccably – his chic and stylish wardrobe are an asset at any party, he makes the perfect choice of foods and liquor to bring his hosts and he can hold an interesting conversation with absolutely anyone.

Pascal tends to come across as very serious. Upon first meeting him, I got the impression that he had no interest in making my acquaintance – which would, of course, be his choice. After having been thrown together under a variety of circumstances, I'd come to realize he was one of the most interesting and enjoyable people to be around. While so many never got beyond niceties and platitudes, Pascal could find an interesting topic and really engage you in conversation versus talking trivialities at you.

I tried a Sauvignon Blanc from California. It was okay. This crew knows I favor white wines for sipping, and some of them know Kim Crawford Sauvignon Blanc is my favorite. As a result, whenever I make it to lunch, my end of the table ends up being the white wine repository. Typically, however, there aren't a whole lot of whites at these luncheons. During times when whites are scarce there are always offers to rectify the situation. I've taken to explaining that "I'm remarkably flexible when it comes to drinking!" The truth is, I'd rather drink a red wine than a white I don't like. I tend to have more of a tolerance for a wider variety of reds, and I drink them a lot more slowly – which is probably not a bad thing.

At the other end of the table, I could see Don gearing up to make a table-wide announcement. He wanted to make us aware that there would be a charity wine tasting in two weeks and was encouraging us to attend. Aside from great company and amazing food and wine, our group does more than its fair share of charitable support and giving. Among us we support a whole host of charitable causes, and to the extent possible, we try to have fun doing it. That's not as easy as it sounds; some of those events are dry as dust.

Often leaders of these organizations are so intent on making potential donors aware of the horrors of the medical or social disease in question they manage to scare and depress everyone into funereal behavior – not the best demeanor at a gala event! People still give; but they don't often come away with fond memories of the evening. These events often equate to "torture in formal dress." To many, formal dress is torture in and of itself, but those well-meaning charity heads can take the mood to a level that makes attendees vow never to return! After receiving the requisite head nods – the group was in, we'd support his event – Don went back to his pleasant luncheon conversation.

Our next course was duck confit. The tiny roast potatoes and brussel sprouts with carrots – also roasted – were superb. No wonder the table was a bit heavier with whites today. The group must have known poultry would be on the menu. Personally, I rarely mind drinking red with fish and poultry or white with beef – as long as they're reds and whites I like. I know that most feel a heavy red overshadows lighter fare, and a more timid white is lost among the bold food tastes of a hearty hunk of beef. On occasion I have experienced the great benefit of pairing just the right wine with the perfect meal, but for the most part, I just want good food with good wine.

My husband, Jon, is one of the few people I know who really enjoys a fine sweet wine. Uninitiated wine drinkers often scoff at anything sweet that isn't served with the dessert course. Jon believes, as do many experts, that a sweet white is best with sushi and foie gras. I still prefer Kim Crawford Sauvignon Blanc – a delightful spring-like fruity blend of grapefruit and apple, decidedly not sweet – with either food. When pressed I can truly enjoy a hearty plum wine with sushi. You won't read this anywhere else – it's not as though I'm considered an expert in wine and food pairing – in fact, I'd venture to say that no one thinks of me that way! Although there's no one who would argue that the most important factor in wine and food pairing is knowing what you like – and drinking it!

Jules and I teased each other about working too hard. Neither of us were able to get to Friday lunch often enough. Once Jon and Olivier jumped into the conversation talk turned wine-specific and I settled down to listen and pick up what I could. Sensing that my proactive role in the conversation had waned, Pascal ventured into, as yet, uncharted territory.

"Have you found yourself more involved in this recent murder than you were in Claire's because of your prior relationship with the victim?" asked Pascal.

Had this been anyone else I would have tensed up immediately. Pascal was different. His interests were neither prurient nor superficial; he really wanted to understand as much as possible about the murder and its impact on me. He would be a sounding board and offer pragmatic advice if the occasion called for it. He would not pompously throw out directives, acting as if he had been the head of the Sûreté Nationale for years; lord knows I see enough of that ridiculous self-aggrandizing behavior more than I'd care to mention! Being reminded of the murder wasn't as concerning as Claire's murder had been – at least not yet – it was more the repetition of answering the same four or five questions for everyone with whom I conversed these days. It was unrelenting. Even Pascal's opening question was a relief from the standard: "How well did you know her," "Do the police think you did it?" "Do you think they'll arrest you?" "Are you close to finding the murderer?"

I spent some time reviewing what I knew with Pascal. He was sharp and didn't need much of a picture painted in order to grasp the whole situation. By the end of my briefing I could tell he had misgivings.

"What?" I asked dreading a response that would send me into a bout of paranoia.

"It's the most difficult thing," Pascal proclaimed. "Dealing with an unbalanced person makes it virtually impossible to use logic in order to find the solution, and without logic, what have we?"

"You make an excellent point, Pascal. My logic seems to be getting me nowhere and yet I find it impossible to abandon."

"Of course, Donna, there is no alternative but to continue

to employ logic," he stated. "However, one must not overlook the bizarre sidetrack, keeping so closely to the trail of logic that veering off into the absurd is not possible. That is, I believe, your best chance at finding your solution – the bizarre side-track that is a direct offshoot of the logic trail."

"Pascal, that's brilliant! You're absolutely right! I cannot become so focused on logic nor so lost in absurdity that I'm unable to see when they are closely connected! That will surely be the sweet spot in solving BJ's murder. I have to look at things differently."

Pascal was beaming – modestly – as I continued on about his contribution to my thought process. He was exactly right, though. The answer could be just before my eyes and I would still miss it because it was unlikely to fit into the way my brain processed data – so I would undoubtedly look right past it, missing it altogether. He was right, but thinking differently was easier said than done!

At the very end of the meal, as we were all getting up to make our departures, Phillippe sidled up to me to ask, "Are you finding that the family appears to be more likely suspects than her business acquaintances?"

"Very honestly, Phillippe, I'm not seeing an abundance of evidence pointing in that direction any more than the other."

"Trust me, Donna, you will."

All in all I had a wonderful lunch. I decided to head home to try reaching Cavrola, rather than make the trek back to the office in time for a 'Friday's at Four' celebration I would be unable to join due to what I hoped would be a lengthy and informative phone conversation.

[CHAPTER 39]

Le Voltaire was so close to home it took less than five minutes from the time I departed to when I pulled into the garage. I made sure the door was closed so the onslaught of welcome bulldogs spilling out into the garage was safely contained. We are very careful about letting 'the girls' out front without leashes; with a bulldog you never know what might peak their interest, the scamper of a bunny rabbit or the flight of a bird, or possibly even the presence of a neighboring dog playing with a ball that they are certain must have been stolen from them. It's possible they'll sit by the nearest tree and keep guard over the squirrel population, but you can't take that chance. On the rare occasion when we let our girls out front they are usually very good about responding to direction – except when they're not. They don't call bulldogs stubborn for nothing; your directive is subordinate to anything and everything that might reasonably distract them, like the whole world.

After my effusive welcome home, I sat with them on the family room floor while they paraded by me with a variety of toys. When the toys got old they made their way over for scratches and kisses followed by play-fighting (bulldogs are such show-offs) and were eventually tired enough to lay down for a snooze. Rituals are so important! And, truth be told, they're comforting, even to humans.

I figured I'd grab my iPad and the nearest phone. I would track Cavrola down. It shouldn't be too difficult since I knew who he was, what he did and where he did it. Sure enough, in about two minutes I had a telephone number. I know I have an address book with all of my Connecticut contacts, but it's been so many years since I've seen it I was better off starting cold. I punched the number into my phone and "dammit" got a voicemail. I might have known. I left an 'upbeat and anxious to reconnect' message in my most sincere voice; it was a lot tougher recording the expected 'so sorry to hear about poor BJ' portion. I resigned to wait for a call back. Luckily, I didn't have long to wait; he must have been screening calls. I answered after two rings.

"Hello, Donna? Donna, is that you?" The sound of Lou's voice really brought me back. I'd first met Lou when I was very wet behind the ears; he was a force of nature in our industry, someone I could learn from but not completely trust. He was an important part of my early career and my youth.

"Yeah, Lou, it's me," I confirmed so we could move on. "How's it going?"

"You know me, Donna, same ole, same ole," he droned his response in the way he always answered that basic question, and then, "really somethin' about BJ, huh?"

"No kidding, Lou, you must be hurting pretty badly, I would think." I tried to sound sincere, although my sympathies did lie elsewhere.

"I'm all right," he reassured me. "It's her son my heart's bleedin' for. Poor guy got a rough break."

"That's putting it mildly," I acknowledged.

" 'Course, you almost took a pretty sizeable hit yourself there, girl," he returned. And I thought I was being provocative. Oh well, he opened the can, now it was up to me to shoo that big clump of worms out into the daylight.

"Yeah, Lou, that's what I need to know. What hit was coming my way?" I cut to the chase, what the hell.

Nothing. That was a first. In all the years I've know Cavrola I've never known him to remain silent after an opening – or even if there was nothing remotely resembling an opening. Lou had been the king of Southeastern Connecticut's community theater – not exactly a major theatrical enclave. Down around Candlewood Lake in Danbury, Lou was the character actor extraordinaire. He was loud and dramatic and never ceased to call attention to himself and whoever he was near. I can recall with vivid clarity numerous occasions when I was lucky enough to be caught in the 'Lou spotlight.'

There was that one incredibly embarrassing BMA Christmas party. BMA stands for Business Marketing Association. Back then, Lou and I were both long-standing members. Knowing how much Lou enjoyed theater, I casually mentioned during the cocktail hour that my husband and I had recently seen *Guys and Dolls*. Much to my dismay, in the midst of a room crowded with BMA holiday revelers (a lot like the dance of the living dead), Lou cleared an imaginary space on the floor, knelt down and started shooting invisible craps as he sang and choreographed the entire scene to the vocals of "Luck Be a Lady Tonight."

Fortunately, most of our members had known Lou for years; they'd come to expect his impromptu performances. Regardless, I did my best to sink into the floorboards. It didn't work; I'd just have to wait for my chance and make a break for it. Turns out this was his signature number – how was I supposed to know he'd played Nathan Detroit on so many occasions? He belted out every word of that whole show tune. He was entranced. Once finished, his beaming countenance was much like that of a Tony recipient and not at all the look of an aging, overlooked, community theater devotee. One glance around the room told me that I was his only – albeit under duress – audience. Apparently he saw something different. You had to love his joie de vivre!

"Lou?"

"Oh, Donna," he sighed, "I don't suppose telling you could hurt anyone now."

"Yeah, Lou," I urged, "It could really help me deal with this thing. Not only has someone I know been brutally and unthinkably murdered" – *unthinkable in the grievous travesty which had occurred to desecrate one of the true pinnacles of beauty in our time, I mean, who would mangle a perfectly good Christian Louboutin that way? Is it just me or am I starting to get seriously twisted?* "I've also got to worry about what damaging scenario she may have set into motion before being murdered. I don't mind admitting to being a little paranoid here; you can see my point can't you?"

"Yeah, I can," he acknowledged. "You have a right to know. I owe you that much."

"Well, thank you, Lou, I'm glad you finally see the logic." I just had to get that last word in. I couldn't keep my big mouth shut!

"Only I worry about any backlash on her boy, Mickey." Skepticism had crept back into his voice.

"Yeah, but Lou--"

"Don't worry, Donna, I've already made up my mind to share what I know with you."

I sighed a huge sigh of relief. I needed to know. I don't think I realized just how much until this very moment.

"I'll start at the beginning," he began. I kept my mouth shut and waited. It occurred to me that the more monologue and the less dialogue, the more productive our phone call would be. If I could just keep my mouth shut!

"You know that BJ, WyCliff, and I were business partners

of a sort?" he began. I remained mute and he continued.

"I'm guessing you've heard that we weren't exactly on the up and up in all of our dealings. I'm not going to deny it, but I want you to know that in retrospect, I'm not feeling very proud of myself," he confessed.

Now I had to say *something*. I couldn't just leave the poor guy flapping in the wind wondering how disgusted I was feeling, wondering if I might mention his admission to the officials on BJ's case.

"Listen, Lou," I assured him, "Frankly, none of that matters unless it impacts me directly. If you've done nothing to hurt me, you have nothing to fear from me."

He chuckled, which seemed odd. Perhaps BJ wasn't the only one who'd taken leave of her senses in that partnership. I waited to see where this was going. Clearly he was trapped in his own ruminations; I thought waiting him out would be best. After a minute or so he continued in a somewhat more whimsical manner "Ah, I needed that. I haven't had any reason to laugh in a long time. Donna, I don't care what you know and what you do with it – assuming you're not cruel enough to use it to hurt Mickey, and I don't think you are."

"God, Lou, why on earth would I ever want to hurt Mickey? I am not in the habit of hurting anyone, for that matter," I responded.

"Of course you're not, Donna," he admitted. "It's just that spending so much time with BJ has really done a job on my head; I forget not everyone's like her."

"Well, I'm not!" I was having trouble letting go of my righteous self-indignation. If I hoped to make this a productive conversation I'd better ramp up my effort to clamp it.

"You know, I'm not making excuses for myself," he offered, "but I never set out to do anything illegal, or anything that would hurt anyone else."

"I thought I knew you well enough to know that for myself, Lou," I offered. "I've always felt you were basically a good person, with a big flair for the dramatic."

"Thank you for that, Donna. That's the nicest thing anyone's said to me in a long time. For the past year, I've been trying to make restitution for what I've done; I've been fighting BJ every step of the way. In fact, I'm surprised the police haven't arrested me yet. She and I were embroiled in a very hostile and long-term battle over our business disasters. I was in Omaha at the time of the murder trying to convince her to come back to Connecticut so we could turn ourselves in together."

"Holy shit, Lou, really?"

"Yeah, some of our "investments" had backfired and either the law or the IRS were minutes away from taking us out. We folded our operation about a year ago when the shit hit the fan; neither one of us has had an honest day's work since."

"That explains why Ron and Sheila were helping her financially," I added.

"That Ron is such a great guy, and Sheila would do anything for Ron," he agreed. "It's not like they could really afford it, and BJ treated Sheila like dirt. Just like her daughter-in-law. I can't think of another woman who'd help her 'til it hurt after being treated so badly."

And no one knew more about how badly BJ could treat people than I did! She was brutal!

"The worst thing was she had bigger and better plans for all of them. She had begun to implicate Ron in our business dealings. She'd started using his check to pay for some of her more highly illegal escapades. All she had to do was tell the poor sap her mortgage carrier had changed and he readily agreed to make the checks out to the worst of the scumbags, which would implicate him in our fraudulent schemes. Then, of course, you know that her plan for Mickey was to wipe him out financially. She hated the new wife and never acknowledged her grandbaby. In her head, Mickey was a young, single guy with a good job – so he'd never miss the money."

It was genuinely shocking. This hateful woman had always defended 'her own' fiercely; to think she would turn against them was unquestionably the most disturbing part of all.

"That's kind of where you come in, Donna," he continued, startling me out of my 'daymare.' "She thought you would be the really big score. It made perfect sense. After stinging you she'd have money and she'd already set Ron up so he would go to jail in her place. She felt that her triumph over you would enable her to overcome her jealousy of you – it was the closest she'd ever come to understanding justice."

"I would be the big score?" I gawked, "I would? How the hell would I be the big score?"

"Actually," he shared, "her plan was pretty clever. She was going to set things up so witnesses would testify that you'd invited her to Omaha to partner with you in a business. She'd been following your career and knew pretty much everything you'd done since leaving Connecticut. She had a total conniption fit each time she read of an appointment or a promotion. Then, when she read you and some partners had bought Marcel, she snapped. I think at that point she had to find a way to hurt you, as soon as the right opportunity presented itself. When she realized she was backed into a hole and needed an out, you became top of mind. She hedged her bet by betraying virtually everyone in her life – but you were to be the big fish."

"I'm still curious as to how that was going to happen." I was sounding like a broken record, even to myself; it must have been shock.

"The lawsuit," Lou stated.

"What lawsuit?"

"You dragged her all the way out here to join you in business, and then you breached your promise. That would be worth upward of a cool mill – and you'd pay it without thinking because you'd want to avoid a scandal," he finished. I was speechless.

"I'm sorry, Donna," he whined. "I should have warned you."

Now I started to laugh. The poor guy thought I was losing it. He tried to console me and grew increasingly nervous as my laughter escalated. I couldn't stop myself or I would have reassured him, but I just kept laughing. I laughed so hard my stomach started to hurt and the tears were shooting out of my eyes. I would have enjoyed this honest to goodness belly laugh considerably more had I not been aware of poor Lou. His suffering seemed to increase with every moment that went by. Time to get myself under control, as difficult as that was going to be. Eventually, after what seemed like a very long time, I was able to pull it together enough to talk. The first attempt at talking through giggles was futile but I persevered; it didn't seem fair to make Lou wait any longer.

"Seriously?" I laughed. "She was getting her big bucks from me?" That was it; I started laughing all over again. And what I had said hadn't helped Lou at all. Finally, I was able to utter something quasi-intelligible.

"Lou, that's the dumbest freakin' thing I have ever heard! I can't tell you how relieved I am to hear that she had nothing at all."

"But Donna, she was having one of her crooked lawyers draw up the contract at the time of her death," Lou cautioned, "and you know she wouldn't hesitate to forge your signature."

"Oh Lou, it's been a long time," I waxed philosophic. "Honey, when you own a business, you learn there are many things to fear. A bullshit claim from a card-carrying lunatic is not even close to being one of them."

"You sound so self-assured," he offered.

"It's been a long time, Lou. We knew each other when I was a kid; so much has happened since then. If I let every empty threat knock me off my pins, it would have been over a long time ago. No, Lou, it takes a lot more than an ill-conceived fairy story to even get my attention. BJ had no idea who she was messing with; she'd have been crushed like a bug."

For just a moment, it occurred to me that I was really sorry BJ had been murdered. I would have liked to see her try to pull that scam on us – I actually shuddered at the thought of how she'd end up. Some might think she couldn't have ended up any worse than she did. If you knew BJ you'd know that dying a mysterious, and maybe even glamorous, death would be far preferable to openly losing a battle with me and being publicly humiliated. Clovis would understand. There it was again, she and Clovis really did have an affinity.

I could tell that Cavrola was relieved. I was glad I could give him that. We talked for a bit longer. He explained how the "famous" business partnership with BJ started out on the up and up, sort of. Then unbeknownst to Lou or WyCliff, BJ started to dabble in fraud. Little things like double insuring parts of a property that were particularly vulnerable to vandalism; and then, when the inevitable happened, double collecting. There were forged rent checks and sometimes mail theft, when a tenant was sent a check of virtually any kind.

After about a year of pulling in some serious dollars through her extracurricular, fraudulent activities, BJ decided it was time to bring Cavrola into the secret. At first Lou was outraged and terrified, but he eventually realized that they were making a killing and no one was the wiser; so he got on board.

After a few years, he could see that BJ was taking huge and unnecessary risks. If she was making good money, she could be making even that much more money. Lou was powerless to stop her, so he sat back and watched. And prayed. Unfortunately, his prayers were not answered and the 'house that BJ built' started to come crashing down on their heads. True to form, BJ looked for any and every out; she found a whole bunch, unfortunately.

We were pretty much talked out at this point. I thanked Lou for helping me with a ton of great information. I assured him that I held no animosity toward him, and we agreed that I could call if other questions arose. I got off the phone feeling that I had answers to many of the most pressing questions. Now it was time to apply those answers to everything else I knew.

[CHAPTER 40]

I was glad to be home. All the time I was on the phone with Cavrola, my "girls" had been with me. As soon as I hung up they sprang into action, letting me know it was time for a walk. Jon and I snapped collars and leashes on and headed to the park, where they sniffed everything in sight until we were all exhausted and ready for home and dinner. For Jon and me it would be more like cocktail hour – a little wine, some olives, maybe some cheese for Jon, and if we allowed ourselves an indulgence, some lovely foie gras and an oven fresh baguette.

Having indulged in more hors d'oeuvres than planned, we kept the actual meal especially light, comprised mostly of salad and cooked vegetables. Afterward, we selected a couple of movies on Netflix and settled down in front of the larger-than-life seventy-inch flat screen, i.e. the love of Jon's life. With our stomachs sated and our bulldogs draped over us, exhausted from their trek through the park, we settled in. I couldn't think of a better way to spend a Friday night. Except maybe in front of a murder mystery – but, as I had found during the investigation of Claire's murder, the thought of watching murder mysteries held no appeal. It just felt wrong when someone we knew had so recently been murdered. I didn't have to be broken-hearted over the victim to feel that when it hits this close to home, it's harder to view any murder as a parlor game.

Knowing we had a lot on tap for the weekend motivated us to be in bed by midnight. After the week we'd had sliding between the sheets was absolute bliss. Murder was tough on a schedule. Life was busy enough, but the extras that had to be jammed in during a murder investigation kept things at a frenetic pace. Keeping up was a challenge.

Saturday morning dawned softly, waking us gently; then the bulldogs converged. It was a new morning and life was too exciting to be believed. Could there ever be a better way to wake up than with three happy, healthy bulldogs who were excited to get their day started? I got myself organized, grabbed my book and went downstairs to feed the throng. It was a bit of a ballet since not everyone ate the same food; keeping them from eating everything but their own food took some fancy footwork. Once the bulldogs were fed and given their post breakfast treats, I got my chance to relax over coffee and toast. After lingering over a meal that lasted almost until my coffee cup was empty, Jazzy grunted her impatience. It was family time! Roxi grabbed a toy and ran frantically back and forth between the kitchen and family room, and Sweet Pea ran upstairs and jumped into bed with Jon. She would either roust him or steal some early morning snuggles. There would be no rest for the weary until we had our promised 'family time.' I took my last sip of coffee and headed into the family room to get things rolling. If you have bulldogs you know they are very demanding companions, and yet, there's no better time for thinking things through than during the self-imposed solitude of family time. Before long there was a thought niggling at the back of my conscious, what had Phillippe said about "looking to family members?" Had he meant blood family or extended family – lord knows she had quite a bit of that. My reverie was broken when Jon came down for his life giving morning coffee.

I asked him, "Do you think I should place much weight on Phillippe's comment about focusing on family members?"

"Maybe."

Thanks a lot!

The rest of Saturday was a maze of errands. We barely made it back home in time to shower, eat a quick meal and dress for an evening at the community theater, a great source of pride for Omaha. As theater aficionados throughout our married life, Jon and I felt extremely fortunate that fate had brought us to a city with such an exceptional local theater.

I wanted to check the review on that night's performance so I grabbed my iPad. Once assured that we were in for a fun evening, I quickly checked Facebook for any important updates.

I immediately spotted a review of that night's play. Something wasn't right. It read like a grisly murder mystery rather than the hilarious comedy I knew it to be. It took a few beats before I realized it was posted as my own personal review, most likely by a true expert in the grisly genre. The blood in my veins ran cold.

After receiving yet another chilling message, neither Jon nor I were much in the mood to enjoy a raucous comedy that evening, so much of the brilliant comedic dialogue was lost to our sobering reality.

Sunday was more 'family time.' Not only do we believe that our dogs deserve the attention they so openly crave, we also believe spending time with them is the best form of r & r for us, soothing the savage breast. We'd never needed that more. Dogs have an uncanny ability to sense the needs of their loved ones, so our Sunday was a combination of peaceful reflection and intermittent clown performances by four-legged acrobats. By Sunday night we were feeling so much better.

[CHAPTER 41]

Even with canine therapy to bolster our spirits, Monday morning came too soon. My alarm brought a pang of sadness as I bade goodbye to the weekend. Sadness flipped to eagerness as I contemplated the information I'd soon be sharing with Warren. I hadn't wanted to sit on important intelligence for a whole weekend. Besides, I was anxious to 'double clear' my name just in case.

Warren had been genuinely interested and appreciative. I could tell she'd taken notes during our conversation. It felt as though my contributions might actually be helping the investigation; I was feeling proud. I suppose my pride got a bit ahead of itself (why does this not surprise anyone?) when I asked Warren somewhat arrogantly, if there was anything else she needed me to help 'resolve.' I swear it was just a momentary flash of bravado – which is not something I'd typically get away with. And I didn't.

"Well," she started, "There is something that would help me." Then she must have thought better of it. "No, I'm not going to ask you for that."

As you may or may not know, the puffed-up ego cannot resist the temptation of being asked for help – particularly by an authority figure. Naturally, I had no alternative but to urge Warren to reveal her need for my skills. My sense of self-importance eagerly awaited the critically important task that would undoubtedly increase the already widespread acceptance of my invaluable expertise. Little did I know, I was the proverbial target with a big old bulls-cye painted on my side!

"Okay," she considered, "I could really use some help in diverting that pain in the behind, Clovis." Now she was on a roll and gaining steam, while I was in shock, virtually frozen with terror. Oh god no, anything but that!!

"She is so exhausting and counterproductive," she went on, "we lose too much valuable time responding to her every preposterous notion. One morning she calls because she thinks she's our prime suspect. No sooner do we talk her off that ledge, and off the phone, then she's calling again to demand our acknowledgement that she is pivotal to the case. I even thought of throwing her in a cell for a night; just to shake her up. But she knows too much about courts and legalities from her journalistic background, and as you can imagine she'd kill for an opportunity to be the center of a huge media coup – whether or not she created it herself! That would only make things worse!"

Damn! Me and my big mouth. How could I say no to her? It was a perfectly reasonable request and she'd asked the right person. The fact that it would make my life slightly more hellish was just something I'd have to endure. Big fat note to self: shut the hell up next time!

I assured Warren I'd do my best to get the psycho off the back of the hard working homicide detectives. We both knew my promises were hollow at best. Neither of us had seen or heard of anything that could keep Clovis from blatantly seeking her just desserts. At best I could hope for a temporary diversion.

Once dressed and organized for work, I made the commute with alacrity. I had had the forethought to set up a meeting and reserve a meeting room for first thing in the morning. I knew not everyone would be available. A lot of our folks start their days early, with client breakfast meetings or breakfast committee meetings for the various boards on which we all serve. With our founder's credo of "paying rent for the space we occupy," we are all very active in giving back to the community. It's virtually impossible to get everyone together at the same time; those otherwise occupied would just have to be briefed by their team members.

Once in the conference room for our briefing, I could see that I had close to a full house. Great. I took the next twenty minutes to fill them in on everything I'd learned. There were about ten minutes of questions and comments and then we adjourned. Mondays were always busy so it was imperative that no time be wasted, especially on non-business business. As usual, I was struck by our amazing crew. Rissa, our account planner, and a team member of Liv's wanted to know what the fracas at Midtown Crossing had been about when BJ's "guys' all ran into each other. Damn! Why didn't I think of asking Cavrola that? I could only share Maria's assumptions. Oh well, there were a number of things I'd still need to find out from both Cavrola and Mickey. Better jot them down.

Rissa had started wondering; had that chance encounter turned hostile at Dèlice been a key factor? Occurring as it had, in the days just prior to B.J's death? Obviously I didn't know, but my instincts told me it was nothing more than a bunch of guys getting caught with their proverbial pants down. None of them had wanted any of the others to know they'd been in Omaha supporting BJ in some form or another. Hard to tell if it was just embarrassment, or something far more lethal. As I contemplated this notion, it dawned on me that I'd found it interesting for another reason altogether. Five men who knew BJ had all come out to Omaha at the same time in connection with her recent move; had there been others that no one knew about yet? I couldn't yet determine the significance of the Dèlice encounter nor could I ignore the importance of knowing whether or not her other supporters had been skulking around as well. I didn't know quite what to think.

I left the meeting with a starter list and the resolve to get more information on each of the key topics. Of course, as was true with so much of this investigation I was heading out blind, uncertain as to what I might find. It was only 9:10 when the realization hit me that I'd have to call Clovis. I swayed just a bit on the long walk back to my work area; this time it wasn't the two hundred year old floors but rather the realization that I was actually inviting communication with the thing I feared almost more than anything else, the official 'chair' of functional dysfunction. It wasn't that you feared the prospect of boredom or annoyance; it was that you feared for your very sanity and the ability to move forward with some semblance of normalcy. Don't doubt it until you've seen it in action! I'd rather face a hungry, agitated grizzly bear in the woods; at least knowledge and logic apply in a grizzly bear confrontation, even if it's just having the knowledge that you're about to be mauled to death.

I called. "Hi Clovis."

"Donna," she half shrieked, half whined. Man, that hurt my head. "It's about time! I wondered when I'd be getting your apology," she ended gruffly.

"And why am I--"

"Well, you nearly got me run over and you humiliated me in front of a political superstar," she shrieked (oh God, back to that)."

"Oh yeah, sorry," I capitulated.

"Really, Donna? Is that all you can say after everything that you've done?" she demanded.

I wanted to help Warren, honest I did. But there was just so much...

"Hey Clovis, I have it on good authority that you're the

prime suspect,"

"What?!" she bellowed. I could tell she was smiling.

"Yeah," I was thinking fast now. That worked, but where could I go from here?

"I've heard it from a few people now," I thought I had a strategy, only time would tell.

"I want to hear everything, Donna, leave nothing out," she cooed. That woman had such a unique way of communicating. I'd be fine as long as the shrieking was kept to a minimum! That was a tall order!

"Well, I don't actually know much." I heard a disappointed sigh and knew I'd have to step up my program if I hoped to survive this call. "I mean, I know quite a bit, but I don't want to worry you, Clovis, I know how sensitive you are."

"Well aren't you just the sweetest thing, Miss Donna. Look at you all worried about me! Well, worry your head no further, I'll just get off the phone and call Detective Warren…"

"NO! Clovis, don't," I shrieked (now she had me shrieking, but Warren would kill me if I drove Clovis to bug her!) "Uh, no Clovis, I, uh, I actually talked to Warren about this." Man, when I lie I really go all the way!

"You talked to Warren about me?" She started to get a little shrieky herself, but the smile in her voice wasn't completely gone. Let's face it, attention is attention!

"Well, we had a complete overview of all new facts, and I mentioned what I'd heard. Not to throw suspicion on you or anything." *I knew I was pretty slick.* "Naturally she couldn't confirm or deny, but I sensed she was leaning closer to confirming."

Silence. Was she still there? I thought I heard breathing. Wow, this was a first, I have never been in Clovis' presence and experienced this kind of silence before. I started to wonder if she'd fallen into a coma.

"Clovis!" I ventured.

Still nothing. Holy crap! I waited.

"Well, Donna," she began. "I can't tell you what it means to me that you are willing to step up and speak the truth. I have always known this whole investigation would revolve around me. Until now no one would give me the satisfaction of an honest assessment. I know I've been hard on you, Donna, but I underestimated you. Maybe I have throughout this whole case." So now I had the key to getting Clovis to love you instead of attack you, and it was so simple. You just had to tell her she might be convicted of murder. I could do that!

"Really, Clovis...."

"No, Donna, don't be modest. It takes guts to tell someone a truth of this magnitude. You have guts!" she gushed all over me. I still didn't want to get too cocky. My story was kind of on shaky ground here.

"Do you want to know the details..."

"No Donna, I really don't need the detritus of the unwashed masses," she declared. "It's enough to know that my concerns and suspicions have all been confirmed. I certainly understand why the good detectives of Omaha have been brushing me off when I've made my daily, and in some cases hourly, reports to them. Naturally, they understand I am a superior intellect and they would never be able to hold their own with me in a one-on-one conversation regarding a murder for which they think I am the prime suspect. They are terrified that I will glean some important information from them and will use it to nullify any case they might be attempting to construct against me. It all makes perfect sense now."

"Gee, Clovis, I'm happy to be of help, and I sure do appreciate your taking it so well," I offered in my best 'aw shucks ma'am' accent (why I was reverting to cowboy twang is beyond me, it happens sometimes – I don't know why).

"Not at all, Donna," she chimed in. "It's just a relief to know where things stand. I will formulate my position and be prepared for any eventuality. It's not like any of them could possibly outsmart me. They don't have the mental capacity to outsmart me any more than you do, Donna."

There it was. She who giveth will undoubtedly taketh away. I was a good person; but I was still dumb as shit. That thought made me smile. Some things would just never change. You had to give the woman credit; she was the master of the 'single shot from out of nowhere.' My hat was off to her! Damn, I did NOT see that one coming.

We finished our call and I felt relief at having fulfilled a promise to Warren and gotten Clovis off her back. I felt certain it would buy Warren some time without instigating a full-on Clovis meltdown. By leaving her with the certainty that she was in fact the center of this universe, peace could reign supreme. It didn't get any better than that!

Things were in a good place. I had briefed 'the teams,' I had fulfilled my promise to Warren and 'tamed the beast;' but perhaps it was best not to get ahead of myself. It was usually during these rare moments of self-satisfaction and pride when that beast reared its ugly head and made mincemeat out of me. Was that a common theme with amateur sleuths or was that just me? Then again, it could just be my good old "raised in New Jersey" paranoia. Anywhere else it would be considered paranoia; if you're from New Jersey paranoia is as natural as sand on a beach.

[CHAPTER 42]

Back at my desk I was multi-tasking. Simultaneously writing a lengthy response to a cryptic and puzzling RFP question and compiling my question list for BJ's acquaintances. In the agency world we view RFPs as the most common form of torture that Marketing Directors are able to inflict on us. Required by government institutions and adopted by public and privately held entities, the RFP is both coveted and dreaded throughout the advertising/communication industry.

Companies expect us to put our blood, sweat and tears into an impersonal list of questions they typically send out to a dozen or more eager and hopeful contenders. Completed tomes submitted a minute past deadline are summarily refused entry. In an industry where interpersonal chemistry is generally considered the reason for being awarded business, we strive to create a compelling and exciting narrative that tells our story and can be convincingly wound around even the most basic questions while providing a 'feel' for our brand persona or essence. It's not like we're manufacturing truck parts – we're selling ourselves – and that's tough to do in a two-dimensional medium, regardless of how compelling our story and our storytellers may be.

On occasion we are perplexed by the best means of responding to a clearly stated question like: How long have each of your helicopter pilots held their flying licenses? Unfortunately, we've seen many an RFP include cut-and-paste questions borrowed from a totally different discipline without benefit of a thorough proofing or editing – we're all busy, right?

In order to advance in the competition, however, our responses must be letter perfect, arriving precisely on deadline. We find ourselves making a lot of value judgments – guessing is never fun when there's a lot at stake.

If the question is ambiguous enough, we are forced to ask for clarification. Frequently, when we do reach out and ask, the response is something like, "Oh yeah, that's not for you; just ignore that one." Which always makes me wonder – are you not even custom-tailoring the torture you inflict on me? It often comes down to: will we guess right or get thrown out on a technicality? They seem to like making us squirm.

Ironically, a little foray into murder is an excellent diversion when facing the overwhelming and sometimes suffocating world of RFP response. Even the best of us tend to get crazed when surrounded by a world where the only control we have is to guess: right or wrong. And so much can rely on that guess. As long as BJ's murder didn't result in jail time or death for me, it was far less hazardous than navigating your average RFP.

Yes, the RFP is the bane of the advertising industry, yet without the RFP there can be no entrée into certain plum accounts, so we celebrate when we're invited to participate. And no matter how challenging, we take enormous pride in crafting a response that reveals our true persona and resonates with key stakeholders. Suffice it to say that compiling a list of murder suspects was a much easier task; taking the odds into account it could also prove to be more productive.

I worked on answers and lists until lunchtime when my stomach threatened mutiny. I thought briefly about potential lunch meetings or phone calls that could expedite things on the investigation and opted instead for a leisurely stroll through the Old Market.

I passed along the cobbled streets by the quirky shops and

restaurants alive with their al fresco diners enjoying every gorgeous moment of a spectacular day. Nestled among these charming old buildings, some looking a little wobbly even though they've clearly stood the test of time, I could feel myself relax. Omaha's Old Market is one of the few genuinely organic old markets. Most downtown old markets are mere reproductions, mirroring and theoretically improving upon what developers believe existed years before thanks to well-meaning civic leaders who believed the past should be bulldozed to make room for modern times. The Omaha Old Market district, however, remains virtually unchanged from when cowboys walked its dusty streets.

When an architect from New York City's ground zero flew out to give a talk, he was most impressed with the organic quality of our old market, and the fact that there were no signs of a history dependent on slaughter houses anywhere in sight. We are organic, yet evolved.

Unfortunately, a cement-headed developer thought it would be cute to name a nearby business park The Stockyards! Really not a reminder of a heritage we'd ever want to tout to businesses or people we're trying to recruit. Any time now he's liable to propose changing the name of Dodge Street to Brothel Row. Everyone thinks they know marketing – so often they forget – first you have to think about the desired outcome!

It was such a gorgeous day! The sun was shining and there wasn't a cloud in the sky; the light breeze kept things comfortable. I was thankful it wasn't slightly stronger and whipping my hair into my eyes, nose and mouth. This day was close to perfect! Immediately upon leaving the platform at the front of Marcel I began to contemplate where I'd search for food. The myriad of planters and flower boxes that bloomed with a magnificent array of colors and fragrances created a feeling as close to paradise as any city center could hope to achieve. Juxtaposed against the elegance of the aged building facades with all their time-worn character and the delightfully authentic cobble-stone streets it was obvious that nothing in Disney's bag of tricks could ever replicate the genuine article. And when I spotted the horse-drawn carriage up ahead, making its way through the intersection of Howard and Eleventh Street, I could almost convince myself that I'd blacked out and awoken in a Dickens novel. Nagging hunger aside, the thought of selecting a restaurant and going inside had lost some of its appeal.

As I neared the corner of Jackson and 11th and saw the glass garage door closed, and fastened I was reminded that the Jackson Street Pub is not open for business on Mondays. On a lovely day like this that was disappointing. Their al fresco dining would have been just the thing to allow me to continue my enjoyment of this glorious day. In the dead of winter their appeal was being the eatery closest to Marcel – we had some damn cold days during the winter!

I proceeded northwest on my jaunt through the Old Market, glancing at some of the cool little shops along the way. Aside from a captivating Old Market, Omaha is all about supporting our artisans. If you need that perfect gift, for the person who has everything, you are sure to find it in one of the many shops or in the artists' coop itself. Failing that you could proceed north to the 'Hot Shops,' where artists and their creations lead and everything else follows.

As I walked I also thought about the investigation and where things stood. It dawned on me that I was feeling a whole lot more confident than I'd been at this point during Claire's murder investigation. Of course, I had more experience this time, and hadn't received any direct death threats. I could honestly admit I was feeling far more useful in aiding the detectives on the case. Things had progressed light years in the past few days. Conversely, you had to ask yourself, how often would someone I knew from Connecticut who had ostensibly moved all the way to Omaha to go into business with me – without telling me – get murdered? Okay, that brought me down to earth a bit. I damn well better be helpful in a murder case that hit this close to home. I could even venture as far as to say it revolved around me. God, even thinking that made me feel too much like Clovis for comfort! I had an involuntary shudder and labored to change the subject in my head.

The Diner. I always enjoyed a nice lunch at the diner. True, it meant I'd forego dining al fresco once again, but they did offer that mid-century retro experience, and I did love my reasonably priced slim platter – does that make me cheap? Once again I found myself drawn to the diner to relax over a "healthy" lunch and a little light reading. It was an opportunity to change the venue completely and recharge my battery. Most folks know that clearing your head and letting your subconscious lead is the best way to solve a perplexing problem – they just don't always allow themselves the luxury. I found that if you sat around and forced yourself to consciously think about a problem – the solution could present itself in flashing neon lights – and you wouldn't so much as notice!

I lingered over a Diet Coke until I finished the chapter I'd been reading. Damn, with the check paid there wasn't much reason to hang around any longer, so I packed up my "stuff" and headed out the door for the return stroll back to Marcel. Halfway back I could feel a thought taking shape; I still needed to find out specifically what each of the guys in the Dèlice 'squabble' had been doing in Omaha at the time of BJ's death, and what all their women thought about it. It occurred to me that Mickey would be in the best position to know everyone's motive, but I hated to bug him any earlier than our next scheduled call. I debated whether to wait or reschedule. Turns out fate had made the decision for me. Checking voicemail I found a message from Mickey requesting that we move our call up to this evening at 7:00 P.M. central time. He had his own reasons for moving things up! His voice sounded okay so I convinced myself it must not be something terrible and settled in to answer two more of the RFP questions assigned to me.

By three o'clock I was so ingrained in RFP responses that when Donny called to ask me a question about our Executive Committee meeting on Friday, I had to really strain to remember what an Executive Committee was. With his usual impatience, Donny waited until I had formulated my first cogent thought before exclaiming, "Geez, I get better response from cadavers that pop up in a fast running stream."

"When the hell have you ever seen a cadaver..."

"Oh I've seen them."

"Bullshit!"

"Okay fine, but what about Friday?"

At this point I was done straining for Donny's sake, "ask Kyle, he's running the show," I offered.

"Fine, where is he?"

"No idea."

And that was the end of our brief interlude and pretty much the end of my concentration. When you're working on a task that's less than a labor of love, it doesn't take much to yank you off focus for good. I cursed Donny and wondered if he'd called just to 'mess me up.' There was that New Jersey again; the nice folks in Omaha were always quick to assure me that my automatic default to suspicion was pointless, because I was among friends who did not think in that devious manner – but when it came to Donny I could never be sure.

Just as I began to regain my concentration, the phone rang. I could tell the caller was from Connecticut, but I had no idea who it could be. I jumped in with both feet anyway.

"Hello?"

"Donna?" I heard the unmistakable voice of Porter Enzo. Wow! Talk about a blast from the past!

"Porter?"

"Huh, I didn't expect you to recognize my voice," he responded. "Heard you've been talking to folks about BJ. I kind of figured you'd get around to me eventually so I thought I'd save you the trouble."

"How are you, Porter?" I decided it would be in my best interest to take control of the conversation.

"Doin' okay," he replied.

"Porter, what can you tell me?" Hell, Porter had been a media sales rep who called on me when I first got into the business and didn't know a bleed ad from a double truck! Lacking knowledge and wisdom born of age, it was crucial that I cop a bit of a 'tude in order to command respect. They tell me my unique talent was in showing enough attitude to get the job done without coming off as completely disingenuous. It's a gift!

"Whadda ya wanna know?" he retorted. I hoped this was not going to be a 'tug of information' war. I had no time for games.

"Why were you in Omaha when BJ was murdered? And what do you know?" I figured I had nothing to lose so I might as well go for it.

"I don't know if you were aware that BJ moved in with a guy just prior to moving to Omaha?" he asked.

"Yeah, I heard something to that effect," I acknowledged.

"That guy was me," he confirmed what I'd been suspecting,

"and then she left, without a good-bye and with the contents of my bank account."

Oh shit. That was one hell of a motive. Could this be the killer reaching out to find out what the cops knew? Get it under control, New Jersey, he's 1,500 miles away; that doesn't pose an immediate threat to safety.

"Wow, Porter, that really sucks." My eloquence was legendary during these candid times.

"No kidding."

"How'd that happen?" I sincerely hoped I wasn't being too flip. Not so much because I'm kind, but more because I thought he'd clam up if I couldn't rustle up a bit of empathy.

"Well, here's why I wanted to call you, Donna," he proceeded. "Everyone thinks I've been mooning over my lost love and desperate to get her back." I nodded my agreement – guess he couldn't see me through the phone – good reason not to use Skype for these more sensitive topics.

"That's a load of crap!" he stated. Geez, maybe he could see through the phone line. "When she left me the first time I took it hard. It's not like she was the great love of my life, but I was at a low point and I needed the support and encouragement. She had a way of making a guy feel like he was a rock star and I bought into it. Then when she stopped all her efforts to build up my ego, it was like taking the ferris wheel to the top and getting kicked off the edge! Blam, she went from "you're the most amazing guy on earth" to "I could not tolerate being around someone as lame as you for even another second." That confirmed it. Her relationship style was very much like her management style. I really understood how he felt.

"I hear ya, Porter."

"I can imagine, Donna. She treated you that way for a long time. At least, for me it was a quick trip up and a quicker trip down. I can't deny I was hurting, but it didn't take me long to realize I'd actually dodged a major bullet. I could finally see how phony she was; so, much of what people saw was intense embarrassment that I could be so gullible."

"But then you took her back after all those years?" I probed. A question like this was tantamount to calling him a moron. I wasn't ready to make that proclamation – yet.

"I took her back because she gave me a sob story – literally. She showed up at my door one day and told me, in between racking sobs, that she'd hit rock bottom, had nowhere to go and no one to help her."

"But Ron and Sheila were paying..."

"Yeah, I know that now. I also know that she needed a few months of living with me to save some of Ron and Sheila's money and to find the numbers and practice the signature of my savings account. And she emptied out my account, as I said."

"Wow again, Porter." I'm not usually a woman of few words, but I guess shock takes its toll on my vocabulary – don't tell Donny!

"Yeah, and I'm guessing, once the cops know that, it'll be a short trip to the top of the suspect list, which is why I wanted to call you. I'd been in touch with Mickey and learned that you've become a homicide expert since moving to Omaha, and the cops use you as a consultant in their difficult cases."

Why correct him and point out that I'd inadvertently stumbled into two murders – within the past year – and I had a feeling the cops stayed close more to 'keep an eye on me' than because I could 'Sherlock' my way to solving their case. The more I corrected people, the more they considered me to be the humble but brilliant homicide sleuth. What can you do?

"I was hoping," he went on, "that you'd put in a good word

for me. That you'd make sure they checked out my entire portfolio, so they would know that what she took, about $300,000 in all, was really just a drop in the bucket when all of my assets are considered."

"Really, Porter? Good for you!" I remarked as I considered that I was clearly in the wrong end of the business.

"Yeah, I've done all right," he acknowledged. "I made some very good investments way back when, and they've made me a wealthy man today. So you see, I would never kill anyone for a measly $300,000! I'll barely notice the loss."

All right, now he was rubbing it in just a bit too much. Enough was enough! He earned himself a shot for that last comment!

"So why'd you come all the way out to Omaha? That's going to make the cops skeptical of your claims of indifference." I slam-dunked that last shot without even grazing the rim! Hmmph, brag to me about your untold wealth, will you? I guess he could see where that got him!

"I never said I was indifferent, Donna," he offered.

Dammit, he was going to take the wind from my sails wasn't he? I could not catch a break!

"I made the trip out to Omaha for a few reasons," he continued. "First, I wanted her to understand that we were through and I never wanted to hear from her again. I told her to keep the money, but I would expect full payback if she ever tried to contact me down the road. She knew I was serious about turning her in to the police if she didn't honor my demands."

That sounded pretty fishy. He came all the way out here to tell her to leave him alone AND he let her keep a huge chunk of money she'd stolen from him. If I didn't know better, I'd think I was watching a soap opera. These things don't happen in real life.

"Okay, and your other reasons?" He must have sensed my distrust, even without the benefit of seeing my disgusted eye roll!

"I know my explanation's a little hard to swallow," he admitted, "which is why I want to share the whole sordid tale so you can pass it along to the officials; you need the whole story."

I grunted my acceptance, encouraging him to finish.

"I had also become aware of her fraud against Ron and Sheila and her blatant theft of Mickey's money. Finally, I had a fair inkling of her plot against you and, in the interest of old feelings, I wanted to warn her she was not covering her tracks carefully enough. I warned her she was playing a dangerous game and this time she may have gone too far. Then I reminded her I was pretty much aware of all of her illegal and unethical behavior. In my opinion, she was in the most potentially dangerous situation of all."

"How did she respond to that?"

"What do you think? She laughed in my face."

"That must have made you violently angry," I pressed.

"Actually, that was a much more positive response than I'd expected. Laughing in my face was the best of the levels of dissention I've experienced at the hands of BJ. It was the violent shrieking and whole body tremors that I feared and dreaded. The laughter was like a kiss and a thank you in her repertoire of responses. When I left Omaha – before I heard about the murder – I left with the feeling that I'd done what I could to warn her of the dangers she was clearly inviting. I'd done my duty and I knew full well that I could do no more. So I left with a clear conscience. When I heard she'd been killed, I felt sad for a short time, but I bore no guilt. Nor was I surprised."

He was right. After hearing the whole story it all made

sense. I could totally see it. He was smart, too; if I told Warren his story I could verify that it was completely consistent with BJ's personality and their relationship. I would gladly do just that. I assured Porter that I would, but that left one more question I had to ask.

"So what was the public fight at Dèlice about?" It would be good to get his perspective.

"Oh, that? That was mostly embarrassment," he responded.

"Embarrassment?"

"Yeah, I know I was embarrassed to have them see me all the way out there in Omaha. I didn't want them to think I was chasing her out of some misplaced feelings of love or something. I think Ron and WyCliff felt the same. I think even Cavrola was a little concerned that we'd all think his feelings for her went far beyond their business partnership."

"I guess that makes sense," I acknowledged, "but why were the rest of them there?"

"Donna, I honestly couldn't hazard a guess," he responded. "You'd have to ask them." I believed him.

At least I had a lot more information and a pretty good handle on why Porter had been there. I also thought Porter was the one whose actions and motives would be least understood by the others, so I probably wouldn't have gotten anything definitive on him when talking to them. He really saved me time and energy by being proactive and calling. I thanked him for the call and assured him I would plead his case with Warren. We rung off with my promise that I'd call to warn him if the conversation on his behalf went badly. I assured him I didn't expect a problem, but I'd be sure to let him know if instincts had failed me this time.

I glanced at the clock; it was almost a quarter after four. Crap! I had wanted to finish one more RFP question before calling it a night, and knowing Mickey would be calling later made me reluctant to hang around the office for too much longer.

I finished answering the question at precisely twenty after five so I packed up and headed for home. Jon and I sipped a glass of wine while preparing dinner; he was checking out a mid-priced Italian Amarone and I had my Kim Crawford. I made a salad and Jon fed the dogs as we discussed the events of the day. We were in a bit more of a rush than normal in our effort to finish in time for my call with Mickey.

[CHAPTER 43]

Mickey called at seven on the nose. After a perfunctory greeting he got right down to the point. A slight note of panic tinged his speech so I knew that my initial read had been inaccurate – this could well be terrible.

"Donna, I'm worried," he began right on cue, "I've learned something that has me more than a little freaked out and I'm not ashamed to admit it."

"God, Mickey, what is it?" I asked.

"I think my wife was in Omaha when my mom got murdered, Donna," he blurted in a groan that was close to a sob. "She's never lied to me before, but she says she was at her sister's with the baby. I'm almost certain she wasn't."

"Hang on," I cautioned, "She told you she was with her sister in Richmond – am I right about that – and you don't believe her even though she's never lied to you before? Now Mickey, is it possible you're jumping the gun here? Did someone tell you they saw her in Omaha? Because maybe they were lying and she wasn't."

"I wish, Donna," he continued. His angst was almost palpable. "I've suspected her involvement for a long time, just based on some comments she's made about my Mom and her treatment of us. It was a vague feeling, but it was growing. Now I think there's hard evidence against Susie, and it's very damning!"

"Evidence? Have the police contacted you?" I was growing more and more curious. I wish he would just spit it out, but I suppose I'd have to let him get there in his own good time.

"I read on Omaha.com that a large orange Armani knock-off designer bag was found at the scene after the murder. They suspect the murderer went back to the scene. Donna, my wife used to have a bag fitting that description. I'm sure I saw it a couple of months ago and now it's missing."

"How do you know it's missing? Did Susie tell you?" I asked.

"That thing took up so much room I considered taking it myself and losing it along the road somewhere. Now it's nowhere in sight. After I read about the bag at the murder scene, I made it a point to search for it – it's nowhere! And don't try to tell me it's a coincidence, Donna, I'm not five-years-old. I'm married with a family and a wife who may be in very serious trouble; I'm not too proud to admit I'm terrified."

"I won't tell you it's a coincidence because I don't believe in coincidence!" I assured him. "I believe you just found the mysterious bag's owner – and it sounds as though you and Susie have a lot of talking to do – fast! You need to find out if the police have questioned her."

"I don't even know how to approach her on this. We've never had a subject we couldn't openly discuss before. I can't tell you how much I hate this!"

"You're young and you've only been married a short time. There will come a time when you aren't all that thrown by the occasional domestic mystery. Some of them are fun to decipher, and some of them are just cases of 'oh, yeah, I forgot to tell you'. Now, having your wife accidentally leave a highly identifiable bag at the scene of a murder over 1,500 miles away from where she was supposed to be is likely to be the biggest domestic mystery you'll ever have to cope with – but you'd better get this sorted out now!"

"So what do I do, Donna?" he pleaded. After everything

else the poor guy had been delivered yet another kick in the gut. Now he faced a confrontation with a wife he'd thought was perfect – the young are so naïve – and the possibility of helping defend her on a murder rap. I assumed he in no way thought she'd actually murdered his mother. I guess when you find out the woman you've trusted for years has been living a double life, even for a short time, that has to take the wind right out of your sails. I wanted to help him, but I honestly didn't know if I could.

"Let me think a minute," I shared, straining for a solution.

"Maybe the best way is to mention the orange bag found at the murder scene. Then watch her face carefully for signs of surprise or even shock at the information."

"Yeah, I could do that, so you think it would be better for me to trick her than to ask her outright? I'm just not good at these things."

"You and most other men, Mickey. No, I don't think you should deceive her. What I think is that you need to get to the bottom quickly so that you can help her. If you ask her outright and she's not ready to share her story, she might evade the issue or lie to buy herself extra time. And Mickey, there is no time. You need a lawyer and you probably need to recommend she turn herself in to Detective Warren before they issue a warrant for her arrest."

"You think they'll arrest her?" he asked.

"Eventually, but the problem is you don't know when. For all you know they could be heading to your house as we speak."

"Oh God, I've got to go and find out what her involvement is in the murder. You're right, if the police find her first it will go hard on her. I want to protect her from the worst of it, no matter what she's involved herself in."

"Then you'd better get off the phone and find out right

away. We can talk again later in the week."

"Okay, Donna, thanks, I should really go talk to her," he agreed. "Oh, and there is just one more thing. I'm so embarrassed. I'm the idiot who wrote the review."

"The play review; about the murder?" I didn't know what to think.

"I'm so sorry, Donna. It was so stupid."

"It's okay, Mickey, I think I can guess why," I offered.

"There's no excuse—"

"Was it right after you figured out that the bag was missing?"

"I knew you'd be able to trace it back to Suzie—"

"Say no more, Mickey. Well, one thing more. Did you author the Facebook threats?"

"Oh, God, no. Facebook threats? Man, I am so sorry about all of this. This must be so difficult for you."

"You've been through quite a bit yourself, let's just put this whole thing behind us. And Mickey, if you need me, don't hesitate to call. Let me know if I can help in any way," I offered as we said our good-byes. I know Mickey was grateful. He assured me that his Dad and Sheila would be plenty of help. He was just sorry he'd have to pester them about this on top of everything else.

Talking to Mickey made me very curious about the murder scene again. I'd seen it once, when we spotted the 'mystery bag,' but now I wondered if seeing it again might crystallize some of the information I'd picked up. Maybe it was time to revisit the scene. I'd think about it overnight and make a decision in the morning. It's not like there was any chance I was heading over there tonight. That's one of the many pet peeves I have about the murder mysteries I so love to read. What moron would head on over to a murder scene unarmed and alone at night, and yet they all do. I get so irritated when they just ask for trouble! They're all supposed to be so brilliant; yet they all do such ridiculously risky things. That was a clear benefit of coming from New Jersey – I saw the potential for danger in everything! Okay, now that the thought had been released into the atmosphere – it might not be the most ringing endorsement for a New Jersey upbringing – but if you're from New Jersey you know what I mean! You can never get the jump on us because we're always anticipating trouble.

I rejoined Jon and "the girls" and we watched House Hunters International in Tuscany before heading up to bed. I mentioned Mickey's wife and the orange bag. Jon just said "hmph." It was enough.

* * *

The next morning I called and left a message for Detective Warren before leaving the house. I wanted to stop by and have the Porter Enzo conversation. I also thought if I played my cards right I might be able to pry loose a little information about Mickey's wife, and whether or not she was on the radar screen. I'd have to be extremely careful not to spill the beans on that one. Hell, I was a professional communicator; this should be no sweat.

I pulled up and parked near the station at precisely eight o'clock. On my way to Warren's office I stopped to chat with Frick and Frack. It seemed like a good time to dig for some info on Mickey's wife; these guys were sharp, but not as sharp as Warren. After five minutes I walked away without knowing much more. I was, at least, able to ascertain that the designer bag had been fairly useless, offering no ID of the owner and no useable fingerprints. Either they knew nothing about the wife or they were much better actors than I'd given them credit for.

I suspected it was the former. That would buy Mickey a little time anyway.

I continued on to Warren's office. When I passed the desk sergeant I waved. I could swear I detected an 'oh man, are you headed for trouble' look and eye roll. It could have been my imagination, but I didn't think so. Upon arrival at Warren's door the reason for "the look" became evident almost immediately. I knocked gently and started into the room only to be greeted by a robust shout.

"Thanks a lot, Leigh!" shouted Warren. "I just spent an hour on the phone with Clovis' attorney; and that's after a two-hour face-to-face with the diva herself at the end of the day yesterday. Good thing you didn't find yourself in a life threatening situation last night – there isn't a cop on the force who would have come to your rescue after two-hours of the screechy baby-doll!"

"Oh God, what happened? I was sure I'd convinced her to steer clear of the police when I told her she was the prime suspect! I'm so sorry; I can't believe I could have misinterpreted her reaction so completely!"

"Oh yeah, she did avoid us after your talk, for about forty-five minutes! Then she decided to hire an attorney and nail down the movie and book rights so a judge couldn't strip her of the right to use this murder as a springboard to global fame."

Oh shit, I gave myself a mental smack to the forehead. How could I possibly miss the likelihood that Clovis would see this as a golden opportunity – and be more anxious than ever to talk about it – to everyone!

"I am so sorry. I guess I'm not as good as I think!" I couldn't humble myself enough. Bringing a massive Clovis attack on someone who asked you to dial her back was like one of the seven deadly sins. If I were Warren, I didn't think I'd forgive me! Crap, that would really put a damper on my plans to dig around for some information. I heard a noise and turned to see Frick and Frack standing in the doorway, laughing their asses off. Those bastards had set me up! They knew all about Warren's wrath and kept their mouths shut so I would walk into the maelstrom unprotected! Goddamn Donny's friends. Oh shit, that meant he would be lying in wait for me when I walked into the office. Hell of a way to start a Tuesday. I turned to Warren with palms upturned. She gave me a perfunctory head nod and indicated I was to have a seat. I hesitated a moment wondering if she wanted to talk or yell some more.

"It's okay, Leigh," Warren assured me, "I didn't really have much hope of getting Clovis off my back. I took a shot. It was probably time for a Clovis marathon anyway; they usually come in two week intervals, so she was pretty much on track."

I felt a little better. I didn't think Warren was really angry, but there wasn't the wonderful camaraderie of our last few meetings, so I wouldn't push my luck by digging for dirt. Who says I don't know when to keep my mouth shut! We'd still have to wait and see if I could pull that off.

I filled Warren in on the whole Porter Enzo perspective. She was clearly riveted to my story. I could tell I was regaining her favor. I did feel guilty about not sharing Mickey's designer bag story. I felt justified in wanting to give the poor kid a chance to run it down before the police became involved, but that didn't stop me from feeling guilty because I knew I should have spilled my guts to Warren right then and there. Oh well, nobody's perfect.

Warren thanked me profusely for filling her in on Enzo – so I felt even guiltier. She acknowledged that the details I shared all made sense and fit what they already knew. She called Frick and Frack in to enlighten them; her appreciation of my involvement in making this so easy and saving the department a lot of legwork was genuine and effusive. I felt like a model citizen, almost.

I took my leave and made a beeline for the office. With my luck a little on the shaky side this morning, I wasn't up for a trip to the murder scene! Speaking of shaky luck, I no sooner stepped through the door when Donny popped out of the Portfolio Room. He wanted to tell me that Clovis was waiting inside so I could review the first half of her memoirs with her – now that she'd added her friendship with BJ, BJ's murder, my involvement in BJ's murder, and her own ordeal of being the prime suspect for said murder. I think I must have started to hyperventilate. The next thing I knew, someone had shoved a chair under me and pushed my head down between my legs urging me to "breathe, Donna, just breathe." When I finally looked up, I could see that Donny was feeling unusually contrite.

"Geez Donna, I was just kidding," he muttered. "Don't you think it was funny?"

"Yeah, Donny, hilarious! The only thing that's keeping you alive right now is the fact that she isn't really here. If I had to deal with that on top of the shock of your adorable little prank, there could be a real medical emergency, and you would not emerge intact."

"Whoa, ouch! Okay, I'll back off. I guess I just thought you were a lot tougher than you are," he deftly floated his insult out as he moved from harm's way and back to his work area. Even under threat of physical harm he still had to have the last damn word!

Getting to my desk that morning was a lot like climbing Mt. Everest. Okay let's face it, I'm never going to know what it's like to climb Mt. Everest, but you get my drift here. It took me a few minutes to get situated. I used the opportunity to run to the ladies' room while my laptop started up. What I saw staring back from the mirror suggested I'd have been better off getting right down to work. I took a deep breath.

Once back at my desk, I set about checking voicemail and e-mail. I was feeling way behind. As I scanned the unread e-mails there was one that grabbed my attention. It was from Sheila, Ron's wife. I wasted no time in opening Sheila's e-mail; things were really getting interesting now.

"Donna," it started, "I'm so worried about Mickey and his family. Something is going on with them. I'm concerned that if I can't help them fix this problem the whole thing will explode, which will just kill Ron. You know Mickey and his new baby are everything to Ron and I can't take the chance that things will get any more out of control. In order to try to help them I thought it would be best to make a trip out to Omaha so I can root out the cause of the problem. I just know there's some connection to the crazy things BJ did before her death. I got in last night and was hoping you'd help me figure things out since you're already in the middle of everything and you obviously know your way around town here. If there's a chance you could meet me for lunch, I would appreciate it more than I can say. So if you are able to help me, please just shoot me an e-mail telling me where and when."

That was a surprise. I did not expect to hear from Sheila, and it was an even bigger surprise to know she was in Omaha and wanted to meet. I immediately sent her a reply, suggesting we meet at the Jackson Street Tavern. I included directions just in case she was driving herself. I also offered to meet further west depending on where she was staying.

Just as I hit send, Kyle came flying over. It was clear he had news.

"Donna, I'm so glad I caught you," he said. "I just came

from having coffee with Maria and Mario."

Kyle took a moment to catch his breath while my curiosity was killing me!

"They were anxious to have me share their revelation with you," he went on, "because you were so nice to call them and give them some hopeful news, and because they're really so very nice."

"Don't keep me in suspense, Kyle, fill me in," I urged.

"Well, you know all this time they've been puzzled by BJ's story about being Mario's girlfriend since she'd moved to Omaha when there was no truth to her claim at all. They couldn't understand how someone who took such pride in her "big city" sophistication could make up a story that could so easily be proven false if anybody really took the time to delve into it."

"Not unlike her story about me, Kyle, and there hasn't really been ironclad proof that she made all of that up," I offered wearily, "proving the truth can be much more difficult than it seems."

"Exactly," Kyle concurred, "which is why they were in a panic. They assumed Mario had somehow been set up to take the fall for BJ's murder. That's why their focus was off."

"So what happened?"

"They were at a big family dinner telling some of their cousins about BJ's murder. They happened to comment that the money she'd spent while in Omaha was a bit of a mystery because rumors were that she'd kind of been run out of Connecticut on a rail, and there was nothing left. Cousin Anthony chimed in with an inside joke. 'Too bad you didn't turn out to be Mario Mantini, maybe you could've done her some real good' he'd commented. That's when the lightbulb went on for both Mario and Maria. It seems that a few years ago one of the big Lotto winners in Council Bluffs was a guy by the name of Mario Mantini. The guy won something like $65 million. Poor Mario Mantino – Maria's brother and Anthony's cousin – began living a nightmare the day that Lotto winner was announced. Naturally, with the names being so close, everyone confused the two, and everyone with a sob story came out of the woodwork to solicit money from Maria's twin. This went on for almost two years. The poor guy almost couldn't go out in public for fear that another destitute individual, who had thrown him or herself on Mario's mercy, was lying in wait to "get back" at the selfish rich guy for not coming to their immediate aid – really makes you think twice about buying the next Lotto ticket – am I right?"

"Yeesss," I coaxed Kyle along with my own thoughts on where this whole thing was going.

"So as soon as Anthony mentions Mantini, Mario and Maria both get a bolt from the blue; of course, BJ needed money so she researched the Omaha metro and fortuitously found a guy with $65 million. Apparently both Mario's were close in age and both were single. She just naturally made the assumption that Mario Mantino from Omaha was her guy – you know, to those east coast pseudo-sophisticates all of us Midwesterners look alike." I rewarded Kyle with the appropriate eye-roll, but in reality, only a handful of easterners would take the time to realize that we don't all look alike.

"So she meets this good looking millionaire and she decides to invent a story about having a relationship with him?" I press. "How does that help her get her hands on all that cash?" As soon as it came out of my mouth I knew the answer.

"You've got it, haven't you, Donna?" Kyle asked.

"She was doing the same thing to Mario that she was doing to me," I responded. "While she was spreading the rumor about her relationship with Mario, she was having her crooked lawyer draw up a pre-nup with a pre-wedding clause. They wouldn't even have to date after a few months of unchecked rumors and a forged pre-nup that was carefully worded she could take him to court for breach of promise and grab a chunk of his winnings without breaking a sweat!"

"That's pretty much exactly right, Donna," Kyle confirmed "I just don't get it about that pre-wedding clause you mentioned. I've never heard of anything like that before; and wouldn't the fact that she'd never dated Mario prove to be an insurmountable barrier?"

"I had my doubts about a pre-wedding clause even existing, much less holding up in court, but so what? Why not just invent whatever you need. That was the brilliance of her plan. She probably never intended to get more than eight or nine million, and she figured for that piddling amount, Mario would probably not bother to enter into a protracted battle over the veracity of the document. That's why she would never go for a huge percentage. She only wanted to make it a minor annoyance for Mario."

"I see your point,"

"It would have been a whole lot more difficult to fake a whole wedding."

"But wouldn't she need witnesses that had, at least, seen them together? Receipts from local restaurants? You know, to add some sense of reality to her claim."

"Once again, the consummate grifter would have a plan. She had met and become interested in Mario by pure coincidence, she led her self-consumed companion, Clovis, to believe. She understood Clovis well enough to comprehend that if she could make it all about Clovis, somehow, that mouth would never stop jabbering about the BJ and Mario relationship all over the city. BJ beseeched Clovis to help her understand what she needed to do for business, for a partnership with me and for a successful relationship with Mario. Clovis bought her whole fantasy hook, line and sinker. When you think about it, there's nothing Clovis won't believe as long as she's the center of the intrigue."

"That is so true," Kyle acknowledged, more than a little impressed with BJ's devious skills.

"I'm sure she was also about to hire an actor who looked just like Mario and begin to parade him all over town, just to reinforce the rumor mill. The fact that Mario was clueless about the whole thing would only lend to her credibility. Folks would think he must be a heartless bastard if he could so completely and cruelly cut her free without any feelings of remorse or residual longing. Yes Kyle, she was good!"

"God, Donna, I think you just answered the last few remaining questions I had," Kyle offered. "It must have happened in exactly that way. How could you know all of that?"

"Once the light bulb went on the rest just followed," I admitted. "I guess she didn't settle for making me her big payoff."

"Nice work, Detective Leigh. Will you call Warren and fill her in on everything?" Kyle asked.

"I can't imagine that Maria would want anyone to speak for Mario besides herself," I offered "I think the honor should be all hers."

"Good point, Maria isn't exactly a shrinking violet no matter who she's addressing," Kyle agreed. "And frankly, she didn't seem to be looking for help when she chronicled her findings for me. I'm guessing Warren might already be briefed, come to think of it. Oh gee, look at the time, I've got to run or I'll be late for my next meeting."

"Before you go, Kyle, let me just fill you in on my lunch date with Sheila."

"Sheila from Connecticut? Sheila, BJ's first husband's new wife?" Kyle wanted to be sure he'd heard right.

I assured him he had and then proceeded to fill him in on her request. By the time he left for his meeting, Kyle knew as much about my lunch with Sheila as I did. He mentioned that he might try to stop by after his meeting, if that was all right. He figured it might be his only chance to get a look at a woman who featured so prominently in a murder right in our backyard. I told him I didn't see a problem with that.

[CHAPTER 44]

I wrote two blog posts with enough time remaining to check e-mails before grabbing my purse and heading to the pub. It was another gorgeous day, and it would be great to meet Sheila and get to dine al fresco finally. Jackson Street, with its English pub-like atmosphere, was the perfect choice. In keeping with a pub theme, the furniture consists of sturdy oak tables, weathered wood and wrought iron bar chairs. Rough stone floors are offset by a long, rustic wooden bar opposite an elegant and time-worn baby grand piano. The overall effect is quite charming, particularly when combined with the enormous glass garage door, open to give me that ultimate al fresco dining experience I'd been craving.

I searched patrons as unobtrusively as possible, hoping to locate a likely Sheila contender. No luck. The hostess greeted me and asked my table preference. I selected a square table very near the open garage door; a light breeze was blowing and it was absolute heaven. The server took my drink order. I hesitated; I couldn't very well order for Sheila. Hell, I'd never even set eyes on her. I didn't know if she'd choose alcohol or stick with a soft drink. Years ago there was never a question – we all drank at lunch. Not anymore.

Business lunches were little more than drinking fests for many years. It wasn't until sometime in the mid-to-late eighties when things started to turn healthy, which was a boon for me since my delicate digestive system preferred abstention from noon cocktails – at the very least. You have no idea how difficult it is to order a Diet Pepsi and sense every critical eye turn your way – only lightweights couldn't handle a drink at lunch! There was nothing worse than being labeled a lightweight in the ad biz. The pressure was intense.

Ironically, it wasn't much later that we learned caffeine in soda wasn't a whole lot better for ulcer-like symptoms than alcohol. Soda just seemed safer, since on a bad day a sip of wine was sure to cause instantaneous heartburn – God, I don't miss those days at all! Luckily my hearty constitution and a very good gastroenterologist have enabled me to enjoy the mysteries of the grape once more – but I try not to push my luck. And these days no one drinks at lunch.

I tried my best to settle in and await Sheila's arrival but my lack of patience, coupled with the fact that I had no idea what she looked like, made it tough. I scanned the menu with its designer sandwiches trying to get my mind off the time.

Just as my iced tea arrived an unfamiliar middle-aged woman ambled in looking around tentatively. She appeared to be about the right age so I waved. She waved back and strolled over.

"Donna?" she asked somewhat tentatively. "I'm Sheila." She put her hand out and we shook. Sheila was a bit of a surprise. I guess after a hideous experience with his first marriage, Ron was looking for something quite different the second time around. Well, he'd found it, at least as far as looks went. No one looked less like BJ than Sheila!

Sheila had a warm and welcoming demeanor that enveloped you like a cuddly old bathrobe. She was as solid in build as she was short in stature. Although I thought Sheila was positively lovely as she appeared before me, I would guess she fretted about losing twenty-five to thirty pounds most of the time. While she was far from being a twig, her curvy figure and her ample chest would go a long way toward earning her some appreciative second glances. It didn't hurt that she had a gorgeous face and long golden blonde hair falling in soft curls around her stunning features. You may recall that my old nemesis BJ was as tall and skinny as a dried out old twig, as flat as an ironing board, had dark tightly curled hair and a face that would undeniably stop a freight train. Seriously, two more different looking women did not exist in the world!

I smiled and scanned the pub for our server as Sheila settled in. By the time I turned back to face her, she was giving the waitress her drink order and asking about the day's specials. We both went for the chicken sandwich with avocado sauce, a personal favorite!

Sheila looked around and commented on my great choice of luncheon places. I wondered if she ever had a negative thing to say. No sooner had that thought crossed my mind than we naturally gravitated into the heart of her concerns about Mickey's family. As we chatted, I learned Sheila had far more depth of character than I'd previously observed.

It occurred to me I might mention my recent conversation with Mickey regarding the orange bag. No need, Sheila was completely up-to-date on Mickey's wife and her trip to Omaha. But here was the shocker. Sheila knew so much because she'd been here herself! She had followed Mickey's wife out to Omaha for fear that Susie was so overwrought she might lose it. Oh, that was not good news. I think Sheila realized her words hit hard because she appeared crestfallen.

I couldn't help thinking Mickey was very lucky his dad had married someone who could care so deeply for him and his family. I started to tell Sheila how terrific I thought she was and she actually started to get all choked up. I felt bad that my comment elicited so much vulnerability so soon into our first face-to-face conversation. Strong women always resent looking weak to others. I could tell her own reaction was frustrating her. I know precisely how that feels from my whole menopausal journey, so I quickly changed to a less emotional topic.

Those of us who were not normally moved to tears were mere playthings once the gods of menopause chose to mess us up! I could envision them looking down at me in raucous fits of laughter as they watched the tears burst forth upon reading of a dog who saved an old man from a fiery death! It was relentless and it came on so fast it was impossible to head off at the pass. Poor Sheila, her family had been through so much. I gave her a few moments to compose herself as I vaguely meandered through some key points of interest in Omaha.

After a few minutes, Sheila joined the conversation, her voice strong and free from the shaky chords that usually precede a tear shower. For the rest of lunch we avoided discussing anything too recent. Sheila probed about my working relationship with BJ; she clearly knew nothing about it. Sure she was married to BJ's ex – but you know how good men are at providing information down to the nth detail; suffice it to say there was a lot she didn't know. I was anxious to learn how Ron and Sheila got together and, in particular, what kind of impact BJ had made on her life.

According to Sheila, in the beginning she had closer contact with BJ because Mickey was just a kid. They saw each other on occasion when one or the other of them had to drop him off or pick him up. Having heard some of the stories about BJ, Sheila had been tentative in their dealings at first. Not surprisingly, she and BJ never developed any kind of rapport. Sheila would try to invite BJ to stay for breakfast, or at least a cup of coffee, on those mornings she arrived early to collect Mickey. BJ would always decline in her annoying imperious manner. Clearly Sheila and her hospitality were not fit for the likes of the great and wonderful diva! Sheila claimed not to be thrown by it, but I knew BJ well enough to know how very nasty even the simplest gesture can be delivered if you try hard enough.

We accepted our server's offer of another round of iced tea before discussing the changes in their relationship during more recent years. Even Sheila became somewhat tense, by her own account, when BJ started weaseling large sums of money out of Ron. Who could blame her? You work like a dog to make a comfortable living, and a big chunk of your hard-earned money goes toward keeping the very woman who treats you with disdain from a perch atop her Manolo Blahnik's, in her decadent lifestyle. And there you are walking around in your Easy Spirits. That's got to be tough! As the incredibly caring and generous person she seemed to be, Sheila didn't appear to have let that get to her – she must have been a saint!

We sipped our tea thoughtfully while Sheila geared up to move to the next phase of her relationship with B.J, when things started getting a lot more serious. Sheila and Ron had been operating on a shoestring. I guess you could say "living on love." Then came the final blow, when Mickey's baby daughter was born. Ron and Sheila scraped together everything they could manage in order to write Ron's son a healthy check as a baby gift. BJ gave nothing.

Sheila was clearly livid at this point in the conversation; the memory alone was raising her blood pressure. Although she held herself in check regarding BJ's puzzling behavior, Sheila confessed to allowing herself a rare moment of complaining to her Bunko partners one night during a break between games.

"I'm sorry to be whining in this way, but I just can't believe her!" lamented Sheila to her closest friends. "Thank you for allowing me to get this out of my system. Do you know how long we've been paying her living expenses? And, of course,

Ron would never ask her to consider moving to a more affordable address now that we're footing the bill. Part of me wants to push him but I just don't have the heart after everything else he's been through with her." Immediately after her mini-outburst, Sheila had felt guilty about airing her family's dirty laundry, but the need to vent had been overwhelming.

That was right about when her friend Margaret starting looking a bit green around the gills.

"Margaret, are you all right?" Jane, the Bunko hostess, asked her. "You look a lot like you did when you drank a mouthful of coffee with curdled milk last year."

That's when Margaret enlightened them all about BJ's living with Porter Enzo. Sheila acknowledged that the roof figuratively caved in on her at that moment. Not only had she and Ron been living extra frugally in order to support BJ's more extravagant lifestyle, BJ hadn't even needed their money, nor had she used it for its intended purpose. Sheila couldn't continue playing Bunko that night; she just felt sick!

At that moment, Sheila resolved to hire a private investigator and find out what else she didn't know. He'd been on the case for about three weeks when he uncovered BJ's plot to indict Ron and WyCliff, letting them take the fall for her latest failed scheme, and the fact that she'd sold the expensive West Hartford house. He also discovered that BJ had wiped out Mickey's entire bank account. That's when it dawned on Sheila that Susie had likely made the same discovery already. She'd noticed some marked changes in Susie's demeanor at around that time. When Mickey packed up in preparation for helping his mom move herself out to Omaha, Susie was supposed to be heading out with the baby to visit her sister. Instead, the baby was at her sister's and she headed to Omaha.

I was getting a really bad feeling about this whole thing.

Now I knew there were two women who were in Omaha at the time of BJ's murder; both had motives to want to harm BJ, and at least one clearly had intent. Then I remembered how certain the detectives had seemed that our murderer was likely to have been a woman. I shuddered to think what this would do to Mickey. The poor guy just could not get a break. He no sooner has the loving family that he's always longed for and his unstable mother gets murdered, most likely by the mother of his newborn child. Some folks seem destined for tragedy and there was nothing they could do to remove themselves from the track of that oncoming train.

I looked over at Sheila and could see from the anguish on her face that I had found the right track. It didn't make me feel any better.

"You know, don't you Sheila?"

"Yes." And she finally allowed herself to break down. My heart went out to her as she struggled to keep her sobbing under control, to no avail. The intensity of her heartbreak was palpable; looking around at the faces of our fellow diners confirmed she was turning a charming al fresco pub on a magnificent day into the E.R. after an eight car pile-up. We had to get out of there. I threw some money down on the table, grabbed Sheila by the arm and murmured, "Let's go!"

Sheila obediently followed my lead as I guided her out onto the sidewalk. Fortunately, when dining at a restaurant with an open garage door in lieu of a wall, getting to the sidewalk doesn't take all that long. Unfortunately, it doesn't afford a bit of shelter from probing eyes even once you're on the outside looking in. I turned to Sheila. "Did you drive here?" She nodded. "Where's your car?"

Sheila guided me over to a dark gray Chevy something.

"Keys," I ordered. She handed me the keys.

Once in the car we were somewhat better off, as Sheila had been forced to park on the top level of the civic garage and apparently none of the vehicles surrounding us were in demand at the moment. We sat, for a time, while Sheila collected herself. Truth be told, I needed to collect myself as well. I heard my cell phone ring. It did not seem like the appropriate time to answer a phone call – so I didn't. I would come to regret that decision.

After a bit Sheila was cried out and I was just wrung out. I asked her, "Are you going to tell me?" She just nodded her head docilely.

Sheila spoke in a gravelly post-sobbing voice, "If you want, we can drive over to the murder scene and I can walk you through the whole thing."

"You were there?!" I asked in horror. She nodded. Oh my freakin' God! This was more than I was prepared for. I didn't know what to do or say; I sat frozen with what must have been a bizarre expression on my face – undoubtedly made more bizarre by my floundering attempt to hide any emotion. After what seemed like an hour Sheila spoke.

"Or we don't have to, if you're nervous."

The funny thing was, I wasn't at all nervous. I was just stunned. Once my brain started to defrost I was able to achieve rational thought (you define rational your way and I'll define it mine!) and I really wanted to head over to the murder scene and have her walk me through from beginning to end. As a life-long mystery reader I should have realized how much an unsolved mystery would weigh on my peace of mind. I did take a moment to ask myself if this was too great of a risk. Was I walking into some kind of trap? I was certain that wasn't the case. I turned to Sheila and nodded. She started the car and I guided her the few blocks over to NoDo and the under-construction office building where BJ had breathed her last.

[CHAPTER 45]

Parking was easy. Neither of the twin office buildings was complete so there were no occupants. Sheila and I made our way to the actual crime scene building. Not certain of what we'd find, the tension multiplied with every step. With the crime scene tape gone and no door yet affixed to the front of the building we were able to walk right in. We glanced in the direction of the shiny new stainless steel elevator doors, but knew they wouldn't be functioning until the building had been properly secured. So we took the stairs. Luckily, it was a low-rise building. Still, we huffed and puffed as we reached the top floor. Neither of us would be running marathons anytime soon.

I wasn't really sure which was the actual office suite – I'm somewhat directionally challenged – but together we found it. The fact that vestiges of crime scene tape still hung stubbornly to the door frame even after they'd been pulled down by the authorities left no doubt we were at the site of BJ's murder. It was no longer a forbidden crime scene. As we moved into the partially constructed space, Sheila's countenance appeared to diminish before my very eyes. Being here was taking a toll on her, and it was palpable.

She walked the perimeter of the space, I assumed to jog her memory of all the details from that fateful day. Her expression changed as she moved about the breadth of the suite – it was like my own private version of a Marcel Marceau performance. A mute woman gliding about as her expression morphed from that of wonder and surprise to that of fear and...was that rage? Okay, that was a bit concerning. I didn't want to see rage.

Luckily, what appeared to be rage turned rapidly into despair; does that sound mean? Trust me, when you're at a murder scene with a woman who was there during the murder, seeing almost anything else on her face is preferable to rage!

I breathed a sigh of relief as I continued my own pacing of the perimeter. I'm certain my face revealed puzzlement and more puzzlement. This was the space that BJ was using as a prop to extort money from me; but I had to admit it was a pretty cool space. The woman knew design; you had to give her that! It looked incredible, sleek and modern, it married all of the newest, chic design trends without going overboard, and appeared to be surprisingly functional. Although predominately white, enough color was splashed here and there to infuse it with an undeniable energy. And it did not clash with the aged character of the building itself. There were work spaces and lounging areas, yet there was a minimalist quality overall. It baffled me that she would go to so much trouble to get a prop looking this perfect. But then, I guess that's the puzzle of the unbalanced mind – you just never know where reality ends and fantasy begins. I had to hand it to her; I would have loved working in the space she had nearly completed.

After we each made several laps around the murder scene, both careful to give the still evident chalk outline of BJ's dead body a wide berth, it was time to hear the long awaited recant of BJ's demise. At this point, Sheila and I seemed to be communicating telepathically. Just as I was about to suggest she begin, she did.

"Susie had hit Omaha by about one o'clock on the day of the murder. She probably had a two hour head start on me – give or take. Now, you have to understand, it never dawned on me that Susie was coming out to murder her. Susie had never spent much time with BJ so she had no idea how damaging that woman could be to a psyche. I didn't flatter myself that I could stop her from running full steam into the abyss, but I could be there to pick up the pieces. By the time I arrived, Susie had found out about this space and was heading over here. I had tried the Midtown Crossing apartment first, and this was my second stop." She paused for a moment here, but I had no questions. After another moment her story continued.

"When I finally got here I saw the two of them in a Mexican stand-off, each facing the other with about ten feet between them. Susie was enraged and BJ appeared to be laughing at her. My heart kind of stopped for a moment. Before intervening I waited, just long enough to find out what was being said. When she saw me, Susie started crying which just about broke my heart. That made BJ laugh all the more. What on God's green earth was wrong with her? Didn't she remember the strength of those post-pregnancy hormones? One woman in my church group told us about a gal she knew in North Carolina who killed her spouse for delivering breakfast in bed with burnt toast! A sane person would not tempt fate in this way! Believe me, I had seen this many times before and it was just not likely to end well. So there I was, Donna, standing halfway between a woman who darn near scared the wits out of me on her best days and an extreme postpartum train wreck just barreling down the track, and I waited. I didn't have to wait long."

I could feel the tension build as Sheila relayed her story. She took a moment to more fully set the scene.

"The place was pretty empty and completely stark white. BJ was dressed in a ridiculous jumpsuit. Its creator had apparently made a feeble attempt at recreating an oversized parachute-jumping overall, complete with parachute pouch hanging off her back. The overall was crafted from magnificent white silk fabric, which could have well been recycled from an actual parachute. Her all red (down to the red soles, of course) Christian Louboutin pumps were sitting on the all-white built in workstation – one of three separated by five or six feet – that were adorning the space. Guess "knock me down" pumps are not the most practical footwear when you're working to construct new office space – I even thought I detected the hint of a limp. Hmmph, who could have guessed that?"

Even at a tense moment such as this, Sheila still managed to hang on to a delightfully acerbic wit – yet another treat I'd recently discovered about her! After a brief moment of respite she continued.

"Susie wore a pair of Levi's, New Balance runners and a loose t-shirt that barely covered the remaining baby weight in her tummy. When BJ spotted me in the doorway, she turned and began to recant their conversation in a tone and manner that mocked Susie's cruelly, while Susie continued to stand there crying."

"Of course, Sheila, I might have guessed. You've come to protect your daughter-in-law!" she said, "perhaps you'd better drag her sorry ass out now before she goes too much further. Oh and you might want to mention to her that I care nothing about her or anyone connected to her. And I certainly don't care about anything she has to say about me."

Sheila stopped again. I looked at her with raised eyebrows.

"Yes, Donna, I can see you picked up on her reference to the fact that Susie was *my* daughter-in-law. Susie didn't miss that, either. She was getting dangerously close to the edge. At this point her tears included some indignant grunts. She was working herself up into quite a state. BJ could see that and did what you would expect from her – she ratcheted up her onslaught. That's when things really started to get ugly."

"To her credit, Susie got a few shots in. At one point she

cried out in anguish, "But how can you ruin your son's happiness in this way; what kind of mother are you anyway?' This earned the fateful retort, 'I ruin my son's happiness? I think he'll have you to thank for that! He so badly wanted a normal family life and then you came along to dash all of his hopes by giving birth to that gnome-like creature! Why, the moment I saw the photos that my darling Mickey pasted all over Facebook, I knew that changeling was no relation to me or my son!"

"Oh crap, that did it. Susie just snapped and countered with: 'Are you calling my baby, YOUR SON'S BABY, a bastard?' she shrieked pretty explosively before going on to finally seal her fate with, 'YOU, standing in that ridiculous, overpriced getup that makes you look like an escapee from a psyche ward? I wonder if you notice all the people staring as you walk down the street – I hope you don't think those are stares of admiration for your style and sophistication – because the second you pass by they all collapse into fits of hysterical laughter. You look like a complete fool! They think it's hilarious that someone so old would try to pull off a suit so outrageously laughable even a twenty year old wouldn't attempt it.' She finished her tirade in blazing pride only to watch a wrench sail by her head. BJ had found some workmen's tools and had thrown one at Susie with enough force to put her lights out once and for all."

"When BJ realized her aim was not good enough to actually kill this blight on her happiness she let out a throaty war whoop, grabbed a large gnarly hammer and charged! Susie, realizing just in time that this was no drill, screamed and ran for her life. BJ chased Susie around the office space gaining intensity as well as distance with each stride. I could see that it was only a matter of time before the two met in a lethal crash, even though BJ's gait was blessedly slow due to that limp. So I did the only thing I could think of, I grabbed the nearest object and sought to stop BJ."

"It worked. Once BJ was down on the floor with blood spurting out of a hole in her forehead, I looked down at my hand – in it was a bloodied Louboutin. Donna, I killed BJ and I...."

At that moment I saw a flash coming from the window. I heard a splat and saw Sheila fall to the floor covered in blood. I hit the floor. Oh my God, Oh my God, what was going on? I couldn't think, I had to get help. I could see that Sheila wasn't moving. I crawled over to my pocketbook and began searching for my cell phone. Need help, have to call 911, oh God.

By the time I found my cell phone and was about to punch 911, I heard activity at the door. Oh God, now they were coming to finish us off? What was happening?

In rushed Babs and Peg.

"Look out," I screeched, "There's a shooter..."

"No," Peg corrected, "That was us." I searched her face in horror.

"You killed...."

"Oh, hell no," Babs interrupted, "That was paint."

"Paint?" I was back to my brilliant conversational style.

"Yeah, remember that paintball photo shoot scheduled for next week?" Peg added. "Well, we had these guns stacked in the conference room all ready to go, so we just grabbed one on the way out the door."

"So she's not dead?" I guess I was a little slow on the uptake, but I was getting there.

"No, Donna, not a chance, but we should probably check to be sure she didn't hit her head," Babs suggested.

"I was looking for you earlier and Kyle said you had gone off to lunch with Sheila," Peg began her explanation. "One of

Liv's team members heard us talk and panicked, Sheila was their number one pick for killer. One of Donny's crew piped in to remind us that, as a woman, she was probably high on the suspect list. At this point we were all starting to get worried so I tried you on your cell. There was no answer (oh shit, why didn't I pick up my phone?) so we tried the pub. That's when we learned that you and 'a woman' had left under some duress. Babs and I figured we had to check out the crime scene – it only made sense. When we saw you both from across the courtyard in the twin building we were sure she was getting ready to take you out – so we acted!"

"Well, I can't say I'm not grateful for your concern and your obvious courage, but did you really have to use *red paint* when you performed your miraculous rescue?" I groaned. Apparently the tension was starting to get to me.

"She's right, Babs," Peg admonished. "You should have grabbed the gun with green paint. Our bad, Donna."

Babs nodded her head in contrition. "Next time we'll be more careful, Donna."

"Great, next time," I mumbled to myself.

We all turned our focus to Sheila, who still wasn't moving a muscle. We got down and slapped her face gently a few times before she started to regain consciousness. As Peg and Babs administered to their patient, I grabbed my cell and called Warren.

"Detective Warren, 'It's a wrap!' That felt awesome!

We were at the station for a long time getting all the details sorted out and helping the detectives work their way through the mountain of paper necessary to wrap a case. I didn't want to worry Jon, so when six o'clock rolled around and it didn't appear as though we'd be finished anytime soon, I gave him a call.

"It's solved," I announced.

"Sheila?" he asked knowingly.

Damn!

[CHAPTER 46]

As we were ready to leave the station, in flew Kyle with a screaming howler monkey behind him.

"Clovis," several of us said at once, and all in the same 'oh crap' tone of voice. It was pretty cool, actually.

"Kyle, you brought Clovis," I announced as if I were telling him he had a bug in his hair. He never got a chance to respond because 'her nibs' was all fired up and ready to blow.

"Donna," shrieking and baby doll whining, there it was again, "How could you? Honestly Donna, how could you do this to me?"

We all looked around, everyone else anxiously awaiting my reply. I waited for Peg to step in and save me once again. No dice.

"Dare I ask? Clovis, what have I done now?" I handed her the straight line she was waiting for.

"You set up a lunch with Sheila and you never called to invite me? Is that correct, Donna, did you fail to offer me an invitation to that lunch?"

"Guilty," I responded.

"What must you have been thinking, Donna? I can't even begin to imagine," she spat out. "Will you never learn?"

"Apparently not, Clovis, was there ever any hope?"

"Oh, don't get smart with me now, Miss, 'I am a real detective and I don't need any help from you self-proclaimed experts!' she barked.

"Real detective, Clovis? In what manner are you a real detective?" I asked, hoping an asteroid would choose now to slam into the earth just precisely in the spot where the little she-devil was standing.

"Not only am I the only person who helped you solve the last murder, when Claire was killed (all eyes darted to Clovis in shock and awe – maybe if you say it out loud, it comes true!) but I am a key individual in the murder of my dear, dear friend BJ, and you cast me off just like yesterday's rubbish," she finished with her usual flourish.

I looked at Kyle and he turned away. So did Babs and Peg. Thanks a lot, guys; you're all so willing to help when I'm in danger of grievous bodily harm, but when I have a real problem you turn away! I guess it's times like these when you learn who your true friends are. In a final desperate attempt I swiftly turned to beseech Warren for help, only to see her back as she headed toward the ladies' room. I contemplated my fate as I heard the faint sound of Frick and Frack chuckling to themselves. That was my last hope; now it was all me!

"Clovis–," was all I could get out before she reloaded her jaw and commenced firing directly at me.

"And another thing, Donna, I've noticed you've managed to get all your facts turned backward and twisted once again. I had to assure Maria, when I ran into her at Lakeside the other day, that she was badly misinformed – I was certain as a result of one of your briefings – and that Mario and BJ had indeed shared an intimate and loving relationship for at least six weeks before her death. When she doubted my veracity, no doubt as a result of your jibber jabbering, I was able to prove my point by explaining that they had gone away together for a long weekend, and BJ called me – we were quite close, you know to tell me how wonderful and romantic it was at the resort I had recommended. You should know better than to doubt me by now!"

"Clovis, I--," I got a little further this time.

"Look, Donna, as you know I have a very full life, and I have no time whatsoever to dilly dally here with you. I can see my words of wisdom are falling on dumb ears – and YES, that double entendre was intended BOTH ways!" she preened triumphantly as she marched vaingloriously out of the station – and I was hoping out of my life!

We shared a collective headshake. Warren had made it back from the loo. Using a weak pretense I walked back to Warren's office with her.

"So what do you think will happen to Sheila, and how about Susie?'

"I think, because of the violence of the attack there will be an inquest, possibly even a trial. Although you can never be absolutely sure about these things, I have a high degree of confidence that the whole incident will be ruled self-defense and Sheila and Susie will be free to go home and forget all about that freakish harridan who passed through their lives."

[EPILOGUE]

The mystery of the orange designer bag had a very simple explanation. It turned out that Sheila and Susie had gone back to the murder scene to check for evidence they might have left behind; everything had happened so fast on the day of the murder, and they hadn't thought of anything but to get the hell out as fast as they could. Realizing the police had already confiscated the evidence, they became shaken. When they rushed out, Susie left her bag behind. It wasn't hard to prove – and it didn't hurt them in the least. Oh, and those Facebook threats? That was something Sheila devised when she thought her best course of action might be to spook me so I'd stop nosing around, but after talking to Mickey she decided it would be smarter to recruit me.

Mickey and Susie went on to have two more children. They named their first son Benjamin John in memory of BJ, although they agreed never to call him BJ.

Mickey's mysterious "buddy," the one who accompanied him out to Omaha, was a guy that BJ had had a short fling with before hooking up with Enzo. The guy was more curious than anything. BJ did not disappoint, she'd met Mickey and his pal for a drink one night and hit on his buddy the moment Mickey hit the means' room.

Ron and Sheila finally had a little cash and were able to buy themselves a beach house on the coast of Costa Rica. His business was going so well, they managed to spend three months a year down in the surf and sun.

WyCliff never married again, but once he was able to get

himself disentangled from his legal woes, he wrote a book about the wild and capricious BJ. Of course, names were changed to protect the innocent – but WyCliff became a bit of a local celebrity. He enjoyed every second of it.

Porter Enzo and Lou Cavrola had gotten together a few times during the investigation to lend each other a bit of support. During one particularly late night of wine and philosophy Cavrola came to two distinct revelations; he would never practice fraud or deceit again and he was falling in love with Enzo. The two shared beachside vows before celebrating with a champagne brunch on the ocean terrace of Ron and Sheila's villa.

The good folks of Omaha and Marcel went back to their normal lives with the knowledge that a good old fashioned Midwestern upbringing was even better than they'd previously thought.

The End

All characters in this book have no existence outside the imagination of the author, and have no relation whatsoever to anyone bearing the same name or names. Some of the important characters are vaguely inspired by individuals known to the author.

Marcel is a fictional ad agency. None of these people exist and none of these incidents have occurred.

ABOUT THE AUTHOR

Robin Donovan is the author of the blog, Menologues, a humorous yet informational look at the trial and tribulations of menopause by someone who's been there. Menologues is republished on two commercial sites: Vibrant Nation and Alltop, and has won regional honors for social media at the AMA Pinnacles and PRSA Paper Anvil awards.

Donovan was born and raised in New Jersey but lived and worked in Connecticut for a number of years before moving to Nebraska in 1999. Starting her career as a high school English teacher, Donovan moved into advertising in the early 80's. In 1999 she accepted a job offer from Bozell, an Omaha based ad Agency. In late 2001, she and three colleagues purchased Bozell from its New York based parent company.

Donovan lives with her husband and three bulldogs, Roxi, Frank and Sadie (Sweet Pea).

The following is an excerpt from the first book
in the Donna Leigh Mysteries Series,
Is It Still Murder, Even If She Was A Bitch?

IS IT STILL MURDER
EVEN IF SHE WAS A BITCH?

A DONNA LEIGH MYSTERY BY
ROBIN LEEMANN DONOVAN

(1st in a series of Donna Leigh Mysteries)

[CHAPTER 1]

Claire Dockens was dead. Wow, that was a shock. When Kyle told me I almost dropped right on the spot. How often is it that someone you've known for years, worked with in the trenches, whose house you've been to several times, drops dead? She wasn't even that old – like early fifties.

If that weren't enough of a bombshell, Kyle's next revelation definitely put me over the edge – "And they say she was murdered." At that point I think I did lose consciousness for a second or two – not enough to make me actually hit the floor – but I'm sure, moments later, I wasn't facing in exactly the same direction as I had been before my momentary lapse.

The next thought that entered my shock-addled head was, "I wonder if they'll suspect me? I mean, it's not like I could stand her."

Then, Kyle said, "Gosh, I hope they won't think I did it."

Kyle Thoroughgood was my colleague and friend at Marcel, the oldest and most revered advertising and marketing consulting firm in Omaha, Nebraska. We'd both been colleagues of the victim a few years prior, and the day that Claire tendered her resignation had been an occasion of mutual celebration. Her mere existence had elicited an intense aggra-vation in both Kyle and me. She'd openly sought to condemn and abuse us for her own personal sport. With Claire as a colleague, we definitely hadn't needed any enemies. Truthfully, Kyle and I were but two of her multitude of victims since verbally abusive banter was her preferred pastime, but with the two of us she'd taken it to a level beyond. She had elevated her abuse to an art form.

That's when we both heaved a sigh of relief. Hell, the list of suspects would be monumentally huge! Sure we'd be on it – but undoubtedly we'd get lost in the shuffle of characters with sufficient motive.

"So how'd they do it?" I tentatively pressed.

"Bludgeoned as she was leaving a charity dinner," Kyle offered.

"Oh god, that really could have been any of us," I shuddered. "With what?"

Still nodding Kyle responded, "Hasn't been released yet. I don't think they're sure. From what I know they haven't found the weapon and the autopsy is scheduled for tomorrow morning."

"Oh yeah, how'd you find out?"

"Facebook."

That's when my partner Liv walked by with her third coffee of the morning. "Gotta run – late for a meeting," she tossed out, and then, "Shit, does coffee come out of silk?" As she frantically swiped at the growing brown stain on her new couture blouse.

"Hey," Kyle pursued "hear about Claire?"

"I read it on Facebook at 2 a.m. last night when I was finishing the proposal for this meeting. Her poor family!"

Leave it to Liv to give the kind, humanitarian response. Liv Danielsen was my partner and fellow owner of Marcel. I'm Donna Leigh. Ten years prior Liv and I had the amazing opportunity to purchase Marcel, the legendary ad agency that had once grown to global status and revenue before being purchased by a somewhat short-sighted holding company and allowed to idle long enough for Liv, two other partners and myself to buy the company. Over the years, our other two partners had eased out and/or retired. Liv and I hand-picked a third partner who had worked with us to reposition the business and shed the "ad agency" persona that was killing every agency unable to make the jump into the future and the world of social media and one-on-one dialogs with customers: Donny Miller.

"Kyle and I are on a mission to identify the murder weapon."

Liv just rolled her eyes and grabbed a damp cloth. She dabbed at her spreading stain while running toward the already packed conference room.

I turned back to Kyle in time to see Donny motoring up the hallway. "I suppose you know about Claire too?"

One thing about Donny; he was connected. If you needed anything you could count on him to hook you up with the best in the city. With his pervasive human network in place it was virtually impossible to be the bearer of any kind of news to Donny, because there was nothing he hadn't already heard.

"Hell yes, two of my high school buddies were cops on the scene. One of them texted me even before the coroner pronounced her dead. I would have run down to check it out – but he didn't think his CO would be too thrilled. I tried you on your cell. Man, this will really be a blow to the Omaha business community. She was unquestionably one of the smart ones, one of the few I could really respect."

"You're kidding."

"Yeah, she didn't know anything. She sure thought she did though. One thing's for sure – they won't have a shortage of suspects. Hey Donna, now that I think of it, you're probably on the list – you too, Kyle."

Now Kyle and I did the eye roll. Typical Donny. But this

time he'd kind of struck a nerve. I could tell by the look on Kyle's face that we were thinking the same thing – would we be getting a visit from a detective anytime soon? Exciting as that may have sounded, we didn't want any public notoriety that would give our clients reason to believe that we could not give them our full focus.

That was when it struck Kyle. He excused himself to call the clients and give them a heads up that the murder victim was one of our former employees. Poor guy, he'd be stuck ducking tough questions while short on information, and forced to appear respectfully sad and inordinately complimentary to a person who made his life hell every chance she got. But that's the way it goes – once a team member always a team member, and even though Claire hadn't been a member of the Marcel team at the time of her death – he wasn't about to speak ill of the dead. Actually, Kyle never speaks ill of anyone. Fortunately for me I can sometimes make him laugh with my blunt and irreverent characterizations of some of our well-deserving colleagues and associates. I'm not as nice as Kyle.

I rolled my eyes at Donny and headed back toward my office passing two puzzled-looking copywriters. One thing was for certain, it would be a while before we lacked a topic of conversation.

Gracie Dancer LLC

www.rldonovan.com